THE KAIRI CHRONICLES

KAYA ABANIAH

AND THE FATHER OF THE FOREST

WAYNE GERARD TROTMAN

www.redmoon.co.uk

KAYA ABANIAH AND THE FATHER OF THE FOREST

Copyright © WAYNE GERARD TROTMAN 2015

This First Edition published in 2015 by Red Moon Productions Ltd. PO Box 1519, Kingston upon Thames, KT1 9UW

ISBN 978-0-9567872-1-7

To my family and friends who helped colour these pages.

Foreword

Kaya Abaniah (*Kah-yuh Abba-na-yuh*) is a boy's name. *Kaya Abaniah and the Father of the Forest* is a unique story, set in the Republic of Trinidad and Tobago. In this two-island Caribbean nation, inhabited primarily by people of African and Indian descent, Trinidadian English is the official spoken language, and Standard English is the official written language. However, Kaya speaks authentic Trinidadian Creole, which is similar, but distinct from Tobagonian Creole. Trinbagonians (Trinidadians and Tobagonians) use Creole in spontaneous conversation, while Trinidadian English is often reserved for more formal speech. Various combinations of English, Trinidadian English, and Creole are not uncommon.

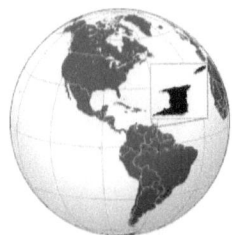

The creole languages of Trinidad and Tobago mix English-derived vocabularies with elements from several African languages. Trinidadian Creole also has influences from French and French Creole, as well as other languages spoken by Trinidad's diverse cultures and ethnicities. These include Spanish, from its proximity to Venezuela, Bhojpuri introduced by immigrants from India, and Cantonese, Hakka, and Mandarin brought by Chinese immigrants. Trinidad Creole is quite different to Jamaican Patois, which is also spoken in this story.

Kindly refer to *Appendix IV*, and the *Selective Glossary*, especially if you are unfamiliar with Trinidad Creole or Jamaican Patois. The extensive glossary explains the fascinating characters of Trinidad and Tobago's folklore, and contains the pronunciations and meanings of many carefully compiled terms and phrases. These include, but are not limited to, Ancient Setian, Canadian, Cyclan, French, German, Jamaican, Japanese, Karellan, Old Cyclan, Osirian, Rastafarian, Setian, Spanish, Swedish, Talisian, Trinidadian, and Urdu.

Table of Contents

1

AGUE

On a hot, humid, moonless night, in the small Trinidadian town of Coconut Grove, Kaya Abaniah lay awake on his bed, covered in a thick woollen blanket, drenched in sweat and shivering uncontrollably. Experiencing fresh waves of feverish chills, Kaya slowly reached for the glass of water on his bedside table. And, between shaky sips, his teeth chattered loudly, and a soft groan escaped his chapped lips. He gulped the tepid water past sore swollen tonsils and shakily placed the glass back on its bedside perch.

With a sigh, Kaya adjusted his pillow. Thinking of nothing in particular, he stared at the four walls, weakly illuminated by the ambient glow of his old computer's LED standby button. In the gloom, his Bob Marley poster, the Birds of Trinidad and Tobago calendar, and the colourful acrylic paintings of local scenery he had meticulously produced were all reduced to morose shades of grey.

Trying to make himself comfortable, Kaya turned to his left and observed his mother, Josephine. She slouched, fast asleep, in the old wooden rocking chair that once belonged to Kaya's grandmother. For the third night in a row, Josephine had watched over her ill son until fatigue finally got the better of her. In Kaya's eyes, the headstrong thirty-six-year-old single-mother did not look a day older than twenty-six, despite the exhaustion she endured due to her busy daily routine.

Always fiercely independent, she had been the subject of much gossip in the village of Tortuga, where Kaya was born. Josephine never told a soul the identity of Kaya's father, and when the constant whispering and innuendo became too much of an annoyance, she left the Montserrat Hills of Tortuga with her infant son and moved in with her mother in Coconut Grove.

In this seaside town, no one dared trouble Josephine, at least not while her mother was still alive. Most people were utterly terrified of Florence Peters, the dark, imposing woman the townsfolk called Mama Flo. According to a popular local legend, Mama Flo, the proud descendant of a powerful African family, had turned an old suitor into a frog after catching him in a compromising position with her best friend. Several stories exist regarding the fate of Mama Flo's former friend, but most inhabitants of Coconut Grove agreed that the poor woman had been turned into a blight-infected silk cotton tree.

Years later, having defiantly vowed never to trust her heart to the whims of men, Mama Flo met Ekon Arius Abaniah, a tall, dark, handsome stonemason from Barbados that everyone, except Mama Flo, called Papa Choonks. However, Josephine's parents would never marry. Their whirlwind romance led to an engagement that abruptly ended, when Ekon was struck down, while hurrying home during an unexpected thunderstorm. The local coroner blamed ball lightning for Ekon's death. There had been several eyewitness accounts of the bizarre natural phenomenon that fateful evening. However, privately, Mama Flo never accepted the coroner's verdict. Long before she peacefully passed away in her sleep, Mama Flo told Josephine that Ekon had been murdered by one of the women he spurned in Coconut Grove. This particular woman, she claimed, was secretly a powerful witch. However, to Josephine's dismay, Mama Flo stubbornly refused to reveal the woman's identity, saying she had no proof of her guilt. In her twilight years, Mama Flo often sat in her old rocking chair, softly singing old-fashioned melancholy songs.

And sometimes, she'd look in awe at Josephine, going about her housework, and she'd whisper sadly, "Poor Ekon. Boy yuh never know ah was makin' dis chile when de Soucouyant take yuh from meh. Buh watch yuh daughter boy, look how she grow up strong like she fadah."

In this day and age, most people would treat the old stories of the Soucouyant, a vampiric witch that roamed the night in the guise of a fireball, as the stuff of folklore. But, Josephine knew better. Mama Flo had raised Josephine alone, and Josephine raised Kaya in a similar fashion. At the first signs of illness, Josephine had given Kaya tea made from what Mr Chen, the pharmacist, called chen pi.

At first, Kaya protested the way most normal fourteen-year-old Trinbagonian boys, in his predicament, would have. "Mammy, I ent drinking Chen pee!"

But, Josephine, the sole proprietor of Josephine's Flower Shop, knew a thing or two about herbs, plants and Chinese medicine.

She explained to Kaya, "Chen pi is de Chinese name fuh dried orange peel. Yuh doh remember yuh granny used to give yuh orange peel tea when yuh were small?"

Of course, Kaya remembered this. He recalled Mama Flo telling his mother on more than one occasion, *"Josephine, doh bother wit any ah dem fancy capsule or tablet. Give de boy orange peel tea fuh de cold an' tuh stop de ague."*

Ague was what people of Mama Flo's generation called fever, and that's exactly what Kaya had now. Orange peel tea, perhaps the most pleasant of Mama Flo's medicinal concoctions, certainly tasted a hundred times better than karaili juice. *Momordica charantia*, known as karaili, bitter melon or bitter gourd is without exaggeration one of the bitterest vegetables known to humanity.

Mama Flo often warned Kaya, *"If you doh drink dis down, crapaud smoke yuh pipe."*

And, he knew if he did not drink the foul-smelling, bitter-tasting mixture, he'd have a painful appointment with a guava whip. Kaya thanked God his mother did not share his grandmother's grim zeal or her unshakeable faith in the dubious medicinal properties of the green, warty-looking menace. But, since Mama Flo's death two years ago, unwilling to take any chances with his precious taste buds, Kaya had developed the habit of ripping up and burning any of the karaili vines and fruit that occasionally sprouted in the garden. The mere memory of the evil taste of karaili made him shiver even more as he tucked himself back into the security of his thick blanket.

Because of his illness, Kaya had already missed the first three days of the college term, and it bothered him that he could not do anything to stop Artimus Corbeau from harassing Raima Khan. Artimus, a fifteen-year-old spoilt rich kid, a class prefect and bully, had the honour of being Kaya's enemy. Kaya delighted in frequently reminding Artimus that corbeaux, pronounced cobo, was the name Trinidadians gave to the local black vulture; an incredibly ugly bird with a tendency to congregate in the vicinity of garbage dumps. Raima also came from a wealthy family, but had no airs and never uttered a rude word or a condescending remark, at least not to Kaya. For this reason, Kaya appointed himself Raima's knight in shining armour. And, the fact that Kaya considered her to be the prettiest girl at Paria College had absolutely nothing to do with it.

A loud crack of thunder woke Kaya. Lying on his back, he opened his eyes to be temporarily confused by silvery-blue flashes and deep shadows dancing on the ceiling. Confusion transformed into fear when Kaya realised that he could only move his eyes. Instinctively, he looked to where he remembered his mother had fallen asleep, but no one occupied the rocking chair. Utterly exhausted from her three-night vigil at Kaya's bedside, Josephine had retired to her room, and not even the thunderstorm could have woken her now.

Nevertheless, Kaya felt a presence in the darkness. Did a thief use the thunderstorm to mask a forced entry into the house? It would not be far-fetched for a criminal to assume that Josephine hid some of the takings from her shop at home. Kaya wanted to call out, but his mouth did not function.

He heard a deep, earthy voice say, "Go back to sleep, Hezekiah."

Hezekiah? Nobody call meh Hezekiah.

"It is your name."

Yeah, buh…. Who is dat?

"I am a figment of your imagination."

Yuh t'ink ah schupid, awa?

"Not stupid. Delirious. You are experiencing a hallucination."

So, yuh mean tuh tell me, dis is ah dream?

"Yes, Hezekiah, you are dreaming."

How come ah dreamin' if yuh askin' meh tuh go back tuh sleep?

"You are in a transitional state between wakefulness and sleep."

Is dat why yuh talkin' funny?

"What do you mean?"

Yuh soundin' like ah real Englishman.

"I am communicating in English, but I am not an Englishman. I am your subconscious mind."

Ah never realise meh subconscious mind could tell lies in perfect English.

"Go back to sleep, Hezekiah."

Kaya was about to think up another witty retort, but the shadow of a man glided towards him, and he felt overpowering fear.

"Your illness is not natural. You will be better by sunrise, but be careful what you eat or drink. There are those who would do you harm."

Kaya noticed that the silhouetted man held something in his right hand, which looked like a baton or cane. He heard a low hum and his eyelids felt suddenly heavy; and, as the thunderstorm headed out to sea, Kaya drifted into a deep, dreamless sleep.

2

FRY BAKES AND BULJOL

Kaya woke slowly. Squinting at his surroundings, he saw bright shards of sunlight streaming into his small bedroom through shuttered windows draped with dark blue curtains. Last night's thunderstorm had swept the usual cocktail of dust and combustion-engine fumes out to sea. Kaya took a deep breath of the cool, moist air that saturated his bedroom with the pleasant scent of wet asphalt from the street outside.

His bedclothes and cotton vest were damp from a night spent in sweaty, feverish throes. But, to his surprise, his fever had completely gone, and he no longer felt ill, just as the mysterious man in his dream had predicted. He could not see the man's face, but Kaya had felt a strong sense of familiarity when he heard the man's voice.

Meh illness wasn't natural, he say. How could illness be unnatural? Ah wonder if he talkin' 'bout Obeah. What ah funny dream.

Groggily, Kaya snatched his old mobile phone from his bedside table noting, with a measure of disappointment, the last text message he received dated the 4th of July, which just read KIT, text-speak for *keep in touch*. While it is true that the 4th of July commemorates the United States of America's independence from the Kingdom of Great Britain, in Trinidad and Tobago, it was the last day of the third college term. Moreover, that was of far more significance to Kaya. Prior to this particular day, much of Kaya's social life involved text messaging. So much so that he had developed the cell-phone generation's ability to touch-type at 50 words per minute, with his thumbs, even while watching his favourite TV show. Kaya's best friend, Eric Andrews, sent that last text message on the 4th of July and had been primarily responsible for Kaya's text addiction. Earlier that day, Eric broke the shocking and unwelcome news that he would be moving to Canada with his family. Eric explained that he only found out about the move two weeks before. He told Kaya he was not at all happy about emigrating, or about the way his parents had sworn him to secrecy just after Sunday Mass. Nevertheless, Kaya felt Eric should have given him the news earlier. After all, they were supposed to be *best friends*.

In the weeks that followed, Kaya occasionally thought, *Ah should really keep in touch wit' Eric.* But sadly, he never did.

Sitting upright, Kaya yawned and stretched, shrugging off thick cobwebs of sleep. With large, warm, dark-brown, cat-like eyes, he stared at his slim reflection in his mirrored wardrobe, stroking his dimpled chin that seemed only to impress his doting mother. Apparently, he had inherited his father's dashing good looks; at least that's what his mother told him. He had a perfectly oval face, prominent cheekbones, brooding eyebrows, a straight nose, full lips and dark, reddish-brown skin. His ears were not large, but they jutted out a bit too much, at least that's what Kaya thought. Kaya had grown used to the crew cut Josephine insisted he had during the two-month school holiday. He decided it made him look manlier than the curly Afro he had before. Pulling a grim facial expression, he flexed his biceps. But, as always, the results were disappointing. While it is true that Kaya's muscles were well defined, he was tall with a very slim athletic build. No matter how much he exercised, he never managed to develop the sheer physical bulk and brute power of his bitter rival, Cobo.

Kaya heard Josephine preparing breakfast in the kitchen, and he marvelled at how much it sounded as if she was engaged in a pitched battle with ill-fated pots, pans, crockery and cutlery. As usual, she hummed a happy tune as she proceeded to make more noise than the automated machines in the bottle factory he once visited in a primary school outing. Kaya did not need an alarm clock to wake him each morning.

Suddenly, the clamour of culinary mayhem stopped; then the anticipated knock came at his bedroom door.

"Kaya, yuh awake?"

"Yeah."

The doorknob turned, and the door gently swung open. Josephine peered into the room. "Yuh feelin' better?"

"Uh-huh."

Josephine approached Kaya. She placed her hand on his forehead and confirmed that his temperature had returned to normal.

"Good," she said, and a warm smile appeared on her oval face, framed by long cornrows of luxuriant black hair.

Josephine wore khaki trousers and a black T-shirt with the green *Josephine's Flower Shop* corporate logo. As usual, Kaya thought his mother looked far too attractive. It was embarrassing. No wonder Delroy Brammer, who called himself Roy Dread, made a point of visiting her shop at least once a week. Josephine tolerated his visits because he always bought her most expensive bouquets, claiming they were for his mother. But she politely rejected his advances. Roy Dread had business cards that professed he was a dealer in African and Caribbean art, but many people unfairly assumed that the charming Jamaican was really a gangster. Kaya was not one of them. Unlike most other adults, Roy Dread took a genuine interest in Kaya's adventures, and Kaya naturally saw the Jamaican in a more positive light.

"Yuh well enough tuh go to college?"

"Yes, Mammy."

"OK den; rise an' shine. Yuh doh wan' tuh be late on yuh first day back."

The aroma of fry bakes and buljol wafted into Kaya's bedroom, and he needed no further incentive to take a quick shower, don his college uniform and take his place at the kitchen table.

Kaya wore a neatly pressed white short-sleeved shirt. Its pocket sported an embroidered monogram bearing the letters *PC*, above the Latin motto: *Excellentia, Scientia, Sapientia*, which meant, *Excellence, Knowledge, and Wisdom.* A charcoal-grey college tie with double diagonal red bands signified his membership of Ocelot House. Rev Dr Conroy McKenney, the founder of Paria College, had established Ocelot House, arguably the most prestigious of the four college houses. The other houses were: Hummingbird, symbolised by the colour blue; Tayra, named after a weasel-like omnivore, with a long neck and bushy tail, and signified by yellow; Mapepire, a name synonymous with local snakes, represented by the colour green. The Paria College uniform also included a monogrammed blue blazer, but like most students, Kaya only wore it to official college functions. And, fortunately, these were very few and far between.

As Josephine often put it, *"In Trinidad, it too blazin' hot tuh be wearin' ah blazer."*

Charcoal grey trousers hid the three-kilogram ankle weights Kaya strapped to each leg. He needed to increase his strength if he wanted to beat

Cobo in the 100 metres race on Sports Day. Dark grey socks and properly shined black shoes completed Kaya's outfit. Kaya recalled the hot August day he went shopping with his mother for his first school uniform. Josephine bought his trousers two sizes bigger than his actual size.

"Ah will take in de waist an' raise de hem," she had told him. "Yuh should be able tuh wear dees pants fuh de nex' two or tree years."

And now, four years later, Josephine stared at her young man with similarly dewy eyes, unable to hide her pride.

Stuffing his face full of bakes covered with buljol, Kaya asked, "What?"

"So ah cyah look at yuh? An' doh talk wit' yuh mouth full."

Kaya rolled his eyes.

"Doh roll up yuh eye. De buljol taste good?"

"Uh-huh," he said, with a broad grin.

The salad of shredded salted-codfish, blended with finely chopped tomatoes, onions and peppers, laced with olive oil, was one of Kaya's favourite dishes. And, Josephine's fry bakes, West Indian breakfast bread made from dough balls fried in hot vegetable oil, were second to none.

"Yuh sure yuh better?"

Kaya nodded, stuffing more food into his mouth before washing it down with hot Milo.

"Yuh had meh worried. Call meh if yuh feel sick at college," said Josephine, raising sympathetic eyebrows.

Kaya nodded, "OK."

"Ah put yuh absence letter in yuh college bag."

"What fuh lunch?"

"Ah was tired dis morning, boy, is corned beef sandwich fuh yuh today."

"Ah like corned beef," said Kaya, eyes bright with anticipation.

"Well, now yuh in Form 4 yuh big enough tuh be makin' yuh own lunch. C'mon, hurry up. Yuh doh wan' tuh be late."

Kaya looked forward to his first day back to college and to joining his new class — Form 4P. At Paria College, each class in the form levels below 6th form was distinguished by one of the four unique letters in the name Paria. So the four Form 4 classes were 4P, 4A, 4R and 4I. In the Republic of Trinidad and Tobago, secondary school and college entry was based on the results of a very rigorous Secondary Entrance Examination. Paria College was among the premier secondary schools in the Republic, maintaining the highest academic standards. Only male and female eleven-year-olds scoring above the 95th percentile were considered for entry into Paria College. Those students were then streamed, with those attaining the highest results being placed in the P-stream. Kaya's exam results had put him in the top two percent of students matriculated.

In his 3rd year at college, after winning a classroom war of words with Lucien Talman, Kaya had been labelled a rebel and sentenced to a week of detention. Students called the tall physics master and Housemaster of Mapepire House, Lucky Shortman; Kaya would defy this *sarcastic bully* at every opportunity. But at home, Kaya was a picture of obedience; he fully appreciated the many sacrifices Josephine made on his behalf. For him, no one could ever be more worthy of his love and respect than his mother. And, as a result, Kaya would never willingly do anything to upset her.

3

THE NEW BOY

Surprises, both good and bad, featured in Kaya's first day back to college. In keeping with the newly built Septimus Corbeau Science Wing, the first and second storeys of the old concrete colonial-style buildings had been given a much-needed coat of white paint, while the ground floor walls were painted dark blue. Doors, windows, supporting beams and ceilings were all decorated in light blue. The four-storey Rev Dr Conroy McKenney 5th Form Block retained its cream exterior, while light-blue stairwells and verandas provided access to classrooms. Broad terraced steps of concrete led from the college playing fields up to the Erebus Apophis Corbeau 6th Form Block, which was off-limits to all but 6th form students.

With dismay, Kaya noted new posters near the entrance of each classroom. They screamed, in bold red letters: *"If your cell phone is seen or heard, it will be confiscated!!!"*

More than the actual warning, it was the use of three exclamation marks that caught Kaya's attention.

"Anybody, who write tree exclamation marks, have ah damn screw loose," he recalled his mother saying.

When he entered his new class, Raima looked over her shoulder and flashed Kaya a warm smile, which he returned, secretly hoping that she wasn't merely amused by his new haircut. Swept to the left side of her oval face, Raima's hair had grown well past her gently sloping shoulders. Graceful and feminine, she had cocoa-brown skin and light brown eyes that exuded calm self-assurance.

Although he considered himself her champion, the truth was that Raima rarely spoke to Kaya. She spent most of her time at college in the protective company of her friends, Shantel Butler and Meenal Baboolal. Like Raima, Shantel and Meenal came from prestigious families and were members of Ocelot House. Sporty Shantel, who excelled at mathematics and science, rarely said a word; her disdainful gaze typically conveyed enough. In contrast, accident-prone Meenal wore braces and spoke far too much.

Kaya believed that both girls disliked him; they certainly did their best to keep him from getting to know Raima better.

In the morning assembly, Kaya had instantly identified a new student. The pale newcomer wore a pristine blazer — a dead giveaway. But his red-banded tie caused concern, as he did not seem athletically inclined, at least not to Kaya. Red-haired, freckled, and bespectacled, the same serious-looking fourteen-year-old boy he spotted in assembly, now stared with inquisitive blue eyes as Kaya sat in the only unoccupied seat in Form 4P.

"Pleased to meet you," the boy said, confidently delivering the Queen's English and extending a hand whiter than any Kaya had ever seen before. "I'm Tom; Tom Baker."

Although Tom had been present for the past three days, his Oxford accent still brought awed silence to the class, and the students observed the introduction with great interest.

Suddenly self-conscious, Kaya gripped Tom's hand firmly and said, "Nice tuh meet yuh, Tom. I'm—"

"Kaya Ah Banana!" shouted Cobo, prompting a roar of derisive laughter.

Cobo had grown even more muscular. The heavily built, light-skinned French Creole teenager had a prominent square chin; black curls covered a large head, set on a short, thick neck, and he stared with cold green eyes. It seemed Cobo had spent the entire school holiday bodybuilding and thinking up clever insults.

"Kaya Abaniah," said Kaya to Tom, "Ah suppose yuh already meet Cobo. But doh mind him. If you were named after de ugliest bird in Trinidad and Tobago, you'd probably have ah inferiority complex as well."

To Cobo's dismay, even more laughter exploded in the class.

"He does seem somewhat acerbic," said Tom, raising a thoughtful eyebrow.

"Doh start wit' dat," said Cobo, to the back of Kaya's head. "Everybody here know Corbeau is French fuh raven."

Speaking to Tom, Kaya said, "Buh in Trinidad, it mean vulture, ah dirty black bird dat live on a rubbish tip."

Playing to his supporters, who overwhelmingly sported the green-banded ties of Mapepire House, Cobo asked Tom, "Shaky Bakey, who yuh go listen to, me or Ah Banana?"

Tom told Cobo, "While it may be true that Corbeau is French for raven, I'd say that vulture fits with what little I know of you."

"What? Like yuh doh like meh callin' yuh Shaky Bakey, awa?"

"No, I do not," said Tom, firmly, a faint pink blush filling his freckled cheeks.

"Tough," said Cobo, and his attentive audience joined him in a chorus of mocking laughter. "At least Shaky Bakey slightly better dan Ginger Baker."

Money has lots of friends, and the Corbeau family has lots of money. In fact, Erebus Apophis Corbeau, Cobo's great-grandfather, was one of Paria College's original patrons and the founder of the athletically competitive Mapepire House. Cobo's father, Septimus, one of Coconut Grove's most prominent citizens, and a Paria College old boy, donated the funds used to build the college's new science wing. As a result, Cobo more or less saw Paria College as Corbeau property.

"Settle down, settle down," boomed Eldred Seymour Gobelyn, the white-haired English language master that Cobo and his cohorts predictably called, Goblin. Wisdom, intelligence and wit, illuminated his hazel eyes, which were set in a face that reminded Kaya of an English Bulldog. "I trust from your high spirits that you are all doing your level best to make our new student feel at ease."

"Yeah, sir," groaned the Mapepires.

"Splendid," said Gobelyn, with gusto.

Gobelyn had been the housemaster of Ocelot House for the last sixteen years. As a result, Cobo and his Mapepire cohorts considered him their sworn enemy. The old rivalry between the ocelot cat and the mapepire snake also partly explained Cobo's animosity towards Kaya and Tom. Tom took the place in Ocelot House vacated by Eric Andrews, Kaya's best friend, who immigrated to Canada with his family. To Cobo, Tom's red-striped tie made him a legitimate target in what he called the House Wars.

"Welcome, Tom Baker, welcome. Paria College is the best institution of secondary learning in Trinidad and Tobago, and we are glad that you have joined us. Welcome, Kaya Abaniah, welcome one and all. Today's exercise will be an analysis of persuasive language. Montano and Edwards, your assistance please," said Gobelyn, beckoning Dale Montano and Cheryl Edwards from their seats at the front of the class. "Kindly distribute these newsletters."

Kaya studied his new timetable intently. Thursday's schedule began with Mr Gobelyn's double English language, followed by religious knowledge with Dr Gerald Harry. The staunchly Presbyterian Paria College principal had earned the nickname, Hairy Harry, because of his thick black beard, bushy eyebrows that joined in the middle, and his exceptionally hairy arms. After the morning break, Kaya had double geography, then English literature.

Ah sure Cobo take de Physics option instead of English lit. Good, ah won't ha' tuh look at his ugly face. After lunch, ah have double Caribbean history with Silly Willy.

"So, is Kaya an African name?" Tom asked Kaya, his eyes bright with inquisitiveness.

"It short fuh Hezekiah — ah Hebrew name dat mean *strength of de Lord*," announced Kaya, proudly.

"That's right; Hezekiah was a king of Judah. He was a successor of King David," confirmed Tom. "Tom is of course, short for Thomas, but no one calls me that; except my dad, when he's angry."

"Nobody call meh Hezekiah," chuckled Kaya, "not even when dey vex."

"You missed the first three days. Did you go abroad for the summer?"

"No, ah didn't go away fuh de school holidays. We doh have summer here. Ah had ah fever, but ah better now. Ah miss much?"

"No, not really," said Tom, passing a handful of the printed A4 sheets to Kaya.

Kaya read the heading: *Wildlife Heritage Trust of Trinidad and Tobago.*

"The Wildlife Heritage Trust," said Gobelyn, "is a non-profit environmental non-government organisation that aims to conserve all natural habitats and wildlife in Trinidad and Tobago. Their emphasis is on the conservation of the Scarlet Ibis, the Trinidad piping guan and the ocelot. Through education, research and advocacy, the WHT aims to combat illegal hunting and habitat destruction. A most noble cause, as I'm sure you will all agree."

Cobo and his Mapepire friends smirked. They were Deron Biggs, distinguished by his muscular physique, pearly-white buckteeth, and extremely dark skin; Mukesh Ahriman, whose jet-black hair, switchblade comb, and staring deep-set eyes gave him an air of unpredictable danger; and short, stocky Kerwin Duff who infamously listed torturing insects as his favourite hobby.

"So, yuh like it here at Paria?" Kaya asked Tom.

"Oh, yes, Corbeau's been a bit of a nuisance, but Raima Khan and a few others have been really nice. She seems to have enjoyed her visit to England in the summer. Have you been to England?"

Raima? He's been talking tuh Raima?

"No.... Buh ah hope to go dere one day. Meh cousin livin' over dere," said Kaya, shrouding his envy with an uncomfortable smile.

Gobelyn continued, "Please read the newsletter carefully, taking note of language and structure. Is the newsletter persuasive? What is your interpretation of it?"

"Mr Gobelyn is head of Ocelot House. He's one ah de best masters at Paria," whispered Kaya.

"Oh, yes, Gobbers and my dad were mates at Oxford's Faculty of English."

"Mates?"

"Yes, you know, buddies. Several very famous writers were members of that faculty. It's the largest in Britain and certainly one of the best in the world," said Tom, adjusting his spectacles that had slid down the bridge of his small nose.

"Yuh father is ah writer?"

"No, Dad's a minister of the Methodist Church," said Tom, matter-of-factly.

"Oh," said Kaya, trying to imagine what it would be like to be a minister's son.

"We swapped the rain for bright sunshine, excellent beaches—"

"It get boring after ah while, trust meh," said Kaya, turning his attention to the newsletter.

"Oh, I don't get bored very easily," said Tom, brimming with enthusiasm.

"So, yuh like sports?" asked Kaya, keeping his eyes on the A4 sheet.

"Love a good game of ruggers — wouldn't miss the Six Nations for anything."

"Huh?"

"You know, rugby?"

"Oh-ho," said Kaya, trying to hide his utter confusion. "Is dat what yuh play?"

"No, I watch it on the telly," said Tom, loosening his tie. "I'm rubbish at ruggers. Phew! I knew it would be hot, but the humidity—"

"Maybe yuh should take off dat blazer before yuh faint."

"I must look a right idiot," said Tom, removing the inappropriate garment.

"Ah bit. So, what yuh play den?"

"Mostly tennis and hockey. I'm OK at tennis, but not very good at hockey. I've heard you're one of the fastest runners in Ocelot House."

Kaya turned to Tom, suddenly intrigued. "Who tell yuh dat?"

"Shantel," said Tom, lowering his voice.

"Shantel?" whispered Kaya, furrows of confusion appearing on his forehead.

"You sound surprised."

Kaya was both surprised and disappointed. He had hoped Raima was the one who had sung his praises.

Hiding his feelings, he said, "Shantel an' she friends doh talk to me much."

"Why's that?"

"Dunno," shrugged Kaya, but deep down he feared it was because his family wasn't prestigious enough.

If anything, Mama Flo's legacy was that in social circles, most people in Coconut Grove kept a safe distance from Kaya and his mother. Underneath the thin veneer of rational thought and acceptance of modern science, ancient superstition still flourished.

"Have you ever seen an ocelot?" asked Tom, his blue eyes bright with zeal.

"Only at de zoo."

"I'd love to see one in the wild, wouldn't you? Maybe we'll see one on the geography class field trip to Blue River Falls next week."

"Yeah, as long as it's through binoculars. Ah doh wan' tuh get bite by no tiger cat."

"I read that people call them that here, but ocelots are obviously much smaller than tigers. Salvador Dali kept one as a pet."

"So, yuh like art?"

"Yes."

"Cool. You'll like Miss Cutlash visual arts class. She's de head of Tayra House. She real crazy."

"Cutlash?"

"Her name is Amita Abilash, buh everybody call she Cutlash."

"Is that local lingo for cutlass?"

"Right."

"I only know a few words of patois. I expect I'll need some help with Trini slang."

"No problem."

Kaya and Tom chatted throughout the class; and, by the end of it, Kaya decided Tom was OK. Gobelyn had tolerated the talking as the boys managed to get all their work done, without distracting the other students. Gobelyn was also secretly quite glad that Tom was making friends, especially one with Kaya's athletic and academic potential.

"Now, young ladies and gentlemen," said Gobelyn, "it occurred to me that a most useful home exercise would be for you all to commit to paper, your most exciting exploits during the August holiday."

Kaya imagined his holiday to have been the most boring in the class. Several students had been abroad. Raima spent her vacation in London; Meenal had a much-anticipated visit to Paris, and Shantel had been to New York. Cobo made much of the fact that his holiday had been spent sailing the Caribbean with his snobbish family. Kaya had never been sailing; in fact, he had never left the shores of Trinidad.

"Your 2,000-word essay will be entitled: *Something to Shout About*," said Gobelyn. "I would like you all to include details of an event, or a personal achievement that filled you with a feeling of success. Do try to incorporate what we've discussed in today's lesson. As an added incentive, the best essay will earn its writer ten house points."

From the back of the class, Curtis Joseph raised his hand for attention.

"Yes, Joseph?" asked Gobelyn.

"Can we make some of it up, sir?"

His question caused more than a few sniggers.

"Indeed, you may, Joseph; as long as your fabrications are not too fanciful. We all recall your incredible accounts of observing icebergs in the Caribbean Sea."

The class roared with laughter, and Curtis smiled with embarrassment.

"Writing with confidence, about what you have experienced, is usually the ticket," added Gobelyn, with a twinkle in his eye.

Kaya recalled the three weeks of the school holiday he spent in the Montserrat Hills of Tortuga. He visited his elderly grandaunt Tantie Rose, who lived with her son Clarence, his common-law wife Beatrice, and their two children, Leandra sixteen and Robin thirteen.

Early every morning, Kaya would run from Tantie Rose's Old Peters House, across the edge of Frederick's Farm, past the cane fields, up the hill to Our Lady of Montserrat Roman Catholic Church, and back again. He did this with three-kilogram weights strapped to each ankle. Even though the Paria College Annual Sports Day was six months away in February, Kaya was determined to beat Cobo in the 100 metres sprint. Kaya had defeated Cobo just once — two years ago, to win his only gold medal in that event. However, the Mapepires claimed that Cobo lost because he had pulled his hamstring while playing football a fortnight before. They had effectively turned Kaya's victory into a hollow one.

Kaya spent most days in Tortuga, exploring the countryside with his cousin, Robin, or producing acrylic paintings of the local scenery. Tantie Rose had two of Kaya's paintings professionally framed and proudly hung them on her living room wall, where every visitor could admire them.

Clarence and Beatrice had taken over Rose's Kitchen, a small family restaurant in the village. Kaya and Robin had dinner there most evenings, but Leandra always managed to find an excuse to spend time away.

Every day, during Kaya's August holiday, Clarence used his formidable charms to persuade diners to order more drinks, and Beatrice, who never tasted anything she cooked, wore swimming goggles whenever she chopped onions. After dinner, Kaya and Robin would return to the Old Peters House and Tantie Rose's candlelit retelling of childhood adventures. Tantie Rose especially loved recounting stories about jumbies — ghosts that roamed the village; and, about Papa Bois — the mythical father of the forest. And Kaya always enjoyed listening to Tantie Rose's tall tales.

From mid-morning, at Paria College, Kaya had been looking forward to eating the corned beef sandwiches his mother had prepared. But at lunchtime, he opened his bag and found to his shock that they were gone. Kaya's lunch had been stolen. Tom offered to share his ham and cheese sandwiches with Kaya, but quickly discovered that he had also been robbed. They even took his apple and his shortbread biscuits.

"Is dat Cobo and de Mapepires," growled Kaya, his brown eyes narrowed with rage.

Cobo and his three stooges, Deron, Mukesh, and Kerwin, strutted into the classroom with broad grins etched on their faces. Cobo looked at Kaya and smirked with disdain.

"I think you're right," said Tom, followed by, "excuse me," when his empty stomach suddenly rumbled loudly.

"Buh wha' trouble is dis?" shouted Marlon Weekes, glaring at the empty sandwich box on his desk. "Who t'ief meh lunch?"

"What dis place comin' to?" said Mukesh, as he straddled a chair, "Like some people cyah even afford tuh buy lunch, dey have tuh steal people food."

Dragging chairs along the concrete floor, so that they screeched annoyingly, the other Mapepires sat like Ba' Johns and did little to hide their glee.

Clenching his fists and walking towards Mukesh aggressively, Marlon demanded, "Is you an' yuh Mapepire friends who steal meh lunch, eh Mooksie?"

Jumping to his feet and gesticulating excitedly, Mukesh retorted venomously, "Who yuh callin' Mooksie, likkle Hummingbird boy?"

"Yuh fadah head!" cried Marlon, spoiling for a fight.

Cobo, Deron, and Kerwin, immediately stood in support of Mukesh, and suddenly several boys wearing blue-banded ties moved forward to assist Marlon.

"Fight! Fight!" exclaimed Dwayne Gopaul, his short arms waving excitedly.

More students quickly converged, including John Byno, one of the class prefects, intent on diffusing the altercation.

"Dey well an' truly gone too far dis time," said Kaya to Tom, "somebody ha' tuh teach Cobo an' dem ah lesson."

Kaya felt a knot in his stomach. Suddenly, the fluorescent tubes on the classroom ceiling brightened then extinguished, drawing surprised gasps from some of the students.

Bhekizitha Duna, the Paria College vice-principal and dean, appeared in the doorway. Known as Shaka Duna, the dark, lean, South African, usually put the fear of God into most pupils, and now you could hear a pin drop. Ignoring the strict no smoking policy of the college, he stood, smoking the finest Virginia tobacco from a calabash pipe with a porcelain bowl, glaring at them like a grim character from a Spaghetti Western.

"Is there a problem here?" he asked calmly, in a raspy, accented voice that fit in with his ominous gunslinger persona.

"No, sir," chimed Cobo and Byno, the two class prefects.

"What are you doing?" asked Shaka Duna, and terror descended on the would-be combatants.

"We were havin' ah debate about boxin', sir," said Mukesh, with a tremor in his voice. "Ah t'ink some of us were gettin' ah bit too excited."

Unmoved by the blatant lie, Shaka Duna glared at Mukesh who now looked as though a Soucouyant had drained him of all his blood. Shaka Duna focussed his piercing gaze on several students, in turn, until the rising tension in the classroom became almost unbearable.

"Anyway, we finish now," said Deron, nervously nudging Cobo and Mukesh towards the exit.

One by one, students silently made their way out of the classroom, until only Kaya and Tom were left.

"How are you feeling, young man?" Shaka Duna asked Kaya.

"Better, sir."

"There are a few nasty bugs going about at the moment, best to take the necessary precautions."

"Yeah, sir."

"I'll have Mr Gulzar change the lamps," said Shaka Duna.

He was the only one who referred to Paria College's groundsman and general handyman in such a formal manner — most people just called him Ranjit. Ranjit Gulzar had been with the college for thirty-one years and famously wore the same tan fedora all that time. He rarely spoke. Shaka Duna walked away, inspiring respectful silence in his wake, and Kaya and Tom breathed loud sighs of relief.

4

THE HIKE

For three days in a row, it had rained heavily in Coconut Grove, but the morning of Paria College's Form 4 Geography Expedition to Blue River Falls was crisp and dry. Even though Kaya had told Josephine he would get up early and prepare his lunch, he woke at 5:00 AM to a cacophony of clashing pots and pans, which emanated from the kitchen. By the time he had a shower and got ready, his breakfast and packed lunch had been prepared.

Kaya wore his white college shirt, blue jeans, which covered his ankle weights, and hiking shoes that his cousin had sent him from England. In his rucksack, he had packed a rolled up plastic rain jacket, a grey cotton vest, a large towel, a baseball cap, sunglasses, a pocket-knife, a notebook, a sketch pad, coloured pencils, his mobile phone, a flashlight, binoculars, a digital camera, two chocolate bars, three small cartons of sorrel and a litre bottle of water that he had frozen and wrapped in old newspapers then placed in a plastic bag. Josephine had insisted that he also packed a pocket Bible, a small box of plasters, spare socks, and an insect repellent spray.

"Yuh didn't have to get up early, Mammy," Kaya protested, "ah was goin' tuh make meh lunch an' everything by meh self."

"Ah know boy, buh' ah was up. So ah say, leh meh just do it one time," said Josephine. She wore a peach coloured cotton robe over her nightdress and leaned against the kitchen counter holding a mug of hot coffee. "So allyuh will have four guides from de Wildlife Heritage Trust, as well as five college teachers?"

"Yeah."

"Good," said Josephine, and she sipped the coffee.

"I'd like tuh join de WHT. Mr Gobelyn is ah member fuh years, an' Tom say he goin' tuh join too," said Kaya, before putting another fork full of scrambled eggs into his mouth.

"Conservation is very worthwhile," said Josephine, sounding sad despite her best efforts.

"Wha' wrong?" asked Kaya.

Josephine composed herself quickly and said, "Yuh could join, but de subscription will have tuh come from yuh allowance. Tuh be ah conservationist yuh need ah sense ah responsibility; an' tuh be responsible yuh need dedication an' personal sacrifice."

"Yes, Mammy," said Kaya, trying to hide his disappointment with a nonchalant smile.

For over a year, he had been saving his money to buy a new bicycle and had hoped Josephine would pay the WHT subscription. But Kaya was willing to use some of his savings for the annual fee as he felt strongly about conservation. It horrified him that the Trinidad piping guan, known locally as the pawi — a bird that is only found in Trinidad, was on the verge of extinction. The leatherback turtle also had *critically endangered* conservation status and the yellow-headed parrot, blue and yellow macaw, West Indian manatee and the ocelot were all at risk. Kaya would simply have to wait a little longer to get his new bicycle.

Several students had opted not to join the Form 4 Geography Expedition to Trinidad's Northern Range. In the end, eighty-three of Paria College's one hundred and five Form 4 students took the hike. They were split into four groups and accompanied by Noreen Adams, the blonde-haired green-eyed bespectacled geography master, whom the students secretly called Spexy; Maurice George, the English literature master, alias Georgie Porgie; biology master Hugo Balgobin, a.k.a. Haemoglobin; Melda Petronella Mallory, the European history teacher nicknamed Obeah Widow and Cyril Williams, the Caribbean history master, known as Silly Willy. Each group had a WHT guide, a college teacher and at least one class prefect, with Obeah Widow floating between the groups.

Florian Hütter, an Austrian, who had made Trinidad his home the past twelve years, led Kaya's group. To Kaya, the tanned European, with his parted, sandy-brown hair swept to the right, seemed to frown even when he flashed a rare smile. Silly Willy, the dark bear-like historian, rarely seen without his trademark dark glasses, supervised the group of twenty-one students that included Tom, Raima, Shantel, Meenal, Cobo, Mukesh, Kerwin, and Deron.

Kaya's sunglasses and the long brim of his baseball cap shielded his eyes from the bright, morning sun. He walked with Tom, listening with interest to Hütter's informative discourse regarding their surroundings, and he kept an eye on Raima, who trekked ahead with Shantel and Meenal. The trio wore pedal-pusher blue jeans and had similar pink rucksacks that stood out from the crowd. The Paria College students had been told they would hike along golden-sand beaches of Trinidad's north coast. Then, two hours later, following the winding Snake River through the rainforest of the Azura National Park, they would arrive at the cool, shaded Blue Pool, at the base of the impressive Blue River Falls.

Hütter and the other WHT guides came equipped with bags, specifically for the rubbish left by careless visitors to the area. And the Paria College teachers encouraged the students to assist them in picking up any discarded food containers and packaging they discovered on the way. Kaya grabbed a small carton from his rucksack, pierced it with a little straw and took a sip.

"Are you sure you have everything?" asked Tom, eyeing Kaya's bulging bag and flashing a wry grin. "What's that you're drinking?"

"Sorrel," said Kaya, handing Tom the small carton.

Tom quickly read the list of ingredients before taking a tentative sip from the straw. His eyes immediately registered his astonishment.

"It's great," said Tom, enthusiastically, offering Kaya the carton.

"Finish it, ah have two more," said Kaya. "Meh mother call sorrel de favoured drink of the pharaohs of Ancient Egypt."

"Yes, I can believe that," said Tom, before sipping on the straw once more. Then, he said, "There's a brilliant new Egyptian gallery at the British Museum, Dad and I went there a couple months before coming to Trinidad." And, calling out to Raima, he added, "You had a great time at the British Museum, didn't you, Raima?"

Flanked by Meenal, who had been speaking incessantly, and Shantel, who remained stoically silent, Raima stopped walking so that Tom and Kaya could catch up.

She said, "Of course, Tom, it was ah interestin' place."

Meenal and Shantel carried on a few paces, hoping that Raima would follow, but she ignored them.

"This sorrel is wonderful stuff, and Kaya was telling me the Ancient Egyptians loved it," said Tom.

"Dat's what meh mother say," said Kaya, raising his eyebrows.

"Actually, ah not surprised," said Raima, smiling calmly, "meh grandmother is Sudanese—"

"Oh, really?" said Tom, suddenly intrigued.

"Yeah, she's from Southern Sudan, which is now the Republic of South Sudan. She came tuh Trinidad with her family in the 60s, during the First Sudanese Civil War."

"Yuh never tell meh dat," said Kaya, just as intrigued as Tom.

"Well, yuh never asked," said Raima, smiling flirtatiously. "In Sudan, they call sorrel *karkadé*, and it's very popular—"

Unable to contain herself, Meenal added, "Sorrel is another name fuh hibiscus, and dat's what dey make sorrel drink from. Meh mother call it hibiscus iced tea, she gives it to meh gran'father fuh he high blood pressure."

Meenal was about to unleash one of her infamous monologues, but Kaya interrupted her.

He said, "Meh mother know ah lot 'bout flowers an' t'ing."

"Yeah, boy," said Raima, smiling in agreement, "Meh mother gets all her flowers from Josephine's Flower Shop."

Of course, Kaya knew this. Raima's mother, Tara, owned a small cake and pastry shop called Patisserie Bougainvillea, which she decorated with flowers from Josephine's Flower Shop. Josephine often told Kaya that Raima's mother didn't need the shop; her family owned very valuable land, and everyone knew Raima's father was an attorney, a senior partner at Ashok Khan and Associates. His clients included Trinidad's elite.

Suddenly, someone snatched Kaya's baseball cap from his head. It was Cobo.

"Gimme meh cap," said Kaya, reaching out, trying to recover his property.

Ignoring him, Cobo quickly passed the cap to Deron, who passed it to Kerwin, who passed it to Mukesh.

Mukesh donned the cap with the brim facing backwards, snaked his arm around Raima's and said, "How many times ah go tell allyuh to leave meh gyulfrien' alone?"

"Leggo meh arm boy, like yuh smoke tampee, awa?" said Raima, quickly untangling her arm.

"Oh, Gawd, gyul, yuh breakin' meh heart," said Mukesh, pretending to be wounded.

Kaya lunged towards Mukesh, with his right hand clenched in a fist. Cobo quickly grabbed the baseball cap from Mukesh's head and joined Deron and Kerwin in blocking Kaya's advance.

"No, Kaya," said Raima, fearing he would try to fight the three larger boys.

Shantel merely sucked her teeth and shook her head in disgust.

Placing the cap back on Kaya's head, Cobo whispered, "Calm down, lover-boy, she outta yuh league."

Kaya glared at Cobo, who smiled contemptuously.

"Corbeau, Ahriman, Biggs, and Duff," barked Silly Willy, "to the front with me now."

"Later, lover-boy," hissed Cobo, turning on his heel.

Kerwin deliberately brushed past Kaya as he joined Cobo, Mukesh and Deron, jogging to the front of the group.

"Make yourselves useful," said Silly Willy, handing the disgruntled Mapepires rubbish bags.

As the groups walked along the beach, the strong, fresh breeze and the thundering waves of the Caribbean Sea charged Kaya's sense of wonder and anticipation. He licked his lips, tasting the salt and sand in the air, and he paused to quench his thirst with the ice-cold water he carried in his rucksack. High above, in the deep-blue sky, he spied a large bird floating on powerful air currents, and he quickly whipped out his binoculars to investigate.

"What is it?" asked Tom.

"That one is the ornate hawk-eagle," shouted Hütter, his Austrian-accented English rising above the din of crashing waves, "they love parrots, pigeons, and mammals such as the agouti. You'll notice the head is entirely white with a brown crown, this tells us it is a young bird. Mature adults have a black crown with reddish-brown sides to the neck."

"Can I have a look?" Tom asked Kaya, eagerly.

"Here yuh go," said Kaya, passing him the binoculars.

"Is dis bird endangered, like de leatherback turtle?" Meenal asked Hütter.

"No, although this eagle is rare locally, it has a wide range and can be found throughout Central and South America. On the other hand, the leatherback turtle is considered critically endangered. Every year, between March and September, leatherback turtles — the largest of the world's sea turtles, nest here on the Azura Beach."

There were fresh tracks in the sand, and Kaya saw that several led to trampled and dug out mounds.

Motioning to the mounds, Hütter continued grimly, "Here you see an example of one of the biggest problems facing the Wildlife Heritage Trust and those dedicated to conserving the endangered animals of Trinidad and Tobago. These mounds are the nests of leatherback turtles, and you'll notice that several of them have been disturbed. This is the work of poachers who have removed the eggs to sell them illegally. The leatherback turtle is a critically endangered species, primarily because their eggs are collected as a delicacy or as an aphrodisiac."

"What is ah aphrodisiac?" asked Curtis.

"Doh worry 'bout dat, Iceberg, yuh too young," said Deron, with a snigger.

Ignoring the laughter, Curtis stared at Hütter, hoping he would give and answer; the Austrian guide had been distracted. Further, down the beach, the leading group made a discovery that caused a lot of commotion among the students. Some of Kaya's group scurried to see what had been found.

"Be careful," Silly Willy shouted after the students, "doh step on de turtle mounds." Then he turned to Hütter and added, "Dis is ah big problem, how yuh will stop people stealin' de eggs?"

"Some of our volunteers work together with other local conservationists to patrol the area during the day. Because of this, turtle numbers have increased in recent years. But some poachers have become more determined. They steal the eggs during the night. They disturb the poor creatures while they are laying their eggs."

Silly Willy shook his head in dismay.

"Ja-ja, there are many problems. On some beaches nearer to towns, there is absolute carnage. Dogs dig up the turtle eggs and eat them—"

"Yuh mean stray dogs?"

"No, sir, these are not stray dogs. They are family pets allowed to roam freely. Even chickens have been seen to join in the daily feast. And, whatever is left by the dogs and the chickens, the corbeaux finishes off, it's just tragic."

"Shameful, jus' shameful," said Silly Willy. "People have tuh be more responsible. Corbeaux ah could understand. But dogs an' poultry? People have to manage their animals."

When Kaya saw what all the excitement was about, it made him feel sick to his stomach. A huge leatherback turtle had been killed the night before. Its head and flippers had been viciously hacked off. Afterwards, as they were quickly ushered away from the scene of the butchered turtle, the WHT guides conspired with the teachers to raise the spirits of the students by distributing free chocolate bars. And, on the whole, this ploy succeeded.

"Thank you, Miss," chorused Raima, Shantel, and Meenal, as Spexy gave them bars of chocolate.

"Wait ahr minute, Abaniah," said Spexy, to an expectant Kaya, "I need tahr get sahm mahr charklet."

"None fuh yuh," laughed Cobo, "losers doh get chocolate; if yuh look around, maybe, yuh go find ah banana."

"Corbeau," came the derisively shrill voice of Obeah Widow, cutting through the laughter of the Mapepires. "I do hope you are not inferring that Abaniah is a monkey."

"No, Miss," replied Cobo, his smile slowly fading.

"That is Mistress Mallory to you, young man," said the attractive, middle-aged black woman.

"Yes, Mistress Mallory. Ah mean no, Mistress Mallory. Ah was only joking; an' ah didn't mean Abaniah is a monkey."

"I am so happy to hear that, Corbeau. Mr Duna is far less tolerant than I am. And, it's likely he would relieve you of your title of class prefect if he believed you were abusing your position," said Obeah Widow, her eyebrows raised high above her staring eyes. "You're not abusing your position, are you, Corbeau?"

"No, Miss…. Mistress Mallory."

"And, what more do you have to say?"

Red-faced with embarrassment, Cobo looked down to the ground and replied meekly, "Sorry Mistress Mallory; it won't happen again."

"Oh, don't apologise to me, Corbeau. Abaniah is the one you offended."

"Sorry Abaniah," mumbled Cobo, unable to mask his humiliation.

Kaya smiled, savouring this rare moment.

"Good," said Obeah Widow. Turning to the dumbfounded Spexy, she added, "Here are some more chocolates."

With a broad smile, Obeah Widow handed Spexy a plastic bag filled with chocolate bars; then she briskly walked away, leaving Kaya's group completely shell-shocked.

Silly Willy, who had been speaking to Hütter, out of earshot, returned and asked, "Everything alright here?"

"Yes," said Spexy, "Ahr ran aht av charklet bars, baht Mistress Mallry braght me sahm mahr."

When Spexy first joined Paria College, a year ago, Kaya could barely understand a word she said. But, he had gradually learned to love her Irish accent and her anecdotal stories of life in the South-West Region's city of Cork.

Turning to Kaya, Spexy said, "Here ye go, Abaniah, catch," and she hurled a chocolate bar at Kaya.

Catching it, Kaya said with a broad smile, "Thank you, Miss."

Kaya tucked the chocolate bar into a pocket in his rucksack and looked forward to having it as an after-lunch snack.

Once Spexy and Silly Willy had walked away, Tom said, "A bit intense, isn't she?"

"Who? Yuh mean Obeah Widow?"

"That's Mistress Mallory to you, young man," said Tom, mimicking Obeah Widow's sharp delivery.

Kaya laughed, "She OK. She doh like people callin' her miss."

"What's Obeah Widow all about?"

"Well, yuh know Sparrow?"

"Er…. If you mean The Mighty Sparrow, the calypsonian, well I obviously don't know him personally, but I've heard of him."

"Well, Sparrow had ah road march, long before ah was born, called *Obeah Wedding*."

"What's a road march?"

"De most popular song on de streets durin' Carnival. Anyway, everybody call it *Melda* because that's de name ah de woman Sparrow was singing 'bout. In de song, Melda was goin' tuh ah Obeah man tuh get spells an' t'ing, tuh get Sparrow tuh marry she."

"What's an Obeah man?"

"Yuh know, ah man who deal with de dead an' magic and all sort ah nastiness."

"You mean like a Voodoo man? A witch-doctor?"

"Ah doh know 'bout no Voodoo; in Trinidad, we have Obeah."

"So is Miss Mallory—"

"Dat's Mistress Mallory tuh you, young man," interrupted Kaya.

"So, Mistress Mallory was seeing one of these Obeah men?"

Kaya laughed, "Nah-nah-nah, at least not dat ah know of. Sometimes is like she could read yuh mind. But, nah boy, we call she Obeah Widow because she first name Melda. An' because she insist on bein' called mistress, an' because she keep goin' on, and on, and on, 'bout she dead husband. Is like she always on a tangent."

"OK…. That sorta makes sense," said Tom, scratching his head.

"Plus, she always wear *Lily ah de Night* perfume—"

"*Lily of the Night*? You don't mean *Lady of the Night*, do you?"

"No-no-no, bredda man, dat is somet'ing completely different."

Tom laughed with embarrassment. He said, "I don't know that one, but then, I don't know much about perfume—"

"It around fuh donkey years, buh only real old ladies like meh gran'aunt wear it. Apparently, Kerwin live near tuh Obeah Widow — he say she move in mysterious ways."

"What do you mean? She's weird?"

"Doh worry tourist, we go make ah Trinbagonian out ah yuh. Eventually."

The boys laughed.

They made their way along the bank of the Snake River, hiking deeper and deeper into the tropical forest. Kaya took many photographs, but most were unsuccessful because of the low light conditions and the limited range of his camera's flash. He was fascinated by the blue-greens and browns he saw, and he found the chorus of bird and frog calls, accompanied by the soothing sound of running river water, to be very refreshing.

Hütter said, "The Azura National Park is home to several protected species, including the pawi, Trinidad's only endemic bird, and the ocelot, our only native wild cat. About half of Trinidad and Tobago's mammals, most of which are bats, can be found here, including the misunderstood and much-slandered common vampire bat. The park's biodiversity is under constant threat by hunters, poachers, pollutants, forest fires and uncontrolled exploitation."

"Save some shots for the ocelot," said Tom, to Kaya.

"Ah doh know anybody who see ah tiger cat in de wild. Ah doubt we'll see any," said Kaya, shifting the weight of his rucksack, which seemed to be getting heavier by the minute.

"Dey usually sleep during de day, an' only come out at night," said Raima.

Meenal seized the opportunity to rattle off a stream of ocelot-related information, and soon she had Raima's and Shantel's undivided attention.

"I think you're wrong," said Tom.

"Boy, ah tell yuh, ah doh know ah single soul who see ah tiger cat outside ah zoo."

"No, I think you're wrong about the girls."

"How yuh mean?"

"You said they didn't like you. I think you're wrong."

"Really? How yuh know so much about girls?"

"Oh, they're not that difficult to figure out, even for a pastor's son."

Kaya laughed, and Tom joined in. Raima gave an inquisitive glance over her shoulder and smiled.

"See?" whispered Tom.

"See what?"

"She likes you."

"Who? Raima?"

"No, Einstein. Shantel."

"Dat gyul doh like me at-all-at-all-at-all," said Kaya, shaking his head.

"What she doesn't like, is the fact that you only pay attention to—"

Suddenly, a gunshot echoed through the forest. Everyone stopped dead in his or her tracks, and no one said a word. Another shot rang out, and then another; and, a blanket of thick silence descended on the forest. Kaya saw Spexy, the geography teacher originally from Ireland, speaking in hushed tones with two of the WHT guides. Pink-faced with fear, she gesticulated wildly. She was terrified, and she wasn't the only one. Most of the students stared wide-eyed as the college teachers and WHT guides tried to reassure them.

Hütter was on his walkie-talkie reporting the incident, when something even more disturbing occurred; Kaya could hear a man wailing in the distance, and he sounded terrified.

"Oh, Gorm, ah t'ink dey shoot somebody," said one of the girls in another group.

Some of the students wanted to run away, but the teachers convinced them they would be much safer in large groups with their guides, than alone in the forest.

"Try to remain calm. We have notified the police, and they are on their way," announced Georgie Porgie, the English literature master.

But before he could say anything else, the man's wailing got louder. He was heading towards them. And, soon it became obvious it was more than one man wailing in apparent terror.

"Oh-Gawd-oh-Gawd-oh-Gawd," they screamed.

The groups of students huddled to one side, away from the path. Kaya suddenly noticed that Hütter and a dark, burly colleague were armed with machetes. He instinctively and protectively moved closer to where Raima was standing. She stared in terror, saying nothing.

"Doh worry, ah sure dey—"

Before Kaya could complete his sentence, three men burst out of tall shrubs, pursued by a large swarm of Jack Spaniards. The man in front had a rifle in his hand and wailed loudly; a dark wet stain in his khaki trousers, suggested that he had recently urinated himself. The three men ran frantically past the group, crashing recklessly through anything in their path.

Terrified students scattered, taking cover behind trees and shrubs. But, the men, and the aggressive paper wasps that pursued them, ignored the hikers and quickly disappeared into the forest in a cacophony of wailing, buzzing and wildly scrambling footfalls.

One of the frantic men screamed, "Run! He comin'-he comin'-he comin', run!"

Kaya wondered, *Who comin'? Who could scare ah man wit' a gun so bad?*

In the distance, he heard another man wailing, "Mercy-mercy, ah-sorry-ah-sorry; no, Papa, no—"

Screams of agony followed. Several girls in the group began to cry in a mixture of shock and confusion. Hütter was on his walkie-talkie again, but Kaya could not hear what he was saying. Spexy and the other teachers did their best to comfort the upset students. For a long, tense moment, they all anticipated coming face-to-face with the men's pursuer. But when no one appeared, the students, teachers and WHT guides slowly began to relax. In typical Trinbagonian fashion, many saw the funny side of the incident. It would be a very long time before the poacher, who peed his pants, was forgotten.

The college group buzzed with speculation about what scared the three men. Some said it was simply the aggressive Jack Spaniards, a few suggested it was the police, others a gangster or rival poacher, but Deron maintained that the men had seen Papa Bois.

"Who is Papa Bois?" asked Tom.

"Meh gran'aunt say Papa Bois is de father of de forest. She say he's ah white-haired African man, with strong muscles an' cow foot."

"Cow foot? You mean cloven hooves, don't you? That sounds like—"

"Doh be fillin' de boy head with nonsense, Abaniah," interrupted Silly Willy. "Baker, Papa Bois is a myth. He is a fictional character in Trinidad and Tobago's folklore. If you're interested, ah could recommend a few books on the subject. It would give you ah fascinating insight into Trinbagonian history an' culture."

Suddenly, the loud sound of a horn echoed to their left, prompting several birds to take to flight. Silly Willy looked at Kaya with dark eyes hidden behind dark glasses and swallowed audibly. The horn blared again. Once more, ominous silence descended on the National Park.

Kaya whispered, "Papa Bois protects de animals in de forest. He have ah hollowed-out bull horn, dat he blows tuh warn de animals when hunters comin'."

After the incident, the teachers and the WHT guides debated whether to abandon the hike, continue, or simply stay put and await the arrival of the police. In the end, they decided to continue. No one wanted to retreat in the direction taken by the poachers, and no one wanted to wait around for the police, so they followed the trail towards the picnic area. Even though the hikers and their guides heard the sound of a horn, few actually believed Papa Bois existed. But, when they discovered several open cages and two machetes, apparently abandoned by the fleeing poachers, many students wondered if the poachers had captured animals in the National Park and someone had subsequently set them free. Hütter and his WHT colleagues collected the discarded items, which they intended to surrender to the police.

"Tell me more about Papa Bois," whispered Tom to Kaya, after Silly Willy had walked to the head of their group.

"Ah t'ink Willy right. Papa Bois is jus' folklore," said Kaya.

"You heard the horn didn't you?"

"Yeah. Ah figure somebody must be playin' ah trick on dem poachers."

"He'd have to be rather brave to play tricks on men with guns."

Kaya related to Tom some of the stories that Tantie Rose told him
during his stay in Tortuga, and Tom listened with interest.

"So he isn't the devil," concluded Tom.

"Of course not. Yuh expect de devil tuh be ah African man?"

"No, of course not," said Tom. "I think he sounds a bit like Pan."

"Peter Pan?"

"No, Pan, the Greek god," said Tom, rolling his eyes.

"Ah doh know much 'bout Greek gods, an' ah doh believe in dem."

"Neither do I, but I have an idea what Pan looks like, and I think the
word panic comes from his name. Apparently, he can be very scary. He
causes panic, just like Papa Bois."

"So, yuh t'ink de poachers see Papa Bois?"

"Naaah."

5

TROUBLE IN AZURA

The hike through the Azura National Park turned out to be more of an adventure, than Kaya and the other students imagined it would be. Once their initial fears subsided, the groups were alive with speculative conversations regarding the gunshots, poachers, discarded animal cages, the mysterious sound of a horn; and, of course, Papa Bois.

"Allyuh see de look on Silly Willy face when dat horn blow?" Kaya overheard Mukesh asking the Mapepires.

"Ah was watchin' Spexy," said Cobo. "She look like she see ah jumbie."

"Yeah, boy, even Haemoglobin look like all de blood drain from he body," said Kerwin, laughing.

"Ah near wet mehself when ah hear dat horn, oui," admitted Deron, "Ah doh care what allyuh say, Papa Bois real. Meh gran'father used to say when he was seventeen he went on ah huntin' trip fuh wild meat, with meh great gran'father and he brothers dem, dong in Moruga. Dey were lookin' fuh agouti, lappe, manicou and deer, buh dey find Papa Bois instead. Dey see 'im as clear as day, wit' he cow foot an' horn. Meh gran'father say all ah dem run like de devil was chasin' dem. Dey never went huntin' again."

"Jeez an' ages Biggs," said Cobo, "men in de Corbeau family hunt all over Trinidad fuh years; an' none ah dem ever see Papa Bois."

"Yuh callin' meh gran'father ah liar?" said Deron, and he wasn't laughing.

"Nah-nah-nah, I ent goin' dere, hoss," replied Cobo, raising his hands defensively. "All ah sayin' is nobody in meh family ever say dey see Papa Bois."

"So, what're you having for lunch?" Tom asked Kaya, interrupting his eavesdropping.

"Ham an' cheese sandwiches ah t'ink. Ah was goin' to make mehself something buh meh mother beat meh to it. Wha' 'bout you?"

"Oh, I have some stew chicken and rice with callaloo. I've grown quite fond of callaloo. You're welcome to have some if you like; it's the least I can do after you shared your sorrel. Maureen is a great cook."

"Maureen?"

"Yes, she's our new housekeeper."

"So, yuh mother doh cook?"

"No, not anymore, she died ten years ago," said Tom, matter-of-factly.

"Oh," said Kaya. "Ah sorry tuh hear dat."

"It sounds like a few of the lads have been on hunting trips with their dads. I've only been fishing with my dad a couple times. What about your dad? Has he ever taken you hunting or fishing?"

"No," said Kaya, wiping sweat from his brow and trying to hide his emotions.

"You never talk about him," pressed Tom.

"Ah never knew him," said Kaya, "he die before ah was born."

"I'm sorry to hear that," said Tom. "I know I'll see my mother again, and I'm sure you'll see your father. I know it's old-fashioned, but I've always believed there's a heaven."

"If dere's no heaven, den dere's no point; dat's what meh granny used tuh say."

"So you'll have some callaloo then?" asked Tom, and Kaya marvelled at how effortlessly he changed the subject. "Maureen makes it with a bit of crab. It's really scrummy."

"OK, yeah, ah love callaloo. We should get tuh de picnic area soon."

But as they walked, Kaya suddenly remembered the mysterious man in his dream.

He remembered him saying *"—be careful what you eat or drink. There are those who would do you harm."*

De fever probably make meh paranoid, thought Kaya, *an' Tom right, oui, callaloo real good.*

As they followed the winding, old, donkey track, along the banks of the Snake River, Kaya sensed that something had been troubling the WHT guides. Away from the teachers and students, they spoke in hushed tones about the Snake River. Kaya could not help feeling that the river wasn't as impressive as he imagined it would be. He had read that there would be eddies and rapids, but the river seemed shallow and slow moving. At two points, during the forest trek, they had crossed the Snake River via narrow old wooden bridges. But it seemed to Kaya they could almost as easily have traversed the shallow water, by hopping on the large smooth stones that protruded from its flow.

At the picnic area, Kaya hoped to produce a few quick sketches before following the old donkey track to the Blue Pool, but after they had eaten, Tom had another idea. Tom insisted that he saw not one but two ocelots about two hundred metres away from the picnic area. He claimed he spied the pair when they climbed down from a vine laden tree in the distance.

Grabbing Kaya's binoculars he announced gleefully, "See? I knew it."

Of course, when Kaya took a look through the binoculars, he could see nothing but greenery and more greenery. He had researched the ocelot on the Internet in the rainy evenings preceding the hike, and his investigations suggested that ocelots were vicious wildcats capable of instinctively attacking pressure points. This opinion directly contradicted Tom's view that ocelots were playful and inquisitive felines, which is why they were once favoured as pets and easy targets for the illegal fur trade.

Tom fearlessly ventured off the path, into the deep green, enthusiastically beckoning Kaya to follow.

"C'mon Abbers," said Tom, "get your camera ready, if we hurry I bet you'll get some half-decent shots."

"Man, we goin' after ah wild animal, jus' remember dat. Ocelots ent no little pussy cats."

"C'mon, stop whingeing, they'll get away," whispered Tom, climbing over the trunk of a fallen tree.

Kaya followed him deeper and deeper into the forest, away from the group. He regretted taking so many things in his rucksack; the grey bag Tom had slung over his shoulder, was much smaller and presumably much lighter than his gear. Kaya had also begun to feel the strain of his ankle weights on the muscles of his legs.

When they got to the bank of the Snake River, Kaya removed his baseball cap, wiped his brow and said, "Boy, yuh sure dey come dis way?"

"Yes, I'm sure," said Tom. "Ocelots can swim, trust me; I read all about them. Look, the river is shallow over here, and we can cross on these rocks."

"Ah have a bad feelin' 'bout dis," said Kaya. "Dem rocks look real slippery, an' how come dis river so shallow? It's rainy season—"

"Do you want to see the ocelots or not?" pressed Tom.

Kaya looked at his watch, "De group will leave de picnic area in fifteen minutes."

"I'm sure they won't leave without us. I'll go first," said Tom, gingerly stepping on the rocks.

"Wait," whispered Kaya, "what's that noise?"

"What noise?" asked Tom, lowering his voice.

Kaya instinctively picked up a small broken branch from the ground and turned towards the sound of movement behind them. He held the branch with both hands, poised for self-defence.

"You won't be able to fight off two ocelots," whispered Tom, ominously.

"I won't be able tuh fight off two ocelots? Ah thought dey were in front of us an' dey cross de river already; an' anyway, ah thought yuh say dey friendly."

"Why are you listening to me? I grew up in Oxford."

Kaya sucked his teeth and tightened his grip on the branch. He felt his heart beating in his chest, and his throat suddenly felt like he had swallowed sandpaper.

The sounds of hesitant movement got louder and louder. Kaya imagined the camouflaged wildcats assessing him from the thick green.

Dey t'ink I'm easy pickings, thought Kaya, *buh dem tiger cats getting' serious buss-head today.*

Kaya slowly raised his trembling arms a bit higher and waited, with bated breath, for the stalkers to emerge.

Suddenly, to Kaya's surprise, Raima Khan burst out of the undergrowth.

"What allyuh doin'?" she asked innocently.

"Kaya was just about to brain you, I think," said Tom, breathing a sigh of relief.

Embarrassed, Kaya lowered the branch and said defensively, "Tom say he see two tiger cats—"

"Yes. If we don't hurry, they'll get away," interrupted Tom, hastily crossing the shallow river.

"Ah t'ink dat boy crazy, oui," said Kaya.

"Yeah, buh we cyah jus' let him go into de forest alone," said Raima, with a mischievous grin.

"They're over here; I can see them," said Tom, trying his best not to shout.

"C'mon," said Kaya to Raima, "hold meh hand."

Without hesitation, he gripped Raima's left hand with his right and carefully stepped on the large smooth stones, using the branch in his left hand like a walking stick. Kaya imagined he was in heaven. But it wasn't a dream; he was holding the hand of the prettiest girl in Paria College.

Raima said, "If we doh see any tiger cats when we get tuh de other side, we turnin' back, OK?"

"With or without Dr Livingstone," said Kaya, jokingly referring to Tom.

Raima laughed, and Kaya deliberately walked slowly, so that he could hold her hand for as long as possible.

"So, where yuh bodyguards?" he asked Raima.

"Meenal and Shantel are not meh bodyguards," said Raima, trying to put on a serious face.

But Kaya just laughed, and she joined him.

Raima said, "Meenal got scared and turned back. Shantel went with her tuh make sure she didn't get lost."

Kaya had been completely engrossed by the sound of Raima's voice, the warmth of her hand, the scent of her bubblegum and a hint of her perfumed shampoo. Any annoyance he felt towards Tom disappeared.

Dat crazy English boy allowed this to happen. Ah holdin' Raima's hand.

But Kaya suddenly snapped out of his puppy-love stupor, when Raima asked, "Wha' wrong, Tom?"

"Don't you hear that?" came Tom's agitated reply.

Kaya not only heard it, he felt it — a rumble that rapidly got louder and louder. And, in an instant, Kaya knew what was happening.

"Run, Raima, run! De river comin' dong!"

As the dark surge of river water rushed towards them, Raima slipped off the rocks, pulling Kaya with her, and Kaya's dream quickly became a nightmare.

6

DROWNING

For a few seconds, which seemed like several minutes, Kaya tried unsuccessfully to make sense of what was going on. A sharp blow to his forehead had caused him to experience difficulty concentrating. But he finally realised that he was holding onto a rucksack, which seemed very odd, as the rucksack was pink — one of the few colours that did not appeal to him. Kaya knew it was of vital importance that he kept hold of the rucksack, but he could not remember why. Nevertheless, he gripped it as if his life depended on it. Kaya gradually became aware of terrible pain in his right forearm. The pain compelled him to release the rucksack, but he knew that no matter what, he had to hold on to it.

How ah go draw or paint with dis pain in meh arm? thought Kaya.

And muscular aches in both legs had him wondering, *How ah go beat Cobo in de hundred metre sprint on Sports Day?*

In his mind, Kaya distinctly heard a deep, earthy voice say, *"Focus, Hezekiah, focus."*

Not you again. De las' time yuh wanted meh to go to sleep. Now, yuh want meh to wake up?

"You are not dreaming, Hezekiah."

Doh tell meh ah hallucinatin' again.

"You are drowning, Hezekiah."

Buh wha' trouble is dis?

"If you have any sense of self-preservation, you will do exactly as I say."

Oh, Gawd, ah t'ink ah buss meh head.

"Listen carefully. You are approaching the branch of a fallen tree that has been lodged in the riverbank. You have to pull yourself and your female companion to the surface—"

Female companion?

"—you have to grab the branch, Hezekiah."

Through the murky water, Kaya saw that the pink rucksack, which he clung to so desperately, was attached to Raima Khan, who still wore it on her back. Raima was underwater, thrashing about in distress, and to his horror, Kaya realised that she was also drowning. Despite ongoing weekly lessons at college, Kaya had not yet learned to swim properly. And the weights strapped to each of his ankles made it difficult for him to keep afloat, but to remove the weights he needed to use both hands. Kaya would have to let go of Raima's rucksack, and he was determined not to do that.

"You have thirty seconds, Kaya. If you miss the branch, both you and your companion will be swept into the rapids. You will not survive."

Tumbling beneath the churning surface of the water, smashing against boulders and the bare, twisted branches of decomposing trees, Kaya began to panic. Disorientated, he had no idea which way was up. But just when he thought he would black out, his head came above water, and he snatched a couple breaths of air. He glimpsed the branch, which he approached at bewildering speed, and then, the relentless current plunged Kaya underwater again.

"Focus, Hezekiah, you have ten seconds."

Ah cyah do it, ah cyah do it.

"You must! Five, four, three, two, one...."

Kaya reached out and desperately grabbed the branch with his left hand. Momentum swung him into the trunk of the fallen tree, and his chest slammed into the rough bark, forcing the breath from his lungs. Miraculously, he maintained his grip on Raima.

She spluttered and sobbed hysterically, "Doh-leh-meh-go, doh-leh-meh-go."

Hearing her plea gave Kaya some comfort. *She alive, she still alive.*

"Hang on! I'm coming! Just hang on!" Kaya heard Tom shouting hysterically from a distance.

The raging water viciously tugged at Kaya, threatening to dislodge him from the dead branch. He saw Raima desperately reaching for protruding roots in the riverbank until finally she grabbed one. It broke, and she screamed. But Kaya still held onto her rucksack vehemently.

The water drove Raima back into the muddy bank. And, fortunately, she grabbed a firm root with each hand. Kaya relinquished the rucksack and experienced excruciating pain from the right side of his torso. Suffering from shock, he had not realised that by maintaining his grasp on Raima in the powerful currents, he had dislocated his shoulder. Unable to move his right shoulder, Kaya held his right arm protectively against his chest.

He watched Raima scramble for safety, muddied and bloodied, but alive. Raima quickly pulled off her rucksack and crawled back to Kaya, grabbing him under both arms. Kaya managed to get his feet firmly planted on the riverbank, and with Raima's help, he pushed himself out of the river's angry flow.

"Oh, Gawd, boy, yuh buss yuh head," wailed a hysterical Raima.

"Ah need mouth…." muttered Kaya.

"What?"

"Mouth-to-mouth resuscitation…."

Deprived of logic, driven by overwhelming panic, Raima immediately complied without thinking. It never occurred to her that Kaya did not need mouth-to-mouth resuscitation. So, she took a deep breath, filled her lungs with air, pressed her warm, full lips on Kaya's and exhaled. A look of blissful contentment instantly came upon Kaya's bloodstained face.

Cherry. She lips taste ah cherry.

"Oh, Gawd, Kaya, doh die boy."

Kaya recalled that he had deliberately walked slowly as they tried to cross the Snake River, and a feeling of guilt descended upon him.

"Is my fault," he mumbled.

Trying to pull him upright, Raima said, "Doh talk schupidness. Yuh have tuh sit up; ah have tuh get yuh rucksack off."

Kaya stared at Raima's pretty face contorted by profound grief, and he noticed that the steady flow of her tears washed away his blood from her cheeks.

"Jus' one more t'ing…." Kaya whispered weakly.

"Anyt'ing boy, anyt'ing…."

"Kiss meh…."

"Oh, Gawd, Kaya…."

Raima immediately kissed Kaya with lips that tasted of cherry-flavoured lip-gloss, and Kaya wondered how Raima's lip-gloss could survive the recent underwater escapade. His eyes rolled back, and he wondered if the tingling feeling, he now felt throughout his body, was what it felt like to die. Or was it love?

"Yuh save meh life boy, yuh save meh life…." said Raima, hugging Kaya close.

Suddenly, a frantic Tom came crashing through the tropical undergrowth. "Oh, my God," he said, "is he dead? Tell me he's not dead."

"He ent dead, buh ah doh t'ink we could move him. Yuh have tuh run an' get help, he head bleedin' real-real bad. Run boy, run…." sobbed Raima.

"Yes-yes, you're right, but first we have to try to stop the bleeding," said Tom, urgently.

"We could use we towels?"

"Yeah, he has a towel in his rucksack, help me get it out."

Tom succeeded in removing Kaya's rucksack, but Raima did not budge. She stared over Tom's shoulder with terrified eyes, too afraid to speak, too horrified to tremble.

Tom turned around, dropped the rucksack and immediately scrambled backwards along the ground with a loud shriek.

At first, Kaya saw what he imagined Tom and Raima had seen. A pair of ocelots emerged from the undergrowth, growling as they trotted towards them. Behind the wildcats, Kaya saw a tall, handsome, black man, with perfectly defined muscles. He wore a brown ragged vest and trousers, and a hollowed-out bull's horn hung from a thin belt of twisted vines around his waist. On his head, were the horns of a ram and instead of feet he had cloven hooves like those of the native red brocket deer. He had snow-white dreadlocks and a goatee beard, strewn with small green leaves. He sported dark tattoos, which ran the length of both of his muscular arms.

Papa Bois, thought Kaya.

But, as the mythological figure approached, striding with confidence towards the three terrified college students, Kaya saw an entirely different image. He saw the same black man, with less-defined muscles. He wore a shimmering skin-tight jumpsuit that reflected the surrounding flora, thereby providing adequate camouflage. Gone were the horns, cloven hooves, white dreadlocks and beard. Instead, Kaya saw that the man sported black hair trimmed very close to the skin. The approaching ocelots remained unchanged.

Raima finally screamed in terror, and Tom tried once more to escape, but stumbled and fell to the ground a whimpering bundle of nerves.

"Neela! Akeeta!" barked the strange man, and the ocelots immediately stopped their approach.

The cats sat and stared at the man as he walked past them. His piercing gaze remaining fixed on Kaya. Kaya had immediately recognised the man's voice. It was the voice of his subconscious mind.

People see an' hear some real funny t'ings when dey dying, thought Kaya.

Raima cried, "Bonjour, vieux Papa. Bonjour, Maître Bois. Ne nous blesser pas, s'il vous plait. Please don't hurt us—"

"Je ne fais que du mal aux coupables, jeune femme," replied the man, "I harm only the guilty, young lady."

The man pulled a small grey metallic tube from a holster on the belt around his waist. Kaya and his companions gasped in unison as the tube suddenly extended to a staff the length of a walking stick. Terrified, Tom softly recited prayers, and Raima continued to sob.

Kaya noticed the sound of a low hum, just like the one he heard on the last night of his fever. Suddenly, he saw quick flashes of light emanate from the top of the staff into Raima's light-brown eyes. She blinked twice, then her eyes rolled back, and she slumped to the ground unconscious. Instantly, immobilised by fear, Kaya felt his heart thumping against the wall of his chest. The man turned the flashing lights to Tom's eyes and Tom immediately collapsed.

Oh, Gawd, ah doh wan' tuh die.

Aiming the light at Kaya, the man announced, "You have suffered an anterior dislocation of your right humerus and mild traumatic brain injury."

"What yuh do to meh friends?" asked Kaya.

"I sedated them. Prolonged elevated stress levels are hazardous."

"Who are you?"

"I am Papa Bois," replied the man, calmly.

"Nah, you're not."

The man just raised a curious eyebrow. Suddenly, Kaya saw bright flashes of light. His eyelids became very heavy, so he closed his eyes and surrendered to oblivion.

7

THE SECRET

Kaya opened his eyes, slowly, allowing the white light of brilliant sunshine to saturate his blurred vision. Suddenly, a dark shadow darted high above, and at first Kaya thought it was a great black hawk, but the distinctive sound of spinning rotor blades soon replaced the ringing in his ears, and he realised that a helicopter had arrived. But, arrived where? Where was he? The sound of the police helicopter, high above the Azura Forest, quickly receded, replaced by the angry roar of the Snake River. Kaya vaguely remembered hitting his head and almost drowning in the river's flow.

Sitting upright, he fearfully placed trembling fingers on his forehead and discovered that his terrible head wound had inexplicably healed. Gone too, were the excruciating pains of a dislocated shoulder and bruised and battered limbs. If not for his wet, bloodstained shirt, Kaya could easily believe that he had imagined the life-threatening events of the last hour. It seemed that the individual who called himself Papa Bois had performed a miracle, but Kaya remained fully aware that things were not always as they seemed.

Miracle or not, something extraordinary had occurred. Kaya's senses fully returned. In fact, they had dramatically improved. It was as if, prior to his encounter with Papa Bois, he had been looking through a dirty glass window with his nostrils pinched shut with a clothespin and his ears stuffed with cotton wool.

Kaya saw Raima sitting at the river's edge, crying, while Tom remained on the ground, lying on his back, eyes closed.

"Get up, Tom, get up."

"Is he gone?"

"Who?"

Stubbornly keeping his eyes firmly shut, Tom cried, "What do you mean, who? Didn't you see him? Didn't you see his horns and cloven hooves?"

"He gone."

"What about the ocelots?"

"Gone."

Finally opening his eyes, Tom exclaimed, "What happened to the gash in your skull?"

"Dat gone too."

"Good Lord, there's only one logical explanation for what happened to your head."

"What?"

"Voodoo."

"Doh be schupid, boy."

"Papa Bois used his black magic. How else do you explain the fact that the big bleedin' gash in your skull has mysteriously disappeared, huh?"

"Ah dunno."

"He spoke to the ocelots, did you notice that? And they listened. I think we're dealing with Satan himself. Wait till I tell my dad—"

"Yuh crazy? Yuh cyah tell him dat. Yuh cyah tell anybody."

"Why not?"

"Because they'll t'ink we crazy."

"But we all saw him—"

"Yuh clothes covered in blood, boy. How yuh go explain dat?" asked Raima, composing herself and wiping away her tears with the back of her hand.

"Ah won't."

Kaya quickly removed his bloodstained college shirt, threw it into the river's swift flow, retrieved the grey cotton vest from his rucksack and put it on.

Raima's blouse was also stained with Kaya's blood. She immediately removed it, revealing the red bathing suit she wore underneath. After throwing her blouse into the fast-flowing river, she turned towards the suddenly awe-struck boys.

"What?" asked Raima.

"Great," said Tom. "You're forcing me to lie, and I don't think Papa Bois will be too impressed by the two of you polluting the river."

"If he's de devil, wouldn't he be happy?" said Kaya.

"Good point."

"I can hear Hütter an' Silly Willy; they'll be here soon. Not ah word about Papa Bois. Agreed?"

"You can hear them? Where are they?" asked Tom.

"About 400 metres, dat way," replied Kaya, pointing to undergrowth to their left.

"And, you can hear them? Does this seem normal to you?"

"Ah agree wit' Kaya, ah doh want nobody tuh t'ink ah seein' t'ings," said Raima. "Ah ent tellin' ah soul about Papa Bois."

"Wha' about you, Tom?

"OK, OK. But—"

"Yuh agree?" pressed Kaya, and his brooding brows narrowed.

"How, in heaven's name, can your disappeared gash be explained? I don't feel well, I think I'm going to be sick—"

"I jus' want tuh go home now, and ah doh want to spend de next six months seein' ah psychiatrist," said Raima, emptying the river-water from her rucksack, before slinging it over her shoulder. "Gawd, ah feel dizzy. Whoever it was we see, ah never want tuh see him again, and ah don't want tuh talk about him, tuh anybody."

Kaya wiped away any telltale traces of blood with his water-soaked towel. "Tom, ah tellin' yuh now; we cyah be tellin' people we see Papa Bois. They go t'ink we crazy, on drugs, or possessed by demons. Yuh ha' tuh t'ink of yuh father, on de front page of every newspaper, tryin' to explain wha' wrong wit' yuh."

Tom held Kaya's stare for a moment. Then, with a heavy sigh, he said, "OK, OK, you're right. They'll think we're bonkers. Not a word about Papa Bois."

That evening, Paria College principal, Dr Gerald Harry a.k.a. Hairy Harry, drove Meenal, Raima, Tom, and Kaya, to their respective homes. He had a lot of explaining to do. By all accounts, Meenal had accidentally walked into a tree and needed to be checked for a possible concussion. At her impressive home, Kaya noticed that a sling supported her mother's right arm, and her father walked with a limp, but he said nothing.

Tom muttered, "Apparently, just one month ago, Meenal's mother reversed into her father with her Range Rover. The accident happened in the car park of the automotive dealership he owns. Sod's law really; he imported that car especially for her. Then, last week, her mother had another accident. The poor woman broke her arm. Meenal says she slipped on a running machine. Today, Meenal whacked her head on a tree branch. She gets so carried away when she's talking...."

From the front passenger seat of Hairy Harry's car, Kaya saw the Firenze red Range Rover that belonged to Meenal's mother, and next to it was the Range Rover that her father owned. A large dent on the driver's door marred the otherwise pristine Buckingham blue paintwork.

Poor 'oman? Unlucky maybe, but poor? No way.

Kaya and Raima remained silent, numbed by the day's shocking events. Kaya slowly inched his hand towards Raima's. He wanted to hold her hand, but a sense of guilt and a sudden fear of rejection got the better of him.

We nearly die today, because ah didn't listen to meh gut feelin'. Raima an' me? Not ah chance.... She only kiss meh because she was in shock an' she feel sorry fuh meh.

Hairy Harry drove the short distance to Raima's home at Royal Palm Avenue, where her worried parents waited impatiently at the gates. Tall palms obscured the house, which was situated at the top of a hill. After calmly thanking Kaya, for saving his daughter from drowning, and suggesting to Raima's mother that they invite the *brave boy* for dinner soon, Raima's father lambasted Hairy Harry for half an hour, repeatedly threatening him with legal action. On the other hand, Tom's dad offered cookies and spiritual counselling. And, Josephine — well, Josephine hit the roof. Long after sending the beleaguered principal packing, with a serious piece of her mind, she continued venting to Kaya.

"First yuh near get shot, den yuh near drong? Ah ha' ah mind tuh sue de damn college."

"De police ketch de poachers," protested Kaya.

"Ah doh care! Why de college have tuh take children tuh a place where it have men wit' guns, eh? An' dey couldn't see de river was dangerous?"

"Mammy, like yuh forgettin' wha' Trinidad like now, an' de teachers didn't send us tuh cross de river—"

"Dis is your first an' last trip tuh dat damn forest. Yuh hear meh? Your last!"

8

MEN IN BLACK

That night, Kaya lay awake in his bed, utterly exhausted but unable to sleep. He could see clearly in the dark. In fact, the LED of his computer's standby button seemed so annoyingly bright, he had to cover it with masking tape. Kaya tried, to no avail, to ignore the scent of cat urine from the garden. And, the myriad sickly sweet fragrances, of the various flowers kept downstairs in his mother's flower shop, did not help at all. But, more than that, the sounds he heard really bothered him. Crickets threatened to drive Kaya mad with their infernal high-pitched racket, as did the deep throbbing soca music from passing cars. Then, there were the nocturnal activities of the newlyweds who lived three houses away. And how his mind raced. With the day's events weighing heavily on his mind, images of water, rushing towards him, constantly jolted him back to agitated wakefulness. He remembered everything vividly — every little detail. That is, everything, until Papa Bois appeared. After the arrival of the father of the forest, there was an impenetrable darkness in Kaya's mind, and he harboured an overwhelming feeling that something terrifying had been erased.

Wha' happened to us? Wha' happened to meh? Wha' he do tuh meh? So, Tantie Rose was right. Papa Bois real....

Gradually, Kaya became distracted by the sound of Josephine shuffling about in the kitchen. He heard cupboard doors being closed, followed by items being placed on the counter. He recognised the sound of the refrigerator door being opened and of liquid being poured. Josephine activated the microwave oven, and it hummed for two minutes before abruptly ending with a ding. Kaya smelt it now.

Milo.

The warming scent of chocolate and malt banished all others, as Kaya listened to every padded footstep Josephine made towards his bedroom in her fluffy slippers.

Like whatever Papa Bois do tuh heal meh buss head, makin' meh see, hear, an' smell better.

Kaya anticipated Josephine's gentle knock on his bedroom door.

"Kaya, yuh awake?" she whispered.

"Yeah," said Kaya, and he switched on the reading lamp on his bedside table.

Josephine gently pushed the door open and stepped in, "Ah had a feelin' yuh would be up, so ah make some Milo fuh yuh."

"T'anks."

Josephine handed Kaya the mug of the warm beverage, which he rested on the bedside table. Then she sat on the old rocking chair next to his bed.

With a sigh, she said, "Meh heart nearly jump outta meh chest when ah see de principal at de front door. T'ank Gawd, nothing happen tuh yuh. T'ank Gawd." And, valiantly holding back her tears, she added with a broken voice, "Boy, ah t'ink yuh granny looking out fuh yuh, oui. Dat woman loved yuh. She really, truly, loved yuh."

"Ah miss her too Mammy."

"Ah didn't mean tuh shout dis evening. Ah hope yuh forgive meh. Yuh mean more tuh meh dan anything in dis world, Kaya. Ah hope yuh know dat."

"Yes, ah know," said Kaya, meekly.

"So tell meh, how yuh manage tuh save Princess Khan from drownin'? Ah real glad yuh taking dem swimmin' lessons at college."

"Princess?"

"Princess, oui. Boy, yuh ha' tuh be rich like royalty tuh live on Royal Palm Avenue," chuckled Josephine.

"Raima not like dat. She doh act hoity-toity," said Kaya, defensively.

"Oh, is so? Tell meh what else yuh know about Miss Raima."

Kaya saw where this conversation was heading, and he did not like it. He did not like it, one bit.

Yuh jus' wouldn't understand, he thought, *Raima not like other rich girls.*

"We were following Tom across de river, when de river come dong."

"Tom is de new boy from England?"

"Yeah."

"Wha' yuh doin' following ah English boy, into de bush, as if he know where he goin'?"

"Well, we see dees two tiger cats—"

"Tiger cats! OK, yuh know what? Drink yuh Milo, quick, before it get cold. In de morning, you and I will talk about what you, de rich girl, de English boy, and de tiger cats, were doin' in de bush. Dat's after I take ah half ah dozen of yuh granny pressure pills."

"Yuh cyah do dat!"

"Buh how yuh mean?"

"Ah sure all dem old pills expire already."

They both laughed.

"Boy, ah proud ah yuh, an' ah sure yuh granny proud too. Yuh save yuh friend from drownin'; an' yuh come home tuh meh in one piece. Dat's the most important t'ing. Drink de Milo, it will help yuh tuh go tuh sleep."

Josephine stood up and walked towards the door.

"Mammy?"

"Yes, son?"

"Yuh t'ink meh father proud too?"

Josephine's smile faded, and Kaya felt she was looking right through him, when she said, "Yes, Kaya, ah sure he proud of yuh too. Very, very proud. It late now, drink de Milo, an' go tuh sleep."

Josephine was about to leave, but Kaya asked, "How did he die?"

Josephine turned to Kaya, stunning him with an unexpectedly anguished expression. Her voice was thick with emotion, when she said, "Ah tell yuh before…. It was ah accident."

"Buh yuh never even tell meh what kinda accident. Yuh never tell meh anyt'ing. Ah doh know ah t'ing about meh own father."

"Ah well and truly sorry, Kaya, buh dere are things yuh still too young tuh understand."

"Ah almost fifteen, an' yuh t'ink ah too young? So when yuh t'ink I'll be old enough?"

"Yuh have tuh trust meh Kaya. I've had to do difficult t'ings. Heartbreaking, unbearable t'ings. But ah will never feel regret because ah will do anyt'ing, anyt'ing at all, tuh protect yuh. Even if yuh never forgive meh. Even if ah have tuh give meh own life tuh save yours."

"What yuh really sayin'? Wha' yuh talkin' 'bout? Yuh won't tell meh who he was, so at least, jus' tell meh how he die. Ah need tuh know, Mammy. Ah need tuh know."

"OK. Alright. Ah will tell yuh, but yuh must swear not tuh tell anyone," said Josephine, sternly.

"OK," said Kaya, softly.

"Swear tuh Gawd, Kaya."

"Ah swear tuh Gawd, ah won't tell ah soul."

Josephine stared at Kaya intently. Then, with a forlorn sigh, she said, "Dey say laugh and cry live on de same street. Well, boy, ah learn dat lesson de hard way. In life yuh ha to expect anyt'ing anytime." With a distant look in her eyes, she sat in the rocking chair that once belonged to Mama Flo. "Ah had fallen out with yuh granny; an' ah was stayin' with Tantie Rose in Tortuga when ah met yuh father. Ah was twenty-one; he was much older, an' ah felt ah was…. Ah felt we were indestructible. Dat's what it's like when you're young. But, of course, we were not indestructible. Yuh father…. Yuh father was ah fugitive, so what we had was secret—"

"A fugitive, yuh mean he was ah criminal?"

"Ah say he was ah criminal? No, yuh father was not ah criminal. He was de kindest, wisest, most gentle human being ah ever knew; an' ah loved him with all meh heart."

"Buh—"

Josephine raised her right hand, motioning Kaya to be quiet.

"Nobody knew ah was seein' him. Ah never told ah soul. But, about two months before yuh father died, two men were in Tortuga askin' all sorta questions. Dey even spoke tuh Tantie Rose. Dey wanted tuh know if anybody saw yuh father. Well, yuh gran'aunt didn't trust dem one bit. So, when dey asked, she told dem, she lived alone. Clarence was at work, and Christina was already trainin' tuh be ah nurse in England; ah was inside, peepin' through de curtains, an' ah watched dem good. Two bald-pated men, white like ghosts, dressed in black suits. Everyt'ing about dem really scared meh. An', when Tantie Rose ask dem if dey were de police, de taller one say, as cool as a cucumber, "No, we are employed by a higher authority." Tuh dis day, nobody could say what dis higher authority is.

"Anyway, after dat, yuh father wanted tuh end it. He never tell meh who de men were, or what dey wanted with him, buh he say it was too dangerous, and he didn't wan' tuh put meh in jeopardy. Of course, dis just made meh want him even more. Ah begged him tuh see meh one last time. We planned tuh spend de day at de beach; but, on de road tuh Maracas, yuh father realised dat de men were followin' us. He slowed dong long enough tuh push meh outta de car, den he drive off like he was flyin' low. Dey chased him. He didn't get too far. Ah saw de car go over ah cliff an' burst into flames."

Josephine paused to gather her composure, and then she continued, "Ah walked, an' walked, an' walked. Ah was in ah daze. Ah just wanted to get as far away from de accident as ah could. Fuh years after, ah felt guilty about walking away; ah suppose, now, ah could see dat ah was in shock. Ah took a taxi back tuh Tortuga; dat was de most difficult journey ah ever took in meh life. Ah couldn't dare show any grief, even though meh heart was burstin', ah was so afraid de men in black would come lookin' fuh meh. Before ah could get tuh de front door, it started tuh rain. Ah doh t'ink it ever rain like it did dat day. An' den ah was sick. Yuh gran'aunt came rushin' out tuh get meh, an' ah vomit all over she new dress. At de time, ah thought ah was just upset, but about ah week later, ah realised ah was pregnant. Well, boy, Mammy didn't talk tuh Tantie Rose fuh five years because of dat."

Josephine paused to hold back the tears, and then she continued, "Of course, de accident was in all de news. De police say dey couldn't identify de body. Burnt, beyond recognition, dey say. But de car, he was drivin', was another matter. That had been stolen de day before. He did dat ah few times.... Buh yuh father was not ah criminal; he would always take de car back afterwards.... Buh not dat last time.... Not dat last time...."

Before Kaya could utter another word, Josephine left the room, closing the door gently behind her. Kaya sat transfixed — too shocked to breathe, too numb to move. He sat like that, for what seemed to be a painful eternity, as anger, confusion, sadness, and grief, gathered together into a large ball that relentlessly grew in the pit of his stomach. Finally, the weight of it dragged him down into the security of his bed. With a heavy sigh, Kaya curled up, under the covers, dizzy and beleaguered by questions.

He switched off the lamp on his bedside table. And, through the shutters of his bedroom window, he peered at the star-filled sky, unable to find solace, completely ill-equipped to console his bitterly crying mother, and yearning for a father he never knew. It seemed a long time since Kaya heard his mother cry — a long time since the death of Mama Flo. He recalled Mama Flo and Tantie Rose, reminiscing about when they were little girls, and sharing memories of the night they saw the stars, dancing, in the heavens above Tortuga. For a long time, Kaya gazed earnestly at the canopy of flickering lights, and he wondered if, somewhere up there, his father still existed. Eventually, sleep got the better of Kaya, but that night, in Coconut Grove, the stars did not dance.

9

BIG PAPPY DINNER

Two weeks later, Raima's father arrived at Paria College in his black Mercedes-Benz S-Class sedan. If not for his receding hairline, greying sideburns, horn-rimmed sunglasses and the fact he was clean-shaven, Ashok Khan looked a lot like Omar Sharif, in Dr Zhivago, at least that's what Kaya thought. He parked outside the college gates where Kaya, Raima, and Devika, Raima's bespectacled younger sister, patiently waited. Josephine had begrudgingly agreed to allow Kaya to accept the Khans' dinner invitation.

Josephine said, "Mammy always used tuh say, *'Cockroach have no right in fowl party.'* Ah doh really like yuh feedin' yuh face wit' dem big pappies; because dey have money, dey feel dey better dan we."

But Kaya knew how much Josephine valued Tara Khan's business. Providing floral decorations for Patisserie Bougainvillea, seven days a week, was very lucrative. Josephine would not risk offending Mrs Khan, despite her aversion towards Trinidad's bourgeoisie.

Devika opened the front passenger door and was about to get in.

But Mr Khan said, "Sugar Plum, let Kaya sit in front. There's more room for his long legs."

"Ah thought Raima wanted tuh sit with she boyfrien' in de back."

Raima rolled her eyes, opened the rear passenger door and said, "Dad, ah doh know wha' wrong wit' dis chile. Kaya, you sit in front."

Kaya sat uneasily in the front seat and discreetly wiped his sweaty palms on his trousers.

"Hello, Mr Khan," he said, with a firm handshake.

"Hello, young man," said Mr Khan.

"Ah ent no chile, I'm eleven," grumbled Devika.

Raima said, "Doh swell up yuh face, yuh look like ah bullfrog."

Devika retorted, "An', yuh look like ah unicorn, wit' dat big zit on yuh big head!"

Mr Khan cleared his throat, and Kaya saw him glare at the reflection of the girls in the rear-view mirror. They immediately stopped bickering. Mr Khan looked at Kaya and smiled, but Kaya could not see Mr Khan's eyes and that unsettled Kaya even more. Kaya had never been in such a luxurious car. And, because he wanted to impress Raima and her family, he felt quite nervous. But all nervousness vanished when Cobo noticed Kaya sitting in the front seat of the Khan sedan. Kaya smiled gleefully, savouring the look of surprise and jealousy on Cobo's red face.

After a short journey, with Kaya's anticipation steadily mounting, Mr Khan guided the Mercedes through large automatic gates, onto the sweeping Indian sandstone drive of 22 Royal Palm Avenue. Kaya never imagined that one day he would be invited to the house that many of Coconut Grove's envious residents referred to as Royal Manor. At the top of a hill, nestled on an acre of landscaped tropical gardens, the Khan residence was a testament to modern luxury, colonial elegance and Trinbagonian upper class excess. A large satellite dish stuck out like a sore thumb, prompting Kaya to imagine that ET would have no difficulty using it to phone home. Nevertheless, with its cathedral ceilings, large bay windows and stone balconies that afforded panoramic views of both Coconut Grove and the Gulf of Paria, Raima's home seemed like a fairytale palace to Kaya. A broad, stone stairway led up to a large covered patio and impressive double doors of the finest Teak wood. The doors opened, and Raima's mother emerged wearing a white summer dress and sporting a welcoming smile.

Kaya was about to get out of the car when he noticed two Doberman Pinschers with docked tails, cropped ears, and spiked collars, racing across the lawn towards the Mercedes. Suddenly terrified, he quickly slammed the car door shut.

"Some hero," scoffed Devika.

With their forepaws pressed against the passenger window, the dogs barked, snarled and growled at Kaya, baring large, intimidating teeth. He was tempted to explain that he had been bitten on the back of his left thigh by a stray dog when he was eight. But he decided that putting on a brave face was a better option. No need to reveal the existence of the small scar that made him feel self-conscious.

Mr Khan muttered, "If these dogs scratch this car, they gettin' neutered tomorrow."

"Don't worry, the dogs don't bite. Abbadon! Calibos! Behave! Lutchman, put the dogs in the kennel please," cried Mrs Khan.

To Kaya, these animals seemed more like minions of Satan than family pets. He looked on, in awe, as Lutchman the gardener, handyman and general dogsbody, swallowed hard and walked towards the viciously barking animals.

Dat is one brave man, thought Kaya. *Buh he so skinny. Skin an' dog bones.*

In unison, the dogs stopped barking, turned and sat staring at Lutchman, who approached cautiously.

Lutchman slowly raised both hands and whistled. "Come now, is kennel time, fuh de two ah you, an' doh gimme no trouble."

Suddenly, the dogs bolted towards Lutchman and leapt on him, knocking him flat on his back.

Oh, Gawd, ah t'ink we better call ah ambulance.

Kaya used this opportunity to get out of the car. Determined not to show fear a second time, he resisted the urge to run to the safety of the house. Mr Khan gripped Kaya firmly by the shoulder.

Smiling broadly, he said, "Come inside, my good fellow, let me show you around the house. We're eager to hear how you saved Raima from certain doom."

"Ah t'ink Lutchman facin' certain doom right now."

Raima giggled, "Doh worry, de dogs jus' playin'."

Ah doh know 'bout dat. It look like de dogs goin tuh eat Lutchman raw, thought Kaya.

Mr Khan observed Lutchman trying desperately to get up as the excited dogs kept him pinned to the ground.

Suddenly, whipping off his sunglasses, he said, "Lutchman! Stop playing with the dogs and put them in the kennel."

At the top of the stairs, Mrs Khan added, "Lutchman loves those dogs; he's taken care of them since they were pups."

Poor Lutchman, thought Kaya.

Once inside the house, the Khans treated Kaya to a tour that had him scarcely believing his senses. Mr Khan proudly explained that the ground floor of the house was made of Carrara marble. Mrs Khan pointed out that Carrara was a town in Tuscany. The Pantheon and Trajan's Column in Rome, Michelangelo's David in Florence, and even the Marble Arch in London were made from marble quarried from Carrara. Kaya was not familiar with any of this, but he had no difficulty deducing that the marble was imported from Italy and cost *plenty money*. Everywhere in the house, classic furnishings contrasted state of the art modern devices. This was most apparent in the impressive entertainment room, which boasted full surround sound, a massive flat-screen television, a projector, various computer game consoles and reference-quality hi-fi audio equipment. The huge satellite dish allowed the Khans to watch television from around the world, and Wi-Fi networking meant that exclusive entertainment could be streamed throughout Royal Manor. Ornately framed family portraits graced the walls of the large lounge, and a monochrome photograph of an African family immediately caught Kaya's attention. He had not forgotten that Raima said that her grandmother was Sudanese.

"That's an old photograph of my grandparents, my mother, my uncle and my two aunties," said Mrs Khan, proudly. "It was taken in a studio somewhere in Port of Spain, a year after they came from Sudan."

"Which one is your mother?" asked Kaya, fascinated by the exotic faces captured in the photographic image.

"Oh, she's the youngest. She was nine when this photograph was taken."

Looking at the image of the young girl, who possessed high cheek-bones and full lips, and consciously trying to speak properly, Kaya asked, "What is her name?"

"Her name is Rita," said Mrs Khan, and noting Kaya's intrigued expression, she added, "Grandpa and Grandma were Catholic.

"She's pretty," said Kaya, sincerely.

"But how yuh mean? Of course she's pretty, she's from Juba," said Mrs Khan, gleefully. Drawing Kaya's attention to a more recent photograph, she said, "Pretty and tall. See how tall she is? Raima has her lips."

Unseen by her parents, Raima rolled her eyes then pouted provocatively at Kaya. Devika shook her head with dismay.

"You see, she's slightly taller than Pa," continued Mrs Khan, showing off a wedding photograph of a young couple — an African woman and a Trinbagonian man of Indian descent.

"So, dey live in Port of Spain?" asked Kaya.

"Well, they moved to San Fernando, two years before I was born. That's where my brothers and I grew up, and a few years after Ashok and I got married, Ma and Pa moved to England. That's where Pa was born.

"They live in Surbiton," added Devika.

Kaya asked, "Is dat near Barnet? Dat's where meh cousin live."

Devika shrugged her shoulders, displayed the empty palms of her hands and made a funny face. She looked to Mrs Khan for an answer, but Mrs Khan had no idea and turned to Mr Khan, "Ashok, you know where Barnet is?"

Mr Khan did not seem confident when he replied, "Well, I think Barnet is North London.... Isn't it?"

"We're not sure," admitted Mrs Khan. "Raima, darling, go look it up on one of the tablets...."

Raima rolled her eyes and whined softly, "Mum...."

"No-no, doh trouble yourself, I'll check it when ah go home," said Kaya.

"OK," said Mrs Khan, eagerly. "Let's go up to the main balcony. From there, you can see where Abercromby sailed into the Gulf of Paria, with eighteen warships, to capture Trinidad from the Spanish crown."

For dinner, the Khans treated Kaya to Tantie's curry chicken and dhalpuri roti; a national dish, brought to Trinidad by indentured labourers from India in the 19th century. The word roti is derived from Sanskrit meaning bread. Dhalpuri, Trinidad's most popular roti, contains a stuffing of ground yellow split peas, toasted cumin, garlic and pepper, rolled flat and cooked on a metal griddle brushed with oil.

"Your auntie is ah really good cook," said Kaya, helping himself to seconds.

"She not meh auntie," said Raima, with a smile.

"Shanti has been the family cook since before Devika was born," said Mrs Khan, "When she was small, Raima couldn't say Shanti. Whenever she tried, it ended up sounding like Tantie, and eventually everybody started calling Shanti, Tantie."

Kaya repeated the compliment, "Well, she's ah really good cook."

"You hear dat, Tantie?" cried Mr Khan.

A grey-haired woman of Indian descent, with a face lined with experience and eyes that betrayed kindness, emerged from the kitchen.

Smiling warmly, she said, "T'anks, Mr Khan." And looking to Kaya she said, "T'anks, young sir. So, who want kurma?"

"Me," chorused Kaya, Raima, and Devika.

Kurma, an East Indian delicacy, which was originally reserved for the Diwali festival of lights, had become such a popular snack that it was now available throughout the year, to be enjoyed by all. During the main meal, Kaya recounted the events in the Azura Forest, taking special care not to mention anything directly relating to Papa Bois. And, for the first time, Kaya felt he could see real admiration in Raima's eyes. He felt like a king. Then something odd began to occur.

"So, Kaya," said Mr Khan, "Raima tells me you joined the WHT. Conservation is something we all feel strongly about in this house."

"Raima told us about your art. Real artists are few and far between, but everyone is a critic," said Mrs Khan. "Creative people are risk takers. True artists tend to be romantics. After all, there are few things riskier than baring your heart and soul to another. There are few things more devastating than a broken heart or more tragic than a lost soul. I think artistic people are

often more socially conscious, and that's one of the reasons I like supporting
local artists. So, if your art is as good as Raima says, I might be interested in
buying a few pieces. I could hang them in the patisserie; that should give you
some good exposure. I hope you're not expensive."

Kaya thought he heard voices whispering, but he effectively hid his
unease.

"T'anks, Mrs Khan, ah could do one 'specially fuh you. Ah never
sell ah painting yet; an' ah wouldn't charge yuh fuh it. It would be ah gift."

"That's very kind Kaya, but if you want to be an artist by profession,
you won't get very far if you give away your work. Most artists can barely
feed themselves. No, I insist on paying for the art you produce, just set a
reasonable price."

"Ah like de ones yuh did in Tortuga," said Raima, "they have lots of
bright colours."

"Yes, Kaya, nowadays there aren't enough paintings of the country.
Everyone seems to be churning out this pretentious abstract nonsense," said
Mrs Khan.

Then, Kaya thought he heard Mr Khan say, *Odd name, Kaya.
Sound like ah girl's name — something to do with marijuana? Ah never
imagine Josephine tuh be de Rasta type."*

Kaya was polite, but firm, when he said, "Kaya, is short fuh Hezekiah, buh nobody call meh dat. Meh mother have plaits; buh dat have nothing
tuh do with weed or Rastas."

Puzzled silence descended on the dinner table.

"Oh, of course not," said Mrs Khan, "why on earth would anyone
think that? I've always admired Josephine's hair. Hezekiah is the name of a
king, right?"

"Yeah, Hezekiah in de Bible, dat's where meh name come from."

It took Kaya a moment to deduce that he had heard Mr Khan's
thoughts.

Then, Kaya heard Mrs Khan thinking, *Why he so defensive? Ah
wonder wha' really happen in de Azura Forest. Raima far too young tuh be
experimentin' wit' boys in de bush.*

Kaya almost choked on his orange juice.

Kaya jus' like all de boys at college, thought Devika, and Kaya heard
her. *All ah them follow Raima around like puppy dogs, but they don't even
know ah exist. Ah wish ah didn't wear froupsy glasses an' look like ah nerd.*

"Ah like yuh glasses," Kaya said to Devika impulsively.

Devika seemed stunned, but she recovered quickly and said, "Yuh
jus' saying dat."

Raima rolled her eyes.

"That's not what you say when someone pays you a compliment, young lady," said Mr Khan.

"T'anks, Kaya," said Devika, sheepishly.

Ah wish he could rescue meh from ah river. Then he could kiss meh like he kiss Raima.

This time, Kaya choked on his orange juice.

Nice boy, but a bit strange. Too bad he's from such a poor family, thought Mr and Mrs Khan.

Wha' happenin' tuh meh? Like somet'ing in de food makin' meh hear what dey t'inking. Dis ent de first time ah eat curry chicken and roti; and ah doh t'ink is de orange juice. What different about dis food?

Kaya remembered the strange dream when he was ill at the start of the college term. He became quite uneasy.

He recalled the stern warning: *"Be careful what you eat or drink. There are those who would do you harm."*

Buh ah cyah believe Raima or she family would want tuh do anyt'ing bad tuh meh.

Raima's thoughts remained a mystery. And, throughout dessert, Kaya heard smaller and smaller snippets of thoughts from Devika and Mr and Mrs Khan; until, to his disappointment, he heard nothing at all.

After dessert, convinced that something unusual had been put in the main meal, Kaya loitered around the kitchen, hoping to get information from Tantie.

When they were alone, Tantie smiled warmly and said, "Ah know why yuh hangin' 'round ah ole 'oman like meh."

Oh, Gawd, like de curry make she psychic too.

"How yuh mean?" asked Kaya, projecting an air of complete innocence.

"Doh skylark; ax meh wha' yuh dyin' tuh ax meh."

"Yuh could read meh mind?" asked Kaya, tentatively.

"Well, ah doh need ah crystal ball," said Tantie, straight-faced. Then, she suddenly started laughing, and she slapped Kaya on the back. "Boy, ah could read yuh like a book."

"Buh how?"

Tantie said, "Sweet chile, it all over yuh face." Then, whispering, she added, "Raima is ah very pretty girl, an' she know it; make sure yuh doh get bazodee. If yuh want she tuh see yuh as ah boyfrien' and not ah frien', yuh ha' tuh be confident. Dat's wha' 'omen like in ah man; an', it doh matter wha' age dey are. Confidence. Mamaguy does only amuse ah 'oman. Tease she ah bit, yes. Buh if yuh spen' yuh time tellin' she how she wonderful, she go lose interest in yuh one time. Doh talk too much. An' doh be too nice — 'omen hate dat. De amount ah mudders tell their boy-chile dem tuh be sweet tuh 'omen an' turn dem into cunumunu...." Tantie paused and shook her head. "Not me. Ah ha' five sons; an', tuh dis day, not one ah dem ha' any 'oman trouble."

For a moment, Kaya remained dumbfounded. Then, he was relieved that Tantie could not read his thoughts.

"So, she interested in meh?"

"Papa yo!" exclaimed Tantie, in mock surprise. "Yuh cyah see? Buh, unless yuh play yuh cards right, she'll be goin' tuh de Christmas Ball wit' somebody else."

"Kaya?" came Raima's voice.

Tantie winked at Kaya.

"T'anks, Tantie," said Kaya.

"Oh, yuh in here," said Raima, as she entered the kitchen, "wha' allyuh talkin' 'bout?"

"Ah was askin' Tantie 'bout she chicken curry recipe."

"What? Like yuh could cook or what?"

"Yes," said Kaya, mildly embarrassed.

"Is so? What yuh could cook?"

"Soup."

Raima chuckled, "Soup? What kinda soup?"

"Nothing special, just chicken soup."

"Hmmm.... Well, yuh will have tuh cook some fuh meh sometime."

"If yuh cut up de chicken, an' peel de potatoes, we have ah deal."

Raima stared into Kaya's dark brown eyes and absent-mindedly licked her lips. Then, with a wry smile, she said, "OK. Deal."

Behind Raima, Tantie gave Kaya a wink of approval.

"So Tantie, what is de secret ingredient in yuh curry?"

Tantie chuckled, "How yuh know ah use ah secret ingredient?"

"Ah figure yuh put something special in it tuh make it taste so nice."

"Ooh Papa! Raima, like yuh frien' here smart too bad." Turning to Kaya, Tantie gently pushed his chin up and down and from side to side. Examining his features, she continued, "Yeah, young sir, is smart yuh well smart. Raima, watch he ears.... Yuh see how dey stickin' out? Uh-hmm, he's ah smart one."

Tantie roared with laughter.

Is mad she mad, oui, thought Kaya.

"Yuh use ah secret ingredient?" Raima asked Tantie.

"Of course. How yuh t'ink meh curry taste so nice?"

"What is de secret ingredient?" asked Raima, now brimming with curiosity.

"Well, if ah tell yuh, it wouldn't be ah secret."

"We ent go tell nobody," said Kaya.

"Oh-ho, is so?" chuckled Tantie.

Raima chimed, "Yes, Tantie, what is de secret ingredient?"

"Ingredients. Is more dan one," said Tantie, proudly. "Yuh see; part ah de secret is tuh start wit' frying whole spices in ghee. Ah always make meh curry fresh, yuh know; curry powder is fuh de people dem dat cyah cook," she chuckled. "Buh meh secret is ah little bit ah dis," Tantie held up a jar of clear, dark honey, in her right hand. "An' ah little bit ah dat," she raised her left hand to reveal a small bottle of rose water.

"Honey an' rose water?" asked Raima, in amazement.

Dat is wha' make meh psychic? thought Kaya.

"How yuh t'ink ah get meh husban'? Dat man was handsome fuh so — he make Raj Kapoor look like Quasimodo." To Kaya's amazement, Tantie laughed as if she had heard the greatest joke ever told; then, she continued, "Dere was only one t'ing he like more dan curry." More laughter ensued, and when she finally caught her breath, Tantie added, "Doh tell nobody meh secret, yuh know."

"We lips sealed, right Kaya?" said Raima.

Kaya nodded, "Yes."

"Wha' allyuh talkin' 'bout?" came Devika's voice, and Kaya saw her standing in the doorway.

"Cookin'," said Raima. "Kaya could make soup."

"Is so? What ah shame yuh doh like soup…." said Devika, matter-of-factly, before turning to Kaya and casually adding, "Buh I love it."

"Who say ah doh like soup?" said Raima, suddenly red-cheeked.

"Las' year, when we went tuh Tobago, an' we had crab soup — everybody like it, except you—"

"Yuh know seafood doh agree with meh," said Raima, to Devika, and turning to Kaya, she said, "Ah like chicken soup. You make chicken soup, right?"

"Yeah," said Kaya, "an' ah not ah big fan ah seafood mehself."

"Why yuh doh tell him how yuh vomit in de middle ah de restaurant," said Devika, with a victorious grin.

Utterly embarrassed, Raima quickly glanced at Kaya before glaring at Devika. "For de same reason ah didn't tell him dat yuh still pee yuh bed."

Devika's grin immediately transformed into a mask of abject horror. "Yuh lie," she wailed as she quickly ran out of the kitchen.

Stunned, Kaya just stared at the empty doorway, feeling oppressed by the uncomfortable silence that now crowded the room.

With a sigh, Tantie said softly, "Why allyuh have tuh embarrass each other like dat?"

"She started it," said Raima, defiantly.

"You and Devika should apologise tuh each other an' apologise tuh young sir. Yuh parents would be ashamed tuh see de two ah yuh act dis way."

Raima turned to Kaya, stared deeply into his eyes and said in a low, sad voice, "Sorry, Kaya…. Ah shouldn't have said that. Ah exaggerated. She was nine, de last time she wet she bed."

Kaya watched Raima's full lips move as she spoke. "Dat's OK," he said meekly, recalling the taste of cherry-flavoured lip-gloss.

Suddenly, the kitchen tap spluttered loudly, jerking Kaya out of a daze. Without breaking eye contact, Raima took two steps backwards. Then, she quickly spun on her heels and exited the kitchen. Kaya heard her calling Devika.

"Yuh see? De both ah dem like yuh," said Tantie. "Well, wha' yuh waitin' for? Go. Now is de time to assert yuhself, young sir."

"Nice talking tuh yuh, Tantie," said Kaya, politely.

"It was ah pleasure meetin' yuh, young sir. Ah hope tuh cook fuh yuh again, soon."

Kaya left the kitchen and made his way towards the lounge. Through large windows, he could see that Mr and Mrs Khan were out on the front lawn, speaking to Lutchman. Once again, he felt uncomfortable.

Dis house so big, an' everyt'ing look so expensive…. Ah doh belong here. Maybe ah should just go….

He walked towards the grand staircase that led up to the bedrooms. "Raima, yuh upstairs?"

Raima came into view at the top of the stairs. She said nothing, but Kaya felt sure that her eyes said, "Come up here."

Immediately, all thoughts of going home vanished. And, without the slightest hesitation, Kaya walked up the stairs. Raima waited, breathing heavily; at least that's the way it seemed to Kaya. Then, without saying a word, she turned and walked towards her bedroom. Mesmerised, Kaya followed.

"Where yuh t'ink yuh goin?" Devika's stern voice startled Kaya. "Yuh can't come up here," she warned.

"Ah come tuh tell yuh ah sorry," interrupted Raima. "Why yuh lock yuh door?"

Kaya noticed Devika's bloodshot eyes. "Dad said we cyah bring boys upstairs," she cried, "Ah goin' tuh tell on yuh — on both ah yuh. I'll tell him how yuh were doin' it in de bush!"

"Doin' what?" demanded Raima.

"Yuh know what!"

"Listen, yuh weren't dere. You don't know what happened."

Devika held up a voice recorder defiantly.

"Dad was lookin' fuh his voice recorder," said Raima. "What is dis?"

"Evidence," spat Devika, "Ah record yuh call wit' Shantel de night after yuh excitin' hike to de forest."

"Yuh little four-eyed troll!"

"Who yuh callin' ah troll? Ah sure Dad would like tuh hear how yuh were kissin' Kaya and how yuh wanted tuh—"

"Shut up!" screamed Raima.

Kaya smiled broadly. *She liked kissing me! She wants to—*

Kaya suddenly became aware that Raima was glaring at him.

He immediately stopped smiling. *Kill me…. She wants tuh kill me.*

"Just wait here," said Raima, and she briskly disappeared into her bedroom.

Before either Kaya or Devika could ask, *what's goin' on?* Raima emerged with a large wad of photocopied paper.

Devika gasped, "What is dat?"

"Insurance," spat Raima, "Ah photocopy yuh diary. Ah sure all de boys yuh write about, would like tuh read it! Ah call dem Legion, for they are many!"

"Yuh female dog!"

"Who yuh callin' ah female dog?"

Man, ah glad ah never had any sisters. Girls vicious fuh so.

"Gimme de voice recorder!"

"Gimme de photocopies!"

"Wait-wait, hang on," said Kaya, "Why allyuh actin' so?"

"Ah doh pee meh bed!" shouted Devika, and the tears began to flow.

"Ah already tell Kaya dat ah make it up," said Raima, meekly.

"She didn't have tuh tell meh, ah knew she wasn't serious," Kaya told Devika.

"Here … have it," said Raima, gently pushing the photocopies into Devika's free hand. "Ah sorry."

Taking the papers, Devika asked, "Are dees de only copies?"

"Swear tuh God," said Raima.

"Alright," said Devika, "Yuh secret safe with me."

"What?"

"Yuh doh ha' tuh worry, Dad will never know."

"Give me de voice recorder," demanded Raima.

"No way! If ah hear anyt'ing about bed-wettin' at college or any-where else, Dad will hear about you an' Master Hezekiah Abaniah."

With that, Devika retreated into her room and shut the door.

For a while, Kaya and Raima just stood there, staring at the closed door. Without averting her gaze, Raima said, "So, yuh want tuh play computer games?"

"Yeah…. OK," said Kaya, continuing to stare at the closed door. "Yuh have another copy of she diary?"

"Of course," said Raima.

"Well, let's play den."

When it was time to leave, Kaya dreaded the possibility that Abbadon and Calibos, the hounds from Hell, were loose. He felt a bit safer being escorted by the Khans.

Walking down the stairway, Mrs Khan said, "Let me show you a bit of the garden. Maybe you could paint here with Raima. I want to encourage her. Her father doh appreciate art, but I do."

"Who say so?" said Mr Khan, "Raima could paint as much as she like, as long as she get a law degree."

On full red alert, Kaya kept a watchful eye for the dogs.

Looking at his watch, Mr Khan said, "Josephine should be here any minute now."

"No," said Kaya, "ah thought…. Ah thought yuh would drop meh home…."

He immediately regretted his honesty.

"So how you'll get home?" asked Mr Khan.

"Well, ah suppose, ah could walk…."

"From here to Mirabelle Street? Nonsense, that's too much of a walk," said Mr Khan, dismissively.

"It not dat far," protested Kaya.

"What about if yuh ride home?" asked Raima.

"Ride home?"

Kaya saw the expectant smiles on the Khan family faces and wondered if Tantie's curry had adversely affected them all. Kaya's old second-hand bicycle had been a broken heap for over a year.

"Yes, Sugar Plum, I think Kaya will enjoy riding home," said Mr Khan.

Just then, Lutchman emerged from around a bend in the garden path, wheeling a shiny new mountain bike. Kaya's mouth dropped open in disbelief. The thin man approached with a black, full-suspension, all-terrain bicycle. It was far better than the bicycle Kaya had been saving to buy. It was well beyond his means.

"Yuh lendin' meh dis bike tuh ride home?" asked Kaya, wide-eyed with awe.

"No, genius," said Devika, rolling her eyes, "De bike is a present fuh you."

Mrs Khan nudged Devika in annoyance.

Mr Khan said, "We would all like to show our appreciation for what you did. It was very brave. If you hadn't kept hold of Raima in the Snake River.... Well, I wouldn't like to even consider what would have happened...."

"How yuh know ah wanted ah bike," asked Kaya, barely containing himself.

"Tom tell meh," said Raima.

Tom? What else Tom tell yuh?

Mr Khan extended his hand, and Kaya shook it with enthusiasm. Without thinking, Kaya kissed Mrs Khan on both cheeks and Raima on one. He looked at Devika, who seemed to be suddenly fascinated with the ground at her feet. He walked towards her, slowly.

"Thank you, Devika," he said.

"Ah didn't do anyt'ing," said Devika, meekly, not daring to look at him, "Is really Mummy an' Daddy yuh ha' tuh t'ank."

"T'anks, anyway," said Kaya, leaning down and gently planting a kiss on her forehead.

Devika's cheeks immediately turned bright red. Then, she looked up at Kaya and smiled.

Suddenly, the sound of loud barks wiped away the smiles. Kaya turned around to see Abbadon and Calibos racing towards him. He wanted to run.

"Lutchman, yuh didn't lock up the dogs?" asked Mr Khan sternly.

The sight of Babooram, desperately running after the dogs with empty dog bowls in each hand, seemed to answer Mr Kahn's question. Babooram, Lutchman's apprentice, was shorter than Lutchman and just as skinny. He had been tasked with feeding the dogs while Lutchman presented the bike to Kaya. Now, only the bike stood between Kaya and the approaching canines.

"Stop," shouted Kaya.

It was an act of desperation that yielded unexpected results. The dogs skidded to a halt; briefly stared at Kaya, then ran away whimpering with fear. They ran past Babooram, almost knocking him over, and disappeared into the kennel. In disbelief, Mr Khan looked at Mrs Khan, and Raima looked at Devika. They had never seen the dogs express fear. All eyes turned to Kaya.

Kaya said, "Sometimes, yuh jus' ha' tuh stand firm."

10

THE LONG WAY HOME

During the weekend, Kaya performed several experiments involving curry, honey, rose water and orange juice, but he could not duplicate the ability to read minds, which he had manifested during dinner with the Khan family. All he got, for his trouble, was a mild case of diarrhoea. Nevertheless, he remained determined not to give up.

On Monday, throughout the morning break, Raima, Meenal, and Shantel, huddled together in the shade of the red Flamboyant tree, in the college courtyard. Kaya and Tom observed the girls from under the canopy that ran the length of the main playing field. Something Raima said, caused Meenal to giggle a lot; even the normally straight-faced Shantel could be heard chuckling loudly.

"Yuh t'ink dey talkin' 'bout me?" asked Kaya.

"Don't you think we should just join them? It's nuts sitting here, trying to read their lips." Tom sighed and nibbled a Rich Tea biscuit.

"Ah doh want she tuh t'ink ah chasin' she."

"Right," said Tom, dryly. "It's such a pity you've lost your amazing superpower."

"Ah regret tellin' yuh 'bout dat. Ah tried all different type ah curry over de weekend, but nuttin' happen. Meh cousin Raya, in Englan', might've been able tuh help meh figure out wha' goin on, as she's ah nurse; buh fuh some reason she not answerin' meh emails."

"Good grief, Abbers, you seriously think that curry makes you psychic?" Tom did his best not to laugh. "That's just daft."

"What?"

"I think you'd say dotish."

"Who yuh callin' dotish?"

"It's the national dish of England, did you know that? With all the curry we eat, if it made us psychic; imagine what we'd be like at football?

But, in case you haven't noticed, England hasn't won the World Cup in a long time. I wonder if they eat curry in Germany."

"Ah said it was probably curry. It could be something else or a combination ah ingredients. Maybe, it was just somet'ing in de house," said Kaya, hotly.

"If I were you, I'd ask Raima if she has a crystal ball or a spirit board."

"Har-de-har-har," said Kaya. "Maybe Papa Bois make meh psychic."

Tom's smile slowly faded. A piece of biscuit fell from his open mouth as he sat on the bench staring at Kaya. "I thought we agreed never to talk about what happened that day, in the Azura Forest."

The college bell rang. Deep in conversation, the girls collected their things and began heading back to their classes.

Kaya stood and said, "Maybe we were wrong. Maybe we need tuh t'ink about wha' really happen. We need tuh understan' who Papa Bois really is."

"I don't know about you, Abbers, but I have trouble remembering that day," said Tom, as they walked towards the biology lab.

Kaya did not reply. Somehow, the day of the hike seemed months ago.

Cobo had been busy during the morning break. At least, that is what Kaya thought, when he sat at his usual place in the biology lab and painfully discovered that someone had placed a thumbtack on his seat.

"Argh!" yelped Kaya, jumping up and extracting the drawing pin from his sore, right buttock.

As expected, most of the class and all of the Mapepires roared with laughter, but Tom, Raima, and other students wearing the red-banded ties of Ocelot House, were not at all amused.

"Be quiet!" shouted Hugo Balgobin, the biology master most students called, Haemoglobin. "Abaniah, what's the problem?"

Cobo sniggered, "Like Ah Banana get ah little surprise."

More laughter ensued.

"You're a childish prat, Cobo," said Tom, angrily.

"Defendin' yuh boyfrien', Shaky Bakey?"

"Another outburst and I'll be issuing detention slips!" warned Haemoglobin, sternly. "Abaniah, what's going on?"

"Nothing sir," said Kaya, red-faced with embarrassment.

Kaya shifted his weight onto his left buttock and focussed on controlling his anger. Suddenly, the overhead lamps hummed and flickered ominously.

"Doh tell meh current goin' again," muttered Deron.

Any laughter abruptly ended when Haemoglobin announced "Congratulations Biggs, you'll be joining Mrs Pascale for detention at 2:40 PM."

Mrs Pearl Pascale, the information and communications technology teacher, was also a 2nd Dan karate black belt master, who earned her nickname of Miss Mow Dem, from a play on the word modem and her ability to knock out violent thugs. The previous year, three youths were hospitalised after attempting to mug her on Carnival Tuesday. The story appeared in the Trinidad Herald newspaper, and consequently, nobody ever messed with her.

Deron shook his head with anger and dismay, but wisely kept his mouth shut. Kaya glanced over his shoulder at Cobo, who confirmed Kaya's suspicions by sporting a smug smile.

Is only jealous yuh jealous, Cobo; ah was invited to Raima house an' dey give meh ah new mountain bike. Dat's wha' eatin' yuh.

Cobo, Deron, Mukesh, and Kerwin, all glared at Kaya. Although it was not his fault, Kaya should have expected retribution from Cobo and his cohorts for Deron's detention. But instead, Kaya turned his attention to his double biology class and looked forward to playing basketball when his classes ended at 2:30.

After basketball, Kaya anticipated taking the long way home on his shiny new mountain bike.

"So, ahm ... Abaniah, wha' else Raima give yuh fuh savin' she from drownin'?" asked Peter Rogers, the lankiest boy in Form 4P.

His high spirits, the result of being on the winning team, in a friendly match between the Hummingbirds and the Ocelots.

"Doh be crude, Rogers," said Kaya, dismissively.

"Ah see yuh ent answerin' meh. Like she ahm ... she really give yuh somet'ing nice."

"Dat's fuh me tuh know an' fuh you tuh find out."

"Is so? OK, man. Ah ha' tuh admit, is ah nice bike. Ah real nice bike. Man, yuh lucky, oui, dem Khan have money fuh so, and yuh in dey good books. Normally, rich people like dem doh even spit on poor people like you an' me."

"Not everybody ignorant, Rogers. We cyah go around punishin' everybody fuh de stupidity of ah few. An' anyway, yuh know how people does act schupid when dey jealous. Dat's where most ah de problems come from."

"Jus' be careful, rich and poor doh mix well in Trinidad."

"Maybe, man, maybe."

"Ahm, yuh goin' tuh de mall fuh ah lime?"

"Nah, not today, too much homework."

"Who yuh t'ink yuh foolin'? Ah sure yuh goin' tuh gallery all over Coconut Grove wit' yuh new bike," said Rogers, flashing a knowing grin.

The boys laughed.

"Alright, ah go dus' it now. Ahm.... Ah ha' all ah dis homework tuh do."

"Ah dus'in' it too. Is ah long ride home," said Kaya, playing along. "Later."

Rogers veered off, towards the college gates, and Kaya imagined he would see Rogers waiting at the maxi taxi stand, a few minutes later as he rode home. It had been a very long time since Kaya had any reason to gallery, which is what some Trinbagonians called showing off. But, at the bike shed, Kaya discovered that both tyres on his new prize had been slashed beyond repair. He just stood there, with clenched fists, gritted teeth and tear-filled eyes, as an unholy rage descended upon him.

Dat's it, ah not takin' anymore ah dis.

Cobo, Deron, Mukesh, and Kerwin, sauntered into the bike shed, seemingly unaware that they had entered the eye of a storm.

"Nice bike, Ah Banana," said Cobo, relishing his victory.

"Watch how he cryin' like ah baby," said Deron, to the other Mapepires. Then, turning to Kaya with the deepest contempt, he spat "Boy, yuh real-real sorf—"

Remarkably, Kaya had never been in any fights at college. As far as jibes and insults went, he had always given as good as he got. But, contemptuous vandalism was different, and now the Mapepires had gone too far. Deron simply did not see the punch coming, and it landed perfectly at the side of his jaw, knocking him out stone cold. It was a lucky punch, and Kaya, who had become an erratic bundle of flailing fists, quickly discovered that he was no fighter when he failed to land another blow. Cobo brought his large right fist down hard on Kaya's shoulder. He had aimed at the back of Kaya's head but had mistimed the punch in his thoughtless haste. However, the blow was enough to throw Kaya off balance and into Kerwin's raised knee. The sobering pain in Kaya's stomach instantly banished any hysteria; then Cobo and Kerwin began a frenzied assault with stomps, kicks, and punches.

"Forget Ah Banana an' gimme ah hand here," cried Mukesh, trying to haul Deron out of harm's way.

Because of the confined space in the bike shed, most of Cobo and Kerwin's blows entirely missed Kaya, and at times, they hit each other. Nevertheless, their onslaught effectively forced Kaya to the ground. He instinctively assumed a foetal position, tucking his chin in and covering his bruised face with bruised hands.

"Stop now, stop! Like is kill yuh wan' tuh kill 'im," Kaya heard Mukesh shout.

A final kick landed on the back of his head, and Kaya felt strangely relaxed. He felt no pain; and, all he could hear was a loud ringing in his ears. Kaya opened swollen eyes to see a world that appeared a pale shade of yellow. He saw Cobo and Mukesh on either side of Deron propping him up and helping him to stumble away. Kaya could tell that Kerwin was complaining about something. His lips moved, but all Kaya heard was loud ringing. When the yellow hue had vanished, so too had the Mapepires. Kaya had a thumping headache, and he felt like throwing up. Moving made his pains worse, so he considered staying on the dusty ground in the bike shed, just a bit longer. He heard movement somewhere behind him, and he wondered if the Mapepires had returned to finish him off.

By some accounts, Roger Delacroix of Form 5A was very handsome. Roger certainly believed this to be the case, and it appeared to Kaya that a few of the lower form girls at Paria also agreed. The fact that many of these girls wore glasses seemed to explain a lot, at least to Kaya. But, as annoying as Kaya found Roger's predilection for narcissism, he had to admit, he was a true Tayra — always generous and compassionate.

"Wha'ppen, Abaniah? Who do dis tuh yuh?" asked Roger, as he helped Kaya to his feet.

"Ah was feelin' sick an' ah faint," lied Kaya.

"Doh talk schupidness, man," said Roger dismissively, "Since when faintin' could give yuh bruised knuckles an' ah black eye? Who fight yuh?"

Kaya shook the dust from his trousers. "Ah OK, ah not ah baby."

"Dis is your bike?" said Roger, eyeing the slashed tyres. "Whoever do dat, need tuh get their tail expelled."

Ah didn't actually see de Mapepires slash de tyres. An' I was de one who start de fight.

"Ah could handle mehself. Alright?" Kaya responded, angrily, while unlocking his bike.

"OK, bredda man, if yuh say so. Yuh wan' tuh use meh cell tuh call somebody?"

"Is OK, ah have ah phone, t'anks."

Kaya could not use his mobile phone to make calls — its keypad no longer worked. It had suffered water damage, which invalidated its warranty; at least that is what the man in the phone shop told him, before offering to dispose of the phone responsibly.

"Alright, Abaniah, you take care."

"T'anks," said Kaya, trying to ignore the pity in Roger's eyes.

Kaya walked home, dragging his vandalised bike along with him and spending the whole humiliating journey wondering what he would tell his mother. He hated lying to Josephine, but if he told her the truth, she would definitely go completely berserk. Kaya had started a fight with the sons of some of Coconut Grove's most prestigious citizens. He had knocked Deron Biggs unconscious. Deron's father, Uriah Biggs, was now an Assistant Superintendent of Police. But, ten years ago, Biggs and other members of Trinidad and Tobago's Specialist Crime Branch had been involved in a massive shootout with a notorious gang of bank robbers. The police assault left one officer crippled, and five gunmen killed, including two shot by Biggs.

Ah wish it was Kerwin dat call meh sorf. He father is ah bookseller; an' ah cyah remember de las' time somebody get kill wit' ah book in Trinidad.

As Kaya approached his home at 18 Mirabelle Street, he heard the *Merry Christmas Polka* blaring from Mr Walker's house. Mr Walker, an elderly bachelor who lived next door, sometimes drank a bit too much. To Kaya's dismay, this was such a time. And, when Mr Walker's spirits got high, he would play his favourite LP record, *Twelve Songs of Christmas* by Jim Reeves — even in the month of October. Mr Walker usually sang along, and this evening was no exception. His off-key voice had all the dogs within earshot howling their disapproval. The Bailey family, Kaya's other neighbours, once owned a Golden Retriever, but one night, after several hours of Mr Walker's sustained frivolity, the dog vanished — never to be seen again. The Baileys believed that the dog had been stolen, but Kaya knew better.

Dat dog run away, oui. Ah t'ink it was either dat or it went lookin' for tonic. Anyt'ing, tuh avoid hearin' Mr Walker sing. De gates lock.... Like Mammy close up early today.

As he opened the front gate, the jolly polka filled Kaya's heart with dread. The sound of Mr Walker's unique vocals guaranteed that Josephine would be in a foul mood. So, Kaya naturally expected to be grounded — at least until his 16th birthday.

11

MASTIFAY

Kaya felt relieved when he discovered that Josephine was neither at Josephine's Flower Shop downstairs nor home upstairs. Eager to establish the full extent of his facial injuries, he rushed to the mirror in the bathroom.

If ah put some ice on meh eye, it might not look so bad.

Kaya opened the medicine cabinet, retrieved two analgesic tablets from a small bottle, and walked to the kitchen where he discovered a note written on the back of a used envelope. Held to the refrigerator door with a little magnet, it announced, *Meeting with web designer. Bring in the clothes from the line. Mauby in the fridge. Macaroni pie in the oven.* Kaya did not need a note to conclude that Josephine had baked a minced beef and macaroni cheese pie, its enticing aroma greeted him as soon as he got to the front door. He poured himself a glass of water, popped the pills into his mouth, and drank.

"Water — a thoroughly underrated drink," Kaya recalled Gobelyn once saying.

He suddenly realised there was a small cut inside of his mouth, and he felt waves of anger when he thought of what the Mapepires had done to him and others. Suddenly, water in an electric kettle on the kitchen counter began to boil.

Ah doh remember switchin' dat on, thought Kaya, and he turned the kettle off.

Strange things had been happening recently, but he just dismissed them as coincidences. Given the frequency of electrical outages and power surges in Coconut Grove, it wasn't that unusual that bulbs often blew, or his computer occasionally switched itself off. He opened the oven and admired Josephine's handiwork. The pie was perfect. Kaya quickly brought the washing in. Then, he sat at the kitchen table, with a small bag of ice pressed to his face. He enjoyed two generous helpings of macaroni pie and rehearsed what he would tell Josephine.

Later that evening, Josephine found Kaya, sitting at the kitchen table, doing his homework and trying not to sulk.

But, although Kaya had succeeded in bringing the swelling down, Josephine's immediate reaction was, "Wha'ppen tuh yuh face?" Deep furrows of concern appeared on her forehead, and she gently turned Kaya's face from side to side, examining his bruises.

"Ah fell," said Kaya, meekly.

"Off de bike?"

Kaya grunted ambiguously. During his fight with the Mapepires, he did fall, so technically he was not lying; at least, that's what Kaya thought. If Josephine wanted to believe he fell from his new bike, he was not going to argue with her.

"How yuh fall off de bike? Look how yuh look like Mastifay," said Josephine, with dismay.

The comment immediately had Kaya thinking of Mama Flo. Mastifay was a notorious hoodlum from the olden days of Trinidad's pan wars. The pitched battles between rival steel orchestras and their bodyguards, in which Mastifay had earned his bad reputation, had occurred long before Josephine was born. With Josephine, then years later with Kaya, Mama Flo shared stories of the pioneers, colourful characters and bloody violence that formed an integral part of steel band history and folklore. Musical innovators, policemen, American military servicemen, who had served in World War II, and Ba' Johns — men who fought with knives, machetes, iron bars and poui — a cured hardwood stick used in stick fighting. Men like Mastifay, a fighter so notorious that calypsonians sang about him in the 1950s.

Kaya recalled Mama Flo singing:

If yuh go an' play
Ba' John in Tunapuna
Yuh bound tuh find
Mastifay on-ah street corner
Yuh better save yuh
Money fuh de undertaker
'Cause Mastifay doh
Take no Ba' John prisoner
Mastifay doh
Take no Ba' John prisoner

Kaya missed Mama Flo terribly, but he still felt the gentle touch of her love and compassion through, her daughter, his mother, Josephine.

"Yuh put antiseptic on yuh face?"

Kaya rolled his eyes. "No, Mammy, ah doh need no antiseptic."

Josephine sucked her teeth loudly. "Doh roll up yuh eye at me, boy; yuh need antiseptic."

She briskly walked to the bathroom and returned armed with cotton wool and a bottle containing a dark liquid. Kaya braced himself for the unavoidable sting.

"Ow!" cried Kaya, when Josephine gently wiped his bruises with the saturated cotton wool.

"So, yuh like de pie?"

"Yes, Mammy."

"Good. Dish out some an' heat it up in de microwave fuh meh. Ah goin' tuh change meh clothes." And, just before she disappeared into her bedroom, Josephine added, "An' Kaya, if ah find out yuh were fightin' at college, you will find out where barley grows."

Kaya already knew where barley grew. Several years ago, having been issued a similar threat, he felt compelled to look it up on the Internet. But, with the risk of severe punishment now looming over his head, he wisely decided not to inform his mother that the cereal grain was currently grown in about 100 countries worldwide, with Russia being its largest producer.

"Ah ha' tuh get new tyres for meh bike," he said, knowing this truth would validate the assumption that he had been injured in a cycling accident.

"Ah cyah hear yuh," Josephine shouted from her bedroom.

"Never mind," responded Kaya, glumly.

In retrospect, he did not want to open, for discussion, any details of an imaginary cycling accident. That would be lying, and Kaya wasn't very good at lying, especially to Josephine. Today, he had allowed anger to get the better of him, and because of it, a line had been crossed with the Mapepires. Consequently, his immediate future seemed grim.

Ah cyah leave meh bike in de shed at college anymore; de Mapepires will vandalise it.

And, as far as self-protection was concerned, Kaya did not know what to do. Deron would certainly want revenge. At Paria College, things were about to get ugly. And it seemed there was nothing Kaya could do about it.

12

AMBUSH

At college, one week later, during the morning break, Kaya was about to leave the men's room when he overheard familiar male voices arguing outside. Impulsively, he hid in a toilet enclosure just before Deron and Mukesh entered the restroom. Inside the closed cubicle, listening intently, Kaya crouched with both feet on the toilet seat while the Mapepires relieved themselves at adjacent urinals.

"Who he knock fuh six, eh? Who he knock fuh six?" repeated Deron, angrily.

Kaya noticed a tiny hole in the closed door and spied through it.

Mukesh finished urinating and immediately became distracted by the image of himself he saw in the wide mirror above the row of sinks. He whipped out the switchblade comb he always carried, and dragging it smoothly through his straight, jet-black hair, he said calmly, "Listen, breds, I was de one dat pull yuh off de ground. Alright?"

"So, little Ah Banana could knock me fuh six, eh? Dat's what yuh saying, eh? Like dat scrawny little boy, could ever lick ah big man like me dong." Deron sucked his buckteeth contemptuously.

Kaya clenched his fists and thought, *Yuh want meh tuh show yuh again?*

Suddenly, the lights in the men's room began to flicker.

Closing and returning his switchblade comb to his back trouser pocket, Mukesh mumbled, "Like jumbie in dis place, man." Then, with confidence, he added "Doh feel ah how, Artimus an' Kerwin give Ah Banana some serious licks. An' now, no man-Jack go mess wit' we."

"He surprise meh an' ah trip an' fall. Yuh know dis," growled Deron. "Cuttin' de bike tyres wasn't enough."

Kaya felt his heartbeat accelerate. *Ah knew it, dey slash de tyres.*

"Shush," hissed Mukesh. He approached Kaya's cubicle and pressed the door firmly.

Kaya held his breath.

"Wha' yuh doin'?" quizzed Deron.

"Somebody in dere," said Mukesh, rattling the locked door.

Kaya psyched himself up for a physical confrontation.

Deron quickly stooped and looked through the gap between the bottom of the door and the floor. He announced, "It empty."

Unconvinced, Mukesh was about to climb the door in order to look down into the cubicle, but the lights flickered again, and he backed away, muttering nervously, "Like spirit ha' diarrhoea."

"Wha' yuh sayin'? Nobody in dere," Deron announced, vigorously washing his hands.

"Yuh better keep yuh trap shut about cuttin' bike tyres, yuh never know who listenin'," said Mukesh, in a low voice. He fidgeted impatiently near the exit.

"Doh stress, mankind, Ah Banana cyah prove nuttin'," said Deron, above the din of the electric hand-dryer. "Yuh not washin' yuh hands?"

Kaya heard Mukesh suck his teeth. "Ax meh dat, nuh." The sound of running water from a tap quickly followed.

"Like yuh 'fraid de soap?" said Deron.

Again, Mukesh sucked his teeth. He said, "Like yuh's meh mudder."

Once again, Kaya heard the loud drone of the hand-dryer.

Leaving the men's room, with Mukesh following close behind, Deron scoffed, "Plenty horrors in store fuh Ah Banana."

Thanks to Roger Delacroix, word soon got around among Paria College students that Kaya had been beaten up. And, within a fortnight, the *bike shed incident* as it had become known, led to a sharp escalation of inter-house animosity. With Tom's help, Kaya avoided the bicycle shed altogether. Reluctant, at first, he eventually accepted Tom's invitation to store his repaired mountain bike at the Methodist parsonage where Tom lived. Every weekday, Kaya would meet Tom at around 7:45 AM; and, the pair would take the short walk to Paria College. And, after college, Kaya would collect his bike and ride home. Occasionally, they would have lunch at the parsonage with Tom's father, the Rev John Baker, but most days, all the members of Ocelot House in Form 4P had lunch together in the college canteen. Kaya, Tom, Raima, Meenal, Shantel, Barry Gangasingh, and Kevin Porter, all sat together. Not to be outdone, the Mapepires also sat in a group. They were Cobo, Deron, Mukesh, Kerwin, Denzil Bari, Kiara Persad, and Abigail Frost. They all took physics with Lucky Shortman, the Mapepire housemaster. Shantel and Barry, the only members of Ocelot House in 4P who took physics as an option, often complained of Lucky Shortman's favouritism.

"Da' man really doin' meh head in," cried Barry. "Ah not feelin' dis parallelogram ah forces at all, an' whenever ah put meh hand up tuh ax ah question, he ignorin' me."

"Doh stress, I'll help yuh," said Shantel. "Doh let 'im beat yuh dong."

"Somebody ought to make a complaint to the school board of governors," said Tom, firmly.

"Ever since de bike shed incident, is like Lucky Shortman and de Gang of Four get worse," said Barry, and all eyes turned to Kaya, anticipating his reaction.

Kaya quietly returned their stares, giving nothing away.

"De las' t'ing we wanted was fuh de bike tuh cause yuh trouble," said Raima, softly.

"Doh blame yuhself fuh anyt'ing, Raima, you an' yuh family very kind. Ah appreciate de present, but ah doh want nobody fightin' fuh meh."

"But, you can't fight them alone," said Tom. "Abbers, the only way to beat these cowards, is to stand united against them."

"Ah agree," said Raima.

"Yeah, buh de way t'ings goin' somebody will end up in hospital," said Kaya, grimly.

"Only if we don't protect each other," said Tom, adjusting his spectacles that had slid down the bridge of his small nose. "Don't you agree Meenal?"

Meenal nodded, "Yes."

She seemed mesmerised, and Kaya noticed that her incessant speaking immediately stopped whenever she came into proximity of Tom.

Having eavesdropped on Deron and Mukesh that morning, Kaya mentally prepared himself for trouble and took the added precaution of removing the ankle weights he always wore. Cycling home from college, he avoided his usual route as much as possible, making his way with urgency and extreme vigilance, constantly on the lookout for the Mapepire Gang of Four. But eventually, with no trace of his enemies in sight, Kaya began to relax, and his mind drifted to his unforgettable dinner at Royal Manor. He had become obsessed with unlocking the secret of his psychic episode, but nothing seemed to work.

Ah wonder if dat big satellite dish dey have, scramble meh brainwaves.

Kaya wiped his sweaty brow with the back of his right hand. He grabbed his water bottle and took a swig.

Raima…. Ah wonder when she'll kiss meh again.

Approaching the increasingly derelict waterfront area of Coconut Grove, Kaya glanced over his left shoulder and discovered to his dismay that he was being followed after all. Riding expensive bicycles of their own, Cobo and Mukesh rapidly gained on him. Raised off his seat, and leaning forward, Kaya applied his full body weight to pumping his bike pedals and increasing his acceleration.

At least is just two ah dem, he tried to reassure himself. *Even if dey ketch up tuh meh, ah might be able tuh fight dem off.*

Ignoring a barrage of obscenities spat by irate motorists, Kaya darted recklessly through rush-hour vehicular traffic. But Cobo and Mukesh followed relentlessly, and despite his best efforts, Kaya could not shake them. Quickly glancing over his right shoulder, he noticed something important that he had not noticed before.

Cobo wearin' ah Bluetooth headset.

In the nick of time, Kaya realised that the Gang of Four had split up and were communicating via mobile phones. Deron and Kerwin had secretly overtaken him and planned to cut across his path as he approached a back-street intersection. Lifting off his seat, standing on his pedals, Kaya jerked his mountain bike onto the narrow uneven pavement, braking and violently leaning left instead of proceeding directly ahead as Deron and Kerwin had anticipated. Frantic and enraged, they swerved to continue the chase and almost collided with Cobo and Mukesh. With fierce pains now wracking his calves and thighs, Kaya continued pushing his bicycle pedals in a desperate bid to escape his pursuers. Suddenly, shifting his weight, he hastily guided his mountain bike off the pavement and down a crooked path flanked on either side by dilapidated sheds. Taken completely by surprise, Cobo and his cohorts missed the turn, and as they skidded to a halt and doubled back, the gap between themselves and Kaya widened. Unlike the Mapepires, he knew this area like the back of his hand. With growing temerity, Kaya sped through narrow alleyways and overgrown lanes, ducking vines and protruding branches, skilfully avoiding broken bottles, discarded cans and other domestic rubbish, overcoming every obstacle on his course. Momentarily dazzled by the sun, which hung low in the sky, casting eerily-elongated shadows on the dusty path ahead, Kaya freewheeled down a small incline before frenetically pedalling along a dry clay track.

Shaking sweat from his face and smiling mischievously, Kaya thought, *Ah go take dem dong tuh de rusty bridge; lemme see if dey man enough tuh follow meh across.*

An old, iron relic from the government-owned steam railway system, the *rusty bridge*, as locals referred to it, had not been used for rail transport since the late 60s. Only the most foolhardy locals ignored the faded *keep off the bridge* sign, to brave the rotted planks that remained. For most, the danger of death from falling off the bridge far outweighed any debatable value it had as a shortcut. And, if the polluted river below did not claim you, there was always the chance that one of the many shady vagrants or illegal squatters in the vicinity would. What remained of the rusted iron structure loomed several metres in the distance. With the Mapepires in hot pursuit, Kaya tried to visualise the route he must take to avoid the missing planks, exposed nails and other hazards on the corroded bridge. Suddenly, a snarling animal leapt out of the bushes, viciously snapping at his heels. Startled and distracted, Kaya swerved and wobbled before regaining his balance and momentum. He immediately recognised the mixed-breed stray dog, which sported a left ear that had been partly chewed off. This particular brown and white pot-hound led a pack of about ten flea-bitten dogs that frequently marauded the waterfront.

"Damn pot hong!" Kaya shouted.

Kaya had ventured into its territory and was summarily ambushed. Mangy, ownerless dogs rushed him on either side, fiercely barking and snarling. Some of the dogs also attacked the Mapepires. Kerwin lost his nerve, swerved and hit the exposed root of a tree. He tumbled off his bike and into a wide, shallow ditch overgrown with stinging nettles. Kaya heard Kerwin's agonised howls above the din of frenzied growls, barks and snarls.

Good. One less Mapepire tuh worry about, thought Kaya.

He grabbed the plastic bottle attached to the down tube of his bike and squeezed it, squirting water into the eyes of the snapping mongrel running alongside him. The leader of the pack yelped, slowed down, and turned its vindictive attention to Cobo. Following Kaya's example, Cobo grabbed his own water canister, but since it was made of metal, he could not use it to squirt the dog. Instead, frustration had him hurling the canister, which hit the alpha male squarely on its nose. With a loud yelp, the stunned mutt finally gave up the chase. For a moment, the pack stood howling and barking, at the four teenagers speeding towards the neglected iron bridge, before they turned to focus on Kerwin. Gradually applying increased pressure on his brakes, Kaya stood on his bike pedals, keeping them level while coasting onto the decaying structure. The planks moaned, cracked, squeaked and split, sending splinters and shards of rotten timber into the shallow, muddy river below.

Eyes bulging with fear, Mukesh skidded his mountain bike to an abrupt halt.

"Whoa-whoa-whoa!" he cried, breathlessly, "Like is crazy allyuh crazy? I ent goin' on dat trap."

"Doh be coward, just take yuh time," said Deron, sternly.

"Ah cyah afford tuh fall in de river, yuh know ah cyah swim good," protested Mukesh.

"Swim? Man, doh make joke, de fall alone go break yuh neck," said Cobo, his green eyes smouldering with contempt. "Now come on, Ah Banana getting' away."

"Coward man keep whole bones," grumbled Mukesh before he reluctantly followed Cobo's lead.

Behind them, Kerwin kept the excited dogs at bay with a long, thin, broken branch.

Shouting, "Mash, dogs, mash!" he wheeled his bike and hobbled as quickly as he could in an attempt to catch up with the other Mapepires.

Midway across the rusty iron bridge, Kaya began to falter. It had been more than a year since he last rode a bike on its rickety planks, and to his dismay, he discovered that several of the wooden beams he had previously used were now missing and most that remained could barely take his weight. To make matters worse, the barking dogs had drawn the attention of some of the area's shiftier characters.

Accompanied by his three brothers, Ras Mohammed, a middle-aged Rastafarian of mixed African and Indian descent, emerged with a bunch of young green coconuts in his left hand. Greyish dreadlocks draped his dark, angular face, but his open khaki shirt revealed a muscular chest and torso uncommon for a man in his early fifties. The middle-aged Rasta reminded Kaya of the individual who called himself Papa Bois. According to Trinbagonian folklore, Papa Bois was capable of assuming other physical forms.

Could dis be Papa Bois? Doh be schupid Kaya, everybody know Papa Bois doh ha' any bredders.

Kaya knew little of the Mohammed men, except for persistent local rumours, which suggested that these squatters counted theft and grievous bodily harm among their hobbies. So, there was no way Kaya would willingly retreat towards them. Snarling, howling and barking, the irritating pothounds followed Kerwin as he limped towards the bridge, his face and exposed arms covered with painful reddish weals. Amid the mounting tension, Kaya got off his bike and slowly inched his way across the decaying structure.

Ignoring Kaya, Ras Mohammed spoke to the Mapepires. "Like is lost allyuh lost, Paria men? Where allyuh really t'ink yuh goin', eh? It ent ha' nuttin' here fuh yuh."

"Doh worry 'bout us, we know where we goin' and what we doin'," came Cobo's hasty response.

The Mohammed brothers found Cobo's words amusing.

"Go home Paria men, it ent safe fuh big shots like you around here," Ras Mohammed shouted over the din of frenzied barking.

"Listen man, we doh want no trouble, we'll cross de bridge an' be on our way," said Cobo, defiantly.

"Doh keep talkin' so proudly; doh let arrogance come outta yuh mouth. De Lord is ah Gawd ah knowledge; an' by him, actions are weighed," said Ras Mohammed, quoting 1 Samuel 2:3 with authority.

Cobo and his stooges briefly exchanged jaded glances before bursting out laughing. Suddenly, from the small of his back, Ras Mohammed whipped out a pistol and fired a single shot into the head of the dominant pot-hound. The dog flew off its feet, landing with a thud in a lifeless heap. Panic-stricken and howling loudly, the remaining stray dogs ran off in several directions fearing for their lives. Scared witless, Mukesh lost his balance and tumbled off his bike, which fell several metres into the murky water below. Screaming in terror, he dangled precariously between two crumbling beams, while Cobo and Deron stood immobilised in a state of wide-eyed shock.

"Help Mukesh. He go fall!" shouted Kaya, at the stunned Mapepires.

Abandoning his bike on the decaying planks and almost losing his footing, Kaya instinctively rushed to Mukesh's assistance. Kaya felt a strange tingling sensation run down his spine as he grabbed Mukesh by the arms and hauled him to safety. Whimpering, Mukesh immediately scrambled off the bridge, leaving Kaya standing alone, utterly amazed by his own show of strength.

Ras Mohammed used his loaded pistol as a pointer when he told Kaya, "Go an' pick up yuh bike before it fall in de river."

"Buh wha' scene yuh really on?" said Kaya, defiantly.

"Disengage yuh mouth, an' engage yuh brain," said Ras Mohammed, with unruffled coldness.

Hesitantly, Kaya complied with Ras Mohammed's stern demand. Carefully stepping on the sturdiest beams, he retrieved his mountain bike. Then, he stood and watched in disbelief as two of Ras Mohammed's brothers casually wheeled Cobo and Deron's forsaken bicycles off the bridge. The third brother approached Kerwin and also wrenched his bike away. Kaya saw that the brother had a pistol tucked into his leather belt. When Kerwin noticed the firearm, he kneeled before the brother and began begging for mercy.

"Gimme yuh cell," ordered the brother.

Kerwin immediately reached into his back pocket and handed him his mobile phone. In turn, Cobo, Deron, and Mukesh offered no resistance when relieved of their mobiles and Bluetooth headsets.

Deron grumbled softly, "Allyuh have no idea who allyuh messin' with."

Ras Mohammed calmly placed his coconuts on the ground. He slowly walked up to Deron and pressed the barrel of his pistol against Deron's nostrils.

"Yuh smell dat, eh, bully boy?" said Ras Mohammed, menacingly. "Yuh t'ink de bullets in meh gun care which backstreet jamette bring yuh into dis world?"

Deron closed his eyes. He began to hyperventilate, and tears trickled down his cheeks.

"Go back de way yuh come, an' doh ever come back here. Ah hate stray dogs, yuh get meh?" said Ras Mohammed.

Cobo stared at Kaya long and hard, but kept his mouth shut. He turned around and headed back towards the main road with Deron, Mukesh, and Kerwin, silently following. Terrified, and uncertain what to do, Kaya began slowly wheeling his treasured mountain bike across the desolate bridge, carefully retracing each step.

"Not you," said Ras Mohammed, to Kaya. Then, looking at him intently, he asked, "Wha's yuh name, Paria man?"

"Kaya."

The brothers chuckled.

"Kaya, what?" quizzed Ras Mohammed.

"Kaya Abaniah."

"Ah t'ought so. Yuh mudder have ah flower shop, right?"

"Yes," replied Kaya, cautiously.

Oh, Gawd, he t'ink we have plenty money because ah have ah expensive bike and meh mother have she own business....

"So, Florence Peters—some people call she Ma Peters—some others call she Mama Flo; dat was yuh gran'mudder?"

"Yes," said Kaya.

"Ah t'ought so," said Ras Mohammed, with a chuckle. "Nuff respect fuh Mama Flo. Nuff respect. Dat was ah real generous lady, Gawd bless she soul. She help we mudder through some desperate times." Turning to his brothers, he asked, "Allyuh remember Mama Flo?"

To which the brothers answered, "Yeah, man." "How yuh mean?" and, "Like we could ever forget dat lady."

Kaya began to entertain the notion that he would not be robbed or murdered on this particular occasion.

"Much respect fuh Mama Flo," said Ras Mohammed, but suddenly his smile faded, and Kaya recognised the unmistakable glint of ruthlessness in the Rastafarian's eyes. "Go now, an' doh come back here. Some bad people livin' here now an' it ent safe. Yuh get meh?"

Kaya nodded, "Yes."

Never daring to look back, and with his knees shaking violently, Kaya carefully wheeled his bike to the other side of the bridge, before mounting it and riding away as quickly as he possibly could.

13

REVENGE

At home, that evening, Kaya tried to replicate his show of strength at the iron bridge to no avail. As with his temporary super-senses, after the incident in the Azura Forest, and the psychic episode during dinner with the Khans, the secret to unlocking this new gift remained a mystery.

Wha' Papa Bois do tuh meh? Ah doh even ha' ah scar tuh show fuh de serious buss head ah get in de Azura Forest. Raima an' Tom see it. Ah didn't imagine it. But somehow, Papa Bois heal meh, an' ah t'ink whatever he do change meh. Accordin' tuh folklore, Papa Bois like ah magician. He could turn into ah deer, or ah hairy man with cow foot. He could appear and disappear; an' he could run fast like de wind. Magic? Ah doh believe in magic; when people doh understan' somet'ing, they start calling it magic. No, ah doh t'ink Papa Bois is a magician or ah Obeah man. Nah, dis ha' some sort ah logical explanation — a scientific explanation. Since de incident in de forest ah not mehself — strange t'ings happenin' all de time. De only way tuh get answers, is tuh go back tuh de forest; ah ha' tuh find a way tuh see Papa Bois again.

After the *rusty bridge ambush*, which is what Kaya called the confrontation with the Mohammed brothers at the waterfront, the Mapepires never dared to follow him home again. Notwithstanding the fact that Kaya risked his personal safety to save Mukesh, tensions continued to escalate between the Mapepires and the Ocelots. Kaya had the support of 6th-formers such as Jaysen Mohammed, Raima's 18-year-old cousin. Jaysen was a college prefect and javelin champion — a proud member of Ocelot House, who felt quite capable of handling Cobo and his Mapepire cohorts. Together with Ocelot House Captain and fellow 6th former Colin Sampson, Jaysen assumed the unofficial role of Kaya's bodyguard; and, at college, Kaya felt relatively safe. But the Mapepires also had their own champions, including Cobo's cousin — Adrian Leotaud, Mapepire House Captain and Trinidad's under-18 Karate Champion. The Gang of Four would not let the loss of their bikes go unpunished, and Kaya even feared reprisals from Deron's father, the

Assistant Superintendent of Police, a man dogged by rumours of murder and corruption.

Nevertheless, a few days later, Kaya scored a minor personal victory against his Mapepire foes. At every given opportunity, they had continued to steal the packed lunches of Form 4 students from rival houses, but Kaya saw a simple way to teach them a lesson. During the morning break, Kaya sneaked past the college prefects and off the college premises. He visited a nearby roti shop; and, with his pocket money, he bought a wrapped, goat roti. Knowing that the spicy curry would effectively mask any untoward taste, Kaya secretly mixed a potent powdered laxative into the curried goat. Sneaking back into college undetected, he left the laced roti in a spare student locker, which he secured with a cheap padlock — one he was certain the Mapepires could easily pick. That afternoon, after the lunch break, Kaya gleefully observed the Gang of Four's growing discomfort and increasing trips to the toilet. The following day, Cobo, Deron, Mukesh and Kerwin failed to attend college. Terms such as *suspected food poisoning, intestinal infection, gastroenteritis,* and *explosive diarrhoea* were used to describe their ailments.

Riding home from college, Kaya darted through the vehicular traffic, which seemed much thicker than usual. And, as he approached the waterfront, Kaya saw the source of the problem — two police vans with flashing lights blocked the main road while armed officers diverted traffic into a narrow side street. There were also three ambulances at the scene with a fourth making a hasty arrival. Curious motorists slowed down, attempting to get information about the presence of the emergency services or hoping to glimpse what had been cordoned off. A large, animated crowd had gathered ahead, but several armed officers kept them at bay, and a sense of danger and suspense permeated the atmosphere.

"Is murder, oui. Murder," said a middle-aged pedestrian to the occupants of an old Mazda that had stopped a few metres ahead of Kaya.

Kaya immediately steered his bike towards the pavement where the woman stood.

"Somebody kill somebody?" he asked the woman.

"Yeah, boy, dey already drag three ah dem from de river. Dey strugglin' tuh reach de fourth."

"Dey kill ah whole family?" asked Kaya, unable to hide his shock.

"Four breddas. De police find ah whole set ah wild bird an' gun in ah shack dat belong tuh dem. Gun fuh so…. Like is smugglin', dey were smugglin'?"

"Buh how you mean? Of course, is smugglin', dey were smugglin; an' it look like somebody ketch up wit' dem," added a female passenger who occupied the back seat of the Mazda.

"So, wha'ppen, somebody shoot dem?" asked Kaya.

"Nah boy, dat's de funny t'ing," said the middle-aged pedestrian, "So far, not ah soul truly know wha' kill dem. Maybe somebody fling dem off de rusty bridge, buh dey cyah find ah trace ah blood anywhere. Not ah single drop. Well, boy, ah wish ah didn't watch dem pull de bodies outta de water. If yuh see how pale dey turn. It crawl meh blood tuh see dem, oui. It still have meh shakin' like ah leaf. Watch meh hand how it still shakin'." The middle-aged woman raised both hands, and Kaya saw that they were trembling. "Yuh better ride home quick, boy, dis ent no place fuh school chirren."

The female passenger said, "Look, gyul, Trinidad gone through, yes, well an' truly gone through; now dey killin' people fuh de fake gold chain hangin' on dey neck. It ent ha' ah safe place in Trinidad now. Dis serious, yes.... Damn serious.... An' before yuh blink, de government go buss another curfew on we tail."

"Buh is like de police treatin' de case like ah big joke," said the middle-aged woman.

The female passenger asked, "So, wha' yuh t'ink really happen to dem?"

"Ah hear Biggs say Soucouyant bite dem," replied the pedestrian.

The female passenger sucked her teeth derisively, "Doh skylark."

"Biggs?" said the driver of the Mazda, "Assistant Superintendent Biggs? Ah hear dat man is de biggest criminal in south."

"Is so? Ah hear Toro is de one yuh ha' tuh watch," said the female passenger.

"Biggs good-good padna, Inspector Thomas Oscar Raymond Ollivierra? He's ah damn crook. If yuh ask me, dis whole t'ing stink ah corruption. Criminals eh go kill four people, an' den leave all dem gun behind. An', yuh see dem bird? People does pay serious money for dem. Serious-serious money. Nah man, everybody know de police is de biggest smugglers in Trinidad. Ah wouldn't be surprised if police kill dem. Ah wouldn't be surprised."

"Keep yuh voice dong nah, man," said the female passenger, "some ah dem in de crowd is undercover police, yuh know dis. Dat's how dey move. Like is ah early grave yuh lookin' for?"

The middle-aged woman, standing on the pavement, sucked her teeth in disgust. "Is true de Mohammed breddas were merchants ah misery, buh it not right fuh Uriah Biggs tuh make joke about dey death. After all, dey have ah mudder too. De poor woman collapse when she find out, oui. Look, de ambulance now come fuh she. Seventy-seven-years-old las' week an' ha' tuh deal wit' dis heartache. Boy, Trinidad not easy, nuh…. It ent easy at all."

Kaya felt a knot growing in his stomach. It seemed as if his fears were becoming a reality. The Mohammed brothers had been murdered, and there was the possibility that Deron's father was involved.

Buh ah cyah believe Biggs father would kill four men over ah bicycle, thought Kaya. *Somet'ing bigger goin' on.*

The impatient driver of an imposing Grand Cherokee Jeep hit his horn, rolled down his tinted window and shouted towards the driver of the Mazda, "Drive yuh car nah, man. Yuh cyah see yuh causin' serious traffic here?"

The Mazda driver, who had been speaking to the middle-aged pedestrian, briskly got out of his old car. He was dark, huge and sweating profusely. In fact, he seemed far too large to have come from such a relatively small vehicle.

"Look nuh, like yuh ah Russian, awa? An' ah damn blind one too. Where yuh wan' tuh rush to, eh? Like yuh cyah see de police block up de road."

"Alright breds, alright…." said the small driver of the big Jeep, activating the Jeep's central locking system and defensively rolling his window up halfway.

"Dat's right, lock yuhself up before ah pull yuh outta yuh seat an' give yuh ah big piece ah meh mind."

"Cool it, bredda man, yuh doh ha' tuh move so—"

"Doh tell meh tuh cool it. De damn air-conditioning in meh car not wukin' an' it hot like Hell, so doh tell meh tuh cool it. Is brave allyuh does get brave when allyuh sittin' in yuh big pappy car."

"Buh A-A, is beat yuh go beat meh now?"

"Because yuh sittin' behind de wheel ah yuh big Jeep yuh feel yuh could intimidate poor people like me? Take ah look at dat Mazda. Watch it good. Now tell meh, it look like ah helicopter tuh you? Where yuh want meh tuh go, eh? Yuh t'ink is Chitty Chitty Bang Bang ah drivin'? Yuh t'ink ah could jus' fly outta here?"

"Alright, breds, ah sorry-ah sorry, doh feel no how…. Ah apologise."

The large man sucked his teeth and lumbered back to his Mazda.

Wiping large beads of sweat from his round face with a stained rag, he grumbled, "Is buy dem so does buy dey license, oui. More money dan sense."

Unable to contain his curiosity, Kaya wheeled his bike closer to the police cordon. He saw Deron's father emerge from a track. Dressed in a dark-coloured short-sleeved suit and sporting his distinctive Panama hat, he was flanked on either side by junior officers. Contrary to the account given by the middle-aged pedestrian, ASP Biggs did not seem to be in a joking mood. Radio and television journalists had arrived, and they jostled to ask the senior police officer questions, but he repelled them with blunt yes and no responses, before being whisked away in an unmarked police car. Kaya could hear the wailing of the woman whose sons had been killed. A young woman tried to console the thin, elderly Indian woman while a tall man of medium build held the woman around her shoulders and steadied her on her feet. Paramedics insisted that she return to the wheelchair that they had provided, but the distraught old woman refused. Then, Kaya saw that the police had retrieved the expensive bikes that belonged to the Mapepires. They were loaded into the back of one of the vans, which already had cages containing exotic birds. Kaya could not help wondering if Deron had told his father about the rusty bridge ambush.

Suddenly, Kaya experienced piercing pains in his temples, and he heard a loud ringing in his ears. He stumbled and leaned against a low wall. Breathing heavily but doing his best not to panic, Kaya looked around the crowd of gawkers, emergency personnel, and pushy journalists. Two men seemed completely out of place, but despite his best efforts, Kaya could not see their faces clearly. It seemed his vision became blurred, and his headache became unbearably worse whenever he tried. Although he could not see their faces clearly, Kaya could tell they were very pale and dressed in black suits. To his dismay, they seemed to be staring directly at him. Kaya had an overwhelming urge to leave; he stumbled away, wheeling his bike against the gathering crowd of onlookers. The further away from the men in black he walked, the stronger he felt. Eventually, Kaya mounted his bicycle and made his escape.

14

ANGELS AND DEMONS

The following day, Kaya had lunch with Tom at the Methodist parsonage. Maureen, Rev John Baker's cook and housekeeper, had made pelau — a popular Creole dish of marinated chicken seared in caramelised sugar and cooked with pigeon peas, diced carrots, tomato chutney, rice and coconut milk. In her forties, and of mixed African and Irish descent, Maureen had kind eyes, chubby cheeks, short loose brown curls and an optimistic disposition, which seemed to manifest itself in the flamboyantly colourful and flowery blouses she always wore. Rev Baker and Eldred Seymour Gobelyn, Kaya's English teacher and the housemaster of Ocelot House joined the boys for lunch.

"Abaniah, I saw on the news that there's been a bit of trouble in your neck of the woods. Did you know those unfortunate men?" asked Gobelyn.

"Ahm…. No, sir," said Kaya, avoiding Gobelyn's piercing grey-eyed gaze.

"Terrible stuff," said Gobelyn, shaking his head with dismay.

"What's that, Gobbers?" asked Rev Baker, adjusting his spectacles.

"You really ought to watch the news, J.B. Growing up on Oxford's Rose Hill estate isn't all that bad when you consider some of the violent crimes that have become so commonplace here. Even the old slums of Jericho would seem tame by comparison."

"Whoever said life on Rose Hill was bad?" chuckled Rev Baker, "My parents worked at Morris Motors, perhaps not an exciting profession when compared to your father's globe-trotting career in oil, but we were happy."

"Indeed. I have vivid memories of your father's 1970 Morris Minor Traveller."

"Oh, how my father loved that car."

"English ash frame…. Top of the line back then."

"Happy times."

"Indeed, happy times."

"So, what did I miss on the telly?"

"Oh yes.... Tragic business.... The police retrieved four corpses from the Paria River — four brothers."

"Terrible.... Terrible...." muttered Rev Baker. "Young men?"

"No-no, the eldest was in his fifties. They also found green-winged macaws, African grey parrots, a channel-billed toucan, and almost ninety Venezuelan bullfinches," replied Gobelyn.

"And a small arsenal," added Tom.

Kaya kept his head down, continued his meal, and hoped that they would change the subject.

"Were these men killed by rivals? Perhaps as a warning?" asked Rev Baker.

"Quite possibly. You know, as well as I do, what extraordinary profits can be made from the illegal trade of wildlife. Globally, it's third after drug trafficking and arms smuggling. Last year, the WHT did an investigation into Trinidad's role as a trans-shipment point for illegal wildlife trafficking. They concluded that it had a monetary value of over $30 billion US."

"That much? Simply astounding," sighed Rev Baker.

"At the same time, the maximum fine for possession of protected animals without a permit is laughably negligible; I tell you, J.B., it's a nightmare. We've already seen the complete decimation of local finch populations; the Picoplat and Bullfinch have been completely wiped out, and the Trinidad Robin is on the verge of extinction. Nevertheless, many bird owners still keep them illegally; corruption is everywhere, and successful prosecutions are rare."

"It is as it's always been, even long before cowry shells were used as currency," said Rev Baker, with dismay. "Instead of loving people and using money, people often love money and use people. I pray for peace; peace in our time."

"As long as the peace-makers are armed with assault rifles, it's highly unlikely we'll ever have peace."

"Oh, yes. Yes, Gobbers, I fear you may be right...."

"Excuse meh, Reverend," interrupted Maureen, "ah jus' goin' tuh de supermarket. De pelau taste good?"

"Absolutely superb, Maureen. Superb!" replied Rev Baker.

And Gobelyn and the boys voiced their approval.

"Good," continued Maureen gleefully, "ah make some cassava pone for dessert. Ah know how much yuh like it, Tom."

"Cool!" cried Tom, his freckled face beaming in anticipation of the spicy cassava and coconut pudding.

"Alright, ah goin' up de road," announced Maureen, her bright red shoes clattering on the polished wooden floors as she made her exit.

"Good to see you two have settled in so well," said Gobelyn, to Rev Baker and Tom. Then, turning to Kaya, he added, "Young Abaniah has helped Tom to settle right in. You know, Abaniah, if you have any problems you can come to me."

"Yeah, sir," said Kaya, trying not to show embarrassment.

"There are murmurs among the students that you've been having a spot of bother with Corbeau and his friends."

"Just Cobo bein' Cobo."

"Hmmm…. I think, at times, the rivalry between Ocelot and Mapepire can get a little out of hand."

"Dey jus' doh want tuh accept dat we better dan dem," said Kaya, straight-faced.

Gobelyn boomed with laughter. Tom and Rev Baker joined in.

"Well said, Abaniah. People who repeatedly attack your confidence and self-esteem are quite aware of your potential, even if you are not. Modesty isn't always a virtue; it can be a hindrance; a careful measure of personal pride builds confidence and ensures success. My money is on you for the races, especially the hundred metres," said Gobelyn.

"Yes, Kaya is quite the runner. It cracks me up watching Cobo and his gang trying to tag him in dodgeball; Kaya's just too fast."

"In Trinidad, we call it scooch, not dodgeball," added Kaya.

"Seems you'll be breaking 100 metres records in a few years," said Rev Baker, to Kaya.

"Ah doh know 'bout dat, ah t'ink Tom does exaggerate."

"I do not," declared Tom, defiantly.

Gobelyn and Rev Baker laughed heartily. Just then, a loud *ding* emanated from Tom's trouser pocket, prompting a conspicuous blush in his freckled cheeks.

"Here we go again," said Rev Baker, whose mood had instantly lost much warmth, "Thomas, you know how I feel about you using that brain-cell fryer at the dinner table. Surely, Miss Baboolal can afford you half an hour's peace to partake of the Lord's bounty."

Kaya raised an eyebrow while Tom briefly fumbled with the mobile phone in his pocket.

Like yuh keepin' secrets from meh, Tomboy. Wha' goin on wit' you an' Meenal?

"I trust you sent an appropriate response?" asked Gobelyn, with a mischievous twinkle in his eye.

"Yes, sir," said Tom, sheepishly.

"Can he do that without even looking at the infernal gadget?" quizzed Rev Baker.

"But of course," chuckled Gobelyn. "Surely, you wouldn't expect any son of yours to be anything but a perfect gentleman."

"Extraordinary," declared Rev Baker.

"Oh, yes; several months ago, one of my students recited Hamlet's soliloquy while texting blow by blow accounts of a recently-aired reality television programme."

"Good heavens," exclaimed Rev Baker.

"My thoughts exactly; the only reality about reality TV is the very real waste of one's time it facilitates."

"Come off it, Gobbers, are you saying this student stood before you, hands behind their back, tapping away while perfectly reciting Shakespeare?"

"Oh, I never inferred that the recital was perfect, J.B. For one thing, I got the impression that Hamlet desperately wanted to naff off to the undiscovered country as soon as humanly possible."

Kaya clearly recalled the incident. It was one of the few times Gobelyn had shown anger, and that afternoon, Abigail Frost spent an hour of detention with Obeah Widow contemplating the error of her ways.

"Several of my teaching colleagues have amassed impressive collections of confiscated mobile devices," continued Gobelyn. "And, I must admit that I have observed a growing tendency in some students to favour speed over accuracy; no doubt an unfortunate side effect of the horrid abbreviations haplessly propagated by speed texters."

"I'm disappointed that you never told me about this problem, Gobbers. I would have had stern words with Thomas had I known."

"Oh, no-no-no, J.B.," said Gobelyn, waving his hands dismissively, "these lads don't use their phones in class. Do you gentlemen?" he added, holding the gaze of Tom then Kaya in turn.

"No, sir," they chorused.

Dat's because meh cell drong in de Snake River, thought Kaya, sadly.

Nevertheless, Rev Baker seemed somewhat unconvinced, at least to Kaya.

"Well, gentlemen, the bird-watching Reverend has twisted my arm into organising a small WHT expedition," announced Gobelyn, swiftly changing the subject. "Our guide, Florian Hütter, claims he can fit six passengers into his Opel, and the lovely Miss Adams has kindly volunteered to join us with her car. At last count, we have four spare seats. So, who's up for a return trip to the Azura Forest?"

Tom and Kaya's smiles slowly faded.

"That sounds great, sir," said Tom, struggling to appear enthusiastic.

"Has that unfortunate incident in the Snake River put you lads off?"

"No, sir, not at all," responded Kaya, "is jus' dat ah doh t'ink meh mother will like de idea."

"Hmmm.... I suppose that's understandable. I could put in a good word if you like — reassure her that we'll keep an eye on you."

"Is not jus' de river, sir, it's de men wit' guns."

"Ah, yes.... Gotcha. Even so, danger still manages to find many locked within the confines of their homes. How things have changed since I first visited Trinidad in my childhood; no one had bars on their windows back then. But the people of this nation are resilient and possess deep faith, I'm certain they'll weather the storm."

"Interesting, hearing a self-confessed atheist speaking of faith," said Rev Baker, with a smug smile.

"Ahh, J.B.; I live in hope that one day you'll accept that I have faith. Deep faith that just happens to be different from yours."

"Still a proponent of ancient astronaut theory?"

"I prefer to call it scientific speculation."

"The Lord — an alien from outer space? Come now, Gobbers—"

"Now-now, J.B., don't put dangerous words into my mouth; being, as you say, a confirmed atheist, I don't profess to have any in-depth knowledge of religion. But, one thing, I do know, is that most religions make reference to angels and demons that come to Earth from the sky. What your faith views as spiritual entities, I believe are no more than flesh and blood. Misunderstood beings with technology so advanced, it seems miraculous."

Dat's what Papa Bois is. Ah sure of it, thought Kaya.

Rev Baker chuckled, "It's an old argument, Gobbers, and we're both old, stubborn, and set in our ways."

"Speak for yourself, Reverend. I'm not old; I just look it."

The men laughed heartily.

"OK then, who's for some of Maureen's delicious pone?" asked Rev Baker, keenly rubbing his palms together.

Gobelyn raised his right hand in the manner of an over-enthusiastic schoolboy.

"Boys?"

"Yes please," said Tom and Kaya, in unison.

"Did you want more mauby, Gobbers?"

"Adam's ale would be fine," said Gobelyn.

"What about you boys?"

"I'm OK, Dad," said Tom.

"No, thank you, Rev Baker," said Kaya.

Rev Baker headed off to the kitchen.

In a low tone, Tom said to Gobelyn, "So, in your opinion, sir, mythical characters such as Hercules could actually be visitors from another planet?"

Hidden by the dining table, Kaya kicked Tom in the shin.

"Ow...." yelped Tom.

"What's the matter?" asked Gobelyn.

"Oh, my leg.... My leg fell asleep," fibbed Tom and his eyes growled, *"Stop that,"* to Kaya.

"Well, to answer your question, consider this quote from the book of Genesis in the Hebrew Bible: 'The sons of God saw that the daughters of men were fair and took them as wives.' I understand that some believe the 'sons of God' to be fallen angels or demons, but it seems unlikely to me that non-corporeal beings would experience lust. In the case of Hercules, his father Zeus was a god and his mother Alcmene a mortal human being. Is it so far-fetched to speculate that these 'sons of God' and even the mighty Zeus could have been no more than advanced extraterrestrials who came to Earth, had their jollies, then buzzed off?"

"Well sir," said Tom, thoughtfully, "I think the 'sons of God' are simply righteous men. My interpretation of relevant Biblical scripture is that the sons of God are the descendants of Seth, Adam's third son, who was righteous, and the daughters of men are descendants of Cain, who committed the first murder by killing his brother, Abel; and, whose descendants were all killed in the Great Flood."

"Hmmm.... An interesting interpretation," said Gobelyn, with a grin, "I must admit, I hadn't thought of that. The Christian Bible is a fascinating document. One, which sadly, many do not take the time to either read or understand."

"Tom, I'm going to need a hand," came Rev Baker's voice from the kitchen.

"Coming, Dad," said Tom, managing not to roll his eyes.

"I suppose, the good news is that they no longer burn people like me at the stake for blasphemy; nevertheless, I'd better change the subject if I want a portion of Maureen's magnificent pone. Off you go, we can continue this conversation another time."

Tom left Kaya and Gobelyn alone at the dining room table.

"Do give it some thought, Abaniah; a trip to the Azura National Park would be the best way to conquer any fears you may have developed. You see, despite what my learned friend may think, I do have faith. I believe we were put on the good earth to evolve through the experience of life. Until the day we conquer our fears; they will forever haunt us. There's time yet — no hurry; the expedition is planned for the last Saturday before college breaks for Christmas. Your mother may feel differently by then."

"Sir?"

"Abaniah."

"Yuh believe Papa Bois could be ah space alien?"

"Papa Bois…. Now there's a model member of the Wildlife Heritage Trust if ever there was one — a supernatural being dedicated to protecting Trinidad's flora and fauna; the original eco-warrior. Could he be extraterrestrial? Why not? There are many myths from a great many cultures regarding strange, otherworldly creatures that could well have been the product of deliberate genetic manipulation. Remarkably, the story of Doctor Frankenstein and his terrible monster is neither unique nor original. Both ancient Egypt and ancient Greece have similar stories that date back thousands of years — but with a twist. You see, the ancient Egyptians and the ancient Greeks did not have a human Frankenstein. No, their versions of Frankenstein were gods who came from the sky. When you consider that Papa Bois, the Trinbagonian father of the forest, and Pan, the Greek god of the wild, are virtually one and the same, isn't it possible that, like Pan, Papa Bois came from the heavens or more accurately, outer space?"

"It make sense."

"Does it?" Gobelyn laughed heartily, "Just speculation, Abaniah, just speculation. Papa Bois may just as easily be the brainchild of an over-imaginative fantasy writer."

"What if he really look like ah regular man? What if he hypnotise people tuh make dem believe he ha' ah cow foot?"

"I suppose it's possible. Why don't you ever exhibit such exquisite flights of fancy in your essays? Need I remind you that house points can be won for assignments as well as for sporting achievements? There is still time to enter this year's English essay competition. Who knows? You could win yourself 30 much-needed points for Ocelot House."

"I'll t'ink about it," said Kaya, unenthusiastically.

"Yes, Master Abaniah, you do that. You do that."

15

BIRTHDAY PARTY

For several weeks, the incidents in the Azura Forest and their shared secret brought Kaya, Raima, and Tom, closer together, much to the dismay of Raima's friends and Kaya's enemies. At Paria College, the three became inseparable. And, when not at college, they used either a popular social networking website or mobile-phone text messaging to keep in close contact. Nonetheless, on the fourth Sunday of November, it was through this social networking website that Kaya learned about Bob Maharaj's eighteenth birthday party. Sixth-former, Bob, of Hummingbird House, only invited young men seventeen or older and attractive girls over the age of fifteen. So naturally, fourteen-year-old boys, such as Kaya and Tom, were not invited. Kaya knew that even if they had met Bob's minimum age requirement, they still would not have been invited as they did not come from wealthy families. Nevertheless, as Kaya discovered from *tagged* photographs taken at the party and displayed on her profile pages, Raima Khan had been invited.

She only fourteen, thought Kaya.

But, there she was, the youngest, prettiest girl at the party, mingling and dancing with sixth-formers such as Colin Sampson and Adrian Leotaud, the House Captains of Ocelot and Mapepire Houses respectively. The fact that her cousin, Jaysen Mohammed, had accompanied Raima was of little consolation to Kaya. Especially, when he discovered that many of her photographs, which had been taken at the party, had been blocked from his view. Her photo album, entitled *Bob's Birthday,* contained twenty-seven images, but Kaya could only access eleven.

Why? What Raima hiding?

On his terribly old computer, Kaya trawled through Raima's pages, at a snail's pace, desperately searching for clues and doing his best to curb his rising frustration. Unable to learn anything of significance from Raima's wall, Kaya turned his attention to Tom's profile, which took an age to load.

"Come on, schupid machine," muttered Kaya, tapping his fingers on the table impatiently.

Suddenly, a loud beep emanated from the computer and the LCD display turned blue. A message appeared on the screen, which read: *A fatal system error is detected. The device will shut down.*

Another beep and the computer switched off.

"Yuh schupid pile ah junk," said Kaya, through gritted teeth.

"Kaya?" came Josephine's voice, from outside his bedroom.

"Yes, Mammy?"

"It too late tuh be talkin' on de phone; yuh should be asleep."

"Ah not on de phone—"

"Well, what yuh doin'? Yuh agree tuh help meh in de shop, bright an' early tomorrow mornin', before yuh go tuh college. Yuh not goin' tuh get up early if yuh stay up talkin' tuh yuhself. Go tuh sleep."

"Yeah, Mammy."

"Right now."

"OK-OK."

To appease Josephine, Kaya switched off his bedroom lights, but as soon as he heard her walk away, he restarted his PC.

Another message appeared on the display, this time it read: *The device did not shut down correctly. Checking disk.*

Kaya shook his fists and snarled at the machine.

Twenty minutes elapsed, and the PC once again displayed: *A fatal system error has been detected. The device will shut down.*

Kaya took a deep breath and resisted the urge to pick up the computer monitor and smash it against the nearest wall. Again, he restarted the machine.

This time, the following message appeared on the screen: *The device has recovered from a serious system error.*

Kaya breathed a sigh of relief.

Then, a new message appeared: *Checking disk for errors. Be patient, this may take some time.*

Kaya looked up to the ceiling, as if searching for divine guidance.

Forty minutes later, the computer finally restarted. Kaya logged in to his social network profile and loaded Tom's pages. Unsurprisingly, he discovered that Raima had left no clues on Tom's profile. Eventually, after his PC had frozen several times, Kaya discovered that both Meenal Baboolal and Shantel Butler had recently been added to Tom's growing list of friend contacts, but the girls had ignored Kaya's friend requests.

Yuh see? Dem gyuls doh like meh at-all-at-all-at-all.

Then, Kaya had an idea: *Maybe ah could find Raima pictures on dey wall.*

Kaya imagined the *Mission: Impossible* theme tune playing in the background as he tried unsuccessfully to view Shantel's photo albums. Shantel had employed maximum security, but perhaps Meenal was careless, at least that's what Kaya hoped. After freezing several times, his Internet browser finally opened Meenal's profile. He was elated to find that Meenal had never heard of the term privacy. Everything could easily be found, her full name — Meenal Omatie Vipadie Baboolal, date of birth, full address, home telephone number, mobile number, shoe size — everything. Kaya navigated through the pages until he found Meenal's photo albums. A few of the titles caught Kaya's attention: *The Day I Broke My Arm; The Day I Broke My Leg; Hospital Visits; My Close Encounter with Jellyfish in Florida; Drama at the Zoo; Mum & Dad — Anniversary Disaster; Chicken Pox; My New Nose;* and, *Parties I was not Invited to.*

The last album on the list seemed promising, and Kaya soon found that Raima had shared several of her photos from Bob's birthday party with her accident-prone friend, Meenal. Kaya tried to skip quickly past the photos he had seen before, but his computer was less than cooperative. So, to speed things along, he switched to title view, which, as the name suggested, only listed the titles of the photographs without actually displaying any images.

The first title, which struck Kaya, was *Passion Wine*. A feeling of dread encompassed him, and he felt a bit ill. It took quite a while before Kaya could bring himself to reveal the image. With bated breath, his heart pounding in his chest, Kaya clicked, *open*; and, ever so slowly, the photograph began to load. He stared at the screen, mesmerised by the browser's slow progress; until finally an image of Raima's face, hair tossed and eyes closed, began to emerge. The slightly blurred shot captured her dancing with wild abandon, a wicked smile traced on her glossed lips. Under different circumstances, Kaya would have enjoyed the sensual provocation of the photograph. However, all he felt was a growing knot in the pit of his stomach and the increasingly crushing weight of waves upon waves of devastating jealousy.

Raima's dark hair obscured someone's face, a face buried in her neck, a face Kaya could not recognise. As his Internet browser gradually revealed more and more of the photograph, it became painfully evident to Kaya that this mystery person was a tall, well-built young man, who held Raima from behind, with strong arms snaked around her waist. Kaya's stomach heaved. He became light-headed and thought he would throw up. He briefly looked away, trying to compose himself, while the image slowly continued to load. The more Kaya saw of the picture, the worse he felt. Until now, he had not realised just how infatuated he had become, and for the first time in his young life, Kaya experienced the full force and debilitating power of unrequited teenage love. All he wanted was for the heartache to go away. Hoping to find solace, Kaya read the picture comments. Instead, he found even more despair and heartache.

You go, girl! commented someone with the alias Trini-girl.

Dat dance look illegal, ladki, posted Samantha Mohan.

Dat's why he arrest meh! added Raima.

@RaimaK, real passion wine, girlfriend, was Shantel's comment.

@ShantelB, wit de hottest hunk in Paria! claimed Raima.

Yuh mean de hottest bulk in Paria! added Meenal.

Ah see yuh finally leave yuh puppy dog in de kennel and yuh find a real man, posted Susan Critchlow.

Doh be rude. Kaya is a nice boy and a good friend, responded Raima.

Emphasis on boy. Make sure yuh lock de kennel, commented Michelle Hunt.

Allyuh too wicked, added Raima.

Jealousy, anger, humiliation, and confusion, punched Kaya where it hurt most — his heart. Nevertheless, curiosity had transformed him into a glutton for punishment. He just had to know the identity of the young man in the photograph, the young man with his arms around Raima, the young man Shantel described as the *hottest hunk in Paria.* Kaya had to look at more photographs. Scrolling down the titles, he found one that caused immediate panic. The image was entitled *Kissing in de Dark.*

With a trembling hand, Kaya slid the computer mouse arrow until it hovered over the word *open.* He right-clicked, only to be startled by a very loud pop that emanated from the back of his old LCD monitor. The moonlight, which filtered into Kaya's bedroom, illuminated a small puff of bluish smoke that streamed out of the air circulation vents of his PC monitor. The monitor had shorted out and tripped the circuit breaker, instantly interrupting the power supply to the electrical sockets and lights.

Kaya opened his bedroom window. He knew he would have trouble sleeping, and the scent of fried capacitors would only make matters worse. Before Josephine realised what had happened, Kaya crept to the fuse box, found the tripped circuit breaker, and he reset it. He stealthily returned to his bed, beaten and in despair. For the last month, Kaya had been building up the courage to ask Raima to the Paria College Christmas Ball, which only fourth-year students and above were allowed to attend. But now, it seemed all but inevitable that Kaya would not be attending the ball at all.

16

ONE RAINY DAY

The following morning commenced with brilliant sunshine and a pale blue sky, marred only by a clump of dark grey clouds that glided inexorably towards the Gulf of Paria's shallow inland sea. At first, Kaya had embraced the moist air, cool breeze, and light drizzle, as the transient manifestations of these passing clouds. But, as he rode his mountain bike to his rendezvous at the Methodist parsonage, Kaya got caught in a terrible downpour. He arrived at Tom's home, wet and deeply despondent. Rev Baker offered to loan Kaya one of Tom's spare college uniforms. He claimed it would not be any trouble for Maureen to dry Kaya's clothes and have them ready for him by lunchtime, but Kaya politely declined. Nevertheless, outspoken Maureen insisted that Kaya would catch pneumonia if he spent the morning soaked to the bone. She persisted until Kaya reluctantly accepted Tom's shirt, which fit fairly well, and his trousers, which were conspicuously two inches too short. As they briskly walked to college, bracing wind and rain under the canopies of borrowed golf umbrellas, Kaya spoke very little. Moreover, although he blamed the inclement weather for his dampened spirits, Tom quickly realised that something else troubled his usually happy-go-lucky friend.

"I guess you've heard about Bob's birthday party last Saturday," said Tom.

"Yeah, ah too young and too poor fuh dat," replied Kaya, bitterly."

"Come on, Abbers, you know what I'm talking about."

"Well, Raima good-lookin' and she rich. Yuh t'ink ah pretty rich gyul ha' time fuh a skinny poor boy like me?"

"Now you're being stupid."

"Oh, yeah?"

"Yeah. Raima is obviously very fond of you."

With his eyes glazed, Kaya burst into insincere laughter.

He mimicked Raima when he said "Dat's why she was kissin' de *hottest hunk in Paria—*"

"You fancy her, don't you?"

"Wha'?"

"Admit it, you like her a lot!"

"Wha' yuh tryin' tuh say?"

"See? That's your problem. You can't even admit you fancy her. Instead of dancing around, all this time, why didn't you just tell her?"

"Oh, is my fault she prefer rich hunks...."

"You're jealous and you're being very unfair. Who said anything about preferring? So, she kissed him — big deal; from what Meenal told me, she also kissed you."

"Meenal and Shantel are your friends; your rich friends, not mine."

"What are you on about?"

"Yuh kno' dey refused meh friend request? Yuh kno' dat?"

"Yes, and do you want to know why?"

"Ah already kno' why—"

"It's because you ignore them, Abbers, and you ignore them because you're only interested in Raima."

"OK-OK, ah admit it; ah like Raima, ah always like she. Yuh satisfied? Ah was goin' tuh ask she tuh de Christmas Ball."

"Listen, I know how you feel—"

"Ah bet yuh goin' wit' Meenal—"

"No, Abbers, not necessarily."

"Why not? It obvious she like yuh, an' you like she."

"She sent a text this morning—"

"Oh, yeah—"

"Late last night, Meenal broke the big toe on her right foot. She won't be dancing at the Christmas Ball this year."

"How come she break she toe?"

"Well, I suppose it was the only bone in her body she hadn't broken before."

Kaya looked down to his feet and the dirty puddles of water on the pavement.

"Wha' yuh t'ink ah should do, Tom?"

"Maybe you should show a bit of compassion and visit Meenal after college with me."

Kaya briefly searched Tom's bespectacled blue eyes before replying sincerely, "Yeah, yuh right. Poor Meenal."

"OK, our first class is ICT with Miss Mow Dem; I think you should use the time to get a grip of yourself. Raima will be in English afterwards. Whatever you do, don't act like a jealous prat; especially if you see Bruce."

"Bruce?"

"Yes, Bruce. Bruce de Freitas. Bruce de Bulk."

"De captain of de football team? So, dat's who she was kissin'...."

"I thought you knew."

"Is dat all she do?"

"Abbers, it was just a kiss, we both know Raima isn't a tart."

"Dey call meh ah puppy dog."

"Well, don't act like one."

Accompanied by Tom, and deeply self-conscious, Kaya entered the information and communications technology suite. Paria College students referred to the ICT suite as the bomb shelter, since it was protected by extra thick steel doors and security shutters. Raima had Principles of Business with Pranit Prakash, also known as Car Crash. And, Kaya felt relieved that Cobo and his cohorts had Chemistry with Pandaros Hooghly, nicknamed Oogly Panda, and Shantel also took this option. He would take Tom's advice and prepare himself for the inevitable ridicule, embarrassment, and emotional discomfort that lay ahead.

As he sat at a workstation next to Tom's, a few girls giggled, and a few boys sniggered. Kaya could not ascertain whether his exposed ankles, his broken heart or other matters completely unrelated to him amused them. Whatever the source of their mirth, they all behaved themselves when Mrs Pearl Pascale entered the room. Here was a woman destined to work in IT, Kaya often mused. Tom thought it was a strange coincidence that Perl and Pascal were the names of programming languages, but not Kaya. Kaya did not believe in coincidences.

Everyt'ing happen fuh ah reason, he thought.

Most students secretly called the black, tomboyish, mildly bowlegged ICT teacher, Miss Mow Dem. She never wore dresses or skirts. She always preferred a plain blouse with dark trousers — widely believed to be of synthetic fabrics, which stretched to allow the unhindered execution of karate kicks and reverse punches.

"Good mornin', students," said Miss Mow Dem, with gusto.

"Good mornin', Miss," came a less than enthusiastic response from the class.

"Today, we'll be learning how to take good digital photographs."

Kaya groaned. The last thing he wanted to think about was digital photography. When he fell into the Snake River, he ruined his camera, and he desperately wanted to erase the painfully lingering mental image of Raima kissing Bruce de Freitas. The thought of it threatened to send him reeling into emotional meltdown.

"So, how would we define a good digital photograph?" asked Miss Mow Dem; and, Curtis Joseph, also known as Iceberg, was first to raise his hand for attention. "Yes, Joseph?"

"Ah good picture not too dark or blurry," said Curtis proudly.

"Iceberg, boy, you smart too bad," grumbled a male student sarcastically. "Compared to you, Einstein is ah duncey-head waste ah space."

"OK," said Miss Mow Dem, "what else?" She looked towards Kaya, ignoring the sparsely raised hands, "Abaniah?"

Kaya did his best to hide his bad mood when he replied, "Nowadays, cameras usually take care ah all de technical t'ings, so anybody could take ah picture dat's bright enough an' in focus, buh dat doh mean it's ah good photograph."

Curtis reacted to Kaya's words with a disapproving pout.

"So, tell us, Abaniah, what makes a good photograph?" pressed Miss Mow Dem.

"Composition," said Kaya, coolly.

Miss Mow Dem calmly said, "Please elaborate."

"De most important t'ing is tuh highlight points ah interest in de photograph. Yuh ha' tuh guide the eyes ah de viewer by controlling balance, structure, and focus. Ah easy way tuh do dis is tuh use de *rule ah thirds*. Yuh divide de image into thirds mentally, so yuh end up wit' nine parts. Make sure yuh put de most interesting elements ah de image on de intersection points or along de four lines...."

"I think we get de idea, but it sounds a bit technical," said Miss Mow Dem, thoughtfully.

"Ah could draw ah diagram," said Kaya, prompting murmurs and sniggers from some of his classmates.

"Please do, Abaniah," replied Miss Mow Dem. "Pay attention," she barked to the class, and everyone suddenly remembered that her entire body was rumoured to be a lethal weapon.

As Kaya walked towards the whiteboard, at the front of the class, he caught the dirty look Curtis Joseph gave him.

Doh gimme no cut-eye, Curtis, ah not in de mood, thought Kaya, angrily, and Curtis immediately yelped, grabbing his face.

"What's wrong, Joseph?" asked Miss Mow Dem.

Several students looked around at Curtis Joseph curiously, including Tom.

"Ow.... Somet'ing burnin' meh eyes," declared Curtis, sadly.

Miss Mow Dem approached him, and suddenly the only audible sound was that of Curtis whimpering.

"Take your hands away from your face," she said, intimidating him with her raptorial stare. "Your eyes seem a bit red; go to de men's room and wash dem out with some water and den hurry back to class."

"Yes, Miss," said Curtis, shakily. He walked past Kaya without even a glance.

Did I do dat? Kaya wondered, and he discerned an unspoken accusation from Tom's blue eyes.

"Please continue, Abaniah," said Miss Mow Dem.

Kaya drew a large rectangle with a black marker on the whiteboard. He added two equally spaced vertical lines and two equally spaced horizontal lines — dividing the rectangle into nine parts. He filled the right side of the large rectangle with a simple drawing of a man's head and shoulders. The image of the man occupied two-thirds of the large rectangle, and his eyes were positioned along the uppermost of the two horizontal lines.

"Yuh see how ah deliberately put de man tuh one side, an' ah put he eyes on de line? Dis is more interestin' than havin' someone in de middle ah de picture," said Kaya, confidently.

"Thank you, Abaniah, well done," said Miss Mow Dem, flashing a rare smile. "Please return to your seat. So, class, what Abaniah has shown us here is dat artistic composition is important for creating a good photograph. And, you don't have to be an artist like Abaniah to apply de *rule of thirds* to your photography; with practice, it should become second nature. Good composition makes de difference between an image dat is engaging, and one dat is boring. De difference between a good photograph and one dat is mediocre or even bad. To create a good digital photograph, we must understand de concepts of lighting, composition, colour, contrast, texture, speed and movement, depth-of-field and distance."

Kaya returned to his seat next to Tom, whose freckled cheeks now sported an emotional blush.

"Did you see his eyes?"

"Whose eyes?" asked Kaya, nonchalantly.

"What do you mean whose eyes? Joseph's — one minute he's giving you a dirty look, the next his eyes are red like the devil's."

"Curtis is ah funny boy, he does come out wit' some funny t'ings jus' fuh attention."

"Did you do something to him?" whispered Tom.

Before Kaya could reply, Miss Mow Dem asked, "Baker, can you name another program we can use to modify our digital photographs?"

Caught completely off guard, Tom blurted out nervously, "Colourshop?"

"Wake up, dunderhead," murmured someone, prompting a spate of unflattering remarks.

"We've had that one," announced Miss Mow Dem, sternly. "You weren't paying attention. Try again."

"Er…. Photo Digital Pro?" said Tom, cautiously.

Miss Mow Dem said to Tom, in a low, calm voice that made him feel even more insecure, "Marvellous. Now login, find de program, create a shortcut on your desktop and open it." Turning to Kaya, she added firmly, "You too, Abaniah. No more chatting." Addressing the whole class, she said, "We'll be experimenting with Photo Digital Pro. First, I want you to create a shortcut on your desktop, den I want you to open de program."

Curtis returned with eyes less red than before.

"Are you better, Joseph, or do you need to see a first aider?" asked Miss Mow Dem, with genuine concern.

"Ah OK, Miss," he replied, softly.

"Everybody know Curtis wearin' contact lenses," Kaya whispered to Tom. "Dust probably went in he eye."

"Yes, you're probably right," replied Tom. "Had any curry, this weekend?"

So now Tom t'ink ah possessed by ah curry-lovin' demon. Man, like today is ah bad day dat only goin' tuh get worse.

Kaya sucked his teeth derisively. He felt betrayed by the prettiest girl at Paria College, but he also worried that he was quite capable of inadvertently taking out his fear and frustration on those around him.

Ah cyah believe ah do dat tuh Curtis. Ever since de incident in de Azura Forest, strange t'ings happening — ah could feel it. Dis is no coincidence — ah changing — buh changing into what?

Later that morning, Kaya and Tom silently took the short walk to Gobelyn's English language lesson in the Form 4P classroom. Since the incident with Curtis in the ICT suite, Tom had not spoken to Kaya. He had decided to err on the side of caution. Kaya entered the classroom and immediately felt disappointed that Gobelyn had not yet arrived. There would be no one present to defend him against the likes of Cobo. So, Kaya braced himself, and he imagined that he wore a futuristic armoured suit that could repel any ray of ridicule. He walked towards his desk, unable to stop himself from staring intently at Raima. At first, she pretended not to notice he had arrived. She continued to look at Samantha Mohan, who wore a yellow-banded tie of Tayra House and occupied absent Meenal's seat. Samantha had been whispering something Kaya could not hear. His superhuman abilities seemed to fail him whenever he wanted them most. And, to his embarrassment, every-one except the secretive pair quietly stared at him with anticipation.

De whole class kno' ah like Raima, he thought, sadly. *An', dey all kno' she was wit' Bruce de Bulk Saturday night. Dey all t'ink ah is some kinda idiot....*

As he came within a few feet of Raima, Samantha, Shantel, and his desk, Samantha finally noticed Kaya's presence and immediately stopped talking.

She looked up to Kaya, with a self-conscious smile that exposed her perfect teeth. "Hello, Kaya," she said nervously.

Kaya did not look at Samantha when he replied bluntly and quietly, "Hello, Samantha." He could not take his eyes off Raima.

Before she hid it with her long hair, Kaya noticed a telltale red mark on Raima's neck, which she had tried to cover with makeup. He imagined a tidal wave of dark-matter particles bombarding his imaginary protective suit, and he allowed the streams of panic to wash over him. After all, Raima was not his girlfriend, and even if she had been his girlfriend, he did not own her.

Unable to keep up the pretence any longer, Raima meekly looked up at Kaya, and a guilt-ridden blush instantly came to her cheeks. Her eyes met Kaya's and immediately he knew, that she knew, that he knew, that she had been kissing Bruce de Freitas at Bob Maharaj's birthday party. Kaya could not bear to look at her any longer. He averted his glazed eyes and sat quietly at his desk. Following behind, Tom occupied the seat next to Kaya's; he slumped into his chair as if he had been burdened with a great weight.

"Hi, Tom," said Samantha, trying to sound chirpy.

Tom replied with uncharacteristic despondence, "Hi, Sam."

He furtively glanced to Raima, who suddenly seemed to find the floor of the classroom quite engaging.

"So, Biggs boy, wha' yuh do on de weekend?" said Cobo, loud enough for Kaya and Raima to overhear.

"Who yuh callin' boy?" said Biggs, disdainfully.

"Ah hear Bob Maharaj had ah serious fete at he house," said Mukesh, playing along with Cobo.

Kaya heard Shantel suck her teeth in disgust; she was sitting next to Raima, so he did not look at her. The guilt he had just seen in Raima's eyes made him sick to his stomach. He just wanted to curl up into a ball and disappear. Kaya knew well beforehand that he would be ridiculed, but this foreknowledge did not make the inevitable humiliation any more palatable. The class had been like a pressure cooker filled with tension.

Cobo announced, loudly, "Ah hear dat was one wicked party!"

This comment lifted the proverbial lid and released a torrent of derisive laughter. Kaya allowed the subsequent taunts and jeers to bounce off of his make-believe armour.

"Ah wonder if anybody here went tuh it," asked Kerwin.

Tom looked towards Kaya, and in his bespectacled blue eyes, Kaya recognised both compassion and apprehension.

"Don't do anything stupid, Abbers," Kaya thought he heard Tom's voice say, but Tom's lips had not moved.

"Yuh had tuh be over seventeen tuh go tuh dat fete, breds," declared Mukesh.

"Raima gyul, yuh alright?" said Cobo, "Ah find yuh well quiet dis mornin'."

"Oh, Gorm, like Puppy Dog wan' tuh cry," Kaya heard Samantha's voice say.

"Ah see yuh hidin' ah bruise on yuh neck gyul, like Soucouyant bite yuh, awa?" teased Kerwin.

"Why dem Mapepires doh shut dey blasted traps?" Shantel's voice said.

Kaya's mind began to reel, and a chink in his imaginary armour started to grow. Very quickly, vital components of his emotional protection fell away. Anger, fear, shame, insecurity, and confusion descended on his head and his heart like a ton of bricks.

"Get a grip, Abbers," said Tom's voice, desperately.

Unable to take it any longer, Kaya stood up and shouted to Tom, "Ah tryin' tuh get ah grip.... Ah tryin'!"

For a few silent moments, Tom stared at Kaya. He was utterly stunned — everyone was; then even more laughter came than before.

Relishing Kaya's humiliation, Kerwin shouted, above the din, "Buh A-A, Ah Banana, like Bob didn't invite yuh to he party, awa?"

There was a roar of laughter so loud that Allister Shen came rushing in from Form 4A next door. The grandparents of the mathematics and music teacher, whom most students called Master Shen, were originally from Kowloon, Hong Kong. However, unlike his grandparents, Master Shen had embraced Rastafarianism and sported long dreadlocks.

"Wha' goin' on here?" waving his small hands to get attention, he shouted, "Cool dong, cool dong!"

Many 4P students failed to notice the short, Oriental teacher, at the entrance to the class; they were far too busy laughing at Kaya. Then, suddenly, Kerwin grabbed his head and screamed in pain. A few, mostly Mapepires, treated Kerwin's odd behaviour as the antics of a clown and continued supporting him with laughter, but the majority, including Kaya, deduced that something was horribly wrong.

Kaya felt a warm liquid fall onto the back of his hand. And, looking down, he discovered two drops of blood. Lifting his trembling hand to his face, Kaya realised to his horror that he had a nosebleed. He saw Kerwin vomit; then, the room began to spin. Above the confused cries of his class-mates, Kaya heard Obeah Widow and Master Shen shouting; and, he saw a look of abject terror on Tom's face.

"If you're doing this, stop it! What's happening to you?" Kaya heard Tom yell.

Yuh cyah see meh nose bleedin'? thought Kaya.

With anger, giving way to panic, Kaya turned around to see Tom's lips moving. All he could hear was a continuous ringing in his ear. Kaya caught a brief glimpse of Master Shen rushing towards Kerwin, who was now on the floor having a fit, while his Mapepire friends went into hysterics around him.

Kaya's knees buckled, and strong arms grabbed him from behind. The sickly-sweet scent of *Lily of the Night*, worn by the person holding him, just made him feel worse.

Barely audible above the incessant ringing, Kaya heard Obeah Wid-ow's shrill voice shouting, "No-no-no, Duff is having a seizure — don't try to restrain him, he'll only get more violent. Byno! Get Mr Mendoza. Quick-ly! He should be in the gymnasium. Someone, help me here; Hezekiah is not well either...."

Kaya thought, *Hezekiah? Nobody call meh dat.*

And, it was the last thing he remembered.

17

THE UNEXPLAINED

"**K**erwin Duff, the son of Nigel and Cicely Duff, the owners of N C Duff Booksellers, suffered sudden unexplained death in epilepsy, according to his death certificate. He died last Monday at Paria College, Coconut Grove, at about 9am. He was fifteen-years-old," said the radio newscaster, solemnly.

Dr Chalmers advised Josephine not to allow Kaya to cycle to school until he received the results of his blood tests. And, as he stared forlornly out of the window of the taxi that drove him to college, Kaya recalled one of the first conversations he had with Kerwin. They had just joined Paria College as wide-eyed Form 1 students.

"Meh mudder own Josephine Flower Shop," Kaya remembered saying.

"Meh parents own N C Duff Booksellers," said Kerwin, matter-of-factly.

"Wha' N C stand for?"

"Nigel an' Cicely — meh parents name."

"Sissy Lee? Yuh mudder name Sissy?" asked Kaya.

Everyone within earshot laughed at Kerwin; and, for many months afterwards, his nickname had been *Sissy Boy*. This led to retaliatory name-calling on the part of Kerwin. Among other things, he mockingly called Kaya, *Abracadabra*, *Abbey Nana*, and *Flower Boy*, but none of his insulting names stuck the way Sissy Boy had stuck to him. Although Kaya had made an innocent mistake, Kerwin never forgave him — even when Sissy Boy had been forgotten. They would never be friends. And now, Kaya feared that Tom believed he had used evil, supernatural abilities to murder Kerwin. They had not had a decent conversation since the incident. On the other hand, Raima had tried to speak to Kaya, several times; but, he stubbornly limited any contact with her. Jealousy had gotten the better of him; not only did he avoid Raima but he also avoided all her friends as well. Kaya had become insular and reclusive. Although he pretended otherwise, Kerwin's untimely death haunted him. His college work suffered, and he found it difficult to sleep at night. Kaya secretly wondered if there was truth in Tom's suspicions. Had he become some sort of psychic assassin?

Several of the Paria College staff and students had not taken Kerwin's death very well. For instance, Cobo and the remaining Mapepires had become very bitter and vindictive. Nonetheless, grateful that Kaya saved him from falling to his doom into the Paria River, Mukesh remained the least aggressive towards him. At least, that's what Kaya thought. Master Shen became withdrawn, and Kaya believed he blamed himself for not knowing what to do during the critical moments when Kerwin stopped breathing. Two days after the incident, the class prefect, John Byno, had related to Kaya how Mr Shen had sobbed bitterly when the desperate efforts of Mr Mendoza failed to revive Kerwin.

Affectionately known as Bulldozer, Bernard Mendoza was the physical education teacher at Paria College and a certified first aider. His father originated from neighbouring Venezuela while his mother hailed from Grenada. And, as his nickname suggested, he had a powerful build. One of Kaya's favourite teachers, Bulldozer had coached him in sprinting and believed he possessed great potential. Bulldozer had also not been himself since the incident; Kerwin had died in his arms. Although rumoured to have been educated in England, Obeah Widow was not British, yet she seemed to be the only person maintaining what the British referred to as, a *stiff upper lip.* Nevertheless, Kaya appreciated that he could have been injured if Obeah Widow had not caught him as he fainted.

Dr Chalmers, Kaya's elderly family doctor, had explained that nosebleeds sometimes led to blackouts. He advised that low blood sugar or low blood pressure could also have caused Kaya to faint, and being drenched, on the morning in question, did not help. There were many plausible scientific explanations for Kerwin's death and Kaya's blackout, yet Tom entertained a supernatural explanation, and he was not the only one.

During the morning break, Kaya had been relieving himself at a urinal in the men's room when Cobo and Deron occupied those on either side of him. Before Kaya could move out of the way, Cobo directed a stream of urine at his legs and managed to splash the hem of his trousers and the tops of his shoes.

"What is wrong wit' you?" shouted Kaya, zipping up his pants and angrily shaking Cobo's urine off his shoes.

"Now yuh could say Cobo pee on yuh," snarled Cobo, and he also zipped up his pants.

Before Kaya could retaliate, Deron reached into his trouser pocket and produced a menacing penknife with a shiny steel blade.

"Jus' cool it, an' listen," he said calmly.

Cobo continued, "Everybody in Coconut Grove know yuh gran'mudder was ah witch—"

"You doh have nothing tuh say 'bout meh gran'mudder, yuh hear meh?" hissed Kaya, and he defiantly clenched his fists.

Deron swiftly brought the knife-edge in line with Kaya's right eye, and the fluorescent, overhead lamp flickered.

"Look nuh, Puppy Dog, unless yuh want meh tuh baptise meh knife on yuh face, yuh better cool it."

"Listen, Biggs, ah doh care who yuh fadah is. If yuh cut meh, yuh not leavin' dis room on yuh own two legs."

"Listen tuh de likkle man, Biggs. Listen good tuh de gun talk. Yuh doh wan' tuh end up like Duff," said Cobo, mockingly. He moved his face close to Kaya's and he added in a low, menacing voice, "Biggs, yuh doh want Ah Banana tuh use he magic an' buss a blood vessel in yuh brain."

"Yuh kno', Cobo, yuh really need tuh start usin' mouthwash," said Kaya, staring defiantly into Cobo's glazed, red eyes, "Yuh breath seriously vampin'."

"Yuh t'ink it funny, Abaniah? Eh, yuh t'ink is ah joke? Duff dead," said Cobo, and his voice faltered. "He dead an' he not comin' back."

"Now, you check dis, Cobo, wha' happen tuh Kerwin, ah wouldn't wish on meh worse enemy — ah wouldn't wish on you."

"Dat's right, Ah Banana.... You and me? We are enemies.... De worse enemies. Yuh come from ah long line ah black witches; an', ah on tuh yuh, likkle man ... ah on tuh yuh. An' mark meh words ... ah go do fuh yuh. Yuh hear meh? Ah go do fuh yuh. So bring yuh magic, bring yuh Obeah, bring whatever de hell yuh want; in de end, is pay yuh go pay fuh wha' yuh do tuh Duff. When ah done wit' yuh, yuh go wish yuh never born."

"Alright, Cobo, so now yuh say what yuh ha' tuh say, ah kno' where ah stand," said Kaya, not showing any fear. Turning to Deron, he said, "An' you Biggs, de nex' time yuh feel tuh threaten meh wit' ah knife, make sure yuh bring ah much bigger knife.... Yuh'll need it."

Cobo and Deron sucked their teeth in unison. For a long moment, they stared at Kaya. Kaya imagined they were deliberating whether or not Deron should just stab him, then and there, in the men's room. Eventually, Deron bared his buckteeth in an unattractive smile; he shook his head dismissively, closed his penknife and put it in his trouser pocket. At that moment, two fifth-formers, who wore the blue-banded ties of Hummingbird House, came into the men's room chatting about a recent football match.

Deron took his cue from Cobo and they both left the room. Kaya breathed a sigh of relief. He gazed at his reflection in the mirror before splashing cold water on his face.

When Kaya left the restroom, he immediately noticed the scent of *Lily of the Night*. He found Deron, not too far away, being challenged by Obeah Widow; and, a crowd of inquisitive onlookers had begun to gather.

"I won't ask you again, Biggs," she said, in her shrill voice, "I would like you to show me the contents of your pockets."

"Buh why, Miss?"

"That's Mistress Mallory to you, young man," she said, eyebrows raised high on her wrinkled forehead.

"Why, Mistress Mallory?"

"I believe you may be carrying an offensive weapon, Biggs," said Obeah Widow, and her eyes narrowed.

"Who tell yuh dat?"

Obeah Widow barked, "Turn out your pockets, do it now!" And, Deron shuddered.

To Kaya, he seemed resigned to his fate, looking down towards his feet, slowly shaking his head with dismay. Deron reached into the back pocket of his trousers and pulled out the lining to reveal its emptiness; then, from the front left pocket, he slowly retrieved a brown leather monogrammed billfold.

"OK. Now the other one," urged Obeah Widow.

Deron glanced at Cobo, who stood several metres away.

Cobo solemnly shook his head as if to say, *"Don't do it."*

Deron pulled a bunch of keys and a few coins from the pocket. His hand trembled, almost imperceptibly, but Kaya noticed. A faint smile cracked Obeah Widow's stony face. With snake-like speed, she grabbed Deron's thigh, causing the crowd to gasp and Deron to yelp.

"What's this?" she growled.

Obeah Widow shoved her hand into Deron's pocket and whipped out his penknife.

"What's this?" she demanded, feverishly opening the knife and brandishing it triumphantly.

"Dat's meh Scout knife, Miss…. Mistress Mallory."

"Deron Biggs," she said, in a tone most people would reserve for speaking to a five-year-old, "you know perfectly well, that this type of knife is not allowed anywhere on the college compound."

Suddenly, the gathered crowd parted; and, like Moses the Lawgiver, Shaka Duna, Paria College vice-principal and dean, walked unhindered to where Obeah Widow and Deron stood.

"Thank you, Mistress Mallory," he said, in his raspy, accented voice.

The dark South African stretched out his right hand, and Obeah Widow closed the knife and placed it in his open palm. He puffed on his pipe and exhaled the smoke of the finest Virginia tobacco. Obeah Widow coughed, and a pained expression wiped the smug smile from her face.

"Come with me, young man," Shaka Duna told Deron.

Once again, the crowd parted to allow Shaka Duna passage; Deron meekly followed, a few paces behind, his head bowed in disgrace.

It was rumoured that Obeah Widow had called for Deron to be permanently expelled. Be that as it may, the college board of governors included Chairwoman Eliza Corbeau, Cobo's mother. She was a close friend of Bertha Biggs, Deron's mother; and many others who were either friendly with or terrified of, Assistant Superintendent of Police, Uriah Biggs — Deron's notorious father. In the end, Deron was kept away from college a mere five days.

During that time, lucky coincidence had Obeah Widow appearing whenever Cobo began to harass Kaya; at least that's the way it seemed to Kaya. Shaka Duna and Obeah Widow were the most feared masters at Paria College. And, of the two, Cobo feared Obeah Widow the most. His wealth and prestige did not matter to her. In fact, there had been widespread speculation in Coconut Grove regarding Obeah Widow's exclusive Bellevue address. In the prestigious gated community, she lived across the street from the Duffs in an old meticulously maintained house, partially hidden behind a high brick wall. Some said that her husband was a wealthy foreigner who left her a fortune when he died. Others suggested that Obeah Widow had won a jackpot in the National Lottery; while a few of the elderly Bellevue residents claimed that Obeah Widow's mother, and her grandmother before that, previously owned the large home. At any rate, no one knew much about the mysterious European history teacher. Kaya once overheard Kerwin saying that Obeah Widow had no visitors and seldom left her house except to go to college. According to Kerwin, cats that ventured onto her property were never seen again, but Kaya dismissed this along with Kerwin's claim that Obeah Widow slept, every night, in a coffin.

18

THE NEW GIRL

Late for college, the following Monday morning, Kaya had been running to his locker when he tripped on his untied shoelaces and fell at the feet of one of Paria's female students. Stunned, he stared at his wide-eyed reflection in gleaming black patent shoes. Slowly lifting his head, Kaya's vision followed long, tanned, perfectly shaped legs, until....

"Stop," said a female voice, with a North American accent. "Don't look up."

Deeply embarrassed, Kaya clumsily scrambled to his feet. "Sorry," he replied, automatically.

Then, he saw the girl's face for the first time and was dumbstruck. Kaya stared into the mesmerising, green, cat-like eyes of a beautiful Eurasian brunette. The new girl had very long hair, parted above her cocked left eyebrow, and her easy smile revealed pleasantly dimpled cheeks.

"I'm not wearing any underwear," she whispered, maintaining eye contact.

"Wha'?" muttered Kaya, and he imagined he could not appear more moronic, even if he tried.

For a second, the gorgeous girl simply stared at Kaya's gradually reddening face, and then she began laughing loudly. "I'm joking," she said, trying to catch her breath, "I can't believe you fell for that." She regained her lady-like composure, offered her slender hand and said, "Hi, my name is Gwendolyn, but everybody calls me Wendy. Wendy Wong." And, as he shook Wendy's hand, Kaya could not help noticing her jasmine perfume or her juicy, lip-glossed lips.

"My name is Hezekiah," he said, self-consciously downplaying his strong Trinidadian accent, "but, people call me—"

"Kaya! Yeah, I recognised you," said Wendy, enthusiastically. "Your picture was in the local paper. You saved that girl.... Eh, what's-her-name, from drowning in a river. You're a hero."

He's even cuter than I thought.

Kaya almost dropped the books he had been taking out of his locker. *She t'ink ah cute?*

"Well—"

"You don't say much, eh?" said Wendy.

But he's shy — maybe too shy, she thought, and Kaya heard her. *I wonder if he's taking what's-her-name to the Christmas Ball.*

Ah not shy....

"I—"

"Great Scott!" said Wendy, glancing at her Mickey Mouse watch. Look at the time. I'm late. Oh, no, I can't believe I'll be late for my first class."

She walked ten paces. And, with each and every step, her short grey pleated skirt and shapely hips waved Kaya a heart-breaking goodbye.

Suddenly, Wendy stopped dead in her tracks and muttered, "Form 4P, Math, in the McKenney Block. The McKenney Block.... Which way's the McKenney Block?"

"We in de same class. Maths with Master Shen," said Kaya, unconsciously sticking out his chest and sucking in his stomach. "C'mon, follow me."

Wendy rushed to keep up with Kaya. She said, "I see from your tie, you're in the red house." Kaya immediately noticed Wendy's green-banded tie, but somehow his attention drifted to her gently heaving chest. "The green matches my eyes, but I really, really hate snakes." Kaya dragged his gaze up Wendy's graceful neck to the warmth of her dimpled smile. "I'm not really into the whole English house stuff. I hope it's not like we're enemies or something, eh?"

"You're in Mapepire House. Mapepire real competitive," said Kaya, "but it doesn't really matter tuh me wha' house yuh in."

"Oh," said Wendy, feigning disappointment, "And, here I thought you liked me."

Suddenly Kaya recalled the words of Tantie. They rang as clearly as church bells on a Sunday morning. *"If yuh spen' yuh time tellin' she how she wonderful, she go lose interest in yuh one time. Doh talk too much. An' doh be too nice — 'omen hate dat."*

"Well, you're still on probation," said Kaya, confidently.

"Whoa, big fella, it's way too early for any kinda probing."

"During your probation, dere's ah thorough examination; yuh could even bring ah friend if yuh doh trust me."

OK, this seems promising. He's not a mouse....

Wendy said, "I think my little joke about not wearing underwear is giving you a completely wrong idea about me."

"Not at all, ah never wear underwear either." Kaya chuckled. "So, wha' part of America yuh from?"

"The Canadian part," answered Wendy, and she casually swept her long hair from her left cheek.

I wonder if it's true what they say about West Indians.

"Absolutely true," said Kaya, with a Cheshire-cat grin.

"Eh? What's absolutely true?"

Kaya suddenly realised he had replied to what Wendy had thought, not what she had said. *Mayday-Mayday-Mayday....* He imagined going down in flames.

Kaya recovered by saying, "It absolutely true dat de best part of North America is de Canadian part."

"Oh, really?" said Wendy, trying to gauge whether Kaya was joking or not. "That's what my dad says. He's Trinidadian. He grew up in San Fernando, but he loves Tronno. My mother's Welsh."

"Wha' about you?"

Wendy frowned when she said; "I'm the reason we're all here. I need discipline; that's what my father says."

"Ah could see dat," said Kaya, with a wry smile.

Ah wonder if ah ask she tuh de ball, wha' she will say.

"No," said Wendy, bluntly.

"No?" asked Kaya, trying to hide his disappointment.

"No, I didn't want to come here. Don't get me wrong, Trinidad seems nice enough, but I had a good life in Tronno."

Kaya tried to look into Wendy's eyes, but, to his surprise, she averted them shyly. Then, without warning, Wendy opened her eyes as wide as she could. She brought her face so close to Kaya's that the tips of their noses brushed. Wendy's dilated pupils turned Kaya's heart to butter.

"What's the matter, eh?" she whispered. "Never seen green eyes before?"

Without waiting for Kaya's reply, Wendy kissed him. Or maybe, he kissed her. It was short, warm, sweet, utterly impulsive, and very confusing.

"Best to get that out of the way," said Wendy, matter-of-factly.

She kissed me....

With both hands, Wendy briefly and gently clasped Kaya's oval face and seemed to examine it the way an archaeologist would a rare artefact. Staring admirably into his dreamy, dark-brown eyes, she licked her lips and added with a soft chuckle, "Hmmm.... Dimple on the chin, devil within."

Kaya arrived at his classroom in an all-consuming daze. He had never met a girl like Wendy before.

"You'd better tie your shoelaces. Wouldn't want you to break something," she said.

"Ah want tuh take yuh tuh de ball," whispered Kaya.

"No," said Wendy.

"No? Why not?"

"Quite frankly, I'm just not that type of girl. Just because I kissed
you, and I'm not wearing any underwear, it doesn't mean I'm easy."

"Yuh really not wearin' any underwear?"

Wendy laughed. "You fell for it again. I'm gonna have a lot of fun
with you; I could tell. Yeah, I know, I'm an insufferable flirt. I'll let you
know about the ball, when your probation ends, Mr Kaya."

Kaya just stood there, at the doorway to Form 4P, thunderstruck.

Wendy entered the classroom, immediately prompting a wall of silence, and
Kaya imagined the attractive Eurasian girl to be the proverbial stranger that
walked into an American Old West saloon. However, once the initial shock
had subsided, the young men of Form 4P expressed their approval of the
attractive newcomer with wolf-whistles and hisses, while greeting Kaya's
late arrival with catcalls, teeth-sucking and general derision.

Cobo pushed Mukesh out of his chair saying, "Yuh better find
somewhere else tuh sit, she sittin' right here nex' tuh me."

"Just settle dong. What impression we givin' our new student?"
asked Master Shen, lacking the good humour he possessed prior to Kerwin
Duff's untimely death. "Keep actin' like barbarians, an' put meh in de mood
tuh deduct house points and issue detention slips." The student chatter
subsided, and Master Shen said, "Have ah seat, Abaniah; we'll discuss yuh
tardiness later."

Kaya sat at one of the vacant chairs next to Tom, who continued to
stare at Wendy and barely noticed his arrival. On the other hand, Raima, who
sat between Meenal and Shantel, did notice Kaya. She smiled, but Kaya
pretended not to see her.

"Oh, it's my fault Kaya's late," said Wendy, stunning the class with
her Torontonian accent, "I had trouble with the key for my locker, and he
kindly stayed and helped me."

"Ah Banana, my hero," mumbled Deron.

"Hmmm. It seems Abaniah has admirably performed de role of ambassador dis morning. Well done," said Master Shen, and his eyes seemed
hollow and his voice subdued. "Class, ah want tuh introduce Miss Gwendolyn Wong—"

"My friends call me Wendy," said Wendy, flashing her winning smile.

"What yuh enemies call yuh?" grumbled Meenal, uncharacteristically.

"Ah, fairest maiden, thine beauty doth maketh mine loins stir, and mine cup runneth over," said Denzil Bari, a very dark, dishevelled boy of Indian descent.

"Bari, if yuh find yuh loins troublesome, is no problem fuh meh tuh remove them from meh class," said Master Shen, and Bari seemed to shrink in his chair. "Tuck in yuh shirt, an' fix yuh tie."

"Buh why yuh ha' tuh embarrass meh so?" muttered Bari, as he slowly complied.

"Any more ole chat from you, and ah will deduct ten points from Mapepire House," said Master Shen, solemnly; and then, addressing the class, he added, "Wendy is from Canada, and ah hope dat we will all be helpful, patient, an' respectful, and generally do our best to be great ambassadors of Trinidad an' Tobago. Please, take ah seat, Wendy."

Wendy eyed the vacant seat next to Cobo, who sported a hungry grin, the one next to Kaya, who tried to act cool as he logged on, and finally the one next to Iceberg, who absent-mindedly picked his nose.

"Sit anywhere," prompted Master Shen.

Wendy cocked her left eyebrow and sat next to Kaya, inciting groans of disapproval from several students. "Guess I'm with you, hero," she whispered, and Kaya couldn't help smiling.

Raima briefly stared in disbelief, while Meenal and Shantel folded their arms and pouted.

"Hello?" said Cobo, in a low voice. "Yuh should sit here, Wendy, near me. In Mapepire House, we stick together."

"Thanks, but that's OK," said Wendy, politely. "I'm fine here."

Kaya, Tom, and the other boys in Ocelot House were quite happy with Wendy's response, but Kaya sensed great animosity from the Mapepires and most of the girls in the class. Kaya had never been able to read Raima's mind, but he did not need a crystal ball to see that she was jealous — very jealous.

Good, he thought.

19

SOCIAL NETWORKING

That afternoon, Kaya rode his shiny mountain bike home on a cloud of extraordinary happiness. His lips tingled with the memory of Wendy's sweet kiss and his heart fluttered at the thought of kissing her again. Somehow, Kaya felt as if he had known Wendy his entire life. He felt completely at ease in her presence; intuitively, she seemed to know exactly what to say, exactly what to do, and exactly when to do it. She dazzled him with her quirky humour and shared interests. On her very first day at Paria College, she had expertly rebuffed the eager advances of other boys and confidently traversed the social minefield laid by envious female students. Kaya could scarcely believe that Wendy took identical study options to his own. An accomplished artist, she astonished Miss Cutlash with her lifelike sketches during their double visual arts class. And, Kaya was both intrigued and impressed by the fact that she sold her artwork and photographs on a dedicated website.

Kaya greeted his hardworking mother at Josephine's Flower Shop; stunning her with an uncharacteristic kiss on the cheek, before happily rushing upstairs to the privacy of his bedroom and the promise of hours of interpersonal cyberspace adventures on his old PC. Kaya hastily logged on to his social networking profile, elated that Gwendolyn Lian Wong had sent him a friend request, which he immediately accepted. He trawled through her photographs and posts, attempting to compile as much information as he could about the new student from Canada. Kaya immediately ascertained that Wendy was *Daddy's girl*. Many of her photographs featured her in the company of her fun-loving father at ice hockey tournaments, rock concerts, Caribana, and even Trinidad and Tobago Carnival. Unsurprisingly, Wendy was very popular. Her friend list totalled almost 2,000, and her name had been tagged to double that number of photographs on the social networking site. Kaya felt deeply flattered that the Torontonian beauty had not yet listed anyone else, from Paria College, as a friend. He was the first. Kaya was particularly interested in identifying Wendy's close male friends. He had a hard time sorting through her photographs with rugged hockey players, tall basketball players, muscular rugby players, and handsome lacrosse players. To his disappointment and bafflement, Wendy seemed to like older, sporty guys — guys like Bruce de Freitas. And, Kaya wondered why she would be interested in a scrawny, Trinbagonian sprinter.

Wendy's many interests included, travelling, netball, art, a Canadian rock band called Rush, UFOs, conservation, quotable quotes, philosophy, mythology, butterflies, chocolate, fashion, modelling, and shoes. In fact, Kaya discovered that Wendy had been on the cover of a teen magazine and had even appeared in a few episodes of a popular Canadian sitcom.

How come she never tell meh dat?

Kaya wondered if Raima had anything to say about the new girl. Since Bob Maharaj's Birthday Party, Raima had become increasingly secretive, hiding many of her posts from Kaya. Nevertheless, Kaya knew he could rely on Meenal's carelessly public profile for information and clues. Navigating to Meenal's wall, Kaya found himself presented with disturbing images of her broken toe.

Poor Meenal....

Kaya soon discovered an online conversation involving Raima, Meenal, Shantel, Samantha Mohan, and several other fourth-form Paria girls.

And, he instantly recalled Rev Baker once saying, *"Envy yearns to find flaws."*

Hi, boys, I'm from Tronno, eh? Look at my perfect teeth and long, long legs.... Ugh!! You see how all the boys were staring at her, with their tongues hanging out? Samantha Mohan wrote.

Tronno! Hahahahahaha!!! Padded bra, short skirt and makeup.... added Susan Critchlow.

Jagabat!!! Kill it, before it multiplies!!! commented Whitney Walker.

Michelle Hunt asked, *How many B's in BIMBO, eh?*

Wait till Obeah Widow sees how short her skirt is, wrote Meenal.

No Yankee going to buss style on me, added Susan Critchlow, *I could do what she do. Dressing to kill, tomorrow. :D*

Cheryl Edwards posted, *Me too!!!*

Me three, added Kimberly de Gannes.

Trini-girl commented, *I can't believe she sat next to Puppy Dog.*

Exactly. Mapepires usually stick with Mapepires, posted Shantel.

Kaya is a nice boy, was Raima's only contribution.

@RaimaK, but Bruce nicer! LOL, posted Samantha Mohan.

A low beep interrupted Kaya's enjoyment of the girls' obvious envy. It was an instant message from Wendy.

Wendy wrote, *Hey, Mr Kaya, welcome to Wendy's world. It's a strange place....* ☺

Yeah, I see you like UFOs. That explains a lot.... responded Kaya.

Exactly what are you inferring?

Don't worry, your secret is perfectly safe with me.

What?!!

I'm an alien too, added Kaya.

Busted.... What gave me away?

The six teaspoons of sugar you put in your iced tea, the way your little fingers stick out, and your antennae....

You noticed the sugar, eh?

Hahahahahaha!!!

Kaya lost track of time, exchanging messages with his pretty new friend all through the night. Flirting gave way to discussions about conservation, art, computer games, music, the possibility of extraterrestrials, and even the meaning of life. Kaya could not believe his luck. Wendy was not just a pretty face; she was very intelligent, and unlike her peers at Paria College, she had travelled the world. Her mother's high-flying job with the United Nations had seen to that. And, for the first time, for almost as long as he could remember, Kaya's last thought, before falling asleep, was not about Raima Khan.

20

FORGOTTEN MEMORIES

Time passed, and Kaya found it more and more difficult to remember what happened during the fateful college expedition to the Azura Forest. Day by day, his friendship with Wendy Wong grew. Raima's attention turned more and more to the moody captain of the college football team — the sixth former named Bruce de Freitas, affectionately known as Bruce de Bulk. Eventually, the kiss Kaya shared with Raima became a faded memory, and as the Paria College Christmas Ball approached, he hoped that Wendy would be his date.

Kaya did not think about the father of the forest at all. In fact, he eventually convinced himself that the strange man, he met on the college trip, was just an old hermit who pretended to be Papa Bois, in order to scare poachers away. Kaya believed that the man's horns and cloven hooves were simply figments of his overactive imagination. After all, he had hit his head hard enough to suffer a concussion at the time when the man emerged. However, all that changed when Kaya bit hard into a kernel of popcorn and broke the amalgam filling in his upper right first molar. The resultant visit to Robert Childs, the dentist, proved to be eventful.

As Kaya sat in the dentist's chair, Dr Childs' dulcet tones, soothing piped music, and his pretty assistant, did nothing to calm Kaya's frayed nerves.

"Don't worry; it's an upper tooth, so I'll be using a very small needle. You shouldn't feel a thing," said Dr Childs reassuringly.

Although it's true that Kaya disliked injections, and usually felt mild anxiety during dental treatment, he could not understand his rising terror. So it came as a complete surprise to everyone, especially Kaya, when he suddenly fainted in the dentist's chair. And, when they revived him, he went completely berserk. The overhead lamp, the chair, the dental tools and instruments all contributed to making Kaya hysterical. Kaya had begun to remember things he had forgotten, and it took Dr Childs, his assistant, another dentist, and a startled patient to restrain Kaya.

"Buh wha' allyuh doin' tuh meh son?" asked Josephine, as she stormed into the examination room.

"Papa Bois…. Ah see Papa Bois," shouted Kaya.

"Oh, Gorm, like he delirious," said the pretty assistant.

"Has he been taking drugs?" Dr Childs asked Josephine.

"Doh be damn schupid," shouted Josephine, "Wha' yuh give him?"

Suddenly Kaya shouted, "Papa Bois!"

The examination lamp directly above Kaya's head got much brighter. The bulb blew with a loud pop, and a box of surgical gloves tumbled from a nearby counter. The air-conditioning fans in the room slowly ceased spinning, and it soon became obvious that the electricity supply to the building had been interrupted. Kaya immediately stopped struggling, but his staring eyes reflected panic.

"Yuh see dat? Yuh see dat? Dat ent drugs, dat is spirit," said the terrified patient, who had assisted in restraining Kaya. "He ent need no doctor; he need ah damn exorcist! Not me an' dat spirit business. Is gone ah gone, oui. Ah goin' straight tuh confession now fuh now."

"But what about your root canal?" asked Dr Childs.

"Root canal? Root canal? Listen, yuh see me an' jumbie? We doh hang at-all-at-all-at-all." The man walked briskly to the doorway; then, before exiting, he looked at Josephine and added balefully, "Madame, if yuh know wha' good fuh yuh, yuh go take de boy tuh see ah priest now fuh now."

Trying to ignore the spooked patient, Josephine leaned over Kaya, lines of concern crossing her face as she gently asked, "Wha'ppen Kaya? Yuh alright?"

"Mammy, ah wan' tuh go home."

"But he has a broken filling," protested Dr Childs.

"Damn de blinkin' fillin'. Ah taking meh son home," said Josephine, with fire in her voice. "Come, Kaya, leh we go."

"Ah hope yuh feel better soon, Kaya," said the pretty assistant.

The electricity supply came back on, and the air-conditioning units began circulating cool air in the tense room.

Dr Childs gesticulated defensively as he said to Josephine, "I assure you, I didn't do anything to the boy. But, he seems quite alright now, and we don't want any infection setting in. Maybe, you could book an emergency appointment for tomorrow or the day after."

Josephine sucked her teeth, pulled Kaya by the arm, and they quickly left.

On the way home, both Kaya and Josephine remained silent. Josephine drove her old Jeep Wrangler faster than usual, and Kaya tried to think up a plausible explanation for his strange behaviour.

Finally, Josephine said, "So, Kaya, yuh goin' tuh tell meh wha' goin' on?"

"Ah doh know, Mammy—"

"Listen to me, dis serious. Ah wan' yuh tuh tell meh de truth. Yuh takin' drugs?"

"No, Mammy," said Kaya, rolling his eyes.

"Right. We goin' straight tuh de General Hospital."

"No. Ah doh want tuh go dere," he said, hysteria in his voice.

"Wha' yuh mean yuh doh want tuh go dere? Yuh t'ink dat yuh behaviour in de dentist surgery normal? Nah, boy, we goin' straight tuh de hospital, now-now-now."

"Remember dat day, on de hike?"

"Yes, wha' about it?"

"Well…. Ah t'ink ah see Papa Bois."

Josephine turned her head to Kaya. He stared deeply into her eyes. And, the fear he saw there, made him shudder. With her attention off the road, Josephine's Jeep slowly began to veer towards oncoming traffic.

"Mammy!" cried Kaya, snapping Josephine's attention back to the road. The driver of an oncoming car blared his horn and swerved to avoid a head-on collision.

Kaya noticed a tremor in Josephine's tightened grip on the steering wheel.

"Yuh believe meh?" he asked her.

"Doh tell ah soul 'bout dis, yuh hear meh?" said Josephine, sternly.

"Buh—"

"Not another word 'bout dis, yuh hear meh, Kaya? Not another word."

Sitting quietly, in the front passenger seat of Josephine's Jeep, Kaya tried to make sense of his mother's unexpected reaction.

She doh even want tuh know what ah remember, he thought. *Maybe, she t'ink ah crazy. Or she worried what people will say. Or maybe … maybe, she know ah really see Papa Bois.*

Kaya stared out the window as they drove through one of the poorer neighbourhoods of Coconut Grove. Rows of ramshackle storefronts merged into walls of optimistically bright colours. Pedestrians of all ages, with dark, sunburnt faces glistening in the noonday sun, went about their business in a carefree manner.

If dey only know, what I know, they'd wet themselves, thought Kaya.

Kaya took a deep breath, not noticing Josephine's quick glance. The dentist chair with its halogen operating light, delivery unit and assistant arm, reminded Kaya of being reclined in a futuristic pod. The man, who called himself Papa Bois, had somehow transported Kaya to another location — one that seemed out of this world.

Kaya recalled waking in the strange environment; feeling drugged, reclined in an elongated regeneration unit. His body, from the neck down, felt immersed in a warm gel-like substance. A cushion supported his head. It made his skull tingle; and, despite being restrained, Kaya had an unusual sense of well-being. The man, who called himself Papa Bois, had a handsome face with prominent cheekbones, brooding eyebrows, a straight nose, full lips and dark, reddish-brown skin. And, a strange sense of familiarity urged Kaya to trust the mysterious stranger.

He asked the man, "Where am I?"

"Your head injury required immediate medical treatment. I have subjected you to targeted accelerated regeneration." Then, taking a chocolate bar from Kaya's rucksack, the man asked, "Where did you get this?"

Kaya observed a solemn intensity in the man's eyes, which scared him.

He replied, meekly, "Dat one was from de WHT guides."

"Who gave it to you?"

"Dey jus' passed dem out—"

"Who gave it to you?" the man repeated, this time with obvious anger.

"Spexy. Spexy give it tuh meh."

"Who is this Spexy?"

"She's ah Irish teacher — Noreen Adams. Dey say, she used tuh be ah nun in Ireland, but she resign. She's meh geography teacher now. She's de one who organised de hike. Is jus' ah chocolate."

"No, Hezekiah, to you it is poison. This confection comprises a mixture of cocoa solids, cocoa butter, vanilla, milk, sugar, soy lecithin, and a tasteless, odourless substance, designed to induce an anaphylactic reaction — a substance developed specifically for you. An ingenious substance synthesised to kill you. I told you to be careful."

"Ah thought dat was meh subconscious mind talkin'."

Man, yuh use ah lot ah words jus' to say somebody put tonic in meh chocolate.

The man sighed, clearly frustrated, "I have introduced an anti-toxin into your bloodstream. It will offer permanent protection against the poison I discovered in the chocolate."

"Who go wan' tuh poison me?"

"A very dangerous criminal."

"Yuh sayin' Spexy is ah criminal?"

"Perhaps."

"Buh wha' reason she or anybody else, have tuh poison me?"

"There are those harbouring old grudges against your family. Perhaps, your mother has warned you about this?"

"What yuh know 'bout meh family?"

"I know a few things. I know your mother sells flowers in Coconut Grove. I know there is much envy in that town. There are also very dangerous individuals residing there. Surely, your mother has told you about this."

"Well, meh granny used tuh talk about t'ings like dat.... She even used to say ah Soucouyant live in Coconut Grove."

"Do you believe this?"

"No way...."

"Do not dismiss the words of the old; they possess wisdom, which comes only with age, and often speak of things that the young are too immature to understand."

"So, it was you who cause de river tuh come dong?"

"No, Hezekiah, illegal loggers are to blame. Their careless, wasteful activities led to a blockage upstream. Discarded logs created a dam, which eventually gave way. I blew my horn to dissuade your groups from venturing too near to the river's edge. It seems, I will need to be more persuasive in future."

"Why yuh doin' dis den? Why yuh helpin' meh, eh? Yuh ah doctor?"

"I have the knowledge required to treat your injury," said the man, placing a warm metal disc on Kaya's forehead.

Kaya studied the man's features. With the exception of his skin-tight jumpsuit and outlandish accent, he seemed like any typical Trinbagonian man of predominantly African descent. Kaya assumed that the man's tight trousers literally made him uptight.

"Who are you?"

"Who do you think I am?"

"Well, yuh ent Papa Bois; dat's fuh sure."

"And, why would you say that?"

"When ah first see yuh, yuh look like Papa Bois. Buh now, ah could see dat you're some kinda scientist. Yuh ah spaceman?"

"Do you believe in the existence of such beings? Beings from other worlds?"

"Yeah."

"Why?"

"Because, de only place ah ever see stuff like this is on space shows on TV," said Kaya, referring to his regeneration pod.

"But everything you see on television, is the product of human ingenuity. Any alien capable of coming to Earth would have technology well beyond the limits of your imagination."

Ah doh know 'bout dat. Meh imagination big fuh so, thought Kaya.

"Is it not odd that you believe in the existence of what you call space men, but a female vampire seems too far-fetched. Perhaps, I am a scientist employed by a foreign government," said the man, taking the disc from Kaya's forehead and placing it on the wall. A robotic voice immediately spoke in a language Kaya could not understand.

"Ah knew it," shouted Kaya excitedly, "you're an alien."

"If I am an alien, presumably from another world, then why are you not afraid?"

"Because, yuh helpin' meh."

"Perhaps, I am keeping you healthy purely to take you to a zoo on another planet, far away. Perhaps, I plan to experiment on you or eat you."

"Naaah…. You're ah good alien."

"Do you not eat cows and chickens and goats and fish and rabbits and pigs and deer?"

"Ah doh t'ink ah ever eat deer or rabbit," replied Kaya, cautiously — suddenly afraid.

"Are you a good human?"

Kaya's panic rose steeply. He began to search the chamber for an exit, but the unbroken walls of metallic grey offered no evidence of a way out. The tingling in his head increased, but this time he began to feel nauseous.

"Do not be alarmed, young Hezekiah. I will not harm you. Nevertheless, you should consider the moral implications of your diet."

Kaya gulped audibly, "Please…. Ah wan' tuh go now."

"Indeed. A few more tests, and I will return you and your friends to the Azura Forest."

Suddenly, Kaya realised that Raima and Tom were in similar pods and seemed to be sleeping, peacefully. For a brief moment, Kaya began to feel agitated again. The tingling in his head increased and he felt his heartbeat begin to slow down. Waves of well-being flooded his mind, and he relaxed.

"Wha' kinda tests?"

"Look to your left. Tell me what you see."

"Ah see ah ball ah light."

"What colour is the light?"

"Red."

The red ball of light silently and fluidly danced two metres above the grey floor.

"What is it?" asked Kaya.

"It is a toy," replied the man. "Now, tell me Kaya, is red your favourite colour?"

"No. Blue is meh favourite colour."

"Would you prefer that the light was blue?"

Kaya shrugged his shoulders. "What makin' it float like dat?"

"Bring it closer. Examine it."

"How yuh mean?"

"This toy responds to thoughts."

"Yuh see? Ah knew yuh were ah alien…." Kaya muttered to himself.

"I am conducting secret experiments for a very powerful foreign government."

"Why yuh tellin' meh dat? No real spy would ever tell meh dat."

"Perhaps, I am lonely."

"Yuh have dem tiger cats fuh company."

"Indeed, but they are poor conversationalists."

Kaya laughed, and the ball of light immediately darted across the chamber, changing from red to brilliant yellow.

"Focus on the light, Hezekiah. Make it blue."

"OK. I'll try."

"A wise man once told me, 'To try is to accept the possibility of failure. Simply do.'"

"Was dat yuh father?"

"Why do you ask?"

"Ah never knew meh father," said Kaya, sadly.

"Oh?"

"He died …. before meh mother had me. She never talk 'bout him."

"Life can often be difficult, but difficulties make us stronger."

"So, who's de wise man den?"

"He was a young man I once knew. A good friend. A very brave soldier."

"Yuh ah soldier den?"

"No, I am simply a scientist."

"Sound like yuh want tuh be ah soldier."

"The scientific work, I am conducting, can help many people. We each have our purpose."

The ball of light slowly turned blue.

"Easy," said Kaya, proudly, and the blue ball glided smoothly towards him.

"Good," said the man. He stretched out his right hand, and the ball instantly changed direction. Despite Kaya's attempts to regain control of it, the man effortlessly caught it, and it dissipated.

"Who are you?"

"I would not be a very good spy if I told you that."

"Ah t'ink yuh want tuh tell meh. Ah t'ink you'll tell meh, and den you'll wipe meh memory."

"My name is Tolan Rapp," said the man. "And, you are correct. For reasons of security, I must erase any memory of this meeting. I will, however, imprint your subconscious with the need to be more vigilant.

"Pleased tuh meet yuh, Mr Rapp," said Kaya, and he shook the man's hand. "See? Ah knew it. Yuh ah alien."

"No, Kaya. I am Scandinavian. Now go to sleep."

21

ONCE IN A BLUE MOON

That night, Kaya regretted not having his broken filling replaced by Dr Childs. Chicken noodle soup was all he could eat. The painkillers he took did little to neutralise his persistent dental pain. And so, long after his nightly correspondence with Wendy Wong had ended, Kaya lay awake in his bed, tossing and turning, and unable to sleep. The far-reaching implications of his recent recollections filled his mind with awe, terror, and confusion. Before his suppressed memories had come flooding back, Kaya had honestly believed that he could tell Wendy anything, anything at all. All the same, Kaya felt that the ramifications of their otherworldly experience in the Azura National Park only concerned Tom and Raima. Their shared encounter with the mysterious Tolan Rapp had created an indelible bond of secrecy, which transcended Kaya's stubbornness, Tom's suspiciousness and Raima's fickleness, a bond that Kaya could no longer ignore.

Earlier that evening, Kaya had spent several feverish hours scouring the Internet for information relating to Papa Bois, but found only the same few passages repeated on various websites. Papa Bois, Trinidad's most widely recognised character of folklore, belonged to the olden days of Kaya's great grandparents. The young people of Kaya's age had little interest in such fantasies; at least, that's what Kaya thought. Be that as it may, something very strange had occurred in the Azura Forest. The mere mention of Papa Bois upset his mother so much, she cried herself to sleep behind her locked bedroom door.

What Mammy not tellin' meh? Ah wish Granny was here now; she woulda tell meh what tuh do. Raima an' Tom doh remember anyt'ing. Ah have tuh get dem tuh remember. Tolan Rapp might be ah Scandinavian name, buh ah doh believe, fuh one minute, dat man is ah secret agent. Ah have tuh go back to de Azura Forest, an' ah have tuh take Raima an' Tom wit' meh.

Kaya stared at the ceiling, illuminated by his desktop PC's LED standby button, thinking about all that he had learned about Papa Bois. Papa Bois, French patois for *father of the forest*, was nature's guardian. And, when

Tolan Rapp first appeared in the Azura Forest, he perfectly fit the description of the horned, muscular man of African descent with cloven hooves. It is said that Papa Bois was a shape-shifter, who used his supernatural abilities to protect the flora and fauna of Trinidad's forests.

Could Tolan Rapp really be Papa Bois? What if Papa Bois was from another world? Wouldn't dat make sense? And, if Papa Bois was from another world, then what about Soucouyant, La Diablesse, Douens and Ligahoo?

Kaya hauled himself out of bed. The generous bowls of soup he had, meant extra trips to the toilet. It was late, and he knew that he needed to sleep, unless he wanted to spend the following day, stumbling around Paria College, like a mindless red-eyed zombie. As he quietly left his room, Kaya felt a cold draught that made him shiver.

Was Mammy so upset she forget tuh close ah window?

A quick check helped to banish most of Kaya's anxiety. All the windows were securely shut; nonetheless, as he walked to the bathroom, he had a feeling that something was not quite right. Kaya yawned, emptied his bladder, flushed the toilet, and, for a brief moment, he felt relieved. However, as he washed his hands, a deathly chill ran down his spine.

"Kaya," came the familiar voice of a woman, but it was not the voice of Kaya's mother. This was an older, more experienced voice; one that for a long time, Kaya had been yearning to hear. And yet, now that he had heard it, the very sound of it filled his heart with dread.

"Granny?" whispered Kaya, suddenly light-headed — his heartbeat going into overdrive. He closed the tap; and, ever so slowly, he turned towards the bathroom door.

"Yes, gran'son," came the woman's voice from an undefined location.

"But...."

How could Granny be here? She....

Kaya could not bring himself to think the word.

Ah wonder if ah take too much painkillers. Maybe ah fall asleep.... Dat's it. Ah well an' truly dreamin'.

Nevertheless, Kaya braced himself for a terrible shock. He slowly opened the bathroom door, allowing the yellow, electric light to flood the hallway. But, to his relief, the dreaded spectre of Mama Flo was nowhere to be seen.

"Come, doux-doux. Hurry, ah doh have much time."

"Where? Where are you?" came Kaya's sheepish voice, as he walked through the dark lounge, unable to stop his knees from trembling.

"Outside. Open de front door, an' come outside."

Despite his grave apprehension, Kaya felt compelled to do as the disembodied voice directed. Stupefied, Kaya retrieved his house keys from his bedroom. However, he questioned everything. Logic screamed that his grandmother could not possibly be directing him; so, he tried his best to resist.

Dis jus' not right…. Dis cyah be happenin'.

Kaya unlocked and opened the front door. He stepped onto the gloomy veranda and peered down into the murky yard below. In the pale blue moonlight, Kaya observed a dark figure standing at the tall steel front gate. Shock, fear, sadness, and bewilderment threatened to overwhelm him completely.

He barely managed to ask, "Buh, Granny … how come yuh here?"

"Come, boy. Come quick-quick. Ah have tuh show yuh somet'ing an' ah doh have much time. Ah cyah protect yuh mother anymore, Kaya; now, it's up tuh you."

"Protect Mammy? Protect she from what?"

"Come, boy, an' stop wastin' precious time."

Time … time … precious time…. What's de time now? When ah see she face, I'll know. I'll look in she eyes an' I'll know if dis is really meh granny.

Kaya approached the gate, but the woman began to walk away slowly.

"Come, boy, follow meh now. Hurry up, time runnin' out."

Kaya unlocked and opened the gate; and then, he began to follow the old woman. Shivering, he rubbed his hands along his biceps. Feeling the goose bumps on his exposed skin, Kaya regretted not putting on a jacket over his cotton vest. He wore his pyjama bottoms and flip-flops; and, he wondered why he left the house, in the first place.

Yeah, boy, ah well an' truly dreamin'.

A lone dog howled, in the distance, but not a soul could be seen anywhere. A moist, cool breeze brought with it the rich, sweet fragrance of Madagascar jasmine. Kaya tried and tried to see the woman's face; the more he tried, the more anxious he became. However, the woman's face always seemed shrouded in shadow. He caught glimpses of her lips, her nose, but never her eyes. Kaya lost track of time. Then, the sounds of lapping water and distant crashing waves snapped him out of a daze. Kaya suddenly realised that he had followed the old woman far away from his house, to a secluded track that led down to the waterfront. Tall bushes were on either side; a blanket of clouds rolled across the sky, obscuring the moon, leaving only thick darkness on the path ahead.

"Wait," said Kaya, with a tinge of bravado, "Ah wan' tuh see yuh face."

The woman immediately stopped walking; and, time itself seemed to have come to an abrupt halt. If a pin dropped, Kaya would have heard it. Then, the woman chuckled and turned slowly, revealing Mama Flo's face.

"Like is forget yuh forget meh? Look at meh face good, boy; look at de dress ah wearin', dis is de same dress yuh cousin send fuh meh from Englan'. Ah only wear it once in a blue moon, so yuh must be forget."

Kaya breathed a sigh of relief, "Granny, is you…. Is really you."

Suddenly, with snake-like speed, the old woman grabbed Kaya by the neck with her left hand, and she hoisted his thrashing body off the path.

With a voice Kaya had never heard before, the woman growled, "No. Silly, superstitious boy; did you really think your wretched grandmother would rise from the dead?"

Kaya's feet dangled as he struggled to continue breathing. He saw it clearly now — hatred and malice in the woman's shark-like eyes. The overhead clouds rolled away, bathing Kaya and his captor in the cold blue moonlight. Much like an insane old hag, the impostor cackled loudly. Her stained teeth and the whites of her eyes glistened as, to Kaya's abject horror, her face began to transform, slowly.

Time tuh wake up, Kaya. Wake up!

"You have your grandfather's eyes, young Hezekiah Abaniah. And, like your handsome grandfather, the last person you will ever see, is me." She cocked her head and smiled coyly.

"Who … are … you?" Kaya managed, before the woman's tightened grip silenced him.

This ent no dream…. Gawd help meh….

"Didn't your grandmother ever tell you about me? About how she stole Ekon from me? Didn't you hear her, weakly calling his name, moments before my poison plunged her into eternal sleep?"

As his eyes rolled back, Kaya thought he caught a glimpse of an object in the sky. Whatever it was, had an orange glow and silently hovered about 100 metres above them.

"I suppose not. Well, no matter," growled the woman. "You'll be joining your naïve grandparents very shortly. I am quite sure, they will be more than happy to tell you all about me." The woman roared with malicious laughter; then a mask of hatred removed any vestige of humanity from her unrecognisable face. "Listen carefully, Hezekiah Abaniah, the next sound you hear will be the blissful sound of your wretched neck snapping."

It was not. Instead, Kaya heard the woman scream in pain as a green energy bolt hit her in the shoulder, knocking her off her feet and hurling

Kaya into nearby bushes. Coughing and gasping for breath, Kaya desperately crawled through the shrubs towards a tree. Looking over his shoulder, he saw the woman raise her right hand. What appeared to be lightning arced from her palm towards her unseen attacker. Frantic now, the woman aimed her deadly weapon at Kaya and fired. Already in motion, Kaya dived behind a tree. A plasma discharge cleaved the tree trunk like a thunderbolt. Kaya rolled out of the way as half of the tree crashed to the ground in flames.

Run, Kaya! Run!

Kaya ran for his life. He did not look back, and he never saw the woman's attacker. But, as he ran, he did see two more unidentified objects approaching from out to sea. These were small saucer-like objects that streaked low, across the water, throwing up sea spray in their wake. Then, something hit him. It slammed into Kaya's back, which immediately felt like it was on fire. Thrown off his feet, he crashed to the ground and tumbled into a ditch. When he finally opened his eyes, he saw a fiery orange ball high above him.

Oh, Gawd…. Soucouyant….

Without warning, it shot away with unimaginable speed. The two silver discs suddenly made impossible ninety-degree turns and vanished in pursuit of the glowing object. Instantly, all the lights from the town went out. And, unable to endure the pain in his back, Kaya slowly slipped into unconsciousness.

22

SLEEPWALKING

Kaya found himself inside the large futuristic cargo bay of an unknown craft, surrounded by strangers at a cocktail reception. Previously, Kaya had only ever seen such parties on television, and those were never as odd as this. Alert military police officers, equipped with cranial attachments, kept watchful eyes on the guests. Most of these guests also wore military uniforms, whilst several bejeweled escorts modeled unusual evening dresses, regal gowns or princely suits. Large black banners hung from the cargo bay's ceiling, displaying glittering golden butterflies. Smaller banners of red, gold and brown depicted an unknown armorial crest. A tall, dark man with long black hair stood apart from everyone else. Neatly cut sideburns, moustache and beard framed the stranger's face — a strong, handsome face, marred only by a conspicuous leather patch that covered his left eye. He wore a dark grey full dress uniform, draped with a gold sash of an unknown military order and sporting six golden butterflies on each lapel. A black cape flowed behind him, and a single medal graced his broad chest — this was no circus strongman.

Instinctively Kaya knew, *Dis man is ah important soldier.*

Kaya's attention moved to the man's beautiful companion, a tanned woman with deep blue eyes and long greenish blonde hair, dressed in layers of gold and brown that shimmered in the artificial light.

Who is dat punk lady?

"Kaya," came a woman's voice from directly behind — a voice Kaya immediately recognised. "Wha' yuh doin' here, boy?"

Expectantly, Kaya turned around to see his cousin Raya, smiling from ear to ear. Although she was nine years older, they had been close, so much so that strangers often assumed that Raya was Kaya's sister, but that was before she went away to England to become a nurse. That was before she got married. And, although they often communicated by video calls over the Internet, Kaya missed his favourite cousin terribly.

"Look at me, Kaya."

Kaya immediately noticed that his cousin's eyes were light brown.

Like she wearin' contacts, awa?

Suddenly, Raya pulled up the hem of her flowing gown and began to twirl, laughing happily.

"Look at me, Kaya. Look! I'm a princess. Princess Soraya!"

Violently, someone grabbed Kaya's shoulder from behind. He spun on his heel to be face to face with a monstrous reptilian humanoid.

With a thick Jamaican accent, the creature snarled, "Well-watch-yah-Kayaman, ah wha' yuh ah do pan road dem I-wahs dey inna starm?"

Kaya had been dreaming. He woke with a gasp and discovered that he was lying on the back seat of Roy Dread's Nissan Bluebird Sylphy. He had slept in such a way that his strained neck ached terribly. Rubbing his eyes and sitting upright, Kaya immediately noticed that the electricity supply had returned to Coconut Grove. He heard distant thunder. And, at regular intervals, the wipers removed the light drizzle that accumulated on the car's windscreen. A compilation of Jamaican reggae music from the 70s played on the car stereo. Roy Dread called it *rockers*. The Rastafarian wore his tam; a black, knitted wool hat with a thin band of green, yellow and red, which covered his long dreadlocks. Beneath the locks, long sideburns, moustache, and beard, a handsome face struggled to emerge.

"Wha'ppen?" asked Kaya, groggily.

In Josephine's presence, Roy Dread made every effort to speak English perfectly. However, whenever he was alone with Kaya, raw Jamaican patois always emerged, and Kaya accepted this as an integral part of their camaraderie.

"Ah wah yu ah aks mi fah? After mi-noh-kno' wah science knock yu out an' put yu out yah dem hours. Ah ooh brok yu 'art ... eee? Mi fine yu out-cha ah-sleep like puss. Yu lucky sa-ah mi fine yu. Ferdamore, ah wah yu did-ah do dong dey pan de watafront dress-up inna pyjama?"

Even so, Kaya had difficulty understanding Roy Dread at the best of times, and this certainly was not the best of times. However, it seemed, according to Roy Dread, that he had no idea what black magic could make Kaya fall asleep at the roadside. He asked Kaya if he had walked to the waterfront in his pyjamas, because of a broken heart.

Kaya began to tremble. Had he dreamt the encounter with the entity impersonating Mama Flo, or did he actually meet a Soucouyant? Did Roy Dread rescue him, or was it someone else — someone like Tolan Rapp? And, what were the lights in the sky? Dream or no dream, something very strange had occurred, and it terrified Kaya. He decided to say as little as possible.

"Ah t'ink ah was sleepwalkin'," said Kaya, meekly.

"Yu kno' say, ten-toe turbo pan road inna pyjama an' slippers. Cha! Road ongle safe fi duppy dis I-wah," said Roy Dread, warning Kaya that the roads of Coconut Grove were only safe for evil spirits, this late at night.

"Yuh cyah tell meh mother."

Roy Dread laughed loudly, startling Kaya. "Coo yah, I an' I noh wan' noh bodderation. Noh cup noh brok, noh coffee noh trow weh," said Roy Dread, advising that since Kaya had not been harmed, everything was fine.

According to Kaya's wishes, Roy Dread parked his red Nissan several houses down from where Kaya lived.

"Trus' de I-man, I an' I nah go su-su su-su. Sista Josie nah go hear nuttin'. Reespec' yu madda, Kayaman; an' fine yuself inna yard wen moon start shine," said Roy Dread, soberly promising not to tell Josephine, and advising Kaya to respect his mother and stay at home at night.

"Alright. T'anks," said Kaya, before suddenly sneezing.

Roy Dread flashed a gold front tooth when he laughed. "Is like sa yu out fi ketch cole. Drink some tonic fi yu structure, an' tek two tablet. Likkle more, I-man forward ah gates fi bunks I res'. Irie."

Roy Dread suggested that Kaya should take an invigorating medicinal food supplement, and a cold remedy, unless he wanted to catch a cold. He was eager to go home to get some much-needed sleep. Everything was all right. Kaya got out of the car, closed the door as quietly as he could, and jogged home in the drizzle. Roy Dread dutifully ensured that Kaya was safely indoors, before driving away. Without waking Josephine, Kaya sneaked back into his bedroom and laid awake replaying recent events, real and unreal, in his mind. But, unable to make sense of it all, he drifted off into a deep, dreamless sleep.

The following morning, Josephine's mayhem in the kitchen woke Kaya as usual. Prepared to dismiss the night's events as pure fantasy, he dragged himself out of bed. Nonetheless, a dull pain in his back prompted him to reconsider. Looking over his shoulder, Kaya viewed his reflection in the mirrored door of his wardrobe. He slowly lifted his cotton vest; and, to his surprise, he revealed strange, reddish, electrical tree-patterns, on the skin of his back. It looked like a representation of lightning; at least that's what Kaya thought. He remembered the mysterious woman's plasma weapon. He recalled being hit in his back.

Ah wasn't dreamin'.

For a moment, he stood there, stunned by the thought, trying his best to consider all the implications. Kaya stared with disbelief at the patterns on his back until he caught a glimpse of his own wide-eyed terror.

Granny was right — Papa Choonks was murdered. Buh ah never even suspect, until now, dat Granny was murdered too, an' de same crazy, jealous woman murder she.

Staring at his sad, exhausted reflection in the mirror, Kaya acknowledged that he had inherited his grandmother's high Carib-like cheekbones and her dimpled chin. Suddenly, he could no longer suppress his profound grief and loss. Silent, bitter tears streamed down his young face.

"C'mon Kaya," came Josephine's voice accompanied by brisk rapping on his bedroom door, "Yuh breakfast on de table."

Startled, he replied hastily, "OK, ah comin'."

Pulling himself together, he used the hem of his vest to wipe his tears before he quickly opened the wardrobe, retrieved his college uniform and got dressed.

Kaya sat at the kitchen table, having scrambled eggs and bacon while Josephine made herself her morning coffee. Still deeply troubled, by his encounter, with the dangerous woman who had impersonated and claimed to have murdered, Mama Flo, Kaya tentatively broached the delicate subject of Mama Flo's love rivals.

"Wha' yuh askin' meh Kaya?" said Josephine, with a sigh, "Yuh know how yuh granny was ah very private woman when it come tuh t'ings like dat. She never tell meh who she t'ink kill Papa Choonks. All ah know is dat de woman live in Coconut Grove."

"Yuh believe she?"

"Well, boy, remember all ah dis happen before ah was even born, buh ah cyah see how any woman coulda kill yuh gran'father wit' lightnin'."

"How dey know it was lightnin'?"

"Well, ah t'ink dey say he was covered in some Licht … ah cyah remember de technical term de coroner use, buh yuh granny call it lightning flowers. She say when she went tuh identify him, de first t'ing she notice was red patterns, all over de right side of his body, dat look like ah fern. She tell meh when she was growing up in Tortuga, one ah Madman Frederick cow get killed by lightnin' an' it had de same marks."

That afternoon, after scouring various informative websites on the Internet, Kaya would discover that the strange patterns were referred to as Lichtenberg figures, and they often appeared on the skin of lightning-strike victims. The patterns are caused by the rupture of capillaries due to the passage of a high voltage electrical current through the body.

"So how come she say somebody kill him?"

"She say de woman was ah witch. She say she had supernatural powers."

"An' wha' 'bout Tantie Rose? Wha' she say?"

"Well, yuh know yuh tantie an' yuh granny had ah love-hate relationship," chuckled Josephine. "She used tuh say: 'When Flo wan' tuh talk, she go talk.' Buh after yuh granny died, she tell meh: 'If Flo wanted yuh tuh know, she woulda tell yuh.' So, dat is it. Ah doh ha' tuh tell yuh how stubborn yuh gran'aunt is."

Kaya suddenly sneezed.

"Like is ketch yuh ketchin' another cold?"

"No, Mammy, ah t'ink is de black pepper. It always make meh sneeze," said Kaya.

However, the truth was that last night's adventure in his pyjamas, in the rain, left him feeling a bit under the weather. Moreover, Kaya just did not find the prospect of being given orange peel tea, at breakfast, appealing.

Just then, the gate buzzer rang.

"Ah hope da' ent Dhanraj again," said Josephine, "Every time dat man argue wit' he wife, de nex' mornin' he wan' tuh buy ah bunch ah roses, early-early before ah open up de shop. Ah ha' ah mind tuh tell 'im tuh come back later. Hurry up an' finish yuh breakfast, Kaya, yuh doh wan' tuh be late fuh college."

Coffee mug in hand, Josephine briskly exited the kitchen grumbling. And, suddenly, Kaya felt afraid. Somehow, he knew that it wasn't Dhanraj at the front gate, and the thought made the hair on his arms and legs stand on end. Kaya slowly walked to the living room where he watched Josephine open the front door, step onto the veranda and peer down towards the front gate. Josephine froze, as if she had seen a ghost; the mug slipped from her hand and shattered on the tiled floor, spilling coffee everywhere.

"Mammy, yuh alright?"

Filled with concern, Kaya quickly approached the veranda only to be stopped dead in his tracks by Josephine's wide-eyed stare. She placed a finger to her lips, silently instructing Kaya to be quiet.

"Good morning," shouted an accented male voice.

Suddenly, Kaya felt a sharp pain in his temples.

"Mornin'," responded Josephine, guardedly.

A feeling of dread overcame Kaya; and, he felt certain he knew who was at the gate. Kaya stumbled into Josephine's bedroom.

He heard the man say, "Please, may we have some words?"

"What it is yuh want?" asked Josephine, sternly.

Kaya slowly pulled back the drapes in Josephine's bedroom just enough to peer through the window unseen. As he feared, two pale men dressed in black stood at the front gate. Only the taller of the two spoke.

He said to Josephine, "Here we are, to discuss your son."

Kaya began having trouble breathing, and his headache became unbearable; then, very quickly, everything turned pale yellow and then pitch black. Something very odd had occurred. Something that should have been utterly horrifying but wasn't. Kaya found himself looking down on his seemingly lifeless body, but he was not afraid. He felt that he was hovering about two metres off the ground; he wasn't confused, alarmed or excited. He noticed that his body, lying on the bedroom floor, was breathing. And, even though this realisation gave him a mild sense of reassurance, Kaya's mind remained preoccupied with other questions.

Who are the men in black, and what do they want?

23

THE SHU-SENYN

In an instant, Kaya found himself hovering above the men in black like a weird, invisible, disembodied spirit. He could see them clearly now, but no one could see him. The two men were much paler than Tom Baker. They were almost identical; except that the one, who always spoke, was about five inches taller than his companion. Their faces were quite plain and oddly devoid of emotion. They had no hair whatsoever, not even eyebrows or eyelashes. Their eyes were grey and seemed lifeless, at least to Kaya. They wore pristine white shirts, black suits and ties. In their left hands, they held identical black hats. And, despite the formidable tropical heat and their unsuitable attire, the men did not sweat at all. Kaya noticed their shoes, which were so shiny he could clearly see Josephine's reflection on them as she approached the gate. Josephine had come down into the yard to speak to the men privately. Despite her outwardly convincing show of confidence, Kaya knew that she was terrified.

"What about meh son?"

"May we come in?"

"No. What about meh son?"

In unison, the men turned only their heads, briefly stared at each other, and then they turned to face Josephine once more.

"Open the barrier and let us in," said the taller of the two, and his voice sounded darker and deeper, like a record playing at the wrong speed.

To Kaya's amazement, Josephine unlocked the gate and opened it without protest.

"Her thoughts are unreadable," said the shorter man, telepathically, and Kaya heard him.

"But her will is pliable," thought the taller man. Kaya heard him too.

Doh let dem in, Mammy.

Suddenly, Josephine snapped out of her daze.

"Hold on, hold on; where allyuh t'ink yuh goin'? Yuh didn't answer meh question," said Josephine, physically preventing any further advance of the men in black.

Once again, the pale men stared at each other.

"The fugitive has trained her to resist," speculated the shorter of the two.

"No. Their liaison was too brief."

"Delicate matters must be discussed," said the taller man to Josephine.

Doh let dem in, Mammy, thought Kaya. *Dey dangerous.*

"Listen, ah ent have time fuh riddles. Either yuh tell meh who yuh are an' wha' yuh want or yuh leave right now," replied Josephine, valiantly masking her terror.

The men reacted by staring blankly at each other.

"I am becoming annoyed."

"Yes, brother, this woman is annoying."

Kaya found that he had no difficulty reading the thoughts of the unwanted guests.

"Our enemies may be her protectors."

"They protected the boy from the Mad Renegade."

"But failed his grandfather."

"He was not special."

"Not like the boy's father."

"The boy may be a threat."

"All threats must be neutralised."

Allyuh kill meh fadah?

For the briefest moment, everything went blank; and, Kaya feared he would return to his unconscious body in Josephine's bedroom. Suddenly, to everyone's surprise, the shorter man slapped the taller one's face. Confused and speechless, Josephine took two steps backwards.

"Have you lost your puny mind?" projected the taller man, angrily.

"Forgive me, brother; I have been compromised."

"Regain control immediately!"

Dumbfounded, Josephine watched as both men casually put their black hats on their heads. They retrieved identical pairs of thick-framed sunglasses and placed them on their faces.

"Buh wha' comess is dis? Like is escape allyuh escape from de madhouse," she muttered.

"Scan for enemy agents," projected the taller of the two.

"Scanning...."

Without warning, the shorter man slapped the sunglasses off of his companion's face. Kaya had discovered that he could mentally manipulate him.

"I no longer have complete control, brother," he said, telepathically.

"This is your final warning — control your errant impulses or I will sedate you!"

Superficially, the men in black exuded stony-faced calm, but Kaya had revealed their Achilles heel. They possessed hidden volatile emotions, precariously reined by conditioned self-discipline.

Once again, the shorter man tried to slap the taller one, but with snake-like speed he grabbed his wrist. Using a small electrical device, he stunned his shorter companion who immediately slumped into his arms.

"Buh wha' trouble is dis? Ah goin' tuh call de police," announced Josephine, and she beat a hasty retreat towards the stairs.

"That would be most unwise," said the taller man.

"Listen, just march yuh tail outta meh gate an' take yuh mute twin wit' yuh," cried Josephine, no longer able to hide her apprehension.

However, the taller man used his stun device to rapidly flash a bright light into Josephine's eyes.

"You have not spoken to us. We are not here," he said, his voice dark and deep.

Josephine immediately sat on the step with a blank expression. But, in retaliation, Kaya caused the shorter man to punch the taller one in the face.

"Forgive me, brother, I know not what I do."

"Do not call me brother."

Once again, the taller man stunned his companion. And, once more, he slumped into his arms. Quickly returning the stun device to his jacket pocket, he maintained a firm grip on his comrade's wrists to prevent further acts of violence. At least, that was his intention. However, Kaya thought the taller of the two deserved more punishment, so the shorter man slammed a bony knee into his groin. While the taller man writhed on the ground, Kaya mentally snapped Josephine out of her stupor and drew her attention to the garden hose.

"Like yuh have wax in yuh ears or what?" shouted Josephine. "Ah tell yuh tuh leave meh yard!" And, she unleashed a sustained burst of water, into the taller man's face. "Yuh could walk, or yuh could swim, make ah choice."

Kaya noticed a twitch in the taller man's left eye and a throbbing vein on his left temple. With blistering speed, the taller man whipped out a futuristic-looking pistol from within his jacket. Josephine immediately dropped the hose and held her hands up defensively.

"I am now overwhelmed by furious anger," said the taller man, with incongruent calmness.

He scrambled to his feet, grasping his tender family jewels with his left hand — pistol in his right trained on Josephine. For a brief moment, the taller man seemed to be in control of the situation; but, things are rarely as they seem; and, life is full of surprises. The shorter man leapt to his feet, placed his stun device at the base of the taller man's skull, and zapped him senseless. The taller man immediately dropped his pistol, turned around with a constipated expression, and collapsed like a marionette with severed strings.

"*Brother, what have I done?*" projected the shorter man.

"*On this day, you have displayed intelligence inferior to that of a comatose pigeon.*"

"*Our mandate is clear, brother.*"

"*Do not call me brother.*"

The shorter man confiscated his comrade's pistol.

"*Termination has not been authorised.*"

"*Threaten, not terminate, you mindless freak of nature. You profoundly stupid moron. I should terminate you!*"

"*You have unresolved issues. Your anger-management conditioning has been compromised.*"

"*Because of your witless actions, we must wipe the memory of the boy's mother, the postman across the street, three youthful pedestrians, and the stupefied neighbour, who, even now, spies from his bedroom window.*"

The taller man flashed startling lights into Josephine's eyes. And, once more, she calmly sat on the step awaiting further instructions.

"*Today is not a good day.*"

The shorter man's powerful feelings of remorse made it increasingly difficult for Kaya to maintain his out-of-body experience. And, he found that he could no longer control the odd visitor. Kaya watched helplessly as strange events continued to unfold.

Disturbed by what he had seen, Mr Walker threw caution to the wind and popped his large head out of his bedroom window. He was a black, stocky, unattractive man, with a broad face, wild greying hair, and long sideburns reminiscent of the 1970s. He wore horn-rimmed bifocals that sat on his bulbous nose. They magnified his staring brown eyes and thick, bushy eyebrows, which made him appear somewhat deranged. Moreover, his enduring love of distilled beverages did not help as far as his crazed image was concerned.

Mr Walker was so drunk — he could barely speak, when he said, "Excuse meh. Excuse meh, Miss … Josephine … deez men … dey troublin' yuh?"

"You are hallucinating," replied the taller man.

"Buh why … yuh come in meh … neighbour yard wit … yuh gun? An' … why … allyuh … dress up … like undertakers? Somebody dead?

Lead me not into temptation, thought the taller man.

"You are inebriated," he said.

"In … ebee … aay … ted?" asked Mr Walker, swaying under the influence of alcohol.

"Indeed, you are intoxicated."

"In … taxi … who?"

"He is almost as stupid as you are," projected the taller man to his companion.

"You have consumed too much alcohol," said the taller man to Mr Walker.

"Oh-ho … doh say … nuttin' … Ah could see … on yuh face, yuh t'ink … ah stinkin' drunk … like … ah skunk. Well … ah ent drunk … like no skunk … wine-lovin' monk … or flunk-lovin' … funk-lovin' punk … Ah jus' … ah jus' … yuh know…. Ah suffer … from de migraine…." slurred Mr Walker, with a rum-induced smirk on his face.

"Indeed. Drink large quantities of a brewed beverage with high caffeine content. All will then be well."

"Cah … feen? How yuh face … white so?

In unison, the men in black turned their heads and silently stared at each other. The taller man pointed his stun device at Mr Walker and flashed brilliant lights into his bloodshot eyes.

"Go to sleep," he said.

Trancelike, Mr Walker slowly did as the taller man commanded.

Returning his attention to Josephine, the taller man said, "You dropped your drinking container; go now and pick up the pieces. We are not here. You have not seen us."

Unable to intervene, Kaya watched as Josephine did exactly as she was told. Just then, the postman approached the front gate.

He asked, "Wha' really goin' on here?"

"We are but two travelling men of sales," replied the taller man.

"What?"

That was the postman's last word before they zapped him. With a demented smile plastered on his face, he joyfully put the post into the mailbox on the gate. Kaya watched as the postman continued with his deliveries, unsettling anyone who saw his insane grin. And, Kaya wondered how long the poor man would remain that way. The sinister men in black, let themselves out of Josephine's yard and closed the gate behind them.

"Because of your foolish actions, we must return," projected the taller man.

"We can intercept the boy while he travels to his institution of learning."

"That operation risks further exposure. And, because of your mindless behaviour, I require immediate regeneration."

"I am truly sorry, brother."

Without warning, the taller man punched the shorter one in the stomach.

"Apology accepted."

A matte black car, with old-fashioned curves, quickly came to a stop on the street just outside Josephine's Flower Shop. The grim sedan had dark tinted windows and was of a make and model Kaya could not identify. Struggling to maintain his covert form, Kaya continued to eavesdrop on the men in black as they communicated telepathically.

"Soon, we may be called upon to capture or kill the boy and his mother," projected the taller man.

"I will be prepared, Shu-Senyn Vets."

"For your sake, I hope so, Shu-Senyn Yerek. Our ca-vus is far less forgiving than I am."

Kaya's mind began to reel.

Is kill, dey mean tuh kill we?

The front doors of the car opened of their own accord; at least that is how it seemed to Kaya. To his horror and confusion, he saw that the vehicle had no occupants. It was driverless; and, an ominous green glow emanated from within. The men sat, and Kaya saw that their seats automatically reclined as the doors closed. The car silently accelerated and was gone in an instant — vanished into thin air. Suddenly, gripped by panic, Kaya found he had returned to the floor of his mother's bedroom. Lying on his back, he stared up at the ceiling, wondering how much longer he had to live.

24

OASIS

"Aliens?" asked Tom.

"Yes, aliens," replied Kaya.

"From outta space?" asked Raima.

"Yes, Raima, from outta space," replied Kaya.

"Aliens from outer space plan to kill you," stated Tom, with unbridled scepticism.

"Yes. Yes. Yes. And, meh mudder too," said Kaya, losing his patience.

"I hate to be the one to tell you, Abbers, but since you hit your head in the Azura Forest, you've been a bit odd."

"Doh talk rubbish, Tom."

"Yuh have any idea why dey wan' tuh kill yuh, Kaya?" asked Raima.

"It ha' somethin' tuh do wit' meh fadah … an' de UFOs ah see last night."

Laughter in the classroom abruptly brought Kaya back to reality. He had been sitting at his desk, daydreaming, awaiting the arrival of Spexy for Wednesday morning's double geography.

"Are you OK?" asked Wendy, "You were mumbling something about aliens."

"Ah was?" Kaya forced himself to chuckle.

"Yeah. Yeah, you were."

"Ah was rememberin' de bad sci-fi movie ah watched late last night."

"Oh really? Was what's-her-name in that? You mentioned her as well as the aliens."

"Yuh mean Raima?"

"I prefer what's-her-name…."

"Raima and me? Yuh know we were jus' friends."

"Yeah, that's what you keep telling me. So, remind me again, exactly why did you stop being friends once she started seeing a certain football captain, eh?"

"Bruce, real, real possessive...."

"Ha!"

As much as he wanted to, Kaya could not find the courage to tell either Wendy or Tom about the recent extraordinary events in his life. He could not help loving Wendy's company and flattering attention. She seemed to be his perfect match, maybe even too perfect. Having been badly burnt by Raima, Kaya naturally resolved to proceed with extreme caution, with the gorgeous newcomer. It seemed almost every boy at Paria College was in line to steal the affection of the young, Eurasian beauty. And, Kaya simply could not understand why she was so interested in him. Surely, she could be with any boy of her choice, but somehow, miraculously, she chose him.

Tom rarely spoke to Kaya now. And, after many attempts, Raima had finally given up. Her genuine desire for reconciliation had hardened into indifference, in the face of Kaya's vindictive neglect and Wendy's intimidating charms. Kaya had successfully isolated himself; jealousy and pride had left him with only one real friend, Wendy. And, his growing paranoia had him wondering if or when, she would forsake him also. So, Kaya imagined what it would be like if he could tell Tom and Raima about his recent encounters. He imagined what it would be like if they were all still the best of friends.

At 8:20, Spexy entered the classroom — ten minutes late, red-faced and nursing her right arm in a sling.

"Wha' happen, Miss?" blurted out Curtis *Iceberg* Joseph.

"Good mahrning, Joseph; good mahrning, 4P," said Spexy, catching her breath and speaking quickly and excitedly, delivering more of her Cork accent than usual, "had a bit of an accident at harm yesterday...."

A chorus of concern rose in the classroom, and Kaya heard Meenal say, "Me too."

"When I slipped in dee baht, it scared dee bejaysus out of me; but, oh my God, I'm OK," continued Spexy, trying to be as reassuring as possible. "My shoulder was just, like, dislocated — no tarn tendons, so I'm very lucky, tarch wood. OK, 4P, settle darn naw. Today, we will continue ahr look at dee location of deserts...."

Kaya recalled that the evil woman, who impersonated his grandmother, had been hit in the shoulder by a mysterious ray of green light.

Ah cyah believe dat was Spexy, he thought, looking at the pretty, blonde, bespectacled, geography teacher.

Nevertheless, Kaya recalled what Tolan Rapp said about the chocolate bar Spexy gave him. He told Kaya that the chocolate contained a poison developed specifically for him.

He said, *"There are those harbouring old grudges against your family."*

Kaya knew that Cobo's animosity towards him stemmed from the legacy of bad blood between his notorious ancestor, Alexandre Gervais-Corbeau and Kaya's third great-grandmother, Arienne. However, the weird woman Kaya recently encountered seemed unrelated to Cobo in any way. He briefly entertained the thought that if Tolan Rapp could impersonate Papa Bois, it could be possible for Spexy to impersonate Mama Flo. However, common sense quickly prevailed.

Spexy is ah alien? Nah, ah doh believe dat.... She jus' Irish. De woman las' night had ah grudge against meh gran'parents. She kill dem; an' now she want meh dead. Buh why now? An' what about de men in black? Ah had tuh ride through all kinda bush in people backyard tuh avoid dem dis mornin'. Wha' really goin' on in Coconut Grove? Like de place crawlin' wit' aliens. An' now, fuh some reason, dey want me an' meh mudder dead. Dis cyah be all 'bout meh gran'father, dat just takin' tabanca tuh ah whole new level.

Kaya chuckled at the absurdity of the thought. Unfortunately, everyone heard him.

"What is so funny, Abaniah? Pray tell," said Spexy, and she wasn't smiling.

Suddenly all eyes were on Kaya.

"Nuttin' Miss, ah remember ah joke," he said, wishing he could disappear.

"Aha, I'm sure we can all do wit' ahr good laugh dis mahrning," said Spexy, peering intently over the rim of her glasses.

Kaya's mind raced as he tried to think of a way out of his current predicament, "Yuh wouldn't t'ink it funny," he said meekly.

"Try me," said Spexy curtly, her green eyes narrowing.

"Ahm...."

Cobo and the Mapepires enjoyed Kaya's obvious discomfort. Tom stared at him briefly then looked away, shaking his head disapprovingly. Kaya turned towards Raima, but she searched the floor avoiding eye contact. The only support seemed to come from Wendy, who smiled at Kaya with reliably warm affection.

"Well, Abaniah? Are ye going tah tell yahr joke ahr naht?" said Spexy.

The class was so quiet you could hear a pin drop.

"Alright," said Kaya, standing up and taking a deep breath. "Ah linguist, ah guide an' ah archaeologist were flyin' over de Gobi Desert when dey plane develop engine problems an' crash. De linguist, who piloted de plane, died instantly. De guide was badly injured, but de archaeologist only had ah few bruises.

Just before he die, de guide tell de archaeologist, "Take meh compass, an all de food, water an' empty bottles yuh could carry; keep headin' south until yuh get tuh ah oasis. Once yuh get dere, fill de bottles wit' water, head south-east, an' if yuh lucky you'll get tuh de nearest village."

Two days after all he water run out, de archaeologist get tuh de oasis. He was so happy he jump in de water; an' when he had enough tuh drink, he start tuh fill de bottles he had. While he was doin' dat, he see ah old bottle partly buried under ah bush. Bein' ah archaeologist, he immediately realise it was ah rare an' valuable find. He dig it out, an' gently rub some ah de mud off ah it.

Poof! Ah genie appear! "Fuh rubbin' meh bottle, an' releasin' meh from tree thousand years ah prison, ah grant yuh tree wishes. Speak yuh first wish an' ah go make it so."

Well, bein' a scientific man, de archaeologist didn't really believe in magic. In fact, he t'ought de genie was only ah hallucination. So, as ah joke he say, "Alright genie, make meh de king ah de desert."

"Shazaam!" say de genie, an' de archaeologist turn into ah king. "Speak yuh secon' wish an' ah go make it so."

De archaeologist was totally amazed. He realise now he could have anyt'ing he want — anyt'ing at all. "Make meh de richest man in de world," he say.

"Shazaam!" say de genie, an' de archaeologist turn into de richest man in de world. "Speak yuh t'ird an' final wish, an' ah go make it so."

De archaeologist thought long an' hard. "Genie, now ah need ah queen; put meh on de arm ah de sexiest, most beautiful woman in de world."

"Shazaam!" say de genie, an' he turn de archaeologist into ah handbag...."

Mukesh snickered, but Cobo immediately silenced him with a slap across the back of his head. Spexy tried to maintain her stern gaze on Kaya, but suddenly burst out laughing. And, with the exception of a few stubbornly belligerent Mapepires, the majority of the class joined her. Raima looked around to Kaya and smiled, it was like bright sunshine on a dark rainy day, and Kaya could not stop himself from smiling back. He realised then, how much he missed her. Tom also stared at Kaya; and, once again he shook his head, but this time he was grinning broadly. Wendy laughed and clapped along with those who did not despise Kaya. She pretended not to notice Raima's furtive glances. She pretended not to feel threatened in any way.

"OK, sit dahn, Abaniah," said Spexy, composing herself. "Ahr bit lang-winded, baht funny al' dee same; nice tarch including dee Gobi Desert, it is dee sarce of many important archaeological finds. Well dahn."

At the end of the class, Kaya and Tom had their longest conversation since the day Kerwin died. And, even though he still could not bring himself to mention any of the strange experiences he recently had, Kaya felt he was well on the road to making amends with his good English friend, Tom Baker.

25

HOT LUNCH

During the Paria College lunch break, under the blazing noonday sun, Wendy gleefully pulled Kaya by the hand, ushering him along nearby shopping avenues. Ignoring all the attempts of eager young men to steal her attention, the attractive Canadian girl navigated through a rainbow maze of discerning bargain hunters, vocal street sellers, pushy taxi touts, and busy, sharp-suited businesspeople — shiny, happy-go-lucky pedestrians from every walk of life.

"Yuh know we'll get detention fuh a week if dey find us outside de college gates?" said Kaya.

"They won't see us," chuckled Wendy. "Only Cupid can see us, and he won't mind."

"Psst...." hissed an older male student from Coconut Grove Secondary School, "Gyul, yuh sweet an' juicy like a Julie mango."

"Family, ah find yuh neck looking bare," said a slim, shady albino, manning a stall laden with all manner of gold trinkets. "Breds, buy ah chain fuh de gyul nah man. How yuh movin' so? Look how she neck lookin' naked."

Before Kaya could respond, Wendy quickly steered him across a main road, giggling as they recklessly traversed steady streams of vehicular traffic that impatiently moved in both directions.

"Where we goin'?" asked Kaya, as irate drivers tapped their horns in the blistering heat. "Yuh know where yuh goin', Miss Canada?"

"Yes, actually I do, Mr Kaya. Today is a very special day," Wendy announced, with a broad dimpled smile, "Today, I'm buying you lunch."

"Why?" asked Kaya, as she dragged him away from the pavement's hustle and bustle into a comparatively dark, relatively secluded, musty arcade.

"Because...."

Without warning, Wendy pounced. Draping her slender arms around Kaya's neck and engulfing him with the warmth of her body, she kissed him desperately.

"Buh wha' slackness is dis?" said an elderly shopper, disapproving-ly. "Is dat what dey teachin' allyuh in school nowadays?"

Stopping to catch her breath, ignoring everyone and everything except Kaya, Wendy said, huskily, "I really wanna go to the Christmas Ball with you. Really...."

"How yuh change yuh mind?" asked Kaya, overwhelmed by the seductive scent of her jasmine perfume and the dizzying promise of her full, tender lips.

"What do you mean? I made my mind up, the very first time I kissed you, silly. You don't know much about girls, do you?"

"Ah know enough...."

Kaya grabbed Wendy's long, dark hair with a gentle tug, causing her to gasp and press her upper body into his. He felt her heart thumping against his chest as he held her in a prolonged, ardent kiss. Not to be outdone, Wendy pulled Kaya even closer, matching his passion, closing her eyes and whispering all the sweet, unintelligible things he very much wanted to hear. Kaya's full lips wandered, eventually resolving to design a tattoo of love on Wendy's exposed neck.

A wildly disgruntled vagrant hurled an empty beer bottle at the young couple. It landed close to their feet and shattered into a thousand tiny pieces, but Kaya barely noticed it.

"We're under attack," Wendy muttered, between stolen kisses.

"Dat's OK," mumbled Kaya.

Kaya was none the wiser, when a police officer challenged the troublesome tramp. Deeply preoccupied, Kaya had not witnessed the frantic scuffle that ensued. He had no idea whatsoever that the beggar grabbed the policeman's baton from its holster and proceeded to whack him over the head with it. Kaya remained oblivious as a curious crowd gathered. He never saw the squad of burly policemen that arrived on the scene, manhandled the nowherian, and hauled him off, kicking and screaming, into a waiting police van.

During those desperate moments, the outside world ceased to exist. Kaya and Wendy were very young and very much in love; at least, that's what Kaya thought. During that blissfully happy hour, they did not have lunch. Wendy's well-meaning offer of a quiet meal had evaporated in the heady steam of teenage romance.

Kaya had remained utterly unaware that two conspicuously pale men, who wore lily-white shirts, black suits, black ties, identical black fedoras, and black horn-rimmed sunglasses, observed him with grey, lifeless eyes that bore no lashes or brows. The Shu-Senyn, as they were called, were patient, exceptionally patient.

26

SIN TIA AND AGONIES

At home, that afternoon, determined to find out more about Mama Flo's mysterious and murderously vindictive love-rival, Kaya phoned his grandaunt, Tantie Rose, who lived in Tortuga.

Kaya's thirteen-year-old cousin, Robin, answered the call. "Hello, good afternoon?"

"Robin, is me," said Kaya.

"Kaya? Hang on ah minute, lemme turn dong de TV. What's up?"

"Yuh know, de usual. College. Meh computer still actin' up."

"Yuh still ha' dat ole t'ing? Hang on, hang on…. Tantie say she want tuh talk tuh yuh, we go chat later…."

"Alright, ketch yuh later…."

"Kaya?" came the sweet singsong of his much-loved grandaunt.

"How yuh goin', Tantie?"

"Well, doux-doux, ah still dey. Yuh remember all de croton we had in front de yard?"

"Yeah."

"Well, bachac eat dem. Not ah single leaf left on any ah dem plant. If yuh stan' still too long, dem ants go eat de clothes right off yuh back."

"Cousin Clarence should put some bait dong fuh dem," suggested Kaya. "Buh, other dan dat, everyt'ing alright?"

"Well no, doux-doux, meh pressure still high. Las' mont', Clarence take meh tuh de doctor — nah we lil' village doctor in Tortuga, de big time one in San Fernando. Ah sit dong so, an' ah seein' everyt'ing cloudy-cloudy. So, he check meh eye; boy, he shine ah big set ah bright light until ah only seein' stars, an' den he say ah ha' cataract — cataract in meh eye. He talkin' 'bout operation. Ah say, t'ank yuh doctor, buh yuh see me? Ah old, an' meh sista waitin' fuh meh on de other side."

"Oh, no, Tantie, doh talk like dat," said Kaya, with heartfelt concern.

"Pappy live tuh be ah hundred an' six, he never ha' problem like dis." Tantie Rose sucked her teeth. "Den las' week ah gone an' slip on de moss near de step. Badang-badap! Ah fall an' mash up meh knee. Boy, if yuh talk 'bout pain, pain fuh so. Ah had tuh go tuh de hospital in Couva. Buh hear nuh, on de way dere, Clarence bunks up he car — is like, cobo pee on we, kya-kya-kya," she laughed. "Well mama yo, is rosary fuh so. Now, ah walkin' wit' ah cane like de Roarin' Lion. Meh knee lancin' meh, buh every man jack goin' tuh church every Sunday. Leandra doh like it, buh ah put meh foot dong; Clarence takin' meh tuh confession with Fadah Buckley, tomorrow, please Gawd. Too much backsliding in dis family. Anyway, doux-doux, how yuh goin'?"

"Ah goin' good."

"Dat's nice ... dat's what ah want tuh hear. Ah know yuh does attend tuh yuh studies. Leandra never home, an' wit' Robin is either TV or computer-computer-computer.... Ah doh kno' what it is dat chile seein' in dat computer. Anyway, boy, ah glad yuh call.... Yuh hear from yuh cousin Soraya, recently?"

"No, wha' happen?" asked Kaya, suddenly worried.

"Well, boy, we doh know. Las' mont', Christina call meh from Inglan, yuh remember Christina?"

"Of course, ah remember Cousin Christie," said Kaya. "Somet'ing happen tuh Raya?"

"Christina call meh from Inglan', in ah state. She say de police call she from London.... Yuh remember she live in Birmingham?"

"Yeah...."

"Well, dey ax she one set ah questions 'bout Soraya an' de boy she marry, from San Fernando, Roman."

"Wha' happen?"

"Listen nuh, we doh know.... Dat is wha' we tryin' tuh find out. Dat is why ah ax yuh if yuh hear from Soraya. Nobody know where she an' she husban' gone.... Is like, dey disappear off de face ah de earth. Poor Christina, she livin' alone in Birmingham, four years now, since Williams die. An' me? Ah cyah even say ah go take ah trip tuh Inglan' tuh keep she company. Ah t'ink ah was studyin' dat when ah slip an' mash up meh knee. Gawd, ha' mercy on dis family.... Meh sister dead, an' meh daughter missin' she only daughter. Mornin', noon and night, is pray ah prayin' fuh meh gran'daughter, oui."

As the initial shock subsided, Kaya remembered the strange dream he had the night before. He remembered he saw Soraya, and she told him she was a princess, but he could not recall anything else.

"Ah keep sendin' she emails, buh de las' reply ah get was back in July."

"Well, boy, everybody worried. Las' week, Christina tell meh de full story, an' ah was glad ah was sittin' dong or else ah woulda fall flat on meh back; de police find one ah Soraya friend — some gyul name Eve, stone dead in dey flat."

"What? Eve was Raya best friend...."

"Lawd know what dem chirren mix up wit'.... De police t'ink dey in real danger."

"How she die?"

"Dey wouldn't say; buh dey treatin' it as a murder investigation, and Soraya an' Roman wanted fuh questioning. Is like, dey feel meh gran'daughter or she husban' could kill somebody," said Tantie Rose, sucking her teeth derisively.

"Doh worry, Tantie, no wonder yuh pressure high."

"Boy, is funny yuh call today, oui. Since yesterday, meh mind run on yuh, jus' like dat, outta de blue; an ah had ah mind tuh call yuh."

"Well, ah call yuh because ah wanted tuh ask yuh somet'ing."

"Is so?"

"Ah wanted tuh ask yuh about Mama Flo."

"Hmmm.... Buh wha' trouble is dis? Jus las' night ah dream Florence. When she die, ah used tuh dream she all de time, buh den de dreams stop an' ah figure she pass on tuh de other side. Buh after de dream las' nite, ah t'inking she still here, lookin' out fuh de family."

"Why yuh say dat?"

"In de dream, Florence come outta ah taxi, fussin' an' frettin', right in front ah de house here in Tortuga. So, ah watchin' she good, from de gallery, wonderin' wha' could have she in such ah state, sweatin' like ah horse, wit' long beads runnin' dong she face. Ah clean forget is dead meh sister dead, oui. Anyway, ah call out tuh she, 'Florence, gyul, look how yuh drippin' wet, come inside from de sun an' dry yuh face, ah now-now boil some mauby, we could have it when it cool.' She watch meh good, from head tuh toe, an' she gimme dat look.... Yuh know dat look she does give before she dress yuh dong? So, now, meh blood boilin'. Ah say tuh mehself, 'She come all de way from Coconut Grove, tuh talk dong tuh meh? Ah ent standin' fuh dat.' Ah get up one time an' ah open de front door tuh go inside. Flo say, 'Rosemary, yuh could turn yuh back on meh, all yuh want, buh doh turn yuh back on meh gran'chile, de messenger ah destruction want what he have. Yuh ha' tuh warn Kaya, yuh ha' tuh warn him. She t'ink she smart, buh she jus' like she name.' Well, doux-doux, ah could give as good as ah get, so ah turn arong tuh give Flo ah piece ah meh mind. When ah look so, no taxi, no Flo, no nuttin'. Is gone she gone, oui. An', jus' like dat, ah wake up in a cold sweat."

"Tantie Rose," said Kaya, tentatively, "who was de woman chasin' after Papa Choonks?"

Tantie Rose chuckled, "Yuh mean women ... plenty-plenty-women. Women, fuh so. Choonks was one handsome man.... Handsome too bad.... An' all de women like him, even me, buh he only had eyes fuh Flo. One t'ing 'bout dat sister ah mine, she was pretty, an' she could cut style, an' of de five of us, she had de best education, but more dan anyt'ing else, she had pride an' she wouldn't chase no man. No-no-no, Choonks was de one doin' all de chasin' while every single woman in Tortuga, an' even ah few married ones too, was chasin' him."

"Mama Flo say one ah de women kill Papa Choonks."

For a moment, Tantie Rose remained silent.

Kaya was about to ask if she was still there, but her voice oozed through the receiver, liquid with grief. "She tell yuh dat?"

"Well, not exactly...."

"Josephine.... Florence make meh swear tuh Gawd ah would never tell Josephine."

"Buh yuh never promise not tuh tell me," said Kaya, pleadingly.

Tantie Rose chuckled. "Boy, is smart yuh smart fuh so. This is de Gawd's honest truth, out ah all de women chasin' Choonks, no matter what he do, two ah dem wouldn't take no fuh ah answer. Both ah dem used tuh threaten Flo, dey even used tuh threaten me. Buh, Kaya, listen tuh meh an' listen good, lightnin' kill yuh gran'fadah. Yuh hear meh? Lightnin'."

"What were dey names?"

"Buh like yuh not listenin'...."

"Tantie Rose, yuh ha tuh tell meh dey names. It important."

"Why it important? De two ah dem dead, an' long gone, donkey years."

"Tantie," whined Kaya.

"Alright den, listen, ah go tell yuh dis once, an' ah doh want yuh askin' meh 'bout it again. De first one was Cynthia Drake, we used tuh call she Sin Tia. She was a light-skin gyul wit' green eyes. Doh ever trust no light-skin 'oman' wit' green eyes, dey heartless an' deceitful fuh so. She was ah singer an' she wanted ev'rybody tuh call she Cindy. Some ah de schupid men used tuh fight over she; ah few even end up in hospital. One fool even kill hisself because ah she. Apparently, he tell she he cyah live without she an' she turn 'rong an' ax, 'If yuh cyah live without meh, den how come yuh still alive?' Like ah damn fool, he run straight home, swallow ah soakin' wet towel, an' choke till he dead. Yuh see, because she fair, Sin Tia figure every man go prefer she; buh Choonks didn't care fuh dat. He didn't care fuh dat at-all-at-all-at-all. Sin Tia marry ah no-good man, wit' more money dan sense. Some say she use Obeah tuh trap him, buh ah doh believe dat. She had she good looks, an' he had no brain. Anyway, she was one dat like tuh drink an' fete, an' one night she drive she husban' big pappy car into ah saman tree, an' dat was de end ah she.

"De odder one was Agnes.... Agnes Talbert. We call she Agonies. Ah t'ink she scare Flo de most; tall an' dark an' pretty fuh so ... straight hair, perfect teeth an' not ah blemish. Agonies was accustom tuh gettin' everyt'ing she want. Sharp as ah razor dat one. She was ah librarian, ah t'ink. Ah gettin' so old now, ah cyah remember nuttin'. If meh head wasn't screw on properly, I'd leave it in ah taxi somewhere. Anyway, dey say Agonies inherit property from she mudder; so, she had everyt'ing.... Except Choonks. Ah few years after Choonks die, she move away an' we never see she again. Somebody say she marry ah rich foreigner an' dey move tuh Coconut Grove. Den one day outta de blue, years later, we see she obituary in de paper. She had ah stroke. Flo never tell meh which ah de two she thought was responsible fuh Choonks death, buh ah figure she thought it was Sin Tia, especially when she start wit' de witch chat.

"Ah doh kno' how Flo get it into she head ah witch could control lightnin'. Is true, when we were small growin' up in Tortuga, we see an' hear all kinda t'ing. Ball ah fire flyin' in de sky. Ligahoo draggin' he coffin an' chain, after midnite; an', Douen playin' hoop, in de bush. In dem days, most ah de lan' behind de house was forest. Josephine doh remember it, buh when she was four or five, Douen come fuh she; buh Papa Bois hisself come an' frighten dem away. Yuh know Papa Bois real? Ah see him wit' meh own two eye."

"Yes, Tantie, ah believe yuh."

"Now Kaya, Flo was meh younger sister, an' even though we could fight tooth an' nail, nobody love dat gyul more dan me. So, what ah tell yuh now not outta spite. After Choonks die, Flo had ah screw loose; an' by de time she pass away, dat screw fall out an' went dong de drain, never tuh be seen again. Lightnin' kill yuh gran'fadah; yuh hear meh, lightnin'."

27

THE REVELATION

Deep into the hot, humid, starlit night, Kaya Abaniah lay awake on his bed, recalling the enlightening conversation he had with his grandaunt, greatly troubled by recent events. Finally, a peaceful, warm blanket of sleep crept upon him. And, in the predawn mist of a tropical rainforest, Kaya found himself walking alone, on a well-used donkey track. The pale light of a waning moon kept the darkness at bay, illuminating the grey nocturnal landscape. Kaya drew comfort from random flashes of the tiny bioluminescent glow of forest fireflies. The trickling, gurgling water, which flowed around mossy boulders and cobbles in a nearby river, soothed his troubled mind. Enthusiastic chirps of arboreal grasshoppers calmed his frayed nerves. Kaya gradually approached a clearing. Emerging from the constraints of the forest canopy, a flicker of light above caught Kaya's attention. He gazed intently into the starry night sky, filling his lungs with dewy air. And, there, hovering below Antares, suspended above Alpha Centauri, a twinkling star moved. At least, it first seemed to be a star to Kaya. But, as it darted and danced, constantly growing larger and larger, Kaya realised it was no star. And, mesmerised by the awesome aerial display, Kaya lost all track of time.

Suddenly, aware of a dark presence behind him, Kaya leapt off the track uttering a startled yelp. The mysterious night-shrouded figure approached, with long steady strides, and cloven hooves crushed the dirt and pebbles that littered the donkey track.

Blocking the dappled moonlight, which filtered through the treetops, and looking down grimly upon Kaya, Papa Bois, the father of the forest, stroked his leaf-strewn goatee beard, cocked an eyebrow beneath his horned forehead, and spoke with a deep, earthy voice. "In the undergrowth may lurk many perils. A steadfast heart does not stray from the path."

Fearfully recalling his recent encounter with the malevolent shape-shifting entity that impersonated Mama Flo, Kaya considered running for his life.

But, before Kaya acted on impulse, Papa Bois calmly said, "The sun has not yet risen. The tall trees still cast dark shadows across the path, making your steps uncertain and your journey treacherous. Now is a time for walking, not running, Hezekiah."

"Mr Rapp, is dat you?" asked Kaya, inching away defensively, trying his best to project composure in the wake of his abject terror.

"Indeed, Hezekiah. I see that my previous attempts, to purge your memory, have been less than successful. Do try not to excite yourself. What I need to tell you is of great import, and if you wake now, it is unlikely you will return to sleep, for several hours."

"Why yuh dress-up like Papa Bois?" asked Kaya, tentatively.

"Since this is your dream, you are better poised to answer that question."

"Ah thought yuh only wear yuh horns in de cemetery, when yuh invokin' de dead," said Kaya, chuckling nervously and trying to ignore the violent thumping of his heart.

Unmoved, Papa Bois stared at Kaya dispassionately. "Do not be misled by my quaint, theatrical accoutrements."

"Dat was ah joke," said Kaya, with a fading smile. "It from ah song."

"It may surprise you to learn that I am quite familiar with the works of the Mighty Sparrow."

"Well, not really," said Kaya, matter-of-factly, "Ah sure yuh ain't schupid, an' Sparrow will always be de calypso king ah de world."

"I am a scientist," announced Papa Bois.

"Dat is exactly what dey call ah witch doctor, in Jamaica," said Kaya, eyeing the tall, dark, imposing folkloric figure with suspicion.

With pursed lips, Papa Bois said, "I assure you, young man, I am not in the business of magic."

Deeply intimidated, Kaya immediately changed the subject. "So, all dis not real?"

"Reality is relative. I am real, and you are also real. The rest is only real when you imagine or perceive it."

Kaya muttered shakily, "It sound like magic tuh me...."

With an audible sigh, Papa Bois said, "It would be wise to familiarise yourself with philosophy and the rudiments of quantum mechanics."

Kaya swallowed audibly. "So, wha' yuh really doing in meh dream?"

"I am here to answer many questions."

And, Kaya thought, *Well yuh could start wit' 'what on earth is quantum mechanics?'*

"Walk with me, Hezekiah. You are in mortal danger."

"Where we goin'?"

Papa Bois paused at a fork in the path. Kaya looked to where the mist-covered donkey track branched to the left. Becoming increasingly crooked and winding, it stretched on in this way for at least two hundred metres until it veered sharply to the right and plunged abruptly into a wall of the black unknown.

"I am taking you to my sanctuary," said Papa Bois, and he motioned to the right branch of the track.

Kaya observed a straight path ahead, sheltered below the deep-green umbrella of rainforest trees barely visible in the dark, distant mist. Once again, he lost track of time as he followed Papa Bois deeper and deeper into the forest. The sound of the river grew angrier, and he felt the cool, refreshing drizzle of freshwater from a waterfall. Since his strange encounter with Papa Bois, in the Azura Forest, Kaya's senses remained enhanced. And, as they approached a network of limestone caves, he easily heard the ultrasound chirps of a colony of bats flying high above. From his right trouser pocket, Kaya removed a slingshot he made in Tortuga from a Y-shaped tree branch, an old bicycle tire inner tube, dental floss and a strip of leather. From his left pocket, he retrieved a steel ball bearing the size of a marble. He loaded the shot into the leather pocket of the catapult, chose his target and took aim, following the bat's swift, erratic flight.

"What are you doing?" asked Papa Bois, rhetorically.

"Ah doh like bats," said Kaya, his eyes narrowed in deadly concentration as he continued to track his fleeting target.

"You fear them. Does your prejudice justify killing them?"

With a sigh and an eye-roll, Kaya tucked his slingshot and ammunition back into his pocket.

Attempting a snobby English impersonation, Kaya said, "I really do love these little chats we have, Mr Rapp. They're spiffing good fun."

"Doh make meh vex, Hezekiah," barked Papa Bois, with a perfect Trinidadian accent that left Kaya dizzy with fear and completely dumbfounded.

Tentatively, Kaya said, "OK…."

"The Trinidadian funnel-eared bat eats insects and is quite incapable of vampirism. I suggest you adopt the Chinese attitude to bats. They regard them as representations of happiness and good fortune."

"Yuh right, bats eat insects; an' ah doh care much fuh insects."

Papa Bois sighed heavily. "You disappoint me, Hezekiah. I thought you valued all life."

Suddenly self-conscious, Kaya averted his eyes meekly. "Like yuh cyah tell is joke ah jokin'."

In a flash of movement that startled Kaya, Papa Bois snatched something from the air with his right hand.

"Come closer. I want to show you something," he told Kaya, calmly.

"What?" asked Kaya, cautiously.

"The main reason I came to this wonderful island."

"De Swedish government send yuh here fuh what in yuh hand?"

For the first time, Papa Bois smiled. It was broad, warm and deeply sincere. "We both know I was not sent here by the Swedish government, Hezekiah."

"OK, so yuh ready tuh admit you're ah alien?"

"I was born in the great Swedish forest of Kolmården," said Papa Bois.

"Sorry, Mr Rapp, buh ah find dat hard tuh believe.

Still smiling, Papa Bois said, "Your acceptance of that fact is not required."

"What it is yuh have in yuh hand?"

Papa Bois stretched out his arm and slowly opened his hand to reveal a grasshopper.

"Yuh come all de way tuh Trinidad, from Sweden, fuh ah cricket?" said Kaya, sceptically.

Shards of light began streaming into the forest, casting long shadows from the sunrise, and the grasshopper took to flight.

"Yuh let it go?" Kaya smirked in disbelief. "Yuh come all de way here; an', yuh let it go?"

Kaya watched the grasshopper soar high into the air.

Fly Jiminy, fly, he thought.

Suddenly, a bat caught the grasshopper in its jaws. At this point, Kaya could no longer suppress gales of nervous laughter.

De bat eat it, he thought. *De bat eat de cricket….*

Slowly, the white dreadlocks, ram's horns and cloven hooves of Papa Bois transformed into Tolan Rapp's neatly trimmed black hair and shimmering boots. Rapp's skin-tight jumpsuit replaced the father of the forest's ragged brown vest and trousers. A broad utility belt housing a small baton appeared instead of the thin strip of twisted, dried vines from which a hollowed-out bull's horn once hung. Having witnessed the fantastic transformation, Kaya finally stopped laughing as anxiety consumed him.

Ah suppose, quantum mechanics could explain dat, thought Kaya, wryly.

Tolan Rapp removed a small silver disc from his belt. "I suggest you prepare yourself for transport," he said, and the disc began to glow.

Somebody sendin' ah Jeep tuh pick we up?

With a blinding flash of plasma energy, Kaya found himself in the silver-walled room in which he recalled receiving medical treatment from the mysterious Tolan Rapp. He felt light-headed and unsteady on his feet.

Trying to mask his shock, Kaya said, "Ah thought yuh say yuh not ah magician?"

"The teleporter converts matter into an energy signature, which it uploads. The uploaded signature is then reconverted and downloaded to a designated location, in its original physical state."

"Yuh coulda save ah lotta time by teleportin' we straight here, instead ah wastin' time strollin' through de forest in de night," said Kaya, cocking an eyebrow. "Ah jus' sayin'...."

"I had hoped our walk was educational," said Tolan Rapp.

Well, ah learn yuh lose yuh cricket, dat's fuh sure....

"You will have to overcome your fears and trust me, Hezekiah. There is absolutely nothing to be gained from pretending to be immature and unintelligent."

"Mr Rapp, ah like yuh, buh you need tuh develop ah sense ah humour."

Buh, doh worry, ah workin' on it, thought Kaya.

"Hezekiah, I will tell you why I am here. After that, you can tell me whether or not my mission is comedic."

"Alright, so yuh say yuh Swedish?"

"I was born in Sweden, but my parents were not Swedish."

With a lump in his throat, Kaya asked, "Dey dead?"

Tolan Rapp's voice was gritty when he said, "Yes, Kaya, they are dead."

"Oh. Ah sorry to hear dat."

Tolan Rapp acknowledged Kaya's sympathy with a sombre nod.

Staring deeply into Kaya's eyes, he said, "My parents were born on Cyclo, planet prime of the Cyclan Confederacy of Neutral Planets. My father was one of Cyclo's greatest scientific minds; and, my mother, her most renowned exobiologist."

It took a while for the gravity of Tolan Rapp's words to fully sink in. Kaya treated the revelation with contained excitement. "So dat mean ah was right. You're ah alien."

"In a manner of speaking, yes. Does that disturb you?"

"No way.... Ah t'ink it cool," announced Kaya gleefully.

"I admire your positive attitude; however, there are many who would do us harm."

"Us? How yuh mean us? What yuh really sayin'?"

Ah related tuh you?

"Your father was also aboard the vessel that brought my parents to Earth."

"Yuh knew meh fadah? Who was meh fadah?"

"Calm yourself, Hezekiah, be patient. I will tell you all that you need to know. If you become too excited, you will wake from this dream. Because of the physical distance between us, much power is required. If our telepathic connection were broken, it would be several days before I could fully recharge my pod and establish another psionic link. By then, it may be too late. So, listen carefully."

"Wait. Please. Ah just have tuh know. Who was meh fadah? What was he name?"

"Torian...."

"Why de men in black kill him?" asked Kaya, his eyes filling with tears. "Why?"

Tolan Rapp said softly, "Please, Kaya, do not cry. You will only wake up."

Sobbing bitterly, Kaya asked, "Why? Why?"

He woke that morning, in his small room, to find his mother, Josephine, sitting in Mama Flo's old rocking chair at his bedside. Josephine gently wiped the tears from his eyes.

"It was just a bad dream, Kaya," she said, with a glassy-eyed smile.

Closing his eyes and trying to compose himself, Kaya replied, "Yes.... Ah know. Ah know."

28

ABSENT FATHERS

Kaya slouched at the breakfast table, morosely staring at his plate, absent-mindedly swirling cooked wieners, diced onions, and tomatoes with his fork.

"Kaya, stop playin' wit' yuh food. Wha'ppen, yuh doh like de Vienna sausage?"

Snapping out of his daydream, Kaya said, "No, it good." He impaled one of the small, short, North American sausages with his fork, and he slowly shoved it into his mouth."

Josephine approached Kaya and gently ran her fingers through his neatly cut hair. "Look, Kaya, ah know yuh still upset yuh friend die...."

Kaya flinched then said bluntly, "Kerwin wasn't exactly meh friend."

"Alright, wha' goin' on den?"

"Yuh know Raya missin'?"

"Of course...."

"An', yuh not worried?"

"Wha' yuh want meh tuh do boy? Every day, ah prayin' fuh Raya. Ah call Cousin Christie twice already dis week; buh at de end ah de day, ah ha' tuh study de t'ings ah could change, not de ones ah can't. Is Raya yuh studying?"

"Yuh doh understan'...."

"Ah doh understand what, Kaya?"

"What is meh fadah name?"

"Buh A-A, dis is wha' yuh swell-up yuh face for?"

"Like yuh forget wha' it like ... growin' up wit'out ah fadah...."

Josephine said sternly, "Boy, doh use dat tone wit' me, alright?"

"Alright," said Kaya, about to leave the table. "Ah'll be late fuh college."

"Stop right dere," said Josephine, and her pointed finger somehow reminded Kaya of a loaded pistol. "I forget wha' it feel like?" she asked, rhetorically. "In school, dey used tuh call meh, *Carnival Baby*. Yuh t'ink ah could ever forget dat? Go tuh de bank on High Street and ask fuh ah woman name Susan Brown. Ask she how she get she first black eye."

Kaya sighed. "Torian. Is dat meh fadah name?"

Josephine could not hide her astonishment. "Who tell yuh dat?"

"So, dat's meh fadah name."

"Who tell yuh dat?" demanded Josephine.

Kaya's eyes narrowed under a heavy frown, and he spoke through gritted teeth. "Papa Bois tell meh inna dream!"

Josephine stopped short of slapping Kaya on the face. She backed away from him and said in a low voice, "Ah never tell ah soul yuh fadah name. Who tell yuh?"

"Ah already tell yuh, buh yuh doh believe meh."

"Papa Bois," Josephine smirked, shook her head, and looked to the ceiling for guidance.

"Tantie Rose say she see him. She say Papa Bois protect yuh once in Tortuga."

"Hmmm. Tantie Rose tell yuh dat?"

"Yuh probably cyah remember," said Kaya, tentatively.

Josephine walked slowly to the kitchen table, pulled a chair and sat next to Kaya. Her voice seemed small and distant when she said, "No, Kaya, ah remember everyt'ing. Like it was yesterday."

"So, yuh know Papa Bois real?"

"Yes."

"An', yuh see Douen?"

"Yes, when ah was small, growin' up in Tortuga. Five of dem. Ah was so scared, boy, ah couldn't move. Dey had dees big, black, staring eyes. Dey surround meh, and one ah dem flash ah bright light in meh eye; buh when Papa Bois appear, dey run off in de bush. Ah never see anyt'ing run so fast. Well, after dat, Tantie Rose take meh tuh Father Buckley, in Tortuga Church. He call dem poltergeist," Josephine shook her head incredulously. "First, he bless meh, den Tantie Rose, den de house, den de yard…. Ah never see dem again. No Douen. No Papa Bois."

"Ah doh t'ink dey are spirits," said Kaya, solemnly.

"Yuh know de ole people say, if yuh talk 'bout Douen, dey will come lookin' fuh yuh?"

"Ah t'ink dey are aliens."

Josephine laughed in disbelief. "Where yuh get dat crazy idea from, Kaya?"

"Mammy, Papa Bois is ah alien, an' he knew meh fadah who was also ah alien too."

"Kaya, boy, yuh were dreamin'," said Josephine, with a warm smile. "Yuh want people tuh t'ink yuh crazy? Maybe dat man at de dentist was right; maybe ah should take yuh to see ah priest."

"Ah t'ink de men in black are aliens too," said Kaya, and he was not smiling.

"Papa Bois tell yuh dat in yuh dream?"

"Ah see dem."

Kaya very much wanted to tell Josephine about his encounters with Papa Bois, the pale-skinned Shu-Senyn, and the murderous woman they referred to as the *Mad Renegade*. All the same, he was quite aware that most of these encounters could easily be dismissed as dreams or hallucinations.

"Aliens?" asked Josephine.

"Yes, aliens," replied Kaya.

"From outta space?"

"Yes, Mammy, from outta space," said Kaya, with an overwhelming sense of déjà vu.

"What yuh t'ink aliens from outer space want wit' us?" asked Josephine, raising a sceptical eyebrow.

"It ha' tuh do wit' your fadah an' mine. Papa Choonks an' Torian."

"So, yuh t'ink Papa Choonks was ah alien too?" chuckled Josephine, dismissively.

"No, buh de woman who kill him might be one."

"Kaya," said Josephine, clearly exasperated, "Yuh fadah die in ah car accident. I was dere, ah see it happen wit' meh own two eye wide open. And, lightnin' kill Papa Choonks. Kaya, one ah de most painful lessons in life, is learnin' dat de people yuh admire de most, are far from perfect. Mama Flo was meh mudder, and ah love her dearly, but she carry ah bitterness in her heart after Papa Choonks die. She jus' couldn't accept dat someone, she love so much, could jus' get hit by lightnin' and drop dead."

"Tell meh 'bout meh fadah," said Kaya, cautiously.

"How yuh mean?"

"What was he like?"

Josephine smiled, and the brightness of it lifted Kaya's heavy heart. "Torian? He was handsome too bad. He was full ah life. He loved every living t'ing, and he knew how tuh make meh laugh. He was interested in conservation jus' like you. Ah t'ink dat's where you get it from.... He could tell yuh de name ah every plant and every tree. He could see de good in everyt'ing...."

"He talk funny?"

"Well, he had ah accent. When ah ask him 'bout it, he jus' say he travel a lot."

"He talk 'bout he family?"

Josephine glanced at the kitchen clock and immediately leapt to her feet. "Oh, Gorm, look at de time, yuh goin' tuh be late, boy. Yuh cyah ride yuh bike tuh college now. Quick-quick, jump in de Jeep, leh we go."

Josephine sat in her old Jeep Wrangler, tapping the steering wheel impatiently, while Kaya quickly closed and locked the tall steel gate that led to the small concrete driveway at the front of her flower shop. Kaya had not seen the approaching postman; in his haste, he bumped into the man, knocking the mail out of his hand. Apologising profusely, Kaya scrambled up the fallen envelopes. He handed them to the silent postman and gasped when he noticed that the poor man still sported a broad, unnatural grin.

"Yuh notice anyt'ing funny 'bout de postman?" asked Josephine, as Kaya sat in the Jeep's passenger seat.

"No. How yuh mean?" replied Kaya, feigning ignorance.

"De last few days, ah find he lookin' like he have ah few screws loose," said Josephine, accelerating quickly and driving off with squealing tyres.

During the short journey to Paria College, Kaya kept a watchful eye on the sunny streets of Coconut Grove, reflected in the rear-view mirrors of Josephine's four-wheel drive. Every day, following the men in black's sinister visit, Kaya lived in fear of an ambush. He felt relieved that their ominous, matt black sedan was nowhere to be seen. However, Kaya could not help wondering if the black-suited visitors were still nearby, watching and waiting for an opportune moment to waylay them. How could he protect himself or his mother, from their murderous intentions?

29

NAMES

Kaya had great difficulty coming to terms with the disturbing implications of Tolan Rapp's dream revelation. Was it true? Was he the hybrid son of an extraterrestrial, and what would Wendy say if he told her? Who was his father, and why was he a fugitive? Kaya wondered if his alien heritage meant that someday he would become a freakish monster, or would he develop cool super-powers. He wondered if foreign scientists would capture and dissect him. He wondered how many aliens and hybrids lived on Earth. He wondered a lot, and it terrified him.

That night, Kaya spent three hours scouring the Internet. Despite all he had been told by his mother, Josephine, and his grandaunt, Tantie Rose, Kaya did not believe Papa Choonks to be the hapless victim of a random lightning strike. He remained convinced that Mama Flo was correct, and Papa Choonks had been murdered. An energy discharge from a weapon of unknown design had caused the misleading Lichtenberg figures found on his grandfather's body. The murderess had the ability to effectively impersonate Mama Flo, and this mysterious individual seemed romantically obsessed with Papa Choonks. According to Tantie Rose, Mama Flo suspected two women — Cynthia Drake, nicknamed Sin Tia, and Agnes Talbert, also known as Agonies. Kaya believed one of these women had faked her death and was still at large.

"Rosemary, yuh could turn yuh back on meh, all yuh want, buh doh turn yuh back on meh gran'chile, de messenger ah destruction want what he have. Yuh ha' tuh warn Kaya, yuh ha' tuh warn him. She t'ink she smart, buh she jus' like she name."

That was what Mama Flo told Tantie Rose in her dream. It was a riddle that Kaya believed held the key to the identity of his grandfather's killer.

She jus' like she name, thought Kaya. *She t'ink she smart, buh she jus' like she name....*

Kaya discovered that Cynthia was one of the names of Artemis, Greek mythological goddess of the moon and hunting. Although the meaning of Artemis remained inconclusive, some speculated it might have derived from *artamos* — *a butcher*. Drake is a male duck; however, in the past, it literally meant *dragon*, which in turn meant *serpent* or *snake*. Was Cynthia Drake the snake that butchered Papa Choonks? In contrast, Agnes, meant *pure* and *holy*, and Talbert was of Germanic origin, derived from *tal*, which meant *valley*, and *berht*, meaning *bright*. Of the two names, Kaya had to conclude that the name Cynthia Drake seemed far more sinister than holy and bright Agnes Talbert.

Sin Tia kill Papa Choonks? Is dat wha' Mama Flo wanted meh tuh know?

Tantie Rose had told Kaya that Sin Tia had green eyes.

Wendy have green eyes, thought Kaya, and he recalled what Tantie Rose said.

"Doh ever trust no light-skin 'oman wit' green eyes, dey heartless an' deceitful fuh so."

However, unlike Raima, who seemed quite happy to callously humiliate him, Wendy offered Kaya nothing but affection. Wendy had dismissed his humiliation and repaired his broken heart. She continued to banish Kaya's strong feelings of inferiority, which had been fostered by the constant bullying of Cobo and his Mapepire cohorts. Wendy's loving attention also countered the painful apathy of many of Paria's most desirable girls.

No way Wendy is de Mad Renegade. Spexy ha' green eyes too, thought Kaya. *Ah always say she too pretty tuh be ah nun....*

Once again, Kaya's suspicions fell squarely on the bespectacled geography master from Ireland. It seemed to make perfect sense. Feeling remorse, after murdering Papa Choonks, Sin Tia could have faked her death in Trinidad, then fled to Ireland and become a nun. Kaya mulled over the facts. Spexy only joined Paria College recently. She had green eyes and was very attractive. She had given Kaya a poisoned bar of chocolate. And the day after Kaya witnessed the Mad Renegade being shot in the shoulder, Spexy showed up at college with her arm in a sling. Kaya felt a knot develop in his stomach. Furthermore, Cobo's name, Artimus, meant *follower of Artemis*, and Cobo was a member of Mapepire House, the house of the snake. Was he more than just a college bully?

30

POUTINE

The following day, at Paria College, away from their inquisitive and disapproving peers, Kaya and Wendy sat silently on the long, slatted, wooden bench, nestling below the galvanised blue canopy that ran the full length of the main playing field, shaded from the merciless lunchtime sun.

"Why don't you let me in?" said Wendy, and she continued to stare into the distance.

"Wha'?" said Kaya, turning to the pretty Canadian girl, trying to snare her green-eyed gaze.

Wendy did not look at him. "I know something's bothering you. Don't you trust me?"

Kaya clasped her warm hand in his. Wendy was always warm; it was as if she had a perpetually mild fever.

"Ah trust yuh," said Kaya, gently.

"Is it something to do with what's-her-name?"

"No, not at all…. Raima was never meh girlfriend," he said, and his brooding eyebrows tilted slightly upwards.

"And, what about me?" said Wendy, turning towards Kaya, and disarming him with glassy, cat's eyes. "I mean, what do you call me, eh?"

"I—"

"Wait, before you say anything, just listen. I like you. I like being with you, and I like flirting with you, but I'm not shallow. And, despite what all the bitchy girls say, I am not a slut—"

"Most—"

"Shush. Everywhere I go, older guys keep making such a big deal about how I look. It's so painfully obvious they just see me as Julie Jailbait. So, the cocky, confident guys are often just dogs with one-track minds. And, the good guys, guys like you, well, they often waste a lot of their time wondering what I see in them or if I'll dump them. The bottom line is that I usually end up alone…."

"Most girls doh like intelligence and dey definitely doh like nice boys, dat's fuh sure," said Kaya, with uncommon cynicism.

"I'm not like other girls…. I thought you knew that."

"I know," said Kaya, without thinking.

I know yuh special….

"Oh, yeah? said Wendy, and a tear ran down her flushed cheek. "You don't even know who you are…."

Oh, no, now you probably think I'm Debbie Downer….

With the back of her hand, Wendy quickly wiped away the tear before putting on a brave face and adding, "I need to pee…. I'll just go to the washroom. I'll see you in class, eh?"

Hormones. Can't help it. At least it only happens once a month…. thought Wendy, and Kaya heard her.

Wendy left hastily. Kaya was far too flabbergasted to attempt stopping her. His mind raced.

She psychic?

Kaya wondered if the Canadian meal, called poutine, which Wendy Wong generously shared with him was responsible. The rich concoction of French fries, fresh cheese curds and brown gravy, was certainly new to Kaya and tasted far better than it looked.

Was Wendy just like him? Was she of part-extraterrestrial parentage? Kaya sometimes imagined that only his mother or an impressionable alien from another planet could truly love him. Despite his outward bravado, years of bullying at the hands of Cobo and the Mapepires and taken its toll. Kaya had become very conscious of his lankiness, and Raima's obvious infatuation with the older, brawnier football captain did not help. However, the after-effects of his encounters with Papa Bois, his growing intuition, and Wendy's attention and admiration were having a profoundly positive effect on Kaya's confidence and self-esteem.

Kaya realised that he had been annoyingly sullen for the past few days, sullen and paranoid. He simply did not know whom to trust. He worried about his mother, and he believed that some of the people he knew were not what they appeared to be.

"Where's your girlfriend?" asked Tom.

Kaya had not seen him arrive.

"She not…."

Is she meh girlfriend?

"She had tuh go tuh de toilet."

Tom sat next to Kaya and said, matter-of-factly, "You know all the girls hate her."

"You hate her?" asked Kaya, calmly.

"Of course not. Do I look like a girl? I'm just saying. Obviously, they're just jealous that most of the lads fancy her. Cobo and the Mapepires are absolutely furious though; they're calling her a traitor, and a few other things that would make Caligula blush."

"Right now, Tom, ah ha' much bigger problems."

"What's going on?"

"Wha' yuh remember 'bout Papa Bois?"

"C'mon, Abbers, you know I don't want to talk about him. I don't ever want to talk about him."

"Why not?"

"Are you serious? Seeing him was an absolute nightmare, like being face to face with Satan."

"He not like dat. Ah mean, he doh look like dat. He hypnotise we or something."

"How do you know that?"

"Ah remember some ah wha' actually happened."

"What do you mean?"

"Wha' yuh remember? T'ink hard."

"Well, you and Raima fell into the river. Then…. Um…. I ran after you, and when I found you, you had saved Raima from drowning. Then Papa Bois came—"

"Yuh remember de tiger cats?"

"Yes, before you fell into the water, I'd seen a pair of them."

"What about afterwards?"

"That was the last I saw of them."

"Yuh havin' trouble rememberin', right?"

"No, I remember he told us we should leave the forest because there were poachers, and it wasn't safe."

"Yuh remember ah had ah big cut on meh head?"

"Where exactly?" asked Tom, trying to find evidence of a scar on Kaya's head. "I can't see anything."

Kaya spent the following fifteen minutes telling Tom about Papa Bois healing his head injury, the mystery surrounding the death of his grandfather, and the strange visit from the Shu-Senyn. Kaya explained that Papa Bois and the Shu-Senyn seemed to possess the ability to manipulate or remove memories by employing advanced technology. He also advised that his grandfather's murderess could expertly mimic others.

"Are you sure you haven't imagined some of this? Let's face it; it's a bit extreme. Even if someone killed your grandfather, why would they want to kill you?"

"Ah hoping Papa Bois go tell meh."

"In your dreams?"

"Most likely."

"Well, what can I say? Good luck with that."

"Ah could tell ah make a mistake tellin' yuh."

"No-no. I'm glad you did. It explains why you've been acting so weird. It explains a lot...."

"So, now yuh t'ink ah crazy, awa?"

"Well, I did see Papa Bois, and Raima did too," said Tom, sweeping a lock of red hair from his troubled brow. "I'm obviously a little loopy as well." He stared at Kaya briefly and asked, "What does your mother think?"

"Ah didn't tell she everyt'ing, she'd want tuh take a one way flight tuh Australia if ah tell she everyt'ing."

"What about Wendy?"

"Not ah word."

"And, until you sign a peace treaty with Raima, I guess you won't be talking to her about this either."

"Are you goin' tuh help meh?"

"Well, I must admit, I'm intrigued by Papa Bois. I mean, what does he want?"

"Well, exactly."

"Yeah, I'll help you. What do you want me to do?"

"Look out fuh strange behaviour. Watch Spexy like ah hawk."

"And the riddle? You said something about the messenger of destruction. Maybe there's something in the Bible. I'll ask Dad, he knows a lot about names and stuff."

"Remember, yuh cyah tell him about Papa Bois."

"Of course not, and I'll ask Maureen about Cindy Drake and Agnes Talbot. She seems to know absolutely everything about everyone."

"It's Agnes Talbert, not Talbot...."

"You're sure? They almost sound the same."

"Actually, ah not sure. Ah didn't t'ink ah dat."

"Well, let's see," said Tom, whipping out his smartphone and tapping the display. "Nuts, I can't get a decent signal. OK, hang on; here we go. Talbot.... It's taking forever to load." In eager anticipation, Kaya huddled closer to Tom, trying to get a clear view of his phone's touchscreen. "Wait for it. Right. Talbot. Surname. Meaning. OK, we're in business. Talbot. English. Norman in origin. Probably derived from the Germanic elements of *tal*, meaning *destroy*, and *bod*, which means *message*." Suddenly, with the exception of his freckles that glowed with a red blush, Tom's face lost what little colour it had. His blue, bespectacled eyes widened as he stared ominously at Kaya. "Messenger of destruction. Talbot literally means, *messenger of destruction.*"

31

PORTRAITS

Kaya had hoped he would meet Tolan Rapp again soon, but night after night, his dreams were filled with nothing worth remembering; at least, that's what Kaya thought. And so, having completed his homework and household chores, he spent a little more than an hour working on his surprise Christmas present for Wendy Wong. True to her word, two weeks prior to the Bob Maharaj birthday party incident, Tara Khan — Raima's mother, had purchased four of Kaya's best acrylic paintings, which she proudly displayed on the walls of her Patisserie Bougainvillea.

Following a family tradition, established by Mama Flo, Kaya donated a small portion of his earnings to a charitable society dedicated to serving the impoverished of Trinidad and Tobago. He used most of what remained to replace his camera, repair his water-damaged mobile phone, and his ailing PC and monitor. He also bought canvases, new brushes, linseed oil, distilled English turpentine, and oil paints. Kaya had embarked on producing an oil-on-canvas fine art portrait of Wendy. As a guide, he used a photographic image, which he had downloaded from her social networking profile. For the past three nights, he eagerly applied himself to his secret artistic task. And, for an hour or so, he tried not to think of either the Mad Renegade or the dangerous Shu-Senyn.

Kaya took a break from his clandestine portraiture, to network with Tom via the Internet. Tom, who had proven to be quite a resourceful detective, confirmed most of the facts Tantie Rose had shared with Kaya regarding Sin Tia and Agonies. Having found the relevant obituaries, Tom verified that a Cynthia Drake had died in a tragic car accident. An old newspaper clipping, replete with graphic photographs, claimed that Cynthia, who had been undergoing treatment for depression, perished when her car collided with a tree. An autopsy revealed her blood alcohol content to be twice the legal limit. Tom also discovered an obituary for an Agnes Hall, née Talbot, of Coconut Grove, but no relevant images. Maureen related to Tom that Agnes's husband, Arthur Hall, had worked at Pointe-a-Pierre within Trinidad's growing petrochemical industry. However, he returned to England three years after Agnes's death. Kaya and Tom ended their communication, resolved to investigate any existing histories further, trace addresses and follow up surviving relatives. Kaya believed one of these women murdered his grandfather and may also have been responsible for the death of his beloved grandmother, Mama Flo.

32

THE BIRD CAVE

During the sombre early hours, a light, rainy season drizzle, cleansed the air and drenched the dusty, pot-holed road that ran outside Kaya Abaniah's modest Mirabelle Street address. He listened to the monotonous, rhythmic drip of rainwater from his ceiling. Unhindered, it fell into a large plastic food container, which Josephine had placed on the floor in the corner furthest from his bed. Tomorrow, if the rain stopped, and the bleaching sun's rays managed to breach the thick cumulus clouds that recently dominated the skies, Kaya would seal the rusty, corrugated, galvanised roof with urethane cement. After all, although he was only fourteen-years-old, he was the man of the house. Several hours ago, Kaya had ended his Internet correspondence with Tom Baker. And, via his repaired mobile phone, he had wished Wendy Wong sweet dreams before concluding their nightly flirt marathon with an audible kiss. Ultimately, fatigue immersed Kaya in the misty depths of slumber, and the enigmatic Tolan Rapp finally returned to Kaya's dreams in the guise of Papa Bois, the father of the forest.

Kaya materialised within a large, pitch-black, cave complex, dazzled and momentarily disorientated by the silvery-blue plasma energy of an alien transporter beam. Immediately, assaulted by the eerie, echoing sounds of fluttering, and blood-curdling shrieks and screeching noises, Kaya raised his hands defensively in the almost complete darkness. The ground felt oddly soggy underfoot, adding to his growing sense of insecurity.

He uncomfortably recalled being told, *"Perhaps, I am keeping you healthy purely to take you to a zoo, on another planet, far away. Perhaps, I plan to experiment on you or eat you."*

Kaya heard the distinctively muffled thud of cloven hooves as Papa Bois ominously approached. Shaking with fear, he observed the light-brown glow of his host's raptorial eyes, and he wondered if he should simply run away.

Papa Bois said, "Welcome to my sanctuary," and his sonorous voice gave Kaya goose bumps. "We are deep within an uncharted cave, at the heart of the Azura Forest. The sounds, you are hearing, are the alarmed calls of Oilbirds. This is their home. The teleporter flash has unsettled them. But soon, they will realise there is no real threat, and their erratic behaviour will cease."

"What is that clicking noise?" asked Kaya.

"Echolocation. These birds forage at night and navigate in a similar fashion to bats."

"Dey endangered?"

"Unique, but not currently endangered. There was a time when these birds, which are commonly known as Guácharos, were also referred to as Devil birds, and their young chicks were captured and boiled to exploit the oil stored in the fat of their bodies. At times, they were even impaled on sticks, set alight, and used as slow-burning torches. Fortunately, that dark period has long passed, and the good people of Kairi have learned to appreciate and protect these unique creatures. They are to be found in the limestone caves of Kairi's Northern Range and in the mountains and hills of the northern regions of South America. They feed on the fruit of the Oil Palm and are the only nocturnal flying fruit-eating birds on this planet."

"Kairi? Yuh mean Trinidad?"

With a calming smile, Papa Bois said, "Yes, Hezekiah, I mean Trinidad."

"Are yuh goin' tuh tell meh 'bout meh fadah?"

"I will attempt to answer all your questions," said Papa Bois. "Come, I will take you to the cutter."

"Cutter?" asked Kaya, unable to mask his apprehension.

Papa Bois chuckled, but it only served to agitate Kaya further. "I refer to my vessel, not the slaughtering implement of an abattoir," he said with a smile. "I assure you, Hezekiah, I am vegetarian. And, furthermore, I have already had a most satisfying evening meal.

Kaya laughed nervously, as, before his eyes, Papa Bois slowly transformed into Tolan Rapp. The alien scientist retrieved his silver baton from his utility belt and extended it to a staff. He activated a dark red glow from its upper tip, which sufficiently illuminated their surroundings.

"This red light will not disturb my fine feathered friends," said Tolan Rapp.

Kaya saw that there were many reddish-brown Oilbirds, the size of pigeons, sporting white spots on their napes and wings. They roosted in bulky nests on ledges high above the cave floor. Several glided about and hovered in the gloom, using low-frequency clicks to avoid colliding with each other or the walls and ceilings of the cave. As they walked, Kaya noted that the musty air carried the moisture of nearby rivers and pools. The ground was soggy, spongy, and strewn with bird and bat droppings and decomposing seeds.

Tolan Rapp explained to Kaya that a combination of holographic imagery and advanced cloaking technology hid his sanctuary from undesired intrusion. He told Kaya that the human beings of the planet Earth were not the only humans in the universe. As well as naturals, there were clones such as the Shu-Senyn, and also artificials, known as Jinzou Ningen — distinguished by their deep-purple eyes and extraordinary physical abilities. The universe teemed with great wonders, dread perils, and intelligent life separated by time, knowledge, and immense distances.

For several anxious minutes, they spiralled down into the humid depths of the shadowy cave, until at last, Tolan Rapp stopped in a sizeable cavern. Large stalactites littered its rocky roof, but Kaya immediately noticed that the stalagmites on the limestone floor had been flattened. Tolan Rapp retrieved a small rectangular object from his utility belt. He activated the device and suddenly a saucer-shaped extraterrestrial craft became visible. The shock left Kaya light-headed. And, for a moment, he stared wide-eyed until finally his slack jaw fell open in awe.

Thunderstruck, Kaya muttered, "Dat's a starship...."

"Not quite," said Tolan Rapp, "it is the Captain's Cutter. And, unfortunately, despite many modifications, it remains incapable of hyperspatial travel."

"Who is de Captain?" asked Kaya.

"I am the Captain," said Tolan Rapp, calmly.

"So, yuh starship in orbit?"

"No. To prevent Cyclan technology falling into enemy hands, my father activated the self-destruct sequence of the Deep Space Explorer Talibah."

"When was dis?"

"In the year 1908. Kian historical documents refer to the Talibah's destruction as the Tunguska event."

"Wait.... Yuh parents come in 1908, how old are you?"

"Obviously, by Kian standards, I am considerably older than I look."

"Kian?"

"In the Cosmic Sea Galaxy, the planet Earth is believed to be a mythical place called Ki, and the people of Earth are known as Kians."

"Mythical? How come?"

"Even in a galaxy far, far away, the governing political bodies of some of the most technologically advanced civilisations encourage a certain degree of ignorance. Deception and privileged secrets are common facets of politics."

Tolan Rapp led Kaya into the silvery-grey space vehicle via a short ramp, and Kaya immediately recalled that he had been in its drab metallic interior before. He simply had not realised it was an extraterrestrial space-craft. Tolan Rapp explained that his parents discovered a Setian spy aboard the Talibah. Prolonged psychic interrogation revealed that the spy had impersonated one of his father's most trusted colleagues. Her mission: to deliver the Talibah, its crew, and their technological secrets, to the Followers of Seti. The spy was Niburian — an ancient race of highly advanced shape-shifters, thought to be the secret mentors and protectors of humanity. Origi-nally a high-ranking Osirian agent, the Niburian had been captured and brainwashed by the Osirians' sworn enemies, the Setians.

"The Osirians and the Setians possess technology that is exceptional-ly advanced," said Tolan Rapp, "far more advanced than my father anticipat-ed. A dampening field protects this planet. It renders much of our Cyclan technology useless."

Naturally, the unfamiliar names and terms used by Tolan Rapp left Kaya utterly confused.

"Who are de Setians?"

"The Setians or Followers of Seti, are the human descendants of Talisian scientists who were marooned on Ki at the dawn of human history. They follow the philosophies of Seti Geb and wish to subjugate mankind utterly. To achieve their insidious aim, they have created a clandestine and extremely powerful society known as the Luminata Prefectara. Their Shu-Senyn clone servants, refer to it as a higher authority, and some informed Kians call it the Illuminati."

"An', who are de Osirians and de Talisians?" asked Kaya, scratching his head and bearing a troubled frown.

"The Osirians follow the teachings of Seti's brother, Osiris Geb. They have allied themselves with the last remaining Niburians and wish to protect mankind. Many thousands of years ago, when the renegade sons of Geb Rey came to Ki and changed human bloodlines forever, the Supreme Emperor of The United Empires of the Planet Talis ruled the Cosmic Sea Galaxy. Since that time, the Cosmic Sea has been turbulent with terrible interstellar conflicts. The Great Ningen Wars, eighteen thousand years ago, brought the tyrannical rule of the United Empires to an end, and mankind, both natural and artificial, to the brink of extinction. The Age of Darkness, which followed, lasted over three thousand years. A democratic, republican, Talisian Commonwealth replaced the United Empires, but corruption and ethnic genocides led to the First Psychic War. Cyclo and several other Talisian planetary colonies demanded and gained neutral independence—"

"So, de Osirians are de good guys?" interrupted Kaya, his mind swimming in a soup of unfamiliar terms.

"From the point of view of Kians? Yes, I suppose. But, remember, we are not Kians. We are Cyclans. The Osirian Colonists and the Followers of Seti classified all the surviving members of my father's scientific expedition as extremely dangerous illegal aliens. You, Hezekiah, are the hybrid offspring of one such alien."

"You are de only Cyclan left?"

"Well, do not forget that you are half Cyclan. But, the Niburian and I are the only survivors of my father's mission."

"Wha'ppen?" asked Kaya, softly.

"The Osirians unleashed fighter vessels from their secret military outposts on Mars, but my father successfully evaded them. However, shortly thereafter, the Niburian impostor escaped confinement, murdered two crewmembers, and sabotaged the Talibah. She had hoped that Setian interceptors launched from the dark side of the moon would capture the ship. But, she had underestimated my father's ingenuity and the versatility of the new power source he had secretly developed. With some difficulty, the Setian vessels were disabled. But, by impersonating my father and members of his crew, the Niburian eventually seized command of the Talibah. Fortunately, my parents escaped with their remaining colleagues, and from this cutter, my father remotely activated the ship's self-destruct. However, the Niburian's mischief caused an unexpected chain reaction. The resultant explosion of the Talibah, near Russia's Podkamennaya Tunguska River, created the largest impact event in Kian recorded history."

"So, de cutter land in Sweden?"

"Yes, in the seclusion of the forest of Kolmården, which is where I was born."

"An', meh fadah?"

"Your father was born in Kolmården."

"What were meh gran'parents like?" asked Kaya, tentatively.

"They were brilliant scientists — noble, kind, and thoroughly dedicated to their humanitarian mission."

"De Mad Renegade is de Niburian, right?"

"Yes. My parents and their three surviving colleagues tracked her escape pod on an uncontrolled trajectory into the Amazon Rainforest. They believed that the shape-shifting Setian agent had perished. However, in 1951, when my father and I came to Kairi, we found to our dismay that the Niburian had been here for some time."

"Meh fadah came with you?"

"Yes, yes of course," replied Tolan Rapp. "The Niburian possessed a modified plasma weapon, and her behaviour suggested that she was mentally ill. For many years, she had been impersonating several of this island's folkloric characters, including Papa Bois, Soucouyant, La Diablesse, and Ligahoo. My father believed she suffered from a form of dissociative identity disorder."

"What dat mean?"

"Since we discovered her presence here, her personality has been characterised by several distinct identities that have alternately controlled her behaviour. My father believed that the Niburian was also psychotic."

"You have ah way tuh track de Mad Renegade?"

"I cannot track her. I can only detect her use of the palm device."

"De plasma weapon?"

"Yes, she used this weapon to murder your grandfather; this is how your family first came to our attention."

"So, why yuh here?"

"It may surprise you—"

Suddenly, an extremely loud peal of thunder woke Kaya from his dream. He sat upright, in his bed, momentarily disorientated. The light drizzle, which had previously ushered him to sleep, was now a raging thunderstorm. Kaya grabbed his mobile phone from his bedside table — it was 4:43 AM. He quickly discovered that he had received a text message from Wendy Wong at 3:35 AM.

Wendy's message simply read, *R U Awake? Scary lightning. I hate lightning. Wish you were here with me.*

33

THE MISSION

The electrical storm quickly swept out to the Gulf of Paria's shallow inland sea, taking its thunder, lightning, and heavy rain with it. The plastic container, Josephine had thoughtfully placed on Kaya's bedroom floor, had overflowed. He used the collected rainwater to douse his mother's exotic collection of indoor potted plants. Kaya placed old ragged towels on the damp carpet, hoping they would soak up most of the moisture. And he glumly wondered if he would ever get rid of the horrible wet-carpet odour that now kept him wide awake.

Kaya tried to make sense of all that Tolan Rapp had told him. A shape-shifting Niburian alien from the distant Cosmic Sea galaxy had killed his grandparents. And, this Niburian was crazy. Kaya desperately wanted to know why Tolan Rapp's parents and their colleagues from the planet Cyclo had come to Earth. What did they want? Soon, fatigue got the better of him. And, once again, Kaya slipped into the enigmatic embrace of yet another lucid dream.

As Kaya looked on in silent awe, Tolan Rapp activated his ship's holographic viewscreen. In the vivid display, Kaya observed two small saucer-like objects. They streaked across the night sky at terrific speeds and were identical to the ones he witnessed just after the Mad Renegade had attacked him.

"An Osirian Guard patrol," said Tolan Rapp, grimly. "They are equipped with terrain-hugging ENDAR, to maintain constant low-altitude flight automatically."

"Dey lookin' fuh yuh?" asked Kaya, and he swallowed audibly.

"Possibly, but it is more likely they are responding to a Sia incursion."

Kaya thought, *How many aliens really hiding on Earth?*

"Who are de Sia?" he asked.

"Some Kians refer to the Sia as Greys. They are small humanoids, with large heads and large eyes. They sometimes abduct humans. Here in Kairi, because of their child-like physical traits, they are ofttimes mistaken for the Douen."

Kaya cut to the chase. "Exactly why yuh come here?"

Tolan Rapp deactivated the viewscreen. Turning to Kaya, he said, "During the Second Psychic War, my father developed a nanoviral treatment, which he believed would rid natural humans of every conceivable illness. Unfortunately, the treatment fell into the hands of Karellan spies—"

"Wait. Who are de Karellans?"

"The most powerful human psychics of the Cosmic Sea," said Tolan Rapp. "I am sorry, Hezekiah, at this point, a full explanation of who they are, and what they represent, would only serve to confuse you further." And, when the disappointment he observed in Kaya's eyes became too much to ignore, Tolan Rapp added sincerely, "In time, through psychic dream training, I will impart to you all the knowledge that is required. There will be no more secrets, no more confusion, just clarity."

"OK, Mr Rapp," said Kaya, meekly.

"The Karellans spent several years secretly corrupting and weaponising my father's work. They systematically transformed his finest medical achievements into instruments of mass murder. A few years later, a young, ambitious Karellan warlord launched an attack against neutral Cyclo. And, when his extensive arsenal of conventional weapons failed to breach superior Cyclan defences, the warlord resorted to highly illegal nanoviral weaponry. Weaponry based on my father's treatment — weaponry for which no defence had been envisaged. Stationed on the Cyclan moon, my parents were spared. Many, living in Cyclo's crowded cities, were not so fortunate."

"How many people die?"

"Official Talisian records claimed that in just six months, three million Cyclan colonists perished. My father later learned that this was a political lie. Human casualties in the first six months following the Karellan attack were in excess of eight million. Of these, five million were children. Unsurprisingly, the very young and the very old were particularly susceptible to nanoviral cancer and other related illnesses. Nine months after the Karellan attack, a further eighteen million human beings had suffered slow, agonising deaths. Without a cure, my father envisioned that at least ninety million people would perish in just two years. And, within seventy years, systemic ecological collapse would render the planet Cyclo unable to sustain human life. Genocide. Genocide, for which my father felt directly responsible."

With a lump in his throat, Kaya asked, "An', yuh hate dem? Yuh hate de Karellans?

"No, Hezekiah. As much as I am appalled by their actions, I will not allow myself to hate the Karellans or any other individuals."

"Yuh must be ah saint; anybody else would wan' tuh get revenge."

"I am no saint; I am just painfully aware that revenge can only be found on the road to self-destruction. It is a product of pride, which brings neither peace nor satisfaction. Beware pride; it would have us seek revenge from those most deserving of our pity. You see, Hezekiah, one of the most devastating symptoms of pride is the unwillingness to forgive. Pride's compassionless and unrealistic expectations invariably lead to bitterness and hatred; it is the enemy of goodness."

For a moment, Kaya took in the words of his mysterious host. He could find no fault in Tolan Rapp's philosophical logic.

"Alright, buh ah still doh understand why yuh parents come tuh Earth, and why you come tuh Trinidad."

"Paranoid, riddled with guilt, but determined to find a cure for the virulent Karellan Immunodeficiency Nanovirus, my father rebelled against the Cyclan authorities and set out in search of the mythical planet Ki."

"Earth, why Earth?"

"Ki produced the most powerful human psychics of the Cosmic Sea. My father considered it to be an exceptional place with answers to many genetic riddles. He believed a cure for KARIN could be found among the naturally-occurring organisms endemic to this planet — life forms, which had not been genetically modified."

Kaya could not mask his scepticism. "Here?"

Tolan Rapp nodded.

"Twenty-one years ago, my father finally discovered a remedy for KARIN." Tolan Rapp motioned with his right hand to a featureless grey wall. Suddenly, several alien characters briefly flashed with an orange glow. "Behold," he said, and a three-dimensional holographic image of a grasshopper appeared. It hovered approximately one metre above a low metallic table, engulfed in a silvery-blue beam of light that emanated from a small grey orb.

"Buh, dat is just ah cricket," said Kaya, unimpressed.

Yuh lucky no bats in dis spaceship.

"My father's KARIN vaccine contains two genetically modified proteins. The first is derived from virus-infected cells extracted from the haemolymph of Coscineuta virens, locally known as the Moruga grasshopper. The second is from this plant, which is endemic to Trinidad."

Kaya watched dispassionately as the image of a small shrub approximately one metre tall, replaced that of the bluish-green grasshopper. The plant had red elongated flowers, slender stems, and tiny, oval leaves.

Dat just look like a wild bush, thought Kaya.

"Unfortunately," continued Tolan Rapp, "this unique species has been extinct in the wild since 1996. It is quite possible that I possess the last remaining living specimens. How ironic. In a distant galaxy, this seemingly inconsequential member of the Acanthaceae family can cure a planet-wide epidemic. It can potentially save billions of human lives, and it was only found here, in the mountain forests of Kairi, this island known as Trinidad."

"Why yuh doh just plant it everywhere?"

With a heavy sigh, Tolan Rapp said, "Oh, I have tried. But, I fear I lack my mother's green thumbs and my father's creative genius. My attempts to reintroduce it into its last known habitat, in the Northern Range, have only resulted in the growth of cross-pollinated hybrids. And, the mutated genes found in these hybrids, have proven unsuitable for vaccine production."

"Yuh cyah store de pattern in yuh transporter memory?"

"It is not that simple. The Captain's Cutter is not much more than a shuttlecraft. Over the years, we have modified it well beyond its intended capabilities. Nevertheless, it will always be limited. The cutter's teleporter employs sophisticated filters designed to neutralise pathogens of any kind. Bypassing the fail-safes and disabling the filters led to catastrophic cellular degeneration in all our simulations. Specialised stasis chambers, matter uploaders, DNA and RNA assemblers, were all destroyed over Russia, together with the Talibah."

Kaya's eyes were glazed when he said, "Buh over ah hundred years gone and pass. It too late to cure all dem people on Cyclo. Billions ah people dead already. In fact, ah doh t'ink any human beings still livin' on Cyclo. Every last one ah dem dead."

Noting Kaya's distress, Tolan Rapp said philosophically, "There is always hope, Hezekiah. Time is not constant. Reality is relative. Our perception of space-time can be thought of in terms of event coordinates relative to our current state of consciousness. Time is, therefore, simply the manifestation of limitless possibilities, perceived by ever-changing consciousness. Where there is no consciousness, there is no time. Time is an illusion. And, like any other illusion, it can be manipulated."

Kaya thought, *What he really talkin' 'bout?*

"To bridge the incredibly great distance between the Cosmic Sea and Milky Way galaxies, my father mentally navigated the Talibah through a traversable wormhole. The ship had been fitted with his prototype dark-matter hyperspatial drive and a unique viridian crystal sub-light propulsion unit. However, an unforeseen reaction occurred. For a microsecond, the Talibah and all aboard had been transformed into an astral shadow, projected at the speed of thought. In that microsecond, two Karellan stealthships, which had been secretly pursuing the Talibah, ceased to exist. The Talibah emerged in the Milky Way, exactly one hundred and seven years, six months, three days, nine hours and fifteen seconds in the past."

"Dey went back in time?"

Tolan Rapp chuckled, "My father eloquently described it as arriving at the appointed moment."

"So, now yuh have de cure, yuh have tuh take it tuh Cyclo."

"I would need the assistance of more enlightened minds to achieve that task."

"Well, yuh on Earth now. Intelligence is like radiation poisoning to most people here."

"This planet has had its share of enlightened thinkers."

"Yuh t'ink so?"

"Indeed. Many enlightened beings have sought to bring wisdom to the humans of Ki. Sadly, the majority of them have been murdered."

"Are you ah enlightened being?"

Tolan Rapp laughed, "No, Hezekiah, I am merely a scientist."

"De Osirians cyah help yuh?"

"The Osirians cannot be trusted."

"Ah t'ink yuh could find good an' bad in everybody. If yuh doh find somebody tuh help yuh, all yuh fadah work in vain, and meh fadah die fuh nuttin'."

"Perhaps," said Tolan Rapp, softly.

"Wha' 'bout de Shu-Senyn and de Mad Renegade? Ah cyah even protect meh mudder—"

"Do not attempt to engage them, it is far too dangerous. I will do everything in my power to protect both you and your mother. Due to hormonal changes in your body, your latent Cyclan abilities have finally begun to surface. However, without training, these talents can pose a threat to you and those around you."

Kaya swallowed hard. He had recalled the look of pain and horror in Kerwin Duff's eyes moments before he collapsed. Uneasily, he recalled the confused laughter and hysterical screams of the witnesses of Kerwin's final fit, and Kaya wondered if Kerwin truly suffered death by natural causes.

Tolan Rapp continued, "I will guide and protect you. But, under no circumstances must you divulge what we have discussed, not even to your mother. Be mindful of your true origin. The fine details of this dream may be forgotten, but the essence of it will remain."

34

THE AWAKENING

Throughout the 70s, 80s, and 90s, scooch had been the highlight of many a lunch break of Form 4 and Form 5 students at Paria College. In contrast, the vast majority of sixth formers, who saw themselves as mature, educated, young men and women, rarely got involved in what they considered to be a childish game. Nevertheless, the beginning of the 21st century saw the gradual demise of scooch. When Kaya joined Paria College, as a wide-eyed first form student, no one had played the Trinidadian version of dodgeball for almost a decade. However, Cobo's cousin, Adrian Leotaud and several other boys in the Mapepire House, reintroduced the game during their fourth year. While most of the college girls were avid spectators, the boys formed three groups: throwers, runners and watchers. Kaya's speed and acrobatic antics meant that he quickly became notorious as the most annoying runner, constantly taunting and embarrassing Cobo and his Mapepire cohorts who were all throwers. Despite their best efforts, they were rarely able to hit Kaya with the tennis ball.

In the weeks that followed Bob Maharaj's birthday party and the death of Kerwin Duff, no one played scooch at Paria College. That was until Sean Charles of Form 4I sneezed loudly just as batsman Deron Biggs was out bowled, losing a decisive cricket match between the Mapepires and the Ocelots. Deron immediately lost his temper, accusing Sean of deliberately distracting him and costing the Mapepires thirty house points. Fortunately, for Sean, PE teacher Bernard *Bulldozer* Mendoza was at hand to mediate. Even so, once Bulldozer's back was turned, as the students made preparations to go home, Kaya heard Deron whisper to Sean that he would get even.

At lunchtime, the following day, as Sean crossed the college football field, Deron got his revenge. He hurled a tennis ball, hitting Sean on the back of his head.

"Ouch!" cried Sean, turning to challenge Deron, "You're ah real idiot, yuh know dat Biggs?"

"Wha'ppen tuh yuh cold, Charlie Boy, like yuh cure overnight?" taunted Deron.

Cobo took this opportunity to throw the ball at Sean from behind, but Sean anticipated Cobo's actions and the ball missed him. Instead, it hit Tom who sat under the canopy, knocking his beloved rich tea biscuit out of his hand before he could take a bite. In anger, Tom grabbed the tennis ball and threw it at Deron who had been laughing. It hit Deron squarely on the nose, and he yelped in agony. Gillian Payne of 4R, who was reputed to be Deron's girlfriend, ran to his assistance, but he made much of telling her to go away.

"You big girl's blouse," shouted Tom at Deron.

As much as Kaya admired Tom's bravado, he somehow knew that Tom had made a terrible mistake. Kaya was not surprised when several Form 4 Mapepire boys, including Deron, Cobo, and Mukesh, began hurling tennis ball after tennis ball at Tom and Sean.

Sean ran for cover as Dwayne Gopaul shouted, "Scooch! Scooch!"

However, Tom just stood there, trying to cover his face and head until Kaya stepped in front of him with a tennis racket and either avoided the balls or knocked them away.

"Scooch ent yuh game, Tom, an' ah no good at tennis," said Kaya. "Take de racket an' do some damage."

"Thanks, Abbers," said Tom, taking the racket, grateful that Kaya would defend him.

As Tom did his best to hit the balls being hurled at him, Kaya stepped onto the field and was greeted by enthusiastic cheers from a gathering crowd of students.

"Since when yuh ha' thirty balls in scooch?" Kaya asked the Mapepires, and the group of spectators laughed.

"No-no, Ah Banana have ah point. Just one ball," said Cobo. Then, looking over Kaya's shoulder, he added, "Yuh alright, Bruce?"

A knot in the pit of Kaya's stomach warned him it was a distraction, but he could not resist the urge to look over his shoulder. To his dismay, Kaya saw Bruce de Bulk, sporting a proud smirk, walking under the canopy with Raima, who seemed self-conscious and ill at ease, at least to Kaya.

Kaya understood why Bruce caused such a stir among the Paria College girls. He was tall, dark, tanned, and muscular. He styled his dark brown hair with a Superman-esque spit curl that brushed his forehead. His brooding brown eyes betrayed very little; he rarely spoke and he possessed a roguish devil-may-care attitude. There was something dangerous about Bruce, and somehow people always seemed to do what he wanted them to do. Bruce de Bulk lived a charmed life.

Suddenly, something hit Kaya hard on the back of his head. His eyes were open, but he could not see, and a loud ringing noise replaced the chorus of concern from nearby observers. Kaya's knees buckled, and he fell to the ground.

In the blackness, Kaya heard a familiar voice say, *"Now, you must remember the techniques that I have been teaching you."*

"Is dat you, Mr Rapp?" thought Kaya.

"Indeed."

"So, is dream ah dreamin' again?"

"No, Hezekiah, you are about to recall memories designed to surface only when you are faced with danger. I suggest you brace yourself for a shock."

"Buh wha' trouble is dis?"

Suddenly, months of experience flooded Kaya's consciousness — experience gained in dreams while Kaya slept at night. Dreams initiated and directed by Tolan Rapp. The mysterious Tolan Rapp had taught Kaya a martial art and form of self-defence, which he called Tay Mo, the way of the open hand.

"Cool! So now ah know karate!" thought Kaya, gleefully.

"No, Hezekiah, although Tay Mo is based on ancient principles also employed by the empty hand concept of karate, it emphatically is not that Japanese form."

"Open hand, empty hand, same difference," mused Kaya.

"You are now physically, mentally, and morally, equipped to deal with your present crisis," announced Tolan Rapp's voice calmly.

"Yeah, ah could see dat," thought Kaya, disappointingly. *"Like yuh give meh conscience steroids, awa? Ah doh even wan' tuh get revenge on de Mapepires now."*

Kaya heard Tolan Rapp say, *"To dispense knowledge without moral guidance would be grossly irresponsible. A wise man once told me, 'To whom much is given, much will be required.'"*

"T'ank yuh, Sensei," thought Kaya.

"Hezekiah, sarcasm is a manifestation of anger, and anger can make you the puppet of your opponents."

"Mr Rapp, please doh call meh Hezekiah, it freakin' meh out."

As he regained consciousness, Kaya began to feel a sharp pain in his head where he had been struck. His breathing quickly went into overdrive. However, a sudden rush of adrenaline banished the pain, increased his strength, heightened his senses and boosted his energy.

"Give him some air," Kaya heard Tom say. "Abbers, are you OK?"

Fully awake, Kaya slowly rose to his feet while the unrepentant Mapepires laughed and jeered.

"Somebody, go an' call Bulldozer, oui; like allyuh cyah see is knock dey knock him out wit' de cricket ball. Ah concussion is ah serious t'ing," said Sean Charles.

"Speak to me, Abbers. Are you OK?" pressed Tom.

"Doh call Bulldozer," said Kaya, bringing his breathing under control, "Ah alright."

"Gimme de ball, Charles," demanded Cobo.

"Oh, yuh want de ball?" came Sean's furious rhetorical question.

Yuh want de ball; yuh want de ball, eh, Cobo? Well, lemme see if yuh could ketch it with yuh teeth, thought Sean, and Kaya heard him.

"Doh do it," said Kaya, firmly grabbing Sean's wrist, preventing him from hurling the hard, solid cricket ball at Cobo's face in vengeful retaliation. "Yuh better dan dat."

For a brief moment, Sean stared into Kaya's eyes, puzzled by what he saw. "Yuh wearin' contact lenses? How yuh eye lookin' funny so?"

"Ah see de light," said Kaya, with a smile, and he took the ball from Sean.

"Ah Banana, doh let meh have tuh take meh ball from yuh," said Cobo, pushing Mukesh out of his path. "Dey will well an' truly ha' tuh call Bulldozer tuh give yuh first aid."

Kaya stretched out his right hand to reveal the shiny new red cricket ball perched on his open palm.

"Here is yuh ball, Cobo. Come an' get it," said Kaya, with a mischievous grin.

"What's the plan?" whispered Tom.

"Yeah, how yuh goin' tuh get revenge?" asked Sean in a hushed tone.

Kaya said calmly, "Ah doh plan tuh get revenge, ah just goin' tuh teach Cobo ah lesson."

"Very good," said Tom, with a freckled smile, "I'm hoping it's a particularly painful and humiliating one."

"Yeah, man," agreed Sean.

"Dat will be up tuh Cobo," said Kaya, observing Cobo's smouldering green eyes, rigid square jaw, tightly clenched fists, and long confident strides towards him.

Increasingly spoiling for a fight, with the gathered spectators from other houses, the Mapepires gradually converged on Kaya in support of Cobo. Both Tom and Sean could not help slowly inching away as rising fear got the better of them. Nevertheless, Kaya stood calmly smiling in the face of the larger boys' bullishness.

"Thank yuh," said Cobo, sarcastically, as he reached for the leather-clad cork ball.

"Doh t'ank meh yet," said Kaya, swiftly moving the ball out of Cobo's grasp, "wait until yuh lesson over."

"Lesson? You goin' tuh teach me ah lesson?" said Cobo, his voice dripping with all the derision he could muster. "Look, lickle boy, gimme meh ball before ah get damn vex."

"The right t'ing fuh yuh tuh do right now, would be tuh apologise," said Kaya, effortlessly moving his hand every time Cobo reached for the ball.

"Apologise? Apologise for what?" said Cobo. Anger and frustration reddened his face and narrowed his eyes into hate-filled slits. "Why should I apologise? At least my parents were married when they had me. At least they wanted me, and at least I know who my father is. If anyone should apologise is you, yuh illegitimate freak of nature. You should apologise for subjecting us all to yuh unwanted presence. After all, it obvious yuh own father didn't want yuh, which is why he didn't stick around."

"Wha' yuh talking 'bout Corbeau?" added Deron with cool, calculated malice, "Ah bet Puppy Dog own mudder doh know who he father is."

Up until that moment, a heightened sense of intuition had Kaya anticipating every move Cobo made, but overconfidence in his newfound physical abilities left Kaya unprepared for this level of verbal assault. Cobo and Deron had crossed that invisible line no one else had ever dared to cross. The Mapepires felt strong in their numbers, and they harboured the confidence of bullies who never experienced retribution.

"Here is your ball," growled Kaya in an almost unrecognisable voice, offering the cricket ball to Cobo.

Cobo's spiteful grin slowly transformed into a bewildered slack-jawed gaze as he watched in disbelief as Kaya tightened his grip and slowly crushed the ball out of shape. Kaya had quickly assessed Cobo with new eyes; eyes trained by Tolan Rapp. He had quickly noted his posture, balance and the potential strength of his arms and legs. He would humiliate Cobo. He would turn his strength against him.

"You freak!" screamed Cobo, and he attempted to land a right hook on Kaya's chin.

Kaya sidestepped swiftly causing him to miss.

"Here, ketch," chuckled Kaya, and he threw the crushed ball into Cobo's rage-red face.

Embarrassed, and surrounded by a small group of Mapepires and other stunned students, Cobo snarled and lunged towards Kaya with a wild flurry of punches, which all missed as Kaya effectively employed the evasive techniques of Tay Mo. Eventually, Cobo overreached and overstepped and fell to the ground at Kaya's feet in a heaving, panting, dishevelled heap.

"Dat's just de first lesson," said Kaya, cocking an eyebrow. "When yuh want ah second lesson, just leh meh know."

Deron immediately took over from his fallen housemate and launched a rage-filled but ineffective attack of his own. Kaya did not parry, he slowly retreated, moving his head and upper body out of the range of Deron's desperate punches.

Suddenly, with his right arm, Kaya jabbed mere millimetres away from Deron's unprotected eyes. "Doh ever have anyt'ing tuh say about meh mudder or meh fadah," warned Kaya.

Deron tried to retaliate, but Kaya jabbed just below Deron's Adam's apple, just stopping short of making physical contact.

"Ah doh wan' tuh talk about dis again," said Kaya.

With bravado, Deron resumed his attack, but Kaya used his momentum against him. He sidestepped and tripped Deron, who crashed hard to the ground.

"Wha' goin' on here?" barked a disdainful male voice that Kaya immediately recognised.

"Ah teachin' lessons; yuh want meh tuh teach yuh ah lesson too?" Kaya responded calmly, not taking his eyes off Deron, who slowly rose to his feet.

The crowd parted, making way for Cobo's older cousin, Adrian Leotaud, Mapepire House Captain and Trinidad's under-18 Karate Champion. The muscular French Creole 6th former had dark, wavy hair, deep-set icy-blue eyes, a crooked nose gained from fighting, and an unexpectedly high-pitched voice. Towering and intimidating, he was amongst the largest and tallest students at Paria College. He looked at Kaya with obvious disdain.

"Like is challenge yuh want tuh challenge me, eh, Banana Head?" said Leotaud, with an incredulous smirk. "Wha'ppen, like yuh watch Karate Kid ah few times an' yuh develop ah death wish?"

All the Mapepires, except Cobo and Deron, laughed in support.

"Obeah Widow comin'," whispered Cobo, in Leotaud's ear. "Unless yuh wan' tuh get expelled, fight Ah Banana somewhere else."

"Ah tell yuh what, Banana Head," announced Leotaud, "Ah might be under-18 Karate Champion, buh ah always eager tuh learn. So, come dong tuh de Community Sports Hall after college on Friday an' we'll have ah contest. If yuh win, I'll make sure no Mapepire ever mess wit' yuh again. Buh, if yuh lose … boy, if yuh lose, yuh might as well transfer yuhself tuh another college."

To everyone's surprise, Kaya laughed.

"Listen," said Leotaud, clenching his fists, about to resort to violence until Cobo grabbed his shoulder and reminded him that Obeah Widow was fast approaching. "Abaniah, hopefully, ah go see yuh Friday. If yuh doh turn up, think about wha' other secondary school yuh wan' tuh go to."

As Obeah Widow approached, the Mapepires and the majority of the other students slowly dispersed.

"Where in blue blazes did you learn those moves?" Tom asked Kaya.

"Ah didn't do anyt'ing," said Kaya. "Ah just move outta dey way."

"Yeah, but it's the way you moved...."

Kaya looked towards Raima, who had been sitting in the shade with Bruce de Bulk under the canopy that ran along the playing field. Once again, Raima suddenly seemed to find her own feet fascinating, while Bruce offered Kaya silent, mock applause. Wendy arrived from the main courtyard, flanked by 4I's Nicole Richards and Gail Angelou, two of the few girls who did not despise her. She took a swig from a fat bottle of red Solo Kola Champagne, before waving happily at Kaya, apparently oblivious to the drama that recently played out on the college football field.

"Abaniah," came Obeah Widow's shrill voice.

"Yes, Mistress Mallory," said Kaya.

"Walk with me, Abaniah."

"I'll see you in class, Abbers," said Tom, his voice wavering with uncertainty as Kaya silently followed Obeah Widow.

35

TREATY OF VERSAILLES

As they walked towards the college staff room, Kaya wondered what punishment Obeah Widow had in store for him. He glanced over his shoulder, flashing a self-conscious smile at bewildered Wendy.

"You showed admirable restraint, Abaniah," said Obeah Widow, to Kaya's surprise.

"Miss?"

"That's Mistress Mallory to you, young man."

"Sorry, Mistress Mallory."

"Apology accepted. You may have noticed that I've been keeping a close eye on you, Abaniah," said Obeah Widow, as she walked up the short flight of concrete stairs, which led to the doorway of the staff room. And, when Kaya hesitated, she added, "Don't worry; you're not in any trouble. Come along."

Uneasily, Kaya followed the attractive middle-aged black woman into the capacious air-conditioned staff room. He fully realised that this was where Paria College masters escaped from their pupils. It, therefore, seemed a rare and unexpected privilege to be invited into this inner sanctum by the strictly officious Obeah Widow. A large boardroom table and high-backed chairs dominated the room. Miniatures of the Trinidad and Tobago flag and the flags of the four college houses adorned the top of a wide cupboard. Kaya noticed that each staff member had been allocated a cabinet and workspace. A wooden rack displayed various books, journals and periodicals and a felt board presented schedules and other pertinent documents. Two well-used sofas, a large wall-mounted flat screen television, a projector, a hi-fi unit and several desktop computers equipped the room for practical, functional and leisure use.

The far end of the main room led to a smaller kitchen area with a sink, electric hob, microwave oven, kettle and refrigerator. The ornate brass hands and Roman numerals on an old, round, over-sized wall-clock reassured Kaya that he had to endure just eight minutes with Obeah Widow. At 1:10 PM, the school bell would signal the end of the lunch break and the promise of Haemoglobin's double biology class. Kaya looked forward to a hasty escape.

"So, I expect you're wondering why I brought you here, Abaniah," said Obeah Widow, staring intently at Kaya's averted eyes, while the old clock ticked loudly.

"Yes, Mistress Mallory," said Kaya, suddenly noticing her Lilly of the Night perfume and low cut dress, but doing his best to mask his suspiciousness.

"Abaniah, as you know, I am not one to mince my words," she said with an unnervingly confident smile, and Kaya gulped audibly. "All is not well at Paria College."

"How yuh mean Miss?"

"Abaniah, you may have noticed I am neither a doe-eyed schoolgirl nor a wizened old maid," said Obeah Widow, continuing to smile uncharacteristically, "Please address me as Mistress Mallory."

Kaya felt the blood rush to his cheeks. "Sorry, Mistress Mallory…. How yuh mean all not well?"

Obeah Widow said, "Now-now, don't be coy, young man," and her smile slowly faded. "In the eighteen months I've been at this college, inter-house rivalry has become a dangerous obsession, bullies maraud the hallways, and a student suffered mysterious sudden death."

Kaya stared at the imposing black woman unable to deliver an appropriate response. He listened to the ticking of the staff room's old wall clock, which now reminded him of a time bomb.

"Abaniah, what I am about to discuss with you is … shall we say, strictly off the record."

"Oh?" asked Kaya, and his voice wavered.

"Can I have your word that my faith in you will not be betrayed?"

"Ahm…. Of course, Mistress Mallory," replied Kaya, and he continued to avert his eyes with respect.

Obeah Widow curled her upper lip. "Look at me when you speak," she said.

Kaya gazed into the unsettling dark eyes of the middle-aged woman. Recalling how she had continued to protect him from Cobo and the Mapepires, he sincerely said, "Yuh have meh word."

"Sit," she said, pulling out one of the boardroom chairs, Kaya sat as instructed and Obeah Widow sat next to him.

Dis 'oman well an' truly creepin' meh out, thought Kaya, in response to her unusual behaviour.

"Relax, Abaniah. It may surprise you to learn that we have much in common, you and I," said Obeah Widow. "You see, I too, grew up without the support of a father."

Kaya squirmed in his chair. "Ah didn't know dat, Mistress Mallory."

"That is perfectly understandable, considering that since my dear mother died, I have never discussed the man with anyone. Oh, to be honest, he abandoned us when I was almost too young to even remember him," she said, waving her hands dismissively. "So, you see, I too have been shrouded by a spirit of rejection and experienced the pain and humiliation of being called a bastard child. I too have suffered the sting of the bully's tongue and the blows of his fists. Some people actually gain great delight from hurting others. Sadly, this is often due to either fear or envy," said Obeah Widow, wistfully. "As a result, I wasted many years consumed by furious anger. Cynicism, sarcasm, negativity and distrust, are but a few manifestations of anger. And, all anger seeks to harm another. The saddest part is that I only recognised it when I met my beloved husband. That is why I would like to help you, Abaniah. I sense much anger in you."

Wow, thought Kaya, *like Obeah Widow worried ah go join de dark side.*

Obeah Widow continued with a chuckle. "You see, my husband helped me to discover laughter. He changed me, thank God. Because of him, I've come to realise that the only really worthwhile things in life are those that would put a smile on my face on my deathbed. Once in a while, someone makes me angry, but it soon passes, and I find myself laughing at him or her again."

Kaya found himself at a complete loss for words.

"Was Kerwin Duff bullying you, just before he collapsed and died, Abaniah?"

Suddenly, caught completely off guard, Kaya felt as if all the blood in his body rushed to his head. "Well.... Ahm.... Ah suppose, yuh could say—"

"Were you angry?" interrupted Obeah Widow, her eyes attempting to stare into Kaya's soul.

Kaya felt dizzy. "Ah doh know wha' yuh mean," he lied.

"Your honesty is required if I am to help you, boy."

The school bell rang, interrupting Kaya's desperate struggle to find his voice.

And, a moment later, Shaka Duna's distinctively raspy South African accent startled Kaya. "Mistress Mallory, when you have a moment—"

"Thank you, Mr Duna," said Obeah Widow, raising her open palm, and not turning to greet the lean college dean, "I have not forgotten our appointment." Not breaking eye contact with Kaya, she added, "If ever you have any further difficulties grasping the finer points of the Treaty of Versailles, please do not hesitate to seek my assistance again, Abaniah. Now, hurry along to Mr Balgobin's class."

"T'ank yuh, Mistress Mallory," said Kaya, nervously. "Ah appreciate yuh help."

Kaya escaped. Skipping three steps at a time, he ran down the stairway from the staff room. Under the canopy, he caught his breath and gathered his thoughts.

Where is Mr Rapp when ah need him?

Wiping beads of perspiration from his troubled brow, he hurriedly made his way to Haemoglobin's biology class.

36

FRIDAY

On Friday afternoon, immediately after double English literature, Kaya swapped his college uniform for a grey T-shirt, black tracksuit bottoms and black-striped running shoes.

"Good choice of attire," said Tom, "if you can't beat Leotaud, you shouldn't have any trouble running away from him."

"Tom, yuh talkin' like yuh expectin' meh tuh lose."

"Remind me again who your instructor is? Oh, I forgot, it's a secret. Listen, even if your mystery teacher taught you every day after the bike shed incident, I don't understand how you could possibly be ready to defend yourself against the likes of Adrian Leotaud. He's bigger, stronger, faster—"

"Yuh talkin' 'bout Leotaud or Colonel Steve Austin?"

"Abbers, unless you have cyborg arms, I can't imagine this fight ending well for you."

Kaya chuckled. "Leotaud might be bigger an' stronger, buh he ain't faster. Yuh see wha' ah do tuh Cobo an' Deron."

"I saw what two bungling idiots did to themselves—"

"Dat is what yuh wearin'?" interrupted Sean Charles, and he gesticulated wildly. "How yuh go buss style when yuh dress up like dat, Breds? Where de headband, de black belt, de kung fu shoes?"

"Ah just goin' tuh put ah stop to de Mapepire harassment. It'll be quick an' nobody will get hurt."

"Oh-ho…. Yuh tell Leotaud? Because, ah hear he say he ent takin' no prisoners. He talkin' 'bout breakin' yuh legs, Dread."

"We shall see," said Kaya, calmly.

Wendy gave Kaya a warm hug and whispered, "Are you sure about this?"

"Yeah, ah sure," replied Kaya, softly.

"I brought a box of bandages, just in case, eh? But the way everyone's talking, I kinda think I should have ordered a hearse."

"Doh worry, doux-doux, ah know what ah doin'."

"Doux-doux? I like that," said Wendy, breaking the hug and landing a quick peck on Kaya's cheek. "Whoever invented the hug was a genius."

Tom and Sean exchanged troubled glances before rolling their eyes.

With his college uniform tucked into the rucksack he carried on his back, Kaya, Wendy and a small band of his supporters made the thirty-minute trek on foot, to Coconut Grove Community Sports Centre, home away from home for Adrian Leotaud, whose Flaming Dragon Academy met six times a week, under the expert tutelage of Sensei Ira *Iron Fist* Thompson. Located in the heart of Coconut Grove, the newly renovated facility offered a 20-metre swimming pool, 18-station gym, impressive multi-purpose studio, sports hall and an outdoor multi-use games area.

Silently intrigued, Kaya read the Flaming Dragon code of honour, which he found posted on the closed door of the studio:

I will realise my full potential.
I will learn from my mistakes and those of others.
I will act without hatred or contempt.
I will maintain an open mind.
I will respect those in authority.
I will be loyal and true to those deserving of my allegiance.
My actions will be lawful and just.
If at all possible, I will subdue my opponents without fighting.
I will be merciful when victorious.
I will be a good example to others.

"Dis deep, man," muttered Kaya to himself. Turning to Tom, he asked the rhetorical question, "How it is, Leotaud could learn karate since he was four an' break every single one ah dees codes?"

Tom shrugged. "He's a prat."

Kaya, Wendy, Sean and the others laughed.

"He's a prat that's still the reigning under-18 Karate Champion of Trinidad and Tobago," added Tom, adjusting his spectacles before stroking his chin thoughtfully. "Are you absolutely sure you're up for this?"

"Ah sure, Tom. It go be alright."

"Shouldn't there be a medic or an ambulance on standby, just in case?" asked Wendy.

"T'anks fuh de vote ah confidence," said Kaya, and he pushed the studio door open.

Suddenly, a wall of jeers greeted Kaya and his small band of mostly Ocelot supporters. The Mapepires had been very busy; at least that's what Kaya thought. It seemed they had spread the word, and Cobo, Deron, Mukesh, and all the members of Mapepire House were present in the crammed studio. They were not alone. It appeared that most Paria College students, their siblings, and even their cousins twice removed, wanted to see Kaya commit suicide by trying to fight the under-18 Karate Champion. In the crowd, Kaya spotted Meenal and Shantel. Meenal leaned against a metal crutch, taking the weight off her bandaged big toe while Shantel immediately began wading through the crowd towards them. Nearby, Kaya saw Raima. Bruce de Bulk had been speaking into her right ear, but she stared directly at Kaya — glassy-eyed, looking like a rabbit caught in headlights.

A brightly lit boxing ring dominated the studio. In its far corner, dressed in the traditional white, brushed-cotton karategi and red competition belt of Iron Fist Thompson's Flaming Dragon Academy, stood Adrian Leotaud — arms crossed, deep-set eyes smouldering and an annoyingly smug grin on his face. Turning his back to Kaya, he revealed the flame-red dragon logo of his martial arts academy. He raised his hands triumphantly and revelled in the deafening cheers of his overwhelmingly Mapepire supporters.

Slowly turning to face Kaya, Leotaud said with his annoyingly high-pitched voice, "Welcome, Abaniah, so glad you can make it. Shall we begin?"

The crowd murmured with restless anticipation as Kaya handed Tom his rucksack, but before Kaya could climb into the ring, an agitated Shantel handed him a folded piece of paper.

"What's dis?" asked Kaya.

"Just read it," replied Shantel, bluntly.

Kaya opened the note, which read:

Dear Kaya,

Please don't do this. You really don't have to prove anything to me. I don't want to see you get hurt. I realise now that I have deeply wounded you, and for that I am very sorry. I hope that someday you will find it in your heart to forgive me.

Love,
Raima

Kaya felt a knot develop in his stomach. He sucked his teeth, crumpled the note and contemptuously threw it to the floor.

Wendy picked up the creased, wrinkled note, read it with an incredulous sneer and muttered, "Wow, I'm surprised she could fit her head through the door. What an ego...."

Shantel rolled her eyes as Kaya hastily climbed into the ring. "What yuh doin'?"

"Wait a minute, Abbers," said Tom, through gritted teeth. "What do you want me to do?"

"This'll be quick, Tom," whispered Kaya, "doh worry yuh head."

"Tom, yuh not goin' tuh do anything? Unless yuh want tuh see his face kicked in yuh need tuh stop him," said Shantel.

"I've already tried," said Tom, with an audible sigh. "I've already tried."

"Let's make this simple," announced Leotaud, "Full contact. No holds barred. Knockout or submission wins."

"No problem," responded Kaya with a wide grin that both astonished and antagonised Leotaud.

Kaya noticed Raima's younger sister, Devika, huddled with a small group of giggling eleven and twelve-year-old girls. They had all changed from their college uniforms into low-cut blouses and jeans that seemed to have been sprayed on. And, they all wore heavy make-up that unintentionally made them look like schoolgirls playing dress-up games.

Adrian so ugly; he like ah caveman. And, Kaya so brave, thought Devika, and Kaya beamed at her with pride. *Dotish, but brave. After Adrian knock him senseless, ah wonder if dey will allow meh to give Kaya mouth-to-mouth resuscitation. If ah lucky, ah might even be able tuh keep one ah he teeth!*

Devika's thoughts wiped Kaya's smile from his face.

"Whoa-whoa-whoa," came a familiar voice over the din of spectators. "What is going on here? What is really goin' on here?"

Glancing over his shoulder, Kaya immediately spotted Miss Mow Dem. Dressed in a dark blue jogging suit; she pushed her way through the crowd with Curtis *Iceberg* Joseph doing his level best to follow her.

Joseph, yuh just love commesse, oui, thought Kaya.

"OK, Abaniah and Leotaud, a quiet word please," said Miss Mow Dem, sternly.

With an insincere smile, Leotaud asked, "Mrs Pascale, how are you today?"

"Leotaud, yuh see right now? You and I will get along so much better if yuh wipe dat schupid grin from yuh face. Now, this is how it is going tuh be. I'll ask de questions, and you just have tuh answer dem. Where is yuh sensei — Sensei Thompson?"

"He not here," came Leotaud's blunt response.

"Right. Ah have to admit, now I am quite confused, Leotaud. Surely, you have no intentions of engaging this child in an unsupervised fight, without qualified adjudication or even the most basic first aid facilities?"

"Well…. Ahm—"

"Because, young man, if that is your intention, I will have you banned, stripped of your title, and singing falsetto in an operatic comedy."

Kaya did well not to burst out laughing.

"Sorry, Miss," said Leotaud, "Ah really don't know what that means…."

"Use yuh imagination, tough guy."

"So, tell meh, exactly what is dis about?"

"Just ah friendly competition, nuttin' tuh stress yuh," said Leotaud.

"Is dat right, Abaniah?" asked Miss Mow Dem, staring intently into Kaya's brown eyes.

"Yes, Miss," said Kaya, "just ah friendly fight."

"Since you are not wearing a karategi, I can only assume dat you don't have one. So, Abaniah, my question to you is, have you actually had any training in karate or any other martial art, for that matter?"

"Ah have de proper training," said Kaya.

"Oh, is dat so? Who is yuh sensei, is his name Bruce, Chuck, Jackie or Jet?"

"Ah know what ah doin', Miss," said Kaya, with calm confidence.

"I see," said Miss Mow Dem. "Something tell meh if I stop dis fight here today, you two will just find another venue. So I will supervise this friendly competition—"

Leotaud began to say, "T'ank yuh, Miss—"

"Ah not finished. This is Kumite, not MMA. You will have a single round lasting three minutes. Any attempt whatsoever tuh deliberately knock out yuh opponent will lead to immediate disqualification. You are both under 18. Therefore, no touch or contact to the head, face or neck, is allowed with hand techniques. The head, the face, the neck, the chest, the abdomen, the back, and the side, are your only scoring areas for controlled foot techniques. Leotaud, yuh listening?"

Leotaud yawned. "Yes, Mrs Pascale."

"Waza-ari, an effective technique such as a punch to the abdomen, will earn you one point. Awasete Ippon, two effective techniques will earn you two points. A decisive technique or Ippon, such as a controlled kick to the head will earn you three points. And, Leotaud, by *controlled* I mean the lightest touch. I certainly do not mean trying to knock Abaniah's head off his shoulders. A sweep immediately followed by an effective technique can also earn you Ippon. But before I let yuh fight Abaniah, he will need to convince me that he is competent. I am not going tuh allow a beginner tuh risk serious injury fighting an expert," said Miss Mow Dem, climbing into the boxing ring. "Excuse us a minute, Leotaud."

Leotaud reluctantly obeyed by slowly exiting the fight area with an exaggerated swagger. He stepped down to floor level and stared at Kaya, stroking his hairless chin and shaking his head derisively.

"Abaniah, show meh what yuh could do," said Miss Mow Dem.

"How yuh mean?" asked Kaya, unable to hide his confusion.

Miss Mow Dem removed her jogging shoes. "Yuh know how tuh fight?"

"Yes."

"OK then, take off yuh runnin' shoes and yuh football socks, ah need to assess yuh techniques."

Kaya complied, removing his inappropriate footwear. He rolled his socks, tucked one in each shoe, and handed them to Wendy.

"Phew, Abaniah, ah could smell yuh toe jam from here," mocked Cobo, prompting further jeers and insults from the Mapepires.

"Like is fight he fightin' she, oui. Well, boy, is dead he dead now," said a girl in the crowd.

"Right," said Miss Mow Dem, loudly addressing the assembled spectators. "The tournament between Leotaud and Abaniah is supposed tuh be a friendly fight, but I am getting the impression that most of you are far from friendly. I expect each and every Paria student to comport themselves with the required respect and dignity befitting Trinidad's best secondary school, so I absolutely do not want tuh hear another insult, condescending remark or slur. Is that clear?"

The laughter and name-calling subsided. No one messed with the grim-faced ICT master.

"I said, is that clear?"

"Yes," grumbled several students.

"Attack me," said Miss Mow Dem, to Kaya.

Miss Mow Dem, an experienced Nidan — 2nd Dan black belt expert, assumed a karate fighting-stance then began bobbing backwards and forwards on her toes in typical point-fighter fashion.

"Meh style fuh defence, not offence," said Kaya.

Miss Mow Dem chuckled, shaking her head. "Yuh might want tuh raise yuh guard then."

Kaya shifted his body weight to his back leg, but he kept his guard low, giving nothing away. "Dat's alright," he said with a confident grin.

Suddenly Miss Mow Dem's smile vanished. She launched a rapid attack with controlled punches that failed to connect with Kaya's chest. Moving with blistering speed, Kaya sidestepped and delivered a decisive punch to the side of Miss Mow Dem's unprotected body, uttering a kiai battle cry. Suddenly, the boxing hall fell silent as shock gripped the onlookers.

"Buh wha' trouble is dis?" muttered Sean Charles, breaking the silence.

Kaya's few supporters clapped and cheered. Leotaud shook his head and attempted to hide his amazement with a jaded smile.

"Hmmm. Well done, Abaniah," said Miss Mow Dem, her eyebrows raised in astonishment. "Perfect technique. It seems I may have underestimated your abilities." Once again, she adopted a karate fighting-stance. "OK. One more time."

Miss Mow Dem launched into punch and kick combinations, briefly forcing Kaya into retreat as he easily avoided each and every blow. Unexpectedly, Kaya tapped Miss Mow Dem across the cheek with his instep. He had executed a controlled round kick so swift that all she saw was a blur. However, control came easily to Kaya — it was an integral part of Tolan Rapp's dream training.

Kaya recalled Tolan Rapp saying, *"Tay Mo is for self-defence, not revenge."*

The crowd roared, and pride briefly got the better of Miss Mow Dem; at least that's what Kaya thought. Her front leg crescent kick missed its target. Kaya saw it coming and instinctively positioned himself to take advantage of her follow-up back leg kicking attack. He swept Miss Mow Dem's front leg. She fell backwards, hard on her shoulders, a moment before Kaya landed a restrained, perfectly executed punch to her exposed solar plexus. And then, he offered his hand to assist his stunned ICT teacher to her feet.

"Sorry, Miss," said Kaya, softly.

"Doh apologise, Abaniah. Impressive, very impressive," said Miss Mow Dem, with an embarrassed smile, dismissing Kaya's offer of assistance.

Kaya heard Wendy's jubilant squeals above the appreciative shouts of the Ocelots. And, to his amazement, he realised that even some of the Mapepires were also cheering. The studio was in an uproar, but predictably, Leotaud, Cobo, Deron, and Bruce de Bulk feigned apathy with slow, rhythmic, unenthusiastic clapping. Raima was no longer at Bruce's side. In fact, Raima was nowhere to be seen. However, Devika and her young girlfriends simply looked up at Kaya admiringly.

Why skin teeth Wendy doh go back tuh Canada, an' leave Kaya alone? thought Devika, and Kaya heard her. *Kaya so talented....*

37

BANANAS

During Kaya's brief assessment bout with Miss Mow Dem, Sensei Ira *Iron Fist* Thompson arrived with a small, grim-looking entourage of mature martial artists. The tall, grey-haired, muscular black man spoke to Adrian Leotaud in hushed tones. Miss Mow Dem excused herself, left Kaya standing alone in the boxing ring, and joined the conversation with the Flaming Dragons.

"That was amazing, eh?" said Wendy, gleefully, "I can't wait to watch Loser Leotaud swallow his pride."

Despite her best efforts, Shantel could not hide her sense of relief.

"Well, Mr Miyagi will be proud," said Tom, "but I hope you realise, you won't be earning any more house points for ICT after today."

Kaya laughed.

"Doh fete too soon, Iron Fist look like he goin' tuh stop de fight," said Sean Charles.

Iron Fist approached Kaya, who still stood alone in the boxing ring. He spoke quickly — almost impatiently. "Yuh name Abu Nada?"

"Abaniah," said Kaya, calmly.

"Abba...." he said, not quite getting Kaya's name. "Alright, ah understan' yuh wan' tuh fight Leotaud?"

"Yeah, sir," said Kaya.

"Hmmm.... Leotaud is one ah meh best students. At thirteen, he was de youngest karateka tuh be awarded a black belt by meh academy. Yuh know he's de under-18 Karate Champion?"

Kaya said, "Yes."

"An', ah assume yuh familiar with meh code."

Kaya nodded.

"Meh senior students will officiate, and Mrs Pascale will referee," came Iron Fist's rapid-fire verbal delivery. "Yuh know de Japanese terms? Hajime means *begin*. Tsuzukete means *continue de match*. Yame means *stop*. It important tuh stop once she call yame. Anyway, ah understan' yuh already know de rules."

Kaya nodded again, "Yes."

"Alright, alright," announced Iron Fist to the expectant spectators in the boxing studio, "Abby Nanah will fight Leotaud in a three-minute match." Rapturous laughter ensued. "De first competitor tuh get eight points, wins de bout."

Leotaud quickly dashed up the four narrow steps leading to the elevated ring. And, firmly gripping the top rope with both hands, he launched himself off his left leg into a reverse vault. He landed in the boxing ring, triumphantly lifting both hands to the appreciative cheers of his many supporters.

"Ready?" Tom asked Kaya.

"Yeah, man. Pass meh de water," said Kaya.

Tom pulled a plastic water bottle from an elastic pocket at the side of Kaya's rucksack. He threw it at Kaya, who effortlessly caught it and quickly took a swig. His thirst quenched; Kaya hurled the bottle back to Tom's waiting hands.

"T'anks," said Kaya.

"Hezekiah, what are you doing?"

"Mr Rapp?" thought Kaya.

"Yes, Hezekiah."

"Ah goin' tuh teach ah bully ah lesson."

"Oh? That may prove somewhat difficult."

"How yuh mean? Ah know karate."

"I have trained you to defend yourself using the Cyclan art of Tay Mo, but you may find it somewhat ineffective while you are under the influence of a psychotropic drug...."

"What?" shouted Kaya, and everyone heard him.

He stood in the suddenly silent boxing studio, trying his best to flash a nonchalant smile. Miss Mow Dem shot a puzzled look at Leotaud, who shrugged with a mixture of confusion and amusement.

"Everything all right, Abaniah?" asked Miss Mow Dem.

Somebody put somet'ing in meh water.... thought Kaya.

Everything was far from all right. Kaya had begun to hallucinate, and he was not sure, which of Miss Mow Dem's two enlarged heads he should address.

"Yes," said Kaya, choosing the wrong head.

"Yuh sure?" asked Miss Mow Dem, suspiciously.

"Yeah, ah sure," said Kaya.

Kaya was never a very good liar.

"Face yuh opponent. Bow. Hajime."

Bristling with aggression, Leotaud immediately launched a low reverse roundhouse kick, slightly clipping the ankle of Kaya's front leg with his heel. Fortunately, despite the effects of the hallucinogen, Kaya had been able to anticipate this first move; nevertheless, distracted by a troupe of man-sized dancing bananas wearing ornate Mexican sombreros, Kaya simply did not see Leotaud's follow-up mid reverse roundhouse kick. It slammed into his ribs. Caught off-balance, Leotaud's high reverse roundhouse heel kick perfectly impacted with the back of Kaya's head, knocking him sprawling to the ground.

"Yame," yelled Miss Mow Dem.

"Well, fight done. Time tuh go home," shouted Cobo.

And, the dancing bananas, the Mapepires, and all of Leotaud's supporters laughed as if they had heard the greatest joke ever told.

"Wha'ppen, Banana Head, like yuh forget tuh eat yuh spinach?" whispered Leotaud, intriguing Kaya with his new corncob pipe and Dixie-cup hat.

Miss Mow Dem, who had disturbingly developed scaly lime-green skin and a deep purple Afro, wore a fluorescent pink tutu. She approached Kaya, accompanied by a mature male karateka with a chicken's head, gigantic hands and long nails painted with light-blue polish.

"Yuh OK, Abby Nanah?" asked the concerned karateka, and he sounded as if he had been breathing helium.

"His name is Abaniah," said Miss Mow Dem, with a voice like thunder.

"Ah OK," said Kaya, rubbing his head and resisting an almost overwhelming urge to run away.

Miss Mow Dem cautioned Leotaud for excessive contact. When the judges deducted a point from his score, the sombrero-wearing bananas began to moonwalk on their spindly legs. Even so, in this first exchange, Leotaud had easily gained half the points required to win the tournament.

Hmmm, it look like Kaya might need mouth-to-mouth resuscitation after all, mused Devika, gleefully.

Something's wrong, thought Wendy, fearfully, and Kaya heard her.

Kaya looked around the boxing studio, which now seemed to be full of cartoon characters. And there, silently standing between Donald Duck and Scooby-Doo, were the men in black — the Shu-Senyn. However, Kaya could not tell if they were real or just figments of his drugged imagination. Kaya tried to control his rising rage; he tried not to dwell on the distinct possibility that someone, he trusted, had poisoned him. Was the Mad Renegade in the crowd?

Batman lookin' real suspicious, thought Kaya.

He chuckled at the absurdity of his predicament as Leotaud appeared before him — a smug, hairy, cross-eyed Neanderthal with a vulgar, gold-toothed smile.

Ah wonder if Leotaud use metal polish tuh brush he teeth?

"Tsuzukete," said Miss Mow Dem.

Once again, Leotaud rushed forward, but this time, Kaya ignored all distractions — real or unreal. Kaya avoided two reverse punches, blocked a dangerous roundhouse kick, counterpunched and scored a point by hitting Leotaud firmly in the abdomen. This really annoyed Leotaud, who immediately retaliated with a hasty tornado kick, but instinct took Kaya out of range of its potentially devastating blow. And, as Leotaud landed, Kaya responded with a flying scissor kick. With his left leg pressed against Leotaud's chest, and his right leg positioned behind his knees, Kaya brought Leotaud down to the mat, flat on his back. A decisive heel kick to his fallen foe's solar plexus earned Kaya an Ippon, bringing his score equal with Leotaud's four points.

"Yame," shouted Miss Mow Dem.

To no avail, Kaya tried to shake the unsettling image of deranged bananas wearing thick-rimmed, dark glasses. The broadly smiling, yellow creatures, performed a traditional Hawaiian hula dance around him. Alarmingly, most of the crowd now appeared to be rainbow-coloured cockroaches. The rest had become oversized, overweight, horse flies. Kaya felt he was losing what little remained of his mind. Before his tainted gaze, Leotaud seemed to transform into a slimy bug-eyed monster, with a smile that only his insectoid mother could appreciate.

"Tsuzukete," said Miss Mow Dem. Little green men played peek-a-boo in her hair, and she sounded like a badly warped, vinyl record.

Monster Leotaud employed caution — feinting, constantly switching his stance, bobbing back and forth while looking like an overactive B-movie reject, at least to Kaya. In Kaya's nightmarish hallucination, Leotaud suddenly began performing an Irish jig. He even wore a lovely green maid's dress and matching green shoes. But, in reality, Leotaud had unleashed a bone-crushing, perfectly executed side kick into Kaya's midsection. Kaya almost lost his lunch.

"Focus, Hezekiah," said Tolan Rapp's voice.

"Go away," thought Kaya. *"Ah doh t'ink yuh name is Tolan Rap; yuh name is Farrell, de spaceman from Hell."*

"Yes, Hezekiah. Tell the annoying man in your head to go away," said an unforgettable woman's voice. *"There is nothing in the water you drank, you know. I'm afraid, dear fellow, the problem is all in your shattered mind."*

"Mad Renegade…." said Kaya, and everyone close to the boxing ring heard him.

"Yame," yelled Miss Mow Dem. "Abaniah, yuh OK?" She stared at Kaya with magenta eyes as big as saucers.

"Yes, Mrs Pascale," lied Kaya, and he smiled wistfully when one of the little green men, who inhabited the ICT teacher's hair, winked at him.

De Mad Renegade is ah shape-shifter. She could be anyone, thought Kaya.

He glanced down at Wendy, who now wore a large, pink, polka dot Minnie Mouse bow in her hair. However, her glassy eyes seemed like open windows that promised boundless compassion. Standing next to her, Tom sported a yellow bowler hat and futuristic silver spectacles that glowed orange.

Tom mouthed, "What is going on?"

"Mad?" said the Mad Renegade's voice. *"You call me mad? You hear and see things that do not exist. You believe you are an alien-human hybrid with psychic abilities. Your symptoms include muddled thoughts, hallucinations, delusions and abnormal behaviour! Now tell me, which one of us is really mad, Hezekiah?"*

"Tsuzukete," said Miss Mow Dem, yanking Kaya's thoughts back to the tournament.

The room began to spin, just as Leotaud launched his vicious attack. Kaya tried to ignore some of what he saw. Limbo-dancing bananas were somewhat disconcerting, especially when your opponent's two arms appeared as four. Kaya did his best to block, but the unknown drug, he had haplessly imbibed, wreaked havoc on his autonomic nervous system and his reflexes.

Like is mad ah gone mad, thought Kaya.

And, when Leotaud scored another point with a perfect reverse punch, Kaya began laughing. He had great difficulty stopping. Leotaud needed just one more point to secure his eight-point victory.

"Yame," said Miss Mow Dem. She warned Kaya, "Like yuh not taking dis seriously. Buck up or you'll lose a point."

"Tsuzukete."

To everyone's surprise, Kaya briefly assumed the role of aggressor. Leotaud had become complacent, and Kaya caught him off guard with a blisteringly fast reverse punch to the ribs. Having earned a total of five points, Kaya could instantly win the tournament if he scored another Ippon. However, Leotaud immediately retaliated, driving Kaya into desperate retreat with a vicious volley of kicks and punches. Kaya sensed that Leotaud no longer cared if he got disqualified; the vengeful Flaming Dragon simply wanted to deliver a massive dose of pain and humiliation. A flying side kick and multiple punches, followed by a spinning crescent kick, followed by a blocked bicycle kick, had Kaya back pedalling to the edge of the fight area. However, just as Leotaud poised to deliver his winning blow, Kaya launched himself forward into a spectacular inverted tornado kick, tapping the back of Leotaud's head with his right instep. Upside down, Kaya hit the canvas with his shoulders, just as a shocked disorientated Leotaud rolled to his side. Kaya recovered quickly springing to his feet.

Ippon!

The Ocelots jumped for joy, and their enemies stared in utter disbelief, as Miss Mow Dem raised Kaya's right arm, victoriously.

"Abaniah wins," said a mysteriously dark voice, and the troupe of demented bananas began to wine.

"Fight done. Time tuh go home," said Sean Charles to Cobo and the Mapepires, and he laughed derisively.

Leotaud and Cobo appeared to be about to combust spontaneously with embarrassment.

"Ah doh believe it," muttered Cobo.

Kaya, my hero, swooned Devika.

Wendy simply looked at Kaya with love in her eyes and the warmest, broadest smile on her face. Kaya laughed and laughed, and the dancing bananas laughed too.

38

DRAGON ASSASSIN

After the Flaming Dragon Tournament, which is how his match with Leotaud became widely known, no one continued to refer to Kaya as *Puppy Dog*, *Banana Head* or even *Ah Banana*. To the vast majority of students at Paria College, he had simply become either *Kaya* or *Abaniah*. In private, and among other things, Wendy called him *doux-doux*, but a growing number of pupils called Kaya, *Dragon Assassin*, and the Mapepires simply did not call him. They said nothing to him at all.

Sean Charles had inadvertently coined the nickname while impersonating a blustery overly dramatic American sportscaster.

"The unrivalled tournament record of Adrian Leotaud, shining star of Iron Fist Thompson's Flaming Dragon Academy, went up in furious flames, when he suffered humiliating defeat by dragon assassin, Hezekiah Abaniah," cried Sean. "With a thunderous tornado kick, Abaniah doused Leotaud's raging fire, in an upset more stunning than the Rumble in the Jungle and more electrifying than the Thrilla in Manila. And this esteemed commentator firmly believes that the world of martial arts will never be the same again."

On Friday afternoon, moments after he had defeated Leotaud, Kaya discovered that his water bottle was missing. His friends had been focussed on the dramatic events in the boxing ring and had not noticed the removal of the bottle from his rucksack. Was the shape-shifting Mad Renegade among the spectators? The voice of Tolan Rapp had told Kaya that the drug, he drank, had been designed to disorientate, not kill. And Kaya wondered if Cobo would go to such great lengths to humiliate him.

As Tom and Kaya walked back to the Methodist parsonage, where his mountain bike was kept, Kaya felt his faculties slowly return to normal. He asked Tom if he had noticed a pair of very pale men dressed in black suits, wearing black hats and sunglasses. Tom explained that he was certain that the Blues Brothers had not been at the fight. Kaya decided not to confess to Tom that he heard voices. He decided not to tell anyone at all.

For the most part, Kaya's ride home from the Methodist parsonage had been uneventful until he noticed a Roman gladiator taking his pet goldfish for a walk. And, being chased for fifteen minutes by an extremely irate lamppost, left Kaya utterly exhausted. Relieved that Josephine had been attending her weekly Zumba dance fitness class, Kaya went straight to bed and slept soundly until the following morning.

39

PRIZES AND SURPRISES

Almost choking, as he did his best not to laugh, Eldred Seymour Gobelyn said, "Master Curtis Joseph, I found your World War II essay to be admirably imaginative and somewhat intriguing; however, your work continues to suffer from a profoundly detrimental lack of research. I daresay, this stunning extract from your epic perfectly illustrates my point."

"Queen Elizabeth I raced through the back garden of Buckingham Palace to the large garden shed, where, unknown to the commander of the German Tiger tank, she kept her secret bazooka...."

Gobelyn found himself unable to continue as the students in the class succumbed to fits of laughter.

"So, Joseph," said Gobelyn, trying unsuccessfully to compose himself, "where should I begin? It may surprise you to learn that Elizabeth I was the daughter of Henry VIII. She was queen regnant of England and Ireland from 1558 until her death in 1603, several centuries before the advent of World War II. Now, it did occur to me that you might have meant Elizabeth II. But, although Her Majesty's public duties commenced during the Second World War, and she remains the only female member of the British Royal Family to have served in the armed forces, Elizabeth II had been heiress presumptive but not queen. Her father was King George VI, the reigning British monarch during World War II. Her mother, who was also called Elizabeth, was queen consort of the United Kingdom and the British Dominions, not queen regnant. Clear as mud?"

Sporadic laughter resumed, and despite the darkness of his sunburnt skin, the redness of Curtis Joseph's cheeks became starkly apparent as he smiled with nervous embarrassment.

"Furthermore," said Gobelyn, shaking his head in dismay, "the Germans never invaded Britain during World War II. So, I have to say, Joseph, I found your detailed account of Nazi stormtroopers crossing the English Channel on coconut-oil-powered jet-skis rather unsettling."

As most of the 4P students rolled with glee, Kaya heard Deron say, "Iceberg boy, it ent yuh fault yuh come from ah parallel universe...."

With a twinkle in his hazel eyes, Gobelyn continued, "You have a great imagination, Joseph — badly let down by your lack of attention to detail. The English certificate of merit and 30 house points, for this year's essay competition, will be awarded to Miss Meenal Baboolal of Ocelot House, for her story entitled, *Trouble in the Azura Forest*. I am told, this creative work was partly inspired by dramatic events during the last college hike. Miss Baboolal cleverly included folkloric figures such as Papa Bois and the Douen, as well as topical issues, such as conservation and poaching, in a very well-written piece. Bravo, Miss Baboolal."

As they clapped, Kaya, Tom, and Raima exchanged uneasy glances. Gobelyn invited Meenal to read her work to the class, and she self-consciously hobbled to the rostrum on her crutches. Several of his classmates seemed unimpressed, but Kaya listened intently to all that Meenal had to say.

The protagonist of Meenal's essay, a 14-year-old girl named Miriam, had been on a college expedition exploring a large cave complex in the Azura Forest, when she responded to the eerie calls of the Douen and became separated from her group. Scared and lost, Miriam stumbled upon the secret hideout of a band of ruthless, heavily armed poachers. They caught and threatened to kill her. However, Papa Bois, who had been observing the poachers' criminal activities for some time, used a cunning combination of trickery and supernatural wizardry to terrify and subsequently imprison them in their cages. He rescued Miriam; and, together, they freed the rare animals and birds the poachers had illegally captured. Nonetheless, the police also had the poachers under surveillance. But when they stormed the cave, intent on making arrests, Miriam helped Papa Bois to escape by creating a diversion. Miriam deliberately fell into a deep pool of water and pretended to be unable to swim, prompting two handsome police officers to rescue her as Papa Bois slipped away unnoticed.

Tom did his best to reassure Kaya that he had said nothing to Meenal about their encounter with Papa Bois. Tom believed that Raima had not said anything either, but Kaya remained sceptical.

"If yuh want de whole world to know somet'ing, tell a woman," Mama Flo often told Kaya.

"Meenal just has a vivid imagination," said Tom.

"She actin' real weird recently," said Kaya.

"Abbers, all girls are weird. The sooner you grasp that universal concept, the better it will be for you," said Tom, matter-of-factly.

The following day, the Paria College students and the proud parents of those receiving awards, assembled in the large auditorium for the Annual Prize-giving Ceremony — one of the few events that required uncomfortable college blazers to be worn. Hot and bothered, Kaya sat sandwiched between his dewy-eyed mother, Josephine, and Meenal and her perpetually beaming mother, Madhula. Wendy took her place in front of them, next to Shantel, who had been accompanied by her parents. Cobo and his mother occupied front row centre, and his Mapepire cohorts huddled together three rows behind. Kaya overheard Deron and Mukesh placing bets on which of the lower form pupils would faint in the sweltering heat. All the sixth-formers, including Adrian Leotaud and Bruce de Bulk, looked down to the stage from their seats in the exclusive balcony.

The proceedings began with a rousing interpretation of the Trinidad and Tobago National Anthem by the Paria College Steel and Brass Band, energetically conducted by Master Shen who tossed his dreadlocks, tiptoed, and even leapt off his feet with enthusiasm. There followed a bland welcome speech by Chairwoman of the Board of Governors, Eliza Corbeau, Cobo's permanently overdressed mother, then a solemn opening prayer by Rev Samuel Cyrus. The Paria College Choir, which included Tom and Raima, led the singing of the popular Christian hymn, *Blessed Assurance*, accompanied by Master Shen on organ; after which, Hairy Harry delivered his ramblingly verbose headmaster's address.

Wendy had glanced at Kaya several times during the opening segments, and this had not gone unnoticed.

"Dat is yuh girlfriend?" asked Josephine, in a whisper, and Kaya rolled his eyes. "Hmmm…. She look cunning…."

"Yuh doh know her," said Kaya, through gritted teeth.

"An' why is dat?" said Josephine, in a honeyed tone. "Invite the pretty young lady to dinner, ah would very much like tuh meet de gyul yuh takin' tuh yuh Christmas Ball."

Kaya had earned himself a certificate of merit and gained 30 points for Ocelot House by winning the forms 4 and 5 art competition. Kaya's entry to the *Most Beautiful Scene in the World* challenge was an impressionistic acrylic painting on canvas board. Entitled, *View from the Montserrat Hills on a Rainy Day*, it depicted a panorama of the Gulf of Paria as seen from the courtyard of Tortuga's Our Lady of Montserrat Roman Catholic Church. Located high on a picturesque ridge in Trinidad's Central Range, Our Lady of Montserrat was arguably Trinidad and Tobago's oldest church, and a very special place to Kaya and his family.

Praising Kaya's dedication to the visual arts, Amita Abilash, affectionately known as Miss Cutlash, commended him on painting from life and on choosing local scenery, with its typical flora and fauna, as the subjects of his artistic expression.

"With Christmas fast approaching, I feel dat Hezekiah Abaniah's choice is even more relevant," said Miss Cutlash. "I didn't know much about this particular location, so I did a tiny bit of research and discovered dat Our Lady of Montserrat was built by Spanish missionaries who arrived in Trinidad in 1687, and it is one of three Catholic missions closely associated with de birth of parang music. Well, I was very pleased to find dat de technical standard of de work submitted in dis year's challenge was very high. However, I was disappointed to find dat so many of our students chose locations from foreign lands to illustrate de most beautiful scene in de world. De overwhelming majority of dees paintings and drawings had been copied from photographs of faraway places. Places dat de artists had never even visited. I found dis very sad — very, very sad; especially when yuh consider dat dere is no shortage of natural beauty right here in Trinidad and Tobago. In fact, I am certain dat the most beautiful scene in de world is to be found right here, in dis country; and, I believe dat Kaya Abaniah will agree with me."

Miss Cutlash presented Kaya with his certificate of merit. And, Josephine and Wendy could hardly contain themselves. Smiling broadly, Kaya absorbed the applause and savoured the proud moment.

Meenal graciously accepted her certificate of merit for the English essay challenge; Shantel won the science award, Bruce de Bulk earned Hummingbird House 30 points for his excellence in football, and Cobo smugly received the prize for cricket. Curtis *Iceberg* Joseph earned the attendance award. During the past year, Curtis had always been punctual and had not missed any time away from college. The Mapepires led with 4,650 points. In second place, Hummingbird House had 4,086 points; the Ocelots were in third place with 3,975, and fourth were Tayra House with 3,845 points.

To present the final award, Vice-principal Bhekizitha *Shaka* Duna took to the stage and approached the podium.

With his deep, South African accent and inimitable gravitas ushering silent awe, Shaka Duna said, "I consider it a great personal privilege to present this year's most prestigious award, the Paria College Spirit Award. The recipient of this honour is that student whose conduct most embodies the following three virtues: heroism, kindness and consideration. The recipient is chosen by nominations from the student body, the faculty and the general public. Here are some of the things people have said about the winning nominee. 'He immediately befriended me and helped me adjust to my new life at college.' 'He risked his safety protecting me from bullies.' 'He saved our daughter from drowning....'"

And, as Shaka Duna continued to read the tributes, Kaya realised where it was all heading, and he self-consciously shrank in his chair.

"And so, it is with great pleasure," said Shaka Duna, "that I present this year's Paria College Spirit Award to Hezekiah Abaniah."

Cobo shook his head disapprovingly, but his mother quickly put a stop to his disrespect with a violent nudge of her elbow. Josephine squealed and clapped with glee, and Wendy had the look of love. All the Mapepires did little to mask their contempt — all except Mukesh. Mukesh had not forgotten that Kaya had saved him from falling from the old iron bridge. He expressed his defiant support with a solemn nod. Uncharacteristically, Shantel simply stared at Kaya with glazed eyes. And, at that moment, Kaya finally accepted what Tom had suggested. In the past, he had been so preoccupied with Raima that he neglected everyone else. Kaya smiled at Shantel, and she glowed.

Standing in the spotlight once more, wallowing in approval, Kaya gazed at a sea of familiar faces. Among them, beaming with pride and feverishly clapping was Spexy. Was she really the Mad Renegade? Could she be a shape-shifting Niburian alien? Circumstantial evidence implicated the pretty Irish teacher, but Kaya could not believe she was a psychotic killer. This was Kaya's proudest moment, and he quickly decided not to mar it with dark thoughts. Kaya earned Ocelot House an additional 150 points with this award, bringing its overall score to 4,125 points and placing it second after the Mapepires. He graciously accepted his trophy from Shaka Duna to rapturous applause.

Later, as Josephine drove Kaya home, she said softly, "Yuh doh know how proud I am, boy; yuh doh know." Then, with a sigh, she added, "Ah spoke tuh Mr Gobelyn...."

"Yeah? What yuh talk tuh him 'bout?" asked Kaya, intrigued.

"He tell meh 'bout de WHT hike tuh de Azura Forest dat yuh want tuh go on."

"Right...." said Kaya, expecting the worse.

"Ah tell him yuh could go."

"What?" said Kaya, in disbelief.

"Ah tell him yuh could go."

"Buh ah thought yuh say—"

"Listen Kaya, yuh just win de Paria College Spirit Award — yuh college most prestigious award. Yuh not ah baby anymore," said Josephine, dewy-eyed. "Tantie Rose and yuh cousins from Tortuga comin' for lunch, de Sunday after next; ah want yuh tuh invite yuh girlfriend."

Kaya's shocked elation turned into concealed concern. Would Wendy still be his girlfriend after an encounter with his relatives from the country? Would he survive the embarrassing tales of his childhood? If Wendy were to be his girlfriend, she would have to accept his family — for better or worse.

40

DREAMS WITHIN DREAMS

Aboard the Captain's Cutter, Kaya awoke within a regeneration pod, and its coffin-like dimensions had him fighting the sweaty threat of panic. But just when he thought he would lose his nerve, a familiar face sporting warm brown eyes that brimmed with wisdom peered down at him.

"Why do you not simply open the pod and exit, Hezekiah?" mentally projected Tolan Rapp.

"How? Ah doh know how...." said Kaya, unable to hide his growing anxiety.

Tolan Rapp's sonorous mental voice encouraged calm. *"Focus, Hezekiah. Focus and remember."*

Kaya centred his thoughts. He willed the Cyclan regeneration pod to open, and it did.

Climbing out of the pod, he asked, "How did I get here?"

"Do not speak, Hezekiah. You possess the ability to project your thoughts, and this is a skill worth perfecting."

"Ah doh know how ah get here," projected Kaya.

"Your thoughts are transparent. All that you see is illusion. You persist in thinking of yourself as a physical form when you are actually consciousness. You are your thoughts. Your thoughts form your reality. I brought you here, just as I have brought you every night for several weeks. I brought you here to continue your dream training."

"How come ah doh remember?"

"The knowledge resides in your subconscious, whence it is revealed when needed. We are currently conversing in a dream within a dream, and you are somewhat disorientated."

"Yes, ah remember. Dis is how yuh teach meh Tay Mo."

"Indeed. However, you have abused your knowledge and may have revealed yourself to our enemies."

"How yuh mean?"

"Your martial arts display did not escape the attention of the Shu-Senyn."

"Buh somebody drug meh—"

"Thereby preventing you from perfectly executing Cyclan fighting techniques and positively confirming their suspicions."

"Dat meh fadah is ah spaceman?"

"Their main concerns are that you are developing psychic abilities and that you are being trained by an illegal extraterrestrial."

"Buh—"

"Hezekiah, it is the hope of the Shu-Senyn that you will lead them to me. That is the only reason they have not yet killed you and your mother."

"Ah was—"

"Very foolish."

"Yuh t'ink somebody poison meh so dat de men in black wouldn't know 'bout meh training?"

"So it would seem. However, it is worth remembering that your water was drugged, not poisoned. They had no intention of causing you permanent harm."

"Buh dat mean whoever drug meh water, know who I am. Dey know meh fadah is an alien."

"Correct."

"Yuh t'ink it was de Mad Renegade dat drug meh?"

"Highly unlikely. I believe you have a protector. An Osirian protector."

"Who?"

"Did one of your peers attempt to dissuade you from fighting?"

"All meh friends try tuh talk meh outta it."

"Oh? Surely one of your friends was more vehement than the others."

"Raima…. She send meh a note…."

"And, is Raima Khan the one to whom you have given your heart?"

"Raima? Nah-nah-nah … she's jus' a gyul."

"Oh? And yet, the mere mention of her name causes your eyes to dilate, your cheeks to redden, and your heartbeat to quicken."

"Buh dat is jus' ah illusion, right? Dis is only a dream, right?"

Smiling warmly, Tolan Rapp added, *"There is no shame to be found in love, it is the true meaning of life that tragically eludes so many."*

"Ah like Raima," admitted Kaya, and he put on a brave face.

More dan she like meh….

"Sometimes people with low self-esteem will try to punish you for caring about them. However, it is possible her affection is greater than you realise. I can assure you, Raima Khan is no Osirian agent, neither is Thomas

Baker. My tests conclusively revealed that they are both Kians. Unlike the Followers of Seti, Osirians do not employ either Kians or clones as agents."

"*Who dey employ?*"

"*Osirians and Niburians — and the Niburian race is all but extinct.*"

"*Yuh t'ink one ah meh college friends is a shape-shifter?*"

"*Although they are few in number, it is a distinct possibility. Niburians are exceptionally powerful beings; who then would be better equipped to deal with a rogue Niburian than another Niburian? You said Raima Khan sent you the note?*"

"*Yes, buh Shantel was de one who actually give it tuh meh.*"

"*Are you certain Raima Khan wrote it?*"

"*Well—*"

"*How well do you know this Shantel?*" projected Tolan Rapp, impatiently.

"*Ah suppose she coulda write de note an' put somet'ing in meh water. She is ah bright gyul — she win de chemistry award.*"

Kaya had imagined that Cobo was the one who drugged him, and even if this were not the case, he could not envision Shantel being the one responsible.

She seem genuinely worried ah would get hurt, thought Kaya.

Kaya certainly could not believe Shantel was a shape shifter.

"*If one of meh friends is ah Osirian agent, ah suppose dey parents will ha' tuh be agents as well.*"

"*I believe so.*"

"*An', yuh sure de Osirians won't help yuh?*"

"*They are interested in my father's work, nothing more,*" projected Tolan Rapp, deep furrows appearing in his brow.

Dis man well stubborn, oui, thought Kaya.

Then he asked mentally, "*Mr Rapp, how yuh fadah die?*"

"*He died protecting me. He died protecting his work.*"

"*Meh grandparents—your parents—wha' really happen tuh all ah dem?*"

Tolan Rapp sighed and said, "I would rather not speak of it." He turned away from Kaya, hiding his glazed eyes. "There were just five survivors, after the Captain's Cutter crash-landed, in the heart of the great forest of Kolmården, on June 30th, 1908. Two couples — my parents, your grandparents and a marine biologist named Salya Krell were all that remained of my father's expedition. My father told me that for several days, the Talibah's explosion had left the skies aglow…."

"Wha'ppen?"

"When I was ten years old, a Setian assassin shot Salya in the back. She had not heeded my father's command and had ventured into the forest without activating her personal shield."

"Was meh fadah there?"

"Yes.... He was always with me," said Tolan Rapp, softly. "Your grandmother protected us. She fought and killed the assassin before he could kill us. And, even though she saved us all, the guilt of having taken the life of that Setian would haunt her for the rest of her life."

"And how she die?"

Tolan Rapp sighed and shook his head with dismay. "A decade later, alone in the forest, she was stung by wasps, developed a severe allergic reaction and succumbed in a matter of minutes."

Kaya's eyes widened with horror, which almost immediately gave way to grief. "Ah never knew dem. Ah never knew meh fadah."

Tolan Rapp placed his hand gently on Kaya's shoulder and said, "Violence is the vulgar failure of reason and intelligence, and Cyclans abhor it. Cyclans seldom have any respect for those employed in the evil business of war. However, my father often spoke of a Talisian warrior who saved his life on the eve of the Karellan attack. During Cyclo's darkest hour, he told my father, 'Verily; a man should not cling to those who have passed, for he will likely neglect service to the living.' These words became my father's tenet for facing death. And, there has been an abundance of death. It is also a philosophy I strive to embrace."

"What was he name?"

"Chi-Ro Jin. He helped evacuate my parents and their staff from Cyclo's moon."

"Did he wear a patch?"

Tolan Rapp stared at Kaya quizzically then said, "No. Why do you ask such a question?"

"Is jus' dat ah had a dream dat meh cousin was at ah funky party wit' military aliens, and one ah de generals had ah eye patch," said Kaya, matter-of-factly.

"Intriguing," said Tolan Rapp, raising an eyebrow.

"Why de Karellans attack a neutral colony?"

"The leader of the Karellan invasion force was obsessed with capturing a Talisian Space Marshal, who had defeated him in several decisive battles. That Space Marshal was Margrave Rin of Taria, the emperor's cousin and heir presumptive. What is particularly interesting is the fact that Rin Mur-Rain defiantly refused to have a cloned implant. Instead, he wore a primitive leather patch over his left eye."

"Yuh ha' a picture of him?"

"I can recognise his features," said Tolan Rapp, and he looked away from Kaya.

"How come; ah thought yuh born in Sweden, not Cyclo?"

"I hold some of my father's memories."

"Yuh have a way ah could see de margrave?" asked Kaya, with anticipation. "Yuh have a way ah could see meh fadah, from yuh memory?"

"Do not ask this of me, Hezekiah," snapped Tolan Rapp in an utterly unexpected flash of anger. "There are memories that are best not shared."

"Yuh doh know how lucky yuh are to know yuh fadah," said Kaya, his sad eyes unable to withstand Tolan Rapp's piercing gaze.

"Forgive me, Hezekiah," said Tolan Rapp, with a gentle sigh. "I received my father's thoughts unintentionally. It is a rare phenomenon, but, at times of profound emotional crisis, there can be a traumatic, involuntary exchange of thoughts between those we Cyclans are close to. For the psychic humans of the Cosmic Sea, this usually only occurs when faced with sudden unexpected death. Cyclans call this experience the *reckoning*. And, the experience can overwhelm even the strongest of us. My reckoning almost killed me."

"Meh fadah was able tuh help yuh?"

"Yes," said Tolan Rapp, almost inaudibly. "Yes, your father helped me. Hezekiah, I am truly sorry that you grew up not knowing him. He would be very proud of the young man you have become."

"Me? Yuh say it yuhself, ah was schupid enough tuh endanger meh own mudder by showing off."

Tolan Rapp smiled warmly. "Beauty makes fools of the wise."

"Huh?"

"Is Wendy Wong jus' a gyul?" asked Tolan Rapp, perfectly mimicking Kaya's Trinidadian accent.

"Yuh makin' fun ah meh now?" asked Kaya, and he was not smiling.

"Be careful with your heart and the heart of others. You are still very young, and even though the young are capable of the purest love, immaturity can spawn callous carelessness. Cherish those you love, but especially those who love you. Avoid the bitterness of misplaced affection; value every kindness and every act of generosity. So often, the discarded love of youth is desperately yearned for in maturity."

Like dis man sufferin' serious tabanca, thought Kaya.

"What yuh know 'bout Wendy?" he asked, tentatively.

"I should ask you that very question. Now, focus on the face you saw in your dream. Focus on the man wearing the eye patch."

"What yuh goin' tuh do?"

"If you have seen the Margrave Rin Mur-Rain, you may be developing psychic abilities beyond those of most Cyclans. I will verify his identity by probing your dream memories."

"Hang on…. What if ah doh want yuh tuh see meh dreams?"

"Don't be silly, Hezekiah."

"How yuh mean? Ah doh want yuh swimmin' in meh brain."

Exasperated, Tolan Rapp sighed heavily. "Do you want to see your father?"

"So now yuh blackmailin' meh?"

Tolan Rapp folded his arms and gazed intently at Kaya — his patience clearly wearing thin.

"Alright-alright…. Do what yuh have tuh do," said Kaya, reluctantly.

"Look into my eyes," said Tolan Rapp, firmly. "Relax. Now think of your dream. Think of the man you saw."

Kaya held Tolan Rapp's unwavering gaze, and he thought of the dream in which he saw his cousin, Raya — the dream in which she announced she was a princess. Kaya recalled the tall black military man. The man seemed young, despite sporting a moustache and beard — too young to be the gallant war hero described by Tolan Rapp. And yet, his self-assured posture, leather eye-patch, long black cape, gold sash and the six golden butterflies on each lapel of his dark grey uniform all suggested that this was no ordinary warrior.

"The Margrave Rin of Taria," announced Tolan Rapp softly, with subdued astonishment. "He wears his full dress uniform and the sash of the Order of the Tordon Raptor; this is no casual party; it is a formal imperial event with members of the Ruling House of the Cosmic Sea."

At Rin Mur-Rain's side, stood a beautiful tanned woman with deep blue eyes and long greenish blonde hair. She wore a dress layered in shimmering gold and brown that matched both her exotic features and the armorial-crested banners that hung from the ceiling.

"I do not recognise this woman," whispered Tolan Rapp.

Once more, Kaya saw his cousin, Raya. Just as before, she wore a flowing green gown with a shimmering intricately embroidered bodice. And, around her neck, Kaya noticed the green pendant that Raya's husband, Roman, had given to her on their engagement. But this time, Kaya saw something that his murky memory of a spent dream had not registered. He saw something surprising.

"Your cousin, Soraya Williams, is pregnant," said Tolan Rapp.

"Officially, she's Mrs Soraya Doyle now," said Kaya, softly, "but she'll always be jus' Raya tuh me. She pregnant? How come ah didn't remember seein' dat before?"

Sternly but calmly, Tolan Rapp said, "Do not speak. These facets are clearer now because you are asleep, and the dream continues. Now concentrate."

Ah cyah believe she pregnant and she ent tell meh nuttin', thought Kaya.

Kaya saw Raya pull up the hem of her flowing gown; with a wry grin, she began to twirl.

Laughing happily, she said, "Look at me, Kaya. Look! I'm a princess. Princess Soraya!"

Violently, someone grabbed Kaya's shoulder from behind. He spun on his heel and found himself face to face with a monstrous reptilian humanoid.

The monster hissed menacingly, "The Saurians are coming."

41

MONSTERS

Kaya awoke with a start, from a dream within a dream. He found himself inside a regeneration pod, immediately beleaguered by an overwhelming sense of déjà vu. Effortlessly, he willed the Cyclan regeneration unit to open and it did.

Climbing out of the futuristic pod, wide-eyed and visibly shaken by the terrifying conclusion of his previous dream, Kaya breathlessly asked Tolan Rapp, "What is de Saurians?"

"They are also known as the Seriak. They are reptilian humanoids that reside in the mythical realms of Talisian fairy tales. According to Talisian myth, the Seriak inhabit only the darkest vilest places and prey on weak children. Only a handful of scientists admit to believing them to be real, and their theories are generally dismissed by Cyclo's scientific community."

"So, ah Saurian like Babooman," said Kaya, dismissively. "Ah bet Talisian parents tell dey chirren de Saurian go get dem if dey doh behave."

"The Seriak are not the elderly bearded men, so often misunderstood by the very young residents of Trinidad's rural communities; they are inhuman monsters — alien invaders that eat children. I am not convinced they are purely mythical bogeymen; my father secretly believed they were real, and your dream seems to confirm their existence."

Kaya smirked disbelievingly, "Yuh t'ink meh dream real?"

"Undoubtedly," said Tolan Rapp, with calm assurance.

"Meh cousin marry ah schoolteacher. She's ah nurse in England—"

"And, in the future, somewhere in the Cosmic Sea, she will become a princess. The golden butterflies you saw on Rin Mur-Rain's lapels and on the large black banners are Arosian Ten-Shi — symbols of the Imperial House of Enki. You have the gift of foresight."

"Yuh really t'ink Raya is ah princess? Wha' happen tuh Roman den?"

"Perhaps he is more than he seems."

"Nah-nah-nah…. Roman might sound like ah Englishman, buh he's ah Trini tuh de bone."

"There is, of course, another explanation. Did you see Roman in your dream?"

"No," replied Kaya, suddenly disheartened by Tolan Rapp's subtle suggestion. "Ah suppose, if ah see de future, somet'ing coulda happen tuh Roman. Raya coulda marry somebody else. Meh gran'aunt tell meh both ah dem missin' in England. De police lookin' fuh dem. Dey find one ah dey friends dead in dey apartment."

"Do not worry about events that you are unable to influence. Perhaps this Roman is a prince."

"From Trinidad?" laughed Kaya.

"Yes, just as I am from Sweden."

"Yuh t'ink Roman is an alien like you?"

"I had always assumed that you and your mother were under Osirian and Setian scrutiny because of your father's Cyclan heritage, but perhaps there is more to the hybrid human interest in your family. It now seems plausible that the Osirians and the Setians have also been observing your cousin and her husband."

"Yuh say ah have foresight. Wha' really happenin' tuh meh?"

"You are changing. Your telepathic abilities are increasing. You are exhibiting the initial stages of psychokinesis — the ability to influence consciousness, energy, and matter through psychic intervention. Your senses and physical abilities have been enhanced. Your mind is expanding—"

"Ah goin' tuh be ah genius?" interrupted Kaya, barely able to contain his glee.

"Let us not jump to conclusions," said Tolan Rapp, calmly. "Your capacity for intelligence is increasing; perhaps soon you will manifest a photographic memory and total recall."

Ah hope ah doh get boring, like you.

"Hezekiah, on Earth, our enhanced abilities can be both a blessing and a curse. We are not so far removed from the self-righteousness of vigilantes, the envy of the weak or the fear and loathing of the paranoid. Witch-hunts are not yet regrettable episodes solely confined to a long-distant past. Be mindful of who you are. There are those who would do you harm. The Osirians and the Setians may attempt to fit you with a transponder — a tracking device. They are miniature and can be ingested or embedded under the surface of the skin."

"OK, ah understan'; I'll be careful. Mr Rapp, who is de Mad Renegade?"

"She is very old and very intelligent — an expert in biotechnology, bioengineering and cloning. Her scientific expertise allowed her to deceive my parents and their colleagues. She is also a spy and assassin who has earned many names — some impossible to pronounce, some too vulgar to repeat. Nevertheless, in coded Setian transmissions, they have referred to her as Golsha Zigg, a Niburian name that my parents believed to be genuine.

"Wha' she really want wit' meh?"

"Since she is insane and manifesting multiple personalities, that is a difficult question to answer with any degree of certainty. Her fixation with you seems to stem from an unhealthy obsession with your grandfather, Ekon Abaniah."

"Ah t'ink she use de name, Talbot, when she knew meh gran'fadah. Agnes Talbot."

"Yes, I know."

"Yuh know, an' yuh didn't tell meh; buh wha' trouble is dis?"

"Leave Golsha Zigg to me, Hezekiah," said Tolan Rapp, sternly. "Pray that you never witness this deranged Niburian in all her fury."

"What else yuh know?"

"I know the danger."

42

BLACK CAKE

As early as September, many Trinbagonians began their Christmas preparations in earnest. For homeowners, whether rich or poor, this usually involved fabricating new Christmas curtains and drapes, purchasing new furniture, decorating the home, and maintaining the garden. With Kaya's help, Josephine repainted the living room and kitchen the colour of butterscotch. They varnished the original hardwood floor and polished it to a specular gloss. Two weeks before the Paria College Christmas Ball, Kaya erected the old Christmas tree that had always been an integral part of every Christmas he could recall. Mama Flo bought the tacky tree in the late 80s. And, following her death, Kaya asked Josephine to promise never to replace it. He lovingly bandaged the broken artificial branches with brown electrical tape before decking the tree with new lights and a mixture of traditional and modern decorations. Fully adorned, the tree did not seem quite so tacky, at least not to Kaya. Admiring his handiwork, he marvelled at how the plastic pine appeared to have grown shorter with each passing year. And, considering the prospect of spending yet another Christmas without Mama Flo, his dear departed grandmother, Kaya fought back the tears.

On Sunday, at around noon, the first of the invited lunch guests arrived. Kaya's cousin Clarence parked his iris grey Nissan Teana alongside Josephine's Jeep on the concrete driveway. Kaya immediately noticed the conspicuous driver's door dent on the otherwise pristine car. He recalled Tantie Rose telling him that Clarence had an accident while taking her to the Couva District Hospital. Nevertheless, Clarence emerged — average height, paunch, short hair, round face, and all smiles, with a bottle of homemade ponche de crème in his left hand. It would take much more than a minor accident to dampen his typically Trinbagonian exuberance. As expected, Clarence arrived with his mother, Tantie Rose, his common-law wife Beatrice, and his children, Leandra and Robin. Willowy Leandra hid her large brown eyes behind mirrored sunglasses. Grinning from ear to ear,

Robin carried a shopping bag filled with Christmas presents, and Tantie Rose wore a long flowery dress that covered her bandaged knee. Proud, dark and tall, with black-dyed, heat-straightened hair, she self-consciously walked with a cane — slowly and deliberately. Clarence assisted her up the flight of stairs to the veranda where Kaya and Josephine boisterously greeted them with warm hugs.

"Where yuh bringin' dat ponche de crème?" asked Josephine, with a grin. "Like yuh cyah see ah getting' fat? Ah on ah diet dis Christmas, boy."

"Is so? Ah cyah see no fat nowhere; like it jump off yuh bone when it see meh comin'. Fat 'fraid meh fuh so, yuh know dat," said Clarence, with his rich, earthy voice. "So, where yuh seein' fat? Like yuh buy ah new mirror? Yuh better take it back one time, ah sure it faulty. Anyway, who tell yuh dis ponche de crème is fuh yuh? Ah tired tell yuh doh listen tuh côté-ci côté-là; all ah dis is mine." Clarence laughed — a deep rumble that caused his pot belly to wobble and his head to bob up and down.

Fourteen-year-old Kaya and his thirteen-year-old cousin Robin behaved like close brothers. But, at sixteen, attractive, self-aware, and very eager to escape the restraints of childhood, Leandra often appeared aloof and condescending. Kaya believed she inherited these mildly negative traits from her light-skinned mother, Beatrice, who had close ties with well-to-do relatives in New York. However, despite her occasional shortcomings, Leandra had no qualms about sitting on the floor and massaging Tantie Rose's troublesome knee. And she still upheld the tradition of bringing along her family's old Monopoly set, which had been tucked away in their bag of presents.

A little later, Tom arrived fresh from Sunday morning worship. Despite having lived under the punishing tropical sun for several months now, he had failed to develop any discernible tan, and remained pale and visibly foreign. At first, Kaya's cousins were uneasy around Tom, but it did not take long for them to conclude that the freckle-faced minister's son from Oxford was OK. Tom joined Kaya and his cousins in a friendly game of Monopoly. But, no sooner had they commenced, Wendy emerged from her father's black sedan, dressed in ordinary dark-blue jeans and a plain purple cotton T-shirt. She wore no make-up and sported a warm smile that could melt any heart of stone. Her arrival momentarily plunged Kaya's relatives into stunned silence. Leandra stared at Wendy, from head to toe, and Beatrice raised her eyebrows.

Finally, Robin whispered in amazement, "Dat's yuh gyulfriend?"

Kaya greeted Wendy with a cheerful "Hi."

"Hi, Kaya," she replied gleefully; then noticing Tom, she added, "Hey, Tom, you beat me here.... I guess I'm finally running on Trinidad time, eh?"

Wendy raised a puzzled eyebrow when she heard the disquieting sound of sporadic gunfire emanating from the living room.

"Dat's meh gran'aunt watchin' de western channel," said Kaya, matter-of-factly. "She like Clint Eastwood fuh so."

Kaya made all the necessary introductions, intriguing his relatives with flattering details about his very pretty Canadian friend.

"Sit down, sit down, ah hope yuh hungry, de food will be ready now fuh now," said Josephine, offering Wendy a generous glass of her homemade sorrel, with crushed ice.

"Thank you," said Wendy, graciously.

She took in the aromas of freshly baked breads and cakes and the mouth-watering scent of pork still roasting in the oven. Wendy could scarcely believe how much food had been laid out. In the dining area, Kaya and Josephine had joined the kitchen and dining room tables together, in order to accommodate all their guests. As usual, for this festive time of year, Josephine, with a little help from Kaya, had prepared a banquet suitable for royalty. Christmas ham and chow-chow, mustard, onion and mayonnaise relish, pelau, Spanish rice, roasted turkey, baked potatoes, macaroni cheese and minced beef pie, pastelles, chicken casserole, stewed pigeon peas, callaloo, homemade hot pepper sauce, and a mixed salad with lettuce, tomatoes, cucumbers and carrots, comprised the main meal offering. For dessert, there was a choice of sponge cakes, spicy sweet breads, custard ice cream, coconut ice cream, and last but not least, four of Josephine's legendary black cakes.

Most Trinbagonian households had their unique variation of the traditional black Christmas cake; however, there was one universally essential ingredient — alcohol, and copious amounts of it. The recipe Josephine inherited from Mama Flo, had a rich fruit and spirit base that called for one pound each of pitted prunes, currants and raisins, to be soaked for one week, in a bowl with one bottle of dark Trinidad rum and one bottle of cherry brandy. Burnt, caramelised brown sugar contributed to the cakes' distinctive blackness; and, once baked for three hours and removed from the oven, another bottle of rum was used, with equal portions, to soak the tops of the cakes. Twenty-four hours later, having absorbed all the rum, the cakes were ready to be served. Josephine had also laid out a variety of exotic drinks, including ginger beer and homemade pommerac wine for the adults, and sorrel, mauby, non-alcoholic fruit punch, and passionfruit juice for everyone.

"Come on, we're playing Monopoly," announced Tom, enthusiastically.

"Wow, you must be joking, eh?" said Wendy, stunning Kaya's cousins with her Torontonian accent and effervescence. "I haven't played Monopoly since the last ice age. Beauty...."

"Tell me about it," said Tom.

Suddenly the sound of *Jingle Bells*, sung by Jim Reeves, began blaring from the house next door.

"Hmmm, like Mr Walker finish he first bottle ah rum early dis mornin'," said Clarence, with a wry grin.

Josephine rolled her eyes. "Lawd, have mercy. Dat man is ah real-real menace. Yesterday it was Jim Reeves, den Johnny Mathis, den Bing Crosby, and den Jim Reeves again. Like he went tuh sleep fuh two hours, den he start again wit' de Merry Christmas Polka, but dis time he had it on de wrong speed. Jim Reeves was soundin' like de Chipmunks."

"Buh wha' trouble is dis? De man play one set ah ole record an' no Nat King Cole? Wha' scene he really on?" said Clarence, and his grin got even broader. "So, why yuh ent invite him fuh lunch, gyul? Dat woulda solve yuh noise problem one time."

"Doh skylark.... Yuh want meh tuh invite dat drunk an' disorderly man into dis house?"

"Doh defame de man character, Josie," chuckled Clarence. "He drunk, but he ent disorderly."

"So why yuh doh take him wit' yuh, back tuh Tortuga, eh?" said Josephine, with her hands on her hips, feigning seriousness. "Yuh could wine an' dine him at Rose Kitchen, an' ah could spend ah day in peace an' quiet here."

"Buh A-A," chuckled Beatrice, joining in the fun. "Like yuh want tuh bring we business tuh ill repute? We doh tolerate drunk people comin' tuh Rose Kitchen. Dey ha' tuh come sober an' leave drunk."

"Ah keep hearin' meh name...." said Tantie Rose.

"Doh worry, Tantie," said Leandra. "Dey only joking."

"Is so? Since when meh name is ah joke?"

"Come, Mammy," said Clarence. "Ah could see yuh getting' crotchety. Wha' happen, like Clint Eastwood only ha' ah small part in dis flim, awa? Lemme rub yuh knee, ah sure it must be lancin' yuh."

"Yeah, son, de tablet dey give meh ent doin' nuttin'. Ah in one set ah pain," said Tantie Rose, and she grimaced. "Rub meh knee good."

As they played the property trading board game, Kaya closely observed Wendy during the friendly banter, trying to gauge her reaction to his relatives. She laughed and seemed to enjoy the friendly exchanges, but Kaya could not help wondering if she would like the present he had made her. He wondered if she would enjoy his surprise.

43

WINDY DAY

Josephine's now-now turned out to be almost half an hour. And, during that time, Leandra managed to amass an enviable property empire that included hotels on Boardwalk and Park Place, as well as several houses on Pennsylvania, North Carolina, and Pacific Avenues. She also owned the Electric Company and Water Works. Wendy's assets included all four railroads, St James Place and Tennessee Avenue. On the other hand, Kaya faced imminent bankruptcy, Tom found himself languishing in jail, and Robin was obliged to pay income tax.

Her pork roasted to culinary perfection, Josephine proudly served her Christmastime Sunday lunch. After Tom had said grace, the gastronomic adventure commenced. Any awkwardness related to the foreign visitors, soon vanished in a hazy wake of animated conversation and deep appreciation of a masterful meal. During the main course, Josephine subtly cross-examined Wendy, judged her reactions and made assessments regarding her character. For her part, Wendy graciously addressed the majority of Josephine's maternal concerns and displayed uncommon maturity, humour, and expert diplomatic flair.

At least it look like she come from ah good family. Dey not hard up, she not ah dunce, an' she have personality. So what dis pretty t'ing from Canada really see in meh son? thought Josephine, and Kaya heard her.

"You know, Kaya is a real ambassador, he really helped me and Tom settle into college, eh?" said Wendy, matter-of-factly. "Isn't that right, Tom?"

"Oh, yeah," said Tom, licking his lips and nodding in agreement. He served himself a second generous helping of delicious stewed chicken. "Some people haven't been so welcoming. I can't wait till Dragon Assassin teaches Cobo another lesson on Sports Day."

"Dragon Assassin?" asked Josephine, and deep furrows appeared on her brow.

Be quiet, Tom, thought Kaya.

And, while Kaya surreptitiously attempted to direct Tom with his eyebrows, quick-thinking Wendy added with a chuckle, "Dragon Assassin is Kaya's online chat ID. I guess it's a boy thing, eh?"

"Ah hope it does not have anyt'ing tuh do with those violent computer games ah keep hearing about," said Josephine, limiting the depth of her Trinidadian accent for the benefit of her foreign guests.

"No-no-no," chorused Kaya, Tom, and Wendy.

Dat doh look like extensions. Ah wonder what she put in she hair? thought Leandra, and Kaya heard her.

Hmmm.... Like quiet cousin Kaya is ah real dark horse. Dis Wendy is ah very nice young gyul, thought Clarence. *Is true, nowadays chirren ole before they time; buh she soundin' like she fourteen goin' on twenty-one. Ah sure Josie feel she too advanced fuh Kaya — look how she watchin' she like ah hawk. Kaya better watch he step.*

Sporting his rarely-seen philosophical face, Clarence said, "So, Wendy, nowadays in dis recession Trinis runnin' tuh Canada left, right an' centre. You an' yuh family move in de opposite direction. How yuh findin' life in Trinidad?"

"It's great, eh? My dad's an energy engineer. Mom works with the UNDP, you know, the United Nations Development Programme. Before we stayed in Tronno, we travelled around a lot. I'm a rink rat.... I suppose I miss skating, going to hockey games with my dad — we just love watching, probably because we're both brutal at playing. And I even miss watching Much."

Wha' she say? thought Tantie Rose. *She ha' tuh slow dong, she talkin' too fas'.*

"Much?" quizzed Clarence.

"It's like a Canadian version of MTV, eh? Except it also has a lotta comedy shows. I also miss Timbits, maple syrup pie, and butter tarts," said Wendy, smiling sweetly. "But I love the beach, and the sun, and the food. And, most people seem really, really happy here. My dad was born in San Fernando, and it's nice to get to know relatives I never met before, eh?"

Hanging on every accented word, Robin appeared to be slowly falling in love with Wendy, at least it seemed that way to Kaya, and Leandra gradually began to pout as Wendy increasingly became the centre of attention.

Alright, we get it — yuh miss de cold, buh yuh like Maracas, so done de chat now, Miss Tronno, thought Leandra.

Wendy turned her gaze towards her, and Leandra replaced her disapproving pout with an innocent smile.

Noticing Robin's enchantment, Josephine said, "Robin, try de pie," and she offered him a slice of her macaroni pie.

Turning to Kaya with a grin, Robin impersonated the junior member of the dynamic duo from a campy cult 1960s television show. He said, "Holy macaroni Batman, is there room for pie?"

"Yes, Robin," said Kaya, impersonating Batman, "there's always room for pie."

Josephine shook her head and rolled her eyes, "Allyuh too idle." She slid the slice of pie onto a corner of Robin's plate.

"T'anks," said Robin, gleefully.

Tantie Rose suddenly exclaimed, "Oh, Gorm, Josephine, yuh know what ah forget? De karaili. Clarence, yuh was suppose tuh remind meh, boy."

Clarence shrugged his shoulders and raised his hands in feigned defence.

"Doh worry, Tantie. We used to have some in de garden, buh it mysteriously disappear," said Josephine, and she eyed Kaya.

Kaya had hoped that Josephine hadn't noticed his zealous eradication of any karaili within a ten-mile radius of their house. Kaya even paid the little girl next door thirty dollars to pull up all the karaili vines in her backyard. Helping himself to callaloo, he pretended to be utterly oblivious of the karaili-centric discourse.

"Ah leave a big plastic bag, right dere on de kitchen counter," said Tantie Rose. She sucked her teeth and grumbled something about growing old and senile. "Anyway, ah go put it tuh one side fuh yuh tuh get it, when yuh come tuh see we on Boxin' Day, please God."

A feeling of dread descended on Kaya. He wondered how much he would have to bribe Robin to dispose of the horribly bitter vegetables that Josephine delighted in cooking if given the opportunity. Robin usually drove a hard bargain with regards to clandestine tasks, and Kaya had already spent most of his savings on Christmas presents.

Tantie Rose entertained the guests with anecdotal stories of Josephine's life in Tortuga. She even mentioned the tale of Josephine's encounter with Papa Bois and the Douen, drawing several nervous glances from Kaya and Tom. However, as the meal progressed, gas got the better of Tantie Rose. Kaya felt certain Josephine's rich pigeon peas stew was culpable. And, when sporadic flatulence began punctuating Tantie Rose's storytelling, Kaya's disposition soured. He secretly thanked God for Mr Walker's blaring music, which masked most of the offending sounds. All the same, Kaya deeply dreaded those quiet moments between songs when his grandaunt's rumbling stomach threatened to let a big one rip.

How totally embarrassing, he thought.

Kaya's heart sank further when he heard Tantie Rose say, "Josephine, ah find yuh pigeon peas real nice. Leandra, gyul, put some more pigeon peas on de side ah meh plate fuh meh."

Kaya fully understood that the passage of gas was a perfectly natural thing. After all, had there ever lived a person who hadn't let one loose, from time to time? Unfortunately, Tantie Rose's gastric emissions did not smell of roses, but of volatile odoriferous sulphur compounds, which Kaya's enhanced Cyclan sense of smell easily detected.

Clarence, Beatrice, Leandra, and Robin were quite used to Tantie Rose's minor explosions, but Kaya feared for Wendy and Tom. He was relieved to see Tom stuffing his face full of ham. Tom loved food. He ate like a horse and seemed blissfully unaware of the explosive cauldron of methane that sat opposite him. Wendy was far less distracted by the feast — she took in everything and kept her thoughts closely guarded. If she knew about his grandaunt's windy moments, she did not let on. Nevertheless, much to his dismay, Kaya noticed Wendy's nose twitch a few times, during the course of the lavish Sunday lunch.

44

GIFTS

After lunch, Kaya anxiously waited for an opportune moment to sneak Wendy into his room. This was a foolhardy and potentially life-threatening ambition, since Josephine had given Kaya strict instructions not to find himself alone with any girl, in any room, under any circumstances whatsoever. Josephine told Kaya that if ever he was caught alone with a young woman, while he was still under the age of sixteen, he should call for an ambulance immediately; since it was likely he would sustain injuries that required emergency medical treatment.

Ah wish somet'ing could distract Mammy fuh just five minutes, thought Kaya, as they resumed the game of Monopoly.

Suddenly, Kaya heard the squeal of tyres, followed by loud metallic thuds in quick succession.

"Oh, no, not again," exclaimed Josephine, and she briskly walked towards the veranda.

"Wha'ppen?" asked Clarence.

"Another car tumble dong in Miss Molly yard, oui," said Josephine. "Come, Clarence, ah doh t'ink Molly an' dem home, an' de driver holdin' she head — she look like she in a daze."

"De passenger still hangin' upside dong, Daddy," observed Robin.

"Leandra, bring meh cell phone from de counter," said Josephine. Ah better call for de police an' ah ambulance."

"Buh wha' trouble is dis? Like she was tryin' tuh fly low 'round de corner," said Beatrice, staring in disbelief at the upside down Volkswagen Beetle in Miss Molly's small, cluttered yard.

Situated on a sharp bend on the other side of Mirabelle Street, Miss Molly's two-storey house had a cramped front garden with no parking area. The ground floor, with its tiny garden, sometimes became the impromptu resting place for inebriated pedestrians or vehicles driven by drunken drivers.

Beatrice, Leandra, and Tom stood watching from the veranda while Josephine, Clarence, and Robin quickly made their way to the stunned driver. They helped her free her young female passenger from the inverted car.

Tantie Rose remained reclined on the settee in the lounge with a small bowl of coconut ice cream on her lap. She stared — mesmerised, at the television screen; utterly enthralled, as Clint Eastwood explained to four, soon to be dead gunmen that his mule did not like people laughing. Kaya smiled mischievously. He had the distraction he had wished for.

"Ah wan' tuh show yuh somet'ing," he whispered to Wendy, gently grabbing her hand and pulling her towards his bedroom.

"What're you doing?" asked Wendy. "The Christmas Ball is Friday, and the hike is Saturday; now's not a good time to risk being grounded by your mother, eh?"

"We'll ha' tuh be quick."

"What?" came Wendy's wide-eyed reaction.

Once alone, in the seclusion of Kaya's bedroom, Wendy said, "We're gonna be in a lotta trouble, eh?"

Kaya said, "We already in ah lotta trouble—"

Wendy quickly draped her arms around his neck and kissed him.

Breaking the kiss, Kaya said breathlessly, "Ah didn't bring yuh here fuh dat...."

"Oh?" said Wendy, and she giggled. "Did you just wanna show me your room? It's very tidy." Noticing a framed photograph on top of a chest of drawers, Wendy added, "You never told me you had an older sister."

"Dat's meh cousin," said Kaya.

"The one that's missing?"

"Yeah."

"She's pretty, eh?"

"Dis is fuh you," said Kaya, motioning towards a 24 by 30 inch canvas, covered with clean muslin, resting on an artist's easel in the far corner of his room.

"What's this?" asked Wendy, both surprised and intrigued.

"Take de cover off," said Kaya, with a smile.

Wendy briefly searched Kaya's brown eyes for clues, before tentatively removing the muslin to reveal his portrait of her. Based on one of her social networking profile pictures, Kaya's oil painting nevertheless depicted an idealised rendition of her most striking features — her cheekbones were more prominent, her lips fuller, and her eyes dreamier. The young woman, in the fine art portrait, stared directly at her beholders — beautiful, confident and mysterious.

"Oh, my God...." whispered Wendy. She slowly turned towards Kaya, and a single tear trickled down her cheek.

Wordlessly, Wendy crushed Kaya in a warm embrace. Her lips briefly found his, but she broke the kiss and began to sob.

"What's de matter?" asked Kaya, utterly bewildered.

Wendy buried her face in Kaya's shoulder. "You're the nicest guy I've ever known," she said, wiping her tears and trying to compose herself. "I mean it. The sweetest, kindest guy…."

"Dat's because ah made of chocolate…." said Kaya, softly.

Wendy chuckled. "You're my chocolate boy."

"An' you're my doux-doux," whispered Kaya.

"You know the girl in the picture is much prettier than I will ever be, eh?" said Wendy, softly.

"Ah could never paint somet'ing prettier dan you…."

Wendy kissed Kaya once more, and his mind began to swim.

He briefly lost track of time, until he heard Josephine thinking, *Buh where Kaya an' Miss Canada? If dat boy take dat gyul to he room, ah go murder him.*

"Robin, where Kaya?" asked Josephine. And Kaya saw her, in his mind's eye. She briefly stopped consoling the driver of the crashed Volkswagen. "Go an' tell him tuh bring de first aid kit."

Kaya broke the kiss and said, "Meh mudder wonderin' where we are."

"That figures," said Wendy, and she began quickly unbuttoning Kaya's shirt.

"What yuh doin', gyul?"

"Something I should have done a long time ago…."

"What?"

Wendy removed a gold chain from around her neck, which had been hidden beneath her purple T-shirt; and, dangling on the chain, was a green gemstone pendant. She draped her arms around Kaya's shoulders, placed the pendant around his neck and hurriedly hid it by buttoning up his shirt.

Kaya's heart skipped a beat. He instantly recalled the pendant Roman Doyle had given his cousin Soraya. Wendy's pendant seemed identical.

"There," said Wendy, "that's my gift to you. Always keep it close to your heart and think of me." She looked at Kaya with the cutest smile.

"Where did you get dis?" said Kaya, doing his best not to appear unsettled.

"It belonged to my grandmother," said Wendy, and she seemed to peer deep into Kaya's very soul, "and now it belongs to you."

Sensing Wendy's burgeoning suspicion, Kaya immediately thanked her and smothered her with a kiss.

"Leandra, where Kaya?" asked Robin, as he came up the stairs leading to the veranda where Leandra stood. Kaya saw it all, in his mind's eye.

"Yuh need tuh go tuh de toilet...." Kaya told Wendy.

"Huh?"

"Go tuh de toilet, quick. Wait five minutes den flush it."

"OK," said Wendy, getting the gist of Kaya's ruse.

Kaya quickly retrieved the first aid kit from the bathroom before Wendy darted into it. He briskly walked to the kitchen and took an ice pack out of the freezer.

"Kaya, wha' yuh doin'?" asked Leandra, suspiciously.

"Ah just getting' de first aid kit," replied Kaya.

"Hurry, Josie want it."

"Yeah, ah know...."

"Where Wendy? She in yuh room?" asked Leandra, spoiling for incriminating evidence.

"No, she in de toilet."

"Oh-ho," replied Leandra, and Kaya could sense her disappointment.

As he crossed the street to the scene of the accident, Kaya recalled Tolan Rapp's words. *"The Osirians and the Setians may attempt to fit you with a transponder — a tracking device. They are miniature and can be ingested or embedded under the surface of the skin."*

Was Wendy's gift a transponder? Was she a cunning spy or an assassin?

Kaya realised he had become paranoid. He had developed distrust towards Spexy and Shantel, and he wondered if Cobo was a Setian agent. Now, he had doubts about Wendy. After all, there was no real reason to doubt that the pendant she gave him was not what she said it was — a pendant that once belonged to her grandmother.

Was Wendy's interest in him a cause for suspicion? Was that the problem? Or was it that he did not feel worthy of her affection?

45

CHRISTMAS BALL

The following Friday, on the eve of the much-anticipated Paria College Christmas Ball, Kaya struggled with anxiety, self-consciousness and self-doubt. This would be his first formal dance, his first Christmas Ball and his first official date. Josephine had her seamstress friend, Tangerine Jean, make Kaya a smart gabardine suit. And, although it was just a bit too big, Kaya did not mind too much. He quelled his nervousness by striking poses in the mirror and doing impersonations of avant-garde pop-culture characters and fictitious Italian gangsters. As Tolan Rapp had predicted, Kaya's memory had become phenomenal. He perfectly recalled lengthy monologues from films, lyrics from songs, and the most mundane trivia. At College, he had become careless — showing off his new-found mental acumen, wowing his teachers and classmates alike.

At 5:40 PM, Josephine and Kaya arrived at Wendy Wong's Battoo Drive address. Her statuesque mother, Rhian, greeted Kaya at the front door of the two-storey upper middle class home and waved to Josephine waiting in her jeep.

"I am pleased to finally meet you, Hezekiah," she said, disarming Kaya with her mild Welsh accent while her piercing blue eyes assessed him. "Come in, Gwendolyn will just be a moment."

"Thank you, Mrs Wong," said Kaya, not yet relaxed enough to lapse into Trinidadianese.

"Here, let me straighten your tie," said Rhian. She moved deliberately and unrushed.

Everything about Wendy's mother exuded calm control, and Kaya could not read her.

"You have a good eye," said Rhian, maintaining eye contact as she adjusted Kaya's college tie. "Your gift to Gwendolyn is an absolute treasure."

"Thank you, Mrs Wong," said Kaya, and Rhian smiled as if he had told her a sweet secret.

At almost six feet, in height, Rhian was slightly taller than Kaya. Her lingering closeness and dark-haired movie-star looks made him uneasy.

However, just when the tension became almost unbearable, Rhian took a step backwards and said, "There. Perfect. Now you look quite regal. Sit. Can I offer you a drink, something very cold with a fizz, perhaps?"

"That would be nice," said Kaya, softly.

"Hello, Kaya," said Kenneth, Wendy's father.

The Oriental man was stocky and about five inches shorter than his wife. Except for a tinge of grey on his sideburns, jet black hair framed his no-nonsense clean-shaven face that beamed with sincerity.

"Hello, Mr Wong," replied Kaya.

"Rhian, Wendy needs you. I'll get Kaya's drink," he said softly. "What will it be, Kaya? Coke?"

"Coke's good."

"I know your mother's waiting, Wendy'll be out in a sec."

Kaya barely had two sips from his drink before Wendy emerged wearing a long red sleeveless gown that left him speechless.

"Hi," said Wendy, with uncharacteristic shyness. She tried to gauge Kaya's reaction.

Kaya swallowed hard. "Hi," he said. The single word had struggled to leave his lips.

He doesn't like it. Why did I listen to Mom, eh? I knew I should've worn my black dress, thought Wendy, and she did a great job of hiding her concerns behind a contagious smile.

"I like yuh dress," Kaya managed to say.

You do? thought Wendy, and Kaya heard her.

Wendy curtsied. "Thank you, kind sir," she said adopting a British accent, which she seasoned with a girlish chuckle.

"It very nice," added Kaya, and he could not help staring.

"Let's not keep Hezekiah's mother waiting," said Rhian.

The Paria College Christmas Ball was held in the large college auditorium. There, the renowned, local DJ, Madman Monstar, mixed dance music from America and Europe, with Trinbagonian parang and the heady tracks of popular soca stars. As expected, Raima arrived with Bruce de Bulk, Cobo had Abigail Frost in tow, and Deron's date was Gillian Payne. Shantel's companion for the evening was Barry Gangasingh, and, contrary to the advice of her doctor, Meenal escorted Tom. By all accounts, a good dancer, Samantha Mohan tried unsuccessfully to teach Tom to wine. That was until Meenal accidentally tripped her. Although Meenal apologised profusely,

Samantha believed that Meenal acted deliberately. Either way, Samantha turned her attention to her previously disregarded date. Although the bandages had been removed from Meenal's big toe, proper dancing was still out of the question. She did manage, nevertheless, to hobble about. She even tried wining on the spot, but wining really was not Meenal's thing.

Raima, on the other hand, caused quite a stir.

"Oh, Lawd, clear de way," said Sean Charles, "like she come out tuh put man-child in de hospital. Raima peltin' waist — left, right, and centre!"

"Gyul, wine," exclaimed Susan Critchlow.

Kaya could scarcely believe his eyes. In his wildest dreams, he never imagined Raima could dance that way. Bruce de Bulk, who was overly preoccupied with looking cool, seemed like a stiff, self-conscious nerd by comparison. For a while, Raima distracted Kaya, and although he did his best not to make it obvious, he felt unexpected pangs of jealousy. For a moment, Raima held his stare. And, in that briefest of moments, he believed that she pretended to be much happier than she was. Kaya believed that her provocative display was designed to show him what he was missing. Raima made him blush.

Not to be outdone, Wendy pushed her own gyrations up a notch.

"Buh wha' trouble is dis?" said the ever-observant Sean Charles.

Meenal shook her head in dismay, Shantel sucked her teeth, Raima developed a pout, and Kaya's mouth fell open.

"Well, look at dat.... Wendy is ah wining specialist...." muttered Sean in disbelief.

Things went from warm to red hot. Gradually, the other dancers formed a ring, allowing the two most attractive girls at Paria College to battle it out. Raima and Wendy — waist versus waist, hip battling hip, and bumper against bumper. To everyone's surprise, the Canadian beauty could hold her own.

"Bruk it up!" shouted Madman Monstar, goading the girls on.

"All ah dis is fuh you?" said Sean, in Kaya's ear. "Ah wish ah had your face, hoss."

Despite their best efforts, the boys simply could not keep up. In fact, no one at the ball could compete with Raima and Wendy. Nevertheless, the girls soon realised that they were evenly matched, and neither of them could claim to be the undisputed Paria Wining Queen. What had started as a competition between two attractive rivals bent on outdoing each other, quickly reverted to two teenagers simply enjoying themselves at a Christmas fete.

"Yuh cyah vex when soca playin'," Kaya recalled his cousin Clarence once saying.

A couple of sixth formers, members of the college football team, began having difficulty containing themselves. They didn't dare trouble Raima; her date, Bruce de Bulk, was their captain. He was big and brooding, and Kaya had never seen anyone mess with him. There was an indefinable cloud of mystery and danger surrounding Bruce. However, despite his victory over karate champion, Adrian Leotaud, many sixth formers had difficulty viewing Kaya as anything but a scrawny fourth form kid that simply got lucky — far too lucky.

They believed Kaya was not man enough for Wendy; and, they told him so, in no uncertain terms. The larger of the two made his move, trying to get behind Wendy.

"Whoa-whoa-whoa, cowboy," said Wendy, stepping away from him without skipping a dance beat.

"Doh feel no way, ah little wine cyah hurt nobody," said the footballer. And, undeterred, he reached for Wendy again.

However, Kaya stepped in front of Wendy, blocking the large footballer's advance. The music immediately stopped, sending Madman Monstar into a mad panic trying to restore it, while the crowd of revellers began to protest. Kaya faced Wendy, maintaining eye contact, with his back to the bully.

Without warning, Kaya shouted, "B for bodyguard!" He spoke so loudly that he startled everyone into stunned silence.

Like is mad he finally gone mad, thought Samantha, and Kaya heard her.

Samantha was not the only one who wondered if men in white coats should have a nice quiet chat with Kaya.

Dey go take he away inna straight jacket, thought Mukesh, who had been unable to find any girl willing to accompany him to the ball.

Having the undivided attention of all present, but never losing eye contact with Wendy, Kaya launched himself into a highly theatrical monologue.

"Behold! Before you, a bawdy bard, cast begrudgingly, betwixt and between, as both benefactor and bandit by the biliousness of fate. This brazen beauty, no banal by-product of blustering bravado, is the badge of a bitter battalion, now beaten, banished. However, this benign, buccaneering bondsman of a bygone barony, stands with bated breath; bewitched, beguiled and burning to beat these belligerent, barbarian brutes, boundlessly bent on butchering blameless babes. Your bona fide bodyguard, forever your bastion; neither bedlam nor bureaucracy shall blunt my bayonet, broadsword or battle-axe. My blood, my brawn and bone, I bequeath you. But, bravura banter briskly becomes brainless balderdash. So, permit me to add with respect that it is my very good fortune to make your acquaintance. I am your humble servant, B."

Silence. You could hear a pin drop. Wendy just stood staring in awe; she was not alone. Eager to douse the unnerving tenseness, Madman Monstar scrambled for his microphone.

"Yuh see? Shakespeare was ah Trini. Make some noise people, give it up for de youth-man," said Madman Monstar, urging everyone in the auditorium to clap.

"That was pretty good," Wendy told Kaya as she joined in the appreciative applause. "Did you actually write that?" she asked tentatively.

"Yeah, wit' ah little help from de Concise Oxford English Dictionary," said Kaya, smiling.

"I'm impressed. Really impressed. You memorised that whole thing. So, kind sir, you would be my bodyguard?"

"Yes, Lady Wendy," said Kaya, with a bow and a mischievous grin. And now, Raima was the one experiencing pangs of jealousy.

For the first time, Kaya saw Bruce de Bulk lose his cool. "Wha' yuh lookin' at?" Bruce said to Raima.

"Nothing. Ah need some water," said Raima, before defiantly walking away.

"Oi, where yuh goin'?" said Bruce, and he briskly pursued her.

Referring to Kaya, the smaller footballer said to the larger one, "Buh wha' de? Like is swallow he swallow ah dictionary. So wha' yuh t'ink de B for, padna?"

"Like yuh is ah real dunce, awa? Is B fuh boo-boo," said the larger footballer, to the smaller one, before setting his sights on Kaya. He said to the back of Kaya's head, "Like yuh fadah is ah glassmaker. Likkle boy, move outta meh way. Yuh cyah see dis is big people fete?"

Then he made the tragic mistake of grabbing Kaya's shoulder, and Kaya's juvenile mischief, instantly turned into mature malice. Faster than the eye could see, he grabbed the footballer's hand, jerking his arm downwards while bending his fingers backwards into an excruciating wrist lock. Kaya effortlessly forced the older bigger youth to his knees.

"If yuh touch meh again, ah go break yuh arm," Kaya whispered into his ear. "Touch meh gyulfriend, ah go break yuh neck. Now yuh better tell yuh friends dem tuh back off, or de next sound everybody hear will be de sound ah yuh bones breakin'."

Kaya projected into the shocked footballer's mind. The bully experienced the traumatic sensation of his neck being broken; then, in his mind's eye, he saw vivid images of his inconsolable mother screaming at his funeral.

His angry friends stopped in their tracks. Dread thoughts clouded their minds. They each saw Kaya utterly devastating them by employing outlandish martial arts techniques. Kaya applied pressure on the footballer's trapped wrist, forcing him to rise slowly, from his knees, to his tiptoes.

He calmly spoke to his victim's sixth form cohorts. "Take yuh friend outside, ah t'ink he need some fresh air, an' ah sure you could do wit' some too."

They did as they were told.

"Dat go teach dem tuh mess wit' de dragon assassin," said Sean, with a chuckle.

Tom whispered into Kaya's ear, "You've been eating curry again, haven't you?"

"What did you say to that moron?" Wendy cautiously asked Kaya. "He looked terrified."

"Ah tell him Ugon Jiwa, de witch doctor, is meh fadah."

46

ABJECT HUMILIATION

For several minutes, Bruce de Bulk wandered the dance floor in search of Raima, who seemed to have disappeared.

"He's such a jerk," said Wendy, "he deserves what he's about to get."

"Wha' yuh talkin' 'bout?" asked Kaya, unable to glean any clues telepathically.

"Look and listen." said Wendy, much like the cat that got the cream.

Bruce still had not found Raima, but Kaya spotted her with her older cousin, Jaysen, and a few of his friends. Unseen by Bruce, they moved in the shadows, on the other side of the auditorium. Madman Monstar had left his soca mix on autopilot, under the supervision of his young assistant while he went to the men's room. However, Jaysen's buxom girlfriend easily distracted the naïve assistant by flirting and jiggling in her low-cut evening gown. She had the mesmerised young man eating out of the palm of her hand in no time. She lured him further and further away from the DJ's equipment until he followed her outside the auditorium. One of Jaysen's friends told Bruce that he had seen Raima in the college car park, and Bruce took the bait. He left the auditorium accompanied by two of his friends. With Jaysen's help, Raima stopped the DJ's music and put on her specially prepared CD.

At first, when the music suddenly stopped for the second time that evening, the confused students and their dates began to protest even more strenuously than before. However, they soon became intrigued by the recorded conversation they heard over the speaker system, and curiosity got the better of them all.

"I thought you were going to the ball with what's-her-name?" came Wendy's unmistakably accented voice.

"Yeah, she probably think so too," said Bruce, callously.

"What's dis, Wendy?" asked Kaya, sternly.

"Shh…. Listen, you'll like it," Wendy told Kaya.

On the recording, she said to Bruce, "Oh, I thought you two were an item, eh? It certainly looked like true love to me."

"Nah, yuh see Raima? She's a nice gyul, but she too young fuh me, ah jus' waiting for de right time tuh break it off wit' she," said Bruce, and all present, in the packed auditorium, seemed to gasp collectively. "Ah not cruel. Ah have ah heart and ah doh really want tuh break hers, buh ah need somebody with more experience."

"Yeah, I see what you mean," said Wendy. "I'm sure she'll appreciate you being so considerate though. By the way, how old do you think I am?"

"Ole enough."

"Old enough for what, exactly?" asked Wendy, coyly.

"Ole enough fuh ah real man."

"Yeah…. How old are you, 17, 18? I guess, at 14, Kaya must seem a bit immature to you."

"Tuh everybody. Yuh deserve tuh be wit' ah real man, not some boy who act like ah puppy dog. So, rude gyul, what is yuh address an' how early yuh want meh tuh pick yuh up fuh de ball?"

"You have a chauffeur?"

"No, baby, how yuh mean? Fuh meh 17th birthday, ah get ah Big Man Wheels — BMW special edition. Leather seats, rims, de works. It real-real nice. Ah know ah gyul like you'll like it.

"I'm sorry; I'll have to decline, yeah, on account of my allergy."

"Allergy? What kinda allergy? Wha' yuh allergic to princess, leather seats?"

"No, I'm just allergic to assholes."

Utterly horrified, Bruce re-entered the auditorium to be greeted with a wall of jeers, mocking laughter, hissing and boos. He did not know it then, but this would mark the acrimonious end of his tenure as captain of the college football team. He would never fully regain the respect of his peers. The humiliation proved too much for Bruce, who quickly left with his tail between his legs.

The DJ's assistant desperately scrambled back to the equipment at that point, but Jaysen had already resumed the music, and he and Raima had disappeared into the laughing crowd.

"When did this happen?" Kaya asked Wendy, and he wasn't amused.

"A week ago. Hey, are you angry with me?"

"Why yuh didn't tell meh?"

"I suppose, I wasn't sure how you'd react. I must admit, it bothered me, you know, not telling you and all…. But I can see now, I made the right decision, eh?"

"Ah comin' back in ah minute," said Kaya, turning to walk away.

"Hey, where are you going?"

"Tuh teach Bruce ah lesson."

"Listen, hotshot, you'd better just calm right down. Guys hit on me all the time; that's what guys do. I just did what's-her-name a favour. One of my friends slit her wrists because of a jerk like Bruce. Her baby brother found her in a bathtub filled with blood. So, what are you planning to do to Bruce, beat him up? Who would you be doing that for? Me? No, I get it. You want to teach Bruce a lesson, as you put it, because what's-her-name picked him over you. That's it, isn't it? Listen, if you two sweethearts have unresolved issues, I think now would be the time to resolve them. I'll be honest with you, which is more than you've been with me. I'm not going to compete with your ghosts of love past, love present, and love yet to come. You will have to make a choice, eh? Because, I'm not going to share you that way. I absolutely refuse to cry myself to sleep each night, wondering if you truly care about me or not."

"Like yuh cyah see," said Kaya, sadly, "Bruce, Cobo, de Mapepires, even Raima.... Dey doh ha' no respect fuh meh."

"The real question is, do you have respect for yourself?"

Over Wendy's shoulder, Kaya saw Jaysen, and his friends, usher Raima out of the auditorium. Jaysen's girlfriend tried to console Raima, but she sobbed bitterly.

47

MOZART

The following morning, the morning of the Wildlife Heritage Trust hike through the Azura Forest, was blessed with a glorious sunrise, preluding sustained sunshine without a rain cloud in sight. Kaya woke before Josephine and had a simple breakfast comprising of a banana and a bowl of cereal with milk. He wore a white T-shirt, which covered the green gemstone pendant Wendy gave him, a blue baseball cap and black tracksuit bottoms that hid his ankle weights. For the trip, Kaya prepared a packed lunch of ham and cheese sandwiches. Previously, for Spexy's geography expedition, insecurity and low self-confidence had led Kaya to fill his rucksack with many unnecessary items. But that seemed a long time ago, and he had changed a lot since then. Thanks to his burgeoning Cyclan abilities, Tolan Rapp's dream training and Wendy's loving attention, Kaya had complete confidence in his ability to protect himself and fulfil his self-appointed role of Wendy's bodyguard. Despite Josephine's anxieties, Kaya could think of no danger in the forest he could not handle. As far as Kaya was concerned, he was the danger.

So, for the WHT hike, Kaya's rucksack was much lighter. Gone were the binoculars, spare cotton vest, notebook, sketch pad, coloured pencils, digital camera, plasters, spare socks and insect repellent spray. Kaya considered leaving his pocket Bible at home.

However, Josephine told him in no uncertain terms, "Yuh not leavin' dis house wit'out yuh pocket Bible."

Josephine also insisted that Kaya gave generous slices of her black cake to Florian Hütter, the WHT guide, and each of the other passengers in his car.

Senior WHT members, Gobelyn, Spexy, and Hütter planned to take the group to the Blue River Falls and the surrounding caves, so Kaya packed a small but powerful LED flashlight, a towel, a plastic rain jacket, his lunch, ice-cold water and a few other drinks. To record the event, Kaya relied on his improved memory and the camera on his mobile phone. In his joggers, he also carried his small pocket knife, his slingshot and a handful of marble-sized ball bearings as ammunition. Kaya hoped to shoot down a few Julie mangoes while on the trek.

After the less-than-perfect Christmas Ball, and a night of restless sleep, Kaya looked forward to smoothing things out and having a romantic walk in the woods with Wendy. He had thought a lot about what Wendy told him. Since he was eleven years old, from the first day he saw her — the first day at Paria College, Kaya nursed a terrible crush on Raima Khan. However, Raima only seemed interested in him after he saved her from drowning. Even so, she managed to find herself repeatedly enjoying the muscular embrace of Bruce de Bulk. While it is true that during the Christmas Ball, Raima did her level best to entice Kaya, he concluded that she did this purely because of the compromising recording Wendy gave to her. Dissatisfied with Raima, Bruce had unsuccessfully pursued Wendy.

From the moment of their very first meeting, Kaya immediately connected with Wendy Wong. She owed him nothing, yet she chose him. She had the attention of all the boys, yet she chose him. Beautiful, mature, sophisticated Wendy had never done anything to hurt Kaya. His mind was made up — there was no doubt. Gwendolyn Lian Wong was the girl for him, and he told her so.

Josephine dropped Kaya off at the Paria College car park just before 7:30 AM. There, he met with the other hikers as agreed. Wendy greeted him with a friendly peck on the cheek. She wore figure-hugging skinny black sweatpants tied provocatively with a white cord at the front, a red T-shirt and a black baseball cap with her hair in a ponytail. She carried a small black and grey rucksack with a pink plastic water bottle tucked in the elastic side pocket.

In Florian Hütter's black Opel Zafira, Gobelyn sat in the front passenger seat; behind him, in the middle row, were Rev Baker, Tom and Shantel, while Kaya and Wendy occupied the converted rear seats. Spexy drove a silver Nissan March hatchback. Miss Mow Dem, Iceberg, Sean Charles, and Barry Gangasingh were her passengers. Jaysen transported Raima, his girlfriend, and Samantha Mohan in his old Toyota. Unexpectedly, Bruce de Bulk arrived in his new BMW with Cobo, Deron, Mukesh, and Adrian. Since Bruce's father and Cobo's mother were both prominent WHT patrons, Gobelyn reluctantly agreed that they could join the hike. Raima and Bruce were history. To Bruce, and the handful of loyal supporters he still had, Raima was now the enemy and so was Wendy. Bruce would seek revenge, and Kaya expected trouble on the hike.

Hütter briskly led the procession of cars with his Opel. Jaysen proceeded behind with Spexy following him and Bruce de Bulk bringing up the rear. Although he had said very little to Raima since Bob Maharaj's notorious birthday party, Kaya still considered Jaysen to be a very good ally. In the days before Tolan Rapp's Tay Mo, Jaysen and his friends effectively protected Kaya against harassment from Cobo and his cohorts. Jaysen, who never really got along with Bruce de Bulk, knew full well how much Kaya liked his pretty cousin, Raima.

Hütter somehow hoped to entertain his passengers with classical music composed by Wolfgang Amadeus Mozart. Even so, Kaya clearly heard the much more preferable pulsating soca music that emanated from the customised car stereo system, which Jaysen was so very proud of. Nevertheless, Kaya thought nothing of Hütter's choice of music; after all, Hütter originated from Austria.

However, Gobelyn said, "Well, this makes a change."

"How so?" asked Rev Baker.

"It's usually the Godfather of Soul," said Gobelyn, with a smile.

"James Brown? Ja, that CD has been skipping of late," said Hütter. "You don't like Mozart? I can change it if you like."

"Mozart's absolutely fine," said Gobelyn, before muttering, "for a lullaby...."

"I don't mind," said Rev Baker. "Maybe, Tom and his friends could do with a nap, after a night of disco dancing. Perhaps you could put something livelier on when we're close to our destination."

Just ten minutes later, while Tom fought a losing battle to keep his eyes open, Rev Baker snored, and Shantel touched down in Dreamland. Wendy's night of wanton wining had taken its toll; she snuggled drowsily on Kaya's shoulder, and he soon lost track of time. Kaya realised he had been asleep for a while, when he woke to the discreet delight of Wendy gently nibbling on his neck. She immediately stole a kiss. Thanks to Mozart, Hütter, Wendy, and Kaya were the only ones awake in the Opel Zafira.

"Did you ever watch old movies with your mom?" Wendy asked Kaya, whispering dreamily.

"Yeah," said Kaya, softly.

"As a kid, it was a real treat for me to watch old movies with my mom and dad. They love romantic classics like *Casablanca*, *Roman Holiday*, *Breakfast at Tiffany's*, and *Gone with the Wind*. Have you seen any of those?"

"Nope," said Kaya, with a mischievous grin, "and frankly, Wendy, I don't give a damn."

Wendy pinched Kaya's shoulder playfully. "Did you ever wonder if someone would ever love you madly?"

"Ah still wonderin' dat," said Kaya, not yet willing to take the conversation seriously.

"For a long time, I wondered what it would be like to be in love. You know, truly, madly, deeply in love," said Wendy.

"Yeah, gyuls does t'ink 'bout dem t'ings," said Kaya. Then, he saw in Wendy's dewy eyes that she was being serious.

"Now I know what it's like, eh, to be in love; because of you, Kaya. I love you...."

Years ago, in the happy days when he still played with toy ray guns and plastic glow-in-the-dark laser swords, Kaya imagined that if any girl ever told him, 'I love you', he would cockily respond, 'I know'.

Hearing the magic words slide off Wendy's luscious lips, he swallowed hard and confessed without a second thought, "I love you too, Wendy."

"Yes, I know," said Wendy.

Kaya and Wendy chuckled softly, before the irresistible lure of their warm lips brought sweet kisses and pleasurable silence.

Although Kaya never imagined that the first time a girl told him she loved him, it would occur in the back seat of a car traversing the potholed road to the Azura National Park, the moment seemed perfect nonetheless. The music of Mozart, Wendy's glazed green eyes, the mild blush across her dimpled cheeks, the husky sound of her voice, her luscious lips, the gentle caress of her cool breath on his neck, and the subtly intoxicating scent of jasmine from her warm skin, were forever committed to Kaya's indelible memory. From that moment on, the music of Mozart would mean love, kisses, and Wendy Wong.

For a while, they kissed as if it would be their last kiss. Finally, Kaya came up for air, with the taste of lip gloss tantalising the tip of his tongue. From the Zafira's rear-view mirror, he caught a glance of Hütter's reflected stare, but the WHT guide quickly returned his piercing gaze to the road ahead and suppressed a knowing smile.

"What's wrong?" asked Wendy, softly.

"Nothing," said Kaya, "Nothing at all."

48

DOWN IN THE PARK

Twenty minutes later, at 8:40 AM, the Wildlife Heritage Trust hiking party arrived at the designated parking area, situated near an old cocoa estate, on the outskirts of the Azura National Park. It was the end of the rainy season, and the Immortelles were in full bloom. The spectacular sight of the twenty-five metre tall trees, with their laden crowns bedecked with flame-orange flowers, caused Rev Baker to gasp with delight.

"If you look closely, you'll spot a few white-necked jacobins," said Gobelyn, to Rev Baker, as they exited Hütter's Opel Zafira.

"Ah yes," said Rev Baker, holding up his compact camera to take snapshots.

"They are among the most striking hummingbirds," said Hütter. "You'll notice their royal blue hoods, viridian green backs, dark wings, white bellies, and white bands on their nape. Quite distinctive," he said, with an uncharacteristic smile.

On this occasion, Hütter planned to guide the hikers along a steeper, faster, less-travelled route to the Blue River Falls. This way held the opportunity to explore a small network of limestone caves that housed a colony of oilbirds. Although this trail avoided the sandy beaches, it afforded opportunities to frolic in shallow limestone pools of clear freshwater that were ideal for swimming.

Looking at the unfamiliar track, winding its way three kilometres uphill to the thunderous Blue River Falls, Kaya remembered the desperate moments he spent fighting for his life in the overflowing Snake River. Thanks to his newly developed total recall, he recollected even the smallest detail with astonishing clarity. It was Kaya's attention to detail that contributed to his growing unease. Gobelyn knew Hütter quite well, and he thought it odd that Hütter chose to listen to Mozart. Then there was all the smiling. On the geography hike, Hütter rarely smiled. Now, he smiled more, spoke less, and what he said was more pessimistic than before. Previously, Hütter felt obliged to pick up every bit of rubbish tourists and hikers carelessly left along the trail; however on this occasion he barely noticed the discarded bottles, cartons and food packaging along the way. Perhaps he was simply tired or in a bad mood; nevertheless, Kaya carefully observed the WHT guide's every move. He also kept a close eye on Bruce, Cobo, Spexy and Shantel, although he had more or less concluded that Shantel was neither a Setian agent nor a Niburian shape-shifter.

Soon, the group approached a ridge that overlooked the mouth of the Blue River and afforded panoramic views of the sand and sea below.

"So, what do you make of the Azura National Park so far, JB?" Gobelyn asked Rev Baker, who had been snapping photographs and taking in the lush scenery. An eastern spur of the Venezuelan Andes Mountains, Trinidad's Northern Range was home to over 400 types of birds. It was a bird-watcher's paradise.

"Stunning, Gobbers, simply stunning," said Rev Baker. "It's even better than the impression Tom gave me, and he spoke very highly of the flora, fauna, and breathtaking vistas here in Azura. I feel twenty years younger."

"You should have seen this place twenty years ago," said Hütter. "A lack of respect for the environment has led to the destruction of much of this area's natural beauty. It has become the adopted home of criminals, squatters, and hermits. There, do you see that?" said Hütter, pointing to a devastated area of forest on the mountain slopes across a bay. "The Azura National Park is a protected area. The destruction you see was caused by illegal slash and burn agriculture. This is a serious problem. Fire constitutes the greatest environmental threat to these ancient forests and their unique wildlife. More effective policing and increased public support for resource protection is required. Much more must be done to preserve this country's natural assets. Much more...."

"I always thought you first came to Trinidad twelve years ago," said Gobelyn.

"Ja-ja, I moved here permanently twelve years ago," said Hütter, "but I first visited the island eight years before that. That's when I first fell in love with Trinidad."

A few minutes later, Gobelyn pointed out an orange-winged Amazon. It was a predominantly green parrot with orange feathers in its wings and tail, which could be seen during flight. Although, not endangered, Hütter grimly advised that the large bird, known locally as the orange-winged parrot, was considered an agricultural pest by members of the local farming community. This type of an exotic bird was often captured and sold in the thriving pet trade.

Suddenly Kaya heard powerful guttural grunts, barks and howls. Initially confused by the sound, he thought there might be a pack of stray dogs in the vicinity, but he soon realised that the racket came from the forest canopy.

"That is the call of a red howler monkey," announced Hütter, sweeping his sandy-brown hair from his sweaty brow. "There is a troupe nearby. The dominant male is reinforcing his territory; they often do this when rain is approaching, so I hope you brought rainwear."

"I can see them," said Tom, "they're over there." He peered through binoculars and pointed to the left.

Kaya did not need binoculars. He easily spied the troupe of ten reddish-brown primates foraging for leaves and fruits, high in the treetops, two hundred metres away.

"They are mostly found in the forested area of the south east," said Hütter, "but we have at least three families resident here in the Azura National Park. Red howlers are among the loudest animals on Earth."

"Yuh t'ink Iceberg is ah red howler?" said Deron, and the Mapepires all laughed.

Ahead of them, Curtis *Iceberg* Joseph trailed several paces behind Spexy and Miss Mow Dem. In hushed tones, the young women remained engrossed in a saucy private conversation. Daydreaming, Iceberg absentmindedly picked his nose, rolled the glob of mucus he extracted between his fingers, and then placed it in his mouth.

Kaya recalled everything he read; he remembered once reading the scientific claim that ingesting nasal mucus constituted a natural way of boosting the human immune system.

Nevertheless, as he observed Iceberg lick sticky mucus from his fingers, Kaya's overriding thought was, *Yuck.*

"Ewww," whispered Raima, both amused and disgusted.

"Dat real repugnant, oui," said Samantha Mohan.

"Somebody really ha' tuh tell Iceberg somet'ing 'bout dat nastiness," added Shantel.

"He so reminds me of a guy from my old school in Oxford," said Tom. "He was also a compulsive nose-picker who ate his bogeys. We called him Roger the Bogey Biter. Eventually, he had to undergo major surgery on his nose."

Samantha Mohan laughed a bit too much while Shantel simply sucked her teeth dismissively.

"No, I'm being serious," said Tom. "Roger the Bogey Biter had never been any good at multi-tasking, but one day he tried to run down the stairs while picking his nose. He tripped and fell — face-first. The doctor told him he was lucky he hadn't killed himself, by sticking his finger in his own brain."

"Ah doh t'ink Iceberg have ah brain," came Shantel's deadpan comment.

Samantha playfully punched Tom on the shoulder and laughed excessively.

"Ah go tell Meenal," whispered Raima, teasingly.

Samantha wore tight jeans, and Jaysen's girlfriend wore a low-cut blouse that barely contained her ample assets. Raima and Shantel sported distractingly skimpy shorts. Poor Barry Gangasingh seemed entranced, at least to Kaya. Kaya did not need telepathic abilities to see that Raima laughed outwardly but cried inside. Bruce, Cobo, and Deron had been making insulting and provocative comments throughout the forest trek. And, when her guard was down, Kaya caught a few sad glances from Raima.

The laughter snapped Iceberg out of his daydream. He reached into his pocket with his nose-picking fingers and retrieved a handful of unwrapped sweets.

"With a smile, he innocently asked, "Anybody want ah sweetie?"

Sean Charles, who had been walking ahead and remained unaware of Iceberg's filthy habit, immediately said, "Pass one here, bredda."

Iceberg generously threw him a few. Sean caught them and immediately popped one into his mouth.

"Oh, no," whispered Raima. Then, she giggled.

"Somebody gimme ah bucket, ah goin' tuh throw up," said Samantha.

Laughter ensued, but Iceberg and Sean remained none the wiser.

"Speaking of sweets," said Gobelyn, "be sure to thank your mother for the Christmas cake, Abaniah, it was the best I've had."

"Ah will let her know," said Kaya, "and t'anks fuh talkin' tuh her 'bout lettin' meh come on de hike."

"As much as I am tempted to take credit where no credit is due," said Gobelyn, "I must confess, I have not spoken to your mother regarding this expedition. In fact, it has been some time since I last spoke to your mother about anything at all. I do hope she is well."

"Yeah, sir," said Kaya, recovering quickly, "she OK. Ah mean tuh say, t'anks fuh offerin' tuh talk tuh her fuh meh."

"Well, it seems my offer proved enough for her to allow you to come," said Gobelyn, with a smile, "and we're glad you're here."

"Yeah, t'anks, sir," said Kaya, convincingly.

Kaya's heart raced. He believed that Golsha Zigg, the shape-shifting Mad Renegade, had impersonated Gobelyn at the Paria College prize-giving ceremony, which meant that she specifically wanted Kaya to join the hike.

She could have taken the form of any one of his companions, or she could be lying in wait, somewhere along the trail, ready to pounce.

Moisture from the waterfall saturated the air, as the group of WHT members followed a narrow ancient path, five metres above a fast-flowing tributary of the Blue River. Dark rain clouds swept overhead. And, with each step, the sound of the Blue River Falls grew louder, punctuated by the sporadic roll of distant thunder. An ominous gloom descended on the forest, and the wildlife became increasingly silent. A feeling of dread consumed Kaya. When he left home, early that morning, Kaya thought he could deal with any danger; but, at any moment, he realised that he could be literally proven dead wrong. Kaya suddenly became desperately concerned about his mother's safety. Intent on communicating with Josephine, he retrieved his mobile phone and immediately realised he had a missed call from her, timed at 8:06 AM that morning.

"Yuh hear meh phone ring while we were in de car?" he asked Wendy.

"No, I think I fell asleep for a while. As divine as it is, the adagio of Mozart's *Serenade No.10 for Winds* knocked me out cold. Is something wrong?"

Kaya noticed he had no mobile reception. "Check yuh phone, tell meh if yuh ha' ah signal."

Wendy pulled her mobile phone out of the front pocket of her rucksack and checked it. "No, doux-doux, no signal. What's happening? You look worried."

"Ah need tuh call meh mudder," muttered Kaya, and he caught up with Tom. "Tom, yuh phone have ah signal?"

Tom checked his phone and said, "No. What's up?"

"Ah need to call meh mudder."

"Well, we are in a forest, maybe there just isn't any reception here, can't it wait?"

"Ah have ah bad feelin'. Ah just wan' tuh know she alright."

Just then Hütter shouted, "C'mon, let's pick up the pace. If we hurry, we could reach the shelter of the caves before the rain comes."

Out of earshot of everyone else except Kaya, Tom whispered, "Is it the Papa Bois is coming to town type of feeling?"

"It worse dan dat," said Kaya, grimly.

"Now would be a good time to start telling me all the stuff you haven't been telling me, don't you think? Nobody becomes a grandmaster of kung fu overnight, no matter how much curry they eat."

"Shh," said Kaya, impatiently. He listened intently for a while, and then he said, "Somebody comin', ah could hear dem."

"Yeah, whispered Tom, "We're on a hiking trail, it's probably just other hikers."

"Ah doh t'ink so," said Kaya, and he developed a nosebleed.

"It's OK, Tom, I've got it," said Wendy, assertively. "I just need a minute with Kaya."

"Are you OK?" Tom asked Kaya, his voice brimming with concern.

"Yeah, I'm fine," said Kaya, pinching his nostrils to stop the flow of blood, "just give us ah minute."

Bruce and the Mapepires, who had been bringing up the rear, overtook Wendy and Kaya.

"Ah hope he buss ah blood vessel in he brain," muttered Cobo, contemptuously.

"Lean forward," whispered Wendy, gently dabbing Kaya's nose with a small towel. "Do you trust me?"

"Yes," said Kaya, softly.

"Do you know who's following us?"

"Ah have ah idea, buh if ah tell yuh, yuh wouldn't believe meh."

"I need you to trust me, Kaya...."

Just then, three gunshots rang out in quick succession. Instinctively, Kaya had tried to shield Wendy, but she immediately grabbed him by the hand.

"Run, Kaya, run!" screamed Wendy, pulling Kaya off the path.

"Hands up! Fling yuh hands up!" shouted a tall, dark man who emerged ahead of the group.

A red bandana covered his head, and another masked his face. He brandished a sawn-off shotgun with smoking double barrels.

Hütter pulled out a concealed handgun from the small of his back, but he was immediately mown down by a hail of bullets from the man's armed accomplices, hidden in the undergrowth. Hütter tumbled off the ridge, rolled down an incline then fell into the fast-flowing river several metres below. Consumed by shock, Kaya caught a glimpse of Hütter's body being swept away as he made a dash into the bush with Wendy.

"Bring dem dong!" shouted the leader above the hysterical screams of Samantha Mohan and Jaysen's girlfriend.

As Wendy urged him to run faster, shots rang out and Kaya immediately heard the lethal bullets whizz past his ear. Over his shoulder, Kaya saw two masked pursuers, armed with pistols, desperately trying to line up clear shots. Without slowing down, Kaya quickly retrieved his slingshot, loaded a ball bearing and fired, hitting one of the men between the eyes. He howled and tumbled into a clump of shrubs. Directly ahead of the second man, Kaya saw the distinctive grey papery nest of Jack Spaniards hanging from a tree.

He fired a perfectly aimed, perfectly timed shot, which dislodged the nest of large aggressive wasps. The nest fell on the head of the running thug, who threw himself to the ground and rolled about frantically trying to avoid repeated stings from the swarm of provoked paper wasps.

Unfortunately, another masked man had overtaken Kaya and Wendy. He stood before them and took deadly aim with a sawn-off shotgun.

To Kaya's horror, Wendy skidded to a halt and barked, "Get behind me. Now!"

Wendy meant to shield Kaya with her body, but Kaya had other plans. He leapt on Wendy, as a shot rang out.

"No!" screamed Wendy.

Kaya felt the impact of the slug as it ploughed through his rucksack. The pain in his back was so great, he had difficulty remaining conscious. Kaya collapsed into Wendy's loving arms, knocking her to the ground under his weight. He had done what he promised himself he would do. He had saved Wendy Wong.

49

PROTECTION

Kaya spent a few agonising seconds, lying face-down on the leafy forest floor, trying to focus beyond the excruciating pain in his back. And, in that brief moment, he considered all that was worth living for. Kaya had been shot, and he wondered why he had not died.

In his mind, he clearly heard a deep earthy voice say, *"Get up, Hezekiah. You must get up now. Death is upon you."*

Mr Rapp, thought Kaya. *Ah t'ink ah need yuh help....*

Wendy had recovered quickly. And she defiantly stood her ground as the murderous criminal levelled the sawn-off barrel of his shotgun with her chest. Once again, Wendy seemed willing to sacrifice herself.

"No, Wendy, no...." cried Kaya.

Suddenly, he heard the dreaded report of the gangster's shotgun, and his broken heart skipped a beat. Desperately scrambling to his feet, Kaya anticipated facing his fatally wounded love. But, to his surprise, Wendy still did not budge. However, the smoking shotgun slipped from the limp grasp of the masked criminal. Dazed, the man stumbled a few feet, clasped his head, vomited then fell to the moist earth and convulsed.

Shocked, Kaya muttered, "Yuh kill him...."

"No, I convinced him that he has severe food poisoning," said Wendy, coolly. "Please don't ever risk yourself to protect me again. I don't think your pocket Bible will save you a second time.

"Yuh psychic," said Kaya, accusingly, and a terrible rage rose from the pit of his stomach.

"Yes, Kaya, I am psychic, just like you," said Wendy, and she swallowed hard.

"So, all dis time, yuh lie tuh meh," said Kaya, brimming with anger.

"Deep down, you've always known I was like you," said Wendy, and a single tear trickled down her cheek. "Listen, I know. It's wrong, and I'm sorry, but sometimes we lie to protect those we love, and I do love you, Kaya."

"No," said Kaya, through gritted teeth. "Ah know wha' yuh want. Yuh use meh as bait—"

Suddenly exhibiting complete control, Wendy cocked her left eyebrow and said, "Can we talk about this later? I need to stop the men behind you from blowing your head off your shoulders."

Two gangsters approached. Armed with pistols, they took deadly aim at Kaya. Wendy focused, and the men immediately dropped their weapons, cried out in pain, and began stumbling about in the bush blindly.

"Oh-Gawd-oh-Gawd-oh-Gawd, ah cyah see," cried one of the men.

Kaya backed away from Wendy, defensively. "Yuh Setian?" he asked.

The question wounded Wendy. Kaya saw the pain in her eyes.

"How could you ask me that? I am an agent of the Osirian Guard," she said, her voice dripping with disappointment. "I was assigned by the Osirian Council of Twelve to protect you."

"Dey send yuh tuh look after meh?" scoffed Kaya.

"Now, listen to me carefully, ordinary guys with guns are the least of our troubles—"

"Dey shoot Hütter. Dey have meh friends—"

"I'm guessing these men are kidnappers. If they're just normal human beings, they can be controlled by psychic suggestion—"

"Why yuh didn't stop dem from shootin' Hütter?"

"I tried," said Wendy, "but another mind worked against me; I think there's at least one Setian spy in our group."

"Yeah," said Kaya, "Hütter was actin' strange."

"I'm not convinced it was Hütter," said Wendy, grimly. "I knew the Setians would be watching you, so I tried to stop you showing off your abilities—"

"Yuh drug meh water when ah was fightin' Adrian."

"Yes. You'd become stronger than we'd anticipated. The Setians are afraid of you, Kaya. So afraid, that twenty minutes ago, their High Commander personally issued a warrant for your containment. Agents of Seti are converging on our location, right now. They mean to take you, Kaya — dead or alive."

Kaya hastily slid his rucksack off his back. Just below the bag's front pocket, he saw the entry hole of the gangster's shot. Worried that his mobile phone had been destroyed, Kaya hurriedly checked the contents of his rucksack. To his relief, he quickly established that his cell phone remained intact; however, the shotgun slug had sliced through the metal casing and batteries of his LED flashlight, before being lodged in the compact pages of his pocket Bible. Kaya checked his mobile phone, but he discovered, to his dismay, that it still had no reception.

"You can't call your mother," said Wendy. "You can't call anyone. Normal mobile phones won't work here; the Setians are jamming the signals. Don't worry, once the containment order had been issued, two of our best agents were sent to protect your mother."

"Yuh expect meh tuh trust yuh now?"

"I expect you to use your common sense. I need you to make an educated guess — that's what trust is. Help is on the way to us, but, to survive, we'll need to work together. There is something else here in the forest, and it's far more dangerous than Setian clones."

"Golsha Zigg, de Mad Renegade," muttered Kaya, grimly.

"Yes, I think she is very close. Protecting you will be no easy task; Osirian shields are not completely effective against Golsha Zigg's plasma weapon, which is why you received injuries when she shot you in the back."

"Yuh mean dat night ah was at de waterfront? You were dere?"

"If I hadn't, you'd surely be dead."

Wendy pulled the pink water bottle from the side pocket of her rucksack. She removed the cap and said, "Here, drink this. It'll make your mind stronger."

Kaya caught the vaguely familiar grassy scent of the liquid. "What is dat?" he asked tentatively.

"It's an Osirian mind amplifier mixed with a natural supplement; I think you call it karaili," said Wendy.

"Karaili? No, t'anks, ah rather die dan drink dat," said Kaya, dismissively.

"That's not funny."

Wendy retrieved a shimmering item of clothing from her rucksack.

"Here," she said, tossing it to Kaya, "put that on."

Kaya caught it. "What is dis?"

"Work clothes," replied Wendy. "It's a camo-shielded bodysuit; you wear it below what you've got on. It absorbs most of the energy from Setian weapons and makes you difficult to be seen. Hurry up, the Shu-Senyn will be here any second."

Wendy did her best to seem nonchalant while Kaya removed his shoes and ankle weights and quickly stripped down to his underwear. She went about retrieving the weapons from the fallen criminals.

"I'll have de shotgun," said Kaya.

Wendy walked towards where the trail overlooked the river. She began throwing the weapons into the fast-flowing water.

"Wha' yuh doin?"

"These weapons were made by men to kill other men," said Wendy, and her green eyes narrowed. "They are absolutely useless against Setian shields."

"Like is crazy yuh gone crazy—"

"When these men finally wake from the deep sleep I've induced, they won't be able to shoot us or anyone else."

"Guns better dan nuttin'...."

"Kaya, do you really think you're ready to kill? Do you understand why the Setians are so afraid of you?"

Kaya grumbled, "Right now, ah 'fraid you."

Kaya quickly donned the Osirian bodysuit, which automatically adjusted to perfectly match his skin tone. To his surprise, he felt completely naked. The bodysuit had a cooling effect and did not restrict movement in any way. He hastily put on his regular clothes on top of the Osirian suit, placed his ankle weights in his rucksack and slipped the rucksack on his back.

"So, wha' 'bout yuh parents, dey agents too?" scoffed Kaya. "An' college, how many agents in college?"

Ignoring the questions, Wendy tossed Kaya a wristwatch and he caught it.

"It's your personal shield controller; twist the face to activate your bodysuit. It also keeps perfect time."

Shaking his head, Kaya clasped the watch around his left wrist.

"Ah cyah believe dat all dis time ah didn't see wha' yuh were up to."

"I was assigned to assess you," said Wendy. "Once I confirmed who you really were; and, that the threat to your life was real, my mission was escalated to shield status. You have to understand, I was ordered not to reveal my identity. Why can't you forgive me?"

"Ah forgive yuh," said Kaya, reluctantly.

No, thought Wendy. *No, you don't. Oh, what does it matter? They'll probably banish me to Siberia, for getting emotionally attached to you.*

"Kaya, listen to me carefully. No matter what happens, no one must know what we are. Osirians and Setians have secretly existed on Earth since the dawn of mankind, and they will stop at nothing to remain secret."

"Yeah, ah know; buh de kidnappers already shoot Hütter, and ah have tuh save meh friends."

Without ah shotgun.... thought Kaya.

"Right now, it's just two of us—"

"Ah ent 'fraid de Shu-Senyn, ah could handle dem."

"Yes, two maybe. But there are six of them closing in on us, and I counted at least three more kidnappers. There is also Golsha Zigg and a Setian spy. We can't take them all on alone Kaya, it'll be suicide, eh?"

Dat explain why yuh t'row 'way all de guns.

"How many Osirians comin'?"

"Four agents," whispered Wendy, motioning Kaya to be quiet.

"Kaya, the Setians do not believe in free will — the Shu-Senyn have been brainwashed and programmed. They can't be reasoned with — they will not deviate from their orders. Don't let their business suits fool you; they're physically much stronger than we are and genetically engineered for combat. I know you've been taught Cyclan Tay Mo, but that's not good enough. The problem with the people of Cyclo is that they're mostly intellectuals, not killers. In war, that's a severe handicap. If you rely solely on your defensive Tay Mo, the Shu-Senyn will kill you," projected Wendy.

"Yuh have ah gun, right?"

"Yes, it's a non-lethal stun weapon; we value all sentient life," projected Wendy.

From her rucksack, she retrieved the stun weapon, which was cleverly disguised as a simple mobile phone. Shaking his head with dismay, Kaya retrieved his slingshot.

"Put that toy away," projected Wendy, *"it will only annoy the clones."*

50

PAPA BOIS AND THE CLONES

Deep within the Azura Forest, in the sweltering heat and sticky humidity, Kaya briskly led Wendy on a steeply inclined tight path along a ridge, which overlooked a fast-flowing tributary of the Blue River. With walls of limestone on either side, the path further narrowed into a natural bottleneck.

"You are under the legal protection of the Osirian Colonies," said Wendy to Kaya, telepathically.

"Dat's very nice," projected Kaya, sarcastically.

"I'm hoping the Setians aren't stupid enough to risk another all-out war by killing us."

"So, de Osirians and de Setians were at war?"

"Oh, yeah, it was almost a lifetime ago since the followers of Seti tried to take over the planet, but maybe you've heard of it. It was imaginatively called World War II. There was a lot more to that war than most people realise. We've held an uneasy truce with the Setians since then."

Kaya and Wendy quickly followed the path through the bottleneck and onto a small plateau. Flanked by a wall of limestone, broken only by the narrow entrance of a cave, the clearing overlooked the river valley and the winding hiking trail. With the aid of a flashlight on her multipurpose mobile phone, Wendy visually checked the cave for nasty surprises. Above the din of the nearby waterfall, Kaya listened intently for any telltale sounds of approaching clones. He discerned nothing alarming. And yet, the dark silence of the cave unsettled him.

"We'll have de advantage here," projected Kaya. *"We have de high ground an' dey will have tuh come one by one, wit' de sun right in dey eye."*

"We also have some cover behind those limestone rocks and a quick escape route into the cave network. I'm impressed," projected Wendy. *"The Baronet has taught you well."*

"Baronet? Wha' baronet? Yuh mean Tolan Rapp? Ah learn strategy from watchin' TV an' playin' computer games."

"You don't know—"

"Ah know de Setians sen' de same clones dat kill meh fadah tuh get meh. Dey doh care 'bout Osirian legal protection."

"Kaya, exactly what has Tolan Rapp told you?"

"He tell meh everyt'ing. He tell meh he doh trust allyuh. Ah know what yuh up to. Yuh want meh tuh lead yuh to him. Well, da' ent goin' tuh happen."

"He hasn't told you everything, Kaya. I am not your enemy. The Osirian Colonies of Ki, the Cyclan Confederacy of Neutral Planets, and the Talisian Empire have a secret alliance. We are bound, by treaty, to assist you."

"So, yuh tellin' meh yuh have Osirian agents in another galaxy?" scoffed Kaya.

"Yes, Kaya, there's a lot you don't know, and it's not my place to tell you. You'll have to ask your teacher."

Of the six clones in the Azura Forest, Kaya sensed only the two he had encountered before — Shu-Senyn Vets and Shu-Senyn Yerek. Wendy called this pair, Tweedledum and Tweedledee. Long before he heard the approaching clones, Kaya felt their presence. Long before he saw their pale faces masked by dark glasses, which hid their stone-cold grey eyes, Kaya heard their disturbing thoughts.

"The boy is special," communicated Vets, telepathically.

"He has been trained by the fugitive," projected Yerek, the shorter of the two.

"Our enemies protect him."

"We must take him, nonetheless."

"Our mandate is clear."

"Yes, brother. We must take him or kill him."

Wendy activated her personal shield and became almost invisible, except that her sudden movements created minor distortions — ripple effects that Kaya could see in direct sunlight.

"They're here," projected Wendy.

She crouched behind an outcrop of rock and aimed her stun device at the bottleneck in the path ahead.

"Activate your shield. Keep an eye on the cave; we don't want any clones sneaking up behind us."

With his heart pounding in his heaving chest, Kaya twisted the face of the Osirian wristwatch. Positioning himself in a shadowy area, behind a tree on the periphery of the clearing, he marvelled at how he had become virtually invisible. Kaya quickly realised that in the dark, the Osirian camo-shields were far more effective at concealment. So, he kept to the shadows and avoided any sudden movement. Kaya observed the grim determination in

Wendy's tight jaw, frowned brow and narrowed eyes. He wondered what motivated her more — love or duty. He found himself admiring her brave beauty. He found himself fearing for her life.

Armed with black futuristic pistols, dressed identically in white shirts, black suits, ties, shoes and hats, Shu-Senyn Vets and Yerek cautiously approached the bottleneck that led to the clearing. A break in the clouds caused brilliant sunlight to shine directly into the thick-rimmed sunglasses that hid their icy grey eyes.

Kaya saw Wendy take aim, and fear and anticipation rose from the pit of his stomach.

However, he heard movement emanating from the cave behind her and suddenly realised, *"They're decoys!"*

Wendy fired. An energy bolt hit Vets in the chest, knocking him off his feet and into the wall of limestone. Yerek, the shorter of the two, immediately shot at Wendy, while two more clones emerged from the cave and also opened fire on her position.

"Kaya, when I stun Tweedledee make a run for it — down the path. Do you understand? Run for it," desperately projected Wendy.

"Right now, ah shotgun would be nice," projected Kaya.

"Serious men are we," announced the clones in unison. "Surrender or be killed."

Pinned down by enemy crossfire, Wendy huddled on the floor as energy bolts pummelled the rocks and shrubs around her. Kaya drew his sling and shot Yerek between the eyes, but the ball bearing simply bounced off Yerek's personal shield, without harming him. However, Wendy was right — Yerek got extremely annoyed. Kaya's foolhardy and futile attack had only served to betray his position to the angry clone. Kaya stumbled backwards as a volley of energy bolts sliced through the air in his direction. Conquering his fear, he focussed his thoughts and his will on Yerek. He had managed to influence this clone mentally, before, and he hoped to do so, again. Two more men in black emerged from the cave and immediately joined their comrades in firing upon Kaya and Wendy. To Kaya's horror, a bolt slammed into Wendy's chest, momentarily deactivating her shield and knocking her to the ground like a rag doll.

"No," shouted Kaya and Yerek in unison.

Under Kaya's telepathic control, Yerek shot the clone that had brought Wendy down. Unfortunately, the three remaining clones responded by targeting Yerek. In quick succession, several energy bolts slammed into Kaya's mental puppet. And, effectively neutralised, Yerek tumbled backwards along the narrow path before coming to an unconscious rest on its verge.

Suddenly, Kaya heard the deafening blast from a bull horn. It echoed from the cave and drifted across the river valley. A blood-curdling animal roar quickly followed, covering Kaya with goose bumps. The three remaining clones turned their heads and looked at each other in a mechanical manner. In unison, they then trained their weapons at the mouth of the cave. Kaya heard the dull thud of approaching cloven hooves and felt elated.

Finally, Mr Rapp.... thought Kaya, and he sighed with relief. *Wha' take yuh so long?*

Papa Bois slowly emerged from the intoxicating gloom of the cave — a monstrously large, horned, hunched-over muscle-bound man-monster. With fiery eyes and a dark, ragged unrecognisable face, shrouded by wild white dreadlocks and a goatee beard, the fearsome creature lumbered, into the light, to tower an impressive nine feet. Kaya's naïve excitement quickly became abject dread, for this was not the Papa Bois he knew — this was something much larger, darker and much more sinister.

Mr Rapp, is dat you?

Presented with the folkloric monstrosity that stood before them, the pale men in black became even paler, and Kaya became light-headed with fear. For an excruciatingly tense moment, the father of the forest stood and stared with scowling red eyes lit with danger.

Finally, Papa Bois spoke with a dark thunderous earthy Trinidadian voice, which oozed power and malice.

"De forest is mine an' all de animals is meh family. Yuh come from tong, tuh make trouble in de country; buh yuh make ah mistake, tuh t'ink Papa Bois easy. Yuh better run quick-quick-quick, 'cause ah vex an' ah hungry."

Indeed, Kaya's heightened sense of self-preservation urged him to run, but he would rather die than leave Wendy at the mercy of Papa Bois and the clones.

The cloned men in black communicated telepathically and Kaya caught some of it.

"We are three."

"It is but one."

"We are ... not enough...."

The three Shu-Senyn opened sustained fire into the broad chest of Papa Bois, forcing him to stumble two steps backwards. With the clones distracted, and remaining under the cloaked protection of his Osirian camo-shielded bodysuit, Kaya stealthily moved to Wendy's side.

"What are you doing?" projected Wendy. *"You have to run, Kaya. You have to run, now."*

"Not wit'out you."

Kaya helped Wendy to her unsteady feet. With a loud growl, Papa Bois charged the man in black who stood closest to him. Being shot at point blank range only seemed to make the towering folkloric figure angrier. Papa Bois clasped the clone on both sides of his head and wrenched it. To his horror, Kaya heard the nightmarish crack of the clone's neck being broken.

Papa Bois held the Shu-Senyn's head, which now faced back towards where Kaya and Wendy stood. Frozen in shock, and barely visible under the protection of their Osirian camo-shields, Kaya and Wendy watched in awe as Papa Bois ignored the frantic shots of the two remaining clones.

"Look. Look good. Like is see yuh cyah see?" said Papa Bois with unmasked derision, into the ear of the dead clone. "Yuh quarry gettin' away."

Whatever doubts Kaya had, instantly evaporated.

"Dis is de Mad Renegade."

"Come on, Kaya, follow me," screamed Wendy telepathically, and Kaya followed the ripples of her frantic dash towards the path.

In a fit of vengeful insanity, two of the remaining clones tried to engage the Mad Renegade in hand to hand combat; however, with a single head-butt, the horned Papa Bois lookalike instantly ended the life of one of the clones. Kaya needed no further invitation. He raced after Wendy towards the bottleneck. But Shu-Senyn Vets, who had been slumped against the wall of limestone pretending to be unconscious, suddenly grabbed Wendy's ankle as she ran past him. Wendy stumbled and fell, and her momentum rolled her down the narrow path, until she came to rest next to the fallen Yerek. Without slowing down, Kaya reached over his shoulder into his rucksack. Vets began to raise his pistol.

Yuh kill meh fadah, thought Kaya, and rage momentarily replaced fear.

Before Vets could fire, Kaya pulled out one of his ankle weight belts and whipped him across the head with it, knocking him unconscious.

"Come on, Wendy, get up," said Kaya, once again helping her to her feet.

Kaya quickly snatched Yerek's sunglasses and pistol.

"Don't put that on," said Wendy, referring to the Setian sunglasses, "it has a two-way telepathic projector. If you wear it, the Setians will know all that you know. You'll hear their thoughts and see what they see, but they could use it to seize control of your mind. Forget the gun; it's useless against Golsha Zigg's shields."

"Ah could use it tuh rescue we friends from de kidnappers."

"Maybe, but the Setians can track it," projected Wendy, grimly.

With a frustrated sigh, Kaya also threw the Setian pistol into the river. *"Right.... one less gun fuh us tuh worry 'bout."*

Kaya watched in terror as the last standing clone launched a perfectly executed kick, which smashed into the head of the Niburian shape-shifter. This desperate act only made her even angrier. Hoisting the clone above her head, with strong tattooed arms, the Mad Renegade hurled him twenty metres, over the edge of the plateau, and to his doom. Kaya saw the clone smash on unforgiving boulders before his broken body was swept away by the fierce currents of the tributary. As Kaya and Wendy ran for their lives, they caught brief glimpses of the clone corpse being flushed downriver. Looking over his shoulder, Kaya soon realised that Golsha Zigg was in hot pursuit.

"She'll catch us," projected Wendy, desperately.

"We ha' tuh jump," said Kaya, telepathically.

Before Wendy could protest, a deadly plasma bolt ignited an adjacent tree, a split second after they ran past it.

In the guise of Papa Bois, Golsha Zigg roared, "Run quick, Kaya; run quick, Wendy. Run quick-quick-quick, because ah vex an' ah hungry."

Another plasma bolt barely missed Kaya and Wendy; it slammed into the path two paces ahead of them. As they desperately ran, Kaya looked out for a clear opening through the trees and shrubs that flanked the old trail. A quick glance over his shoulder confirmed Kaya's fears — the Niburian shape-shifter had been steadily gaining on them, and she now had a clear shot.

"Jump!" projected Kaya.

He instinctively grabbed Wendy's arm — violently hauling her with him as he leapt off the path. A plasma bolt singed his baseball cap, just as the wind snatched it off his head. For a few seconds, Kaya experienced the surreal exhilaration of flying through the air. He let go of Wendy, seconds before impact with the river water silenced her scream and plunged him into cold, wet, murky confusion.

51

THE DARK AND THE DEEP

Kaya fought his way to the surface of the fiercely foaming river and gasped for air. For a few agonising seconds, he could not see Wendy, nor could he hear her thoughts.

Instead, as panic threatened to overwhelm him, Kaya heard the distinctive voice of Tolan Rapp. *"Are you afraid, Kaya? That is good. That is very good. Immerse yourself in fear, do not resist it. Let your bones shake and your heart quiver. Learn from it. Only by fully experiencing fear, can you ever hope to control it. For soon, you will arrive at that fateful hour, when controlling your fear, could mean the difference between life and death."*

Kaya briefly wondered whether he had truly received a projection from his Cyclan mentor or had Tolan Rapp's words simply been a hysteria-induced figment of his subconscious mind. The river was shallower than he anticipated and its course stronger than he had hoped. Its forceful tide dragged and pulled Kaya as he struggled to stay afloat. Kaya feared Wendy had crashed into one of the many boulders that littered the riverbed. And, when he finally saw her barely visible outline — face down, arms outstretched, being ushered away by dispassionate currents, he knew his fear had been justified. Kaya held a deep breath and dove into the underwater flow, using his arms and legs to propel him closer to his unconscious girlfriend. The rucksack on his back hindered his progress, but there was no time to lose — Wendy would slip away and be drowned if he delayed to remove his burden.

"Wake up, Wendy, wake up," projected Kaya, to no avail.

In the submerged gloom, Wendy's camo-shielded body was difficult to discern. Kaya reached out blindly and caught nothing. He needed to breathe — his head throbbed painfully. He launched himself forward with a powerful flutter kick and reached out once more. His fingertips brushed against Wendy's ankle. A few strenuous strokes and Kaya came alongside Wendy, held her waist and launched himself up to the surface with her in tow. Kaya gulped for air. However, Wendy remained unresponsive as he battled to keep her head out of the depths. Wendy's eyes were closed, her cheeks appeared hollow and pale and although she was not bleeding, a prominent bruise marred her forehead. Instinctively, Kaya performed mouth to mouth resuscitation on Wendy. Eventually, she spluttered and gasped, but she did not open her eyes. Kaya continued to administer the breath of life, but Wendy unexpectedly responded by transforming Kaya's efforts to revive her, into a passionate kiss.

"Mmmm.... As much as I love kissing you, maybe getting out of the river should be our priority, eh?" projected Wendy, languorously.

Surprised and relieved, Kaya broke the kiss. The tips of their noses touched as he stared into Wendy's dewy-green eyes and did his best to hide his elation. She was not bleeding; however, Kaya noticed that Wendy's pupils were unevenly dilated — she had suffered a concussion.

"Ah wasn't kissin' yuh," projected Kaya, and Wendy misinterpreted the cause of his unusually sombre mood.

"Whatever," said Wendy, telepathically. "You want to be angry with me? Fine, but I know you still love me — I'm psychic, remember?"

Kaya took a deep breath and plunged below the murky surface of the surging water. He twisted and turned, using his arms to free himself of his restrictive rucksack, which he abandoned to the powerful stream. Wendy did the same, and they set about battling the currents, steadily inching towards the nearest riverbank. Kaya took solace from the knowledge that bull sharks no longer frequented these northern rivers, as they did centuries ago. Shark attacks were unheard of in Trinidad and Tobago. A brilliant flash of silvery-blue light and a deafening thunderclap heralded a sudden downpour of torrential rain.

"Great.... I suppose we can't get any wetter...." said Wendy, telepathically.

"Ah t'ink we lose de Mad Renegade," projected Kaya, squinting as raindrops beat relentlessly against his face.

"Fat chance," projected Wendy. "Oh, my head really hurts.... She's toying with us, like a cat with mice. She's been known to do that to amuse herself, eh? Niburians are the most dangerous beings in the universe, and, this one is totally bonkers."

As they swam towards land, Kaya saw a fiery orange ball streak across the dark clouds in the brooding, slate-coloured sky, one hundred metres above them.

He recalled the words of Tolan Rapp, "For many years, she had been impersonating several of this island's folkloric characters, including Papa Bois, Soucouyant, La Diablesse, and Ligahoo."

"So, de Mad Renegade's ah Soucouyant now?" projected Kaya.

"Chem hasguhnar…. No, I get it…. That's not a fiery old lady flying through the sky. That's a supe-sushippu…. Oh, my head is spinning…."

"Yeah, yuh hit yuh head…. Yuh ha' tuh see ah doctor. Where de other Osirian agents?"

"Oh, I think they're winging their way here…. Ugh, you're right … I don't feel too good…."

Where Mr Rapp when ah really need him? thought Kaya.

"Rapp? That's his Swedish alias…. He's probably protecting your mother, where else would he be? That thing, up there — it's a modified escape pod from the Cyclan Deep Space Explorer Talibah. Golsha Zigg can operate it remotely. Did I tell you she's a genius? She's managed to create superior shields based on matter transfer beam technology. She projects it from her pod. That's why the Shu-Senyn guns had no effect. You'd need a heavy cannon, to knock it out."

"So, she up dere, lookin' down on us?"

"She often uses the pod as a distraction — a decoy. She's probably on the ground, somewhere; trying to track us, mentally, using the pod's ENDAR."

"We ha' tuh stop her."

"I can't, but maybe you can."

"How yuh mean?"

"Compared to yours, my telepathic ability is very limited. It's the same for all Osirians and Setians. The sun robs us of our psychic powers. We take supplements to compensate. Even so, our abilities could never match those of the psychics from the Cosmic Sea."

"Ah not from de Cosmic Sea."

"But your grandfather was, eh? And, some of the women on your mother's side of your family have latent abilities that manifest in their sons — abilities beyond those of stormbringers. Soter-like abilities."

"What is ah stormbringer?"

"There is so much he hasn't told you, eh? Stormbringers are among the most powerful psychics of the Cosmic Sea."

"OK, so what is ah soter?"

Wendy shook her head with dismay. *"The soter is the chosen one."*

Lightning illuminated their watery surroundings with a flash of silver and blue. And, for a second, Wendy's camo-shielded outline seemed to glow, at least to Kaya. Wendy was an exceptional swimmer. Kaya marvelled at how effortlessly she glided through the water. The intermittent symptoms of her concussion notwithstanding, Wendy appeared to be completely at home in their aquatic environment, so much so that Kaya imagined her to be a dark-haired, green-eyed, dimpled-cheek mermaid.

"I was born in Atlantis," projected Wendy.

Although he could not decide whether or not she was joking, Kaya chuckled. *"Yuh t'ink I am de chosen one? Dat's why yuh interested in meh?"*

"No, Kaya, you are definitely not the soter, of that I am certain," projected Wendy, with anger. *"If Golsha Zigg doesn't kill us both, you'll probably figure it all out, soon enough."*

Wendy had already complained of a headache and dizziness, and Kaya knew that irritability was another symptom of a concussion. Wendy had manifested mild confusion, the pupil of her left eye was much larger than that of her right, and she had expressed her thoughts with an unusual mixture of languages.

"So how yuh go stop ah Niburian?"

"With your mind, Kaya, with your mind. And, Kaya, from now on, stay away from trees; she's been known to mimic trees."

Amid the constant roar of the nearby Blue River Falls, the relentlessly pounding rain and the irregular peals of thunder, Kaya heard a loud splash — about one hundred metres behind them. Looking over his shoulder as he swam, he saw a monstrous creature about eight metres long, slithering across the river's darkly surging surface. At first, Kaya thought he had seen a giant green anaconda, the world's largest, heaviest species of snake, which Trinidadians called Huille. Also referred to as water boas, these massive constrictors were excellent swimmers, known to ambush unsuspecting prey in rivers by dropping upon them from overhanging tree branches. However, what Kaya saw was only half snake. Golsha Zigg had transformed into another terrifying character from the pantheon of Trinidad and Tobago's folkloric entities. She had become Mama Dlo, the mother of the water — the female counterpart of Papa Bois, the father of the forest. Her upper body was that of a dark, beautiful West African woman, with an ornately tattooed face, luxuriantly long jet-black hair, and an incongruously forked, serpent-like tongue. Below her torso, Mama Dlo was all snake, laterally undulating in a swift serpentine method, steadily gaining on Kaya and Wendy.

According to Tantie Rose, a quick-witted person could escape Mama Dlo by removing their left shoe, placing it on the ground upside down, and then beating a hasty retreat by briskly walking backwards.

Kaya recalled Wendy's recent comment, *"Fat chance."*

"Swim fast, Wendy. Swim!" projected Kaya.

Kaya observed the terror in Wendy's eyes. With a loud crack, Mama Dlo whipped her serpentine tail and accelerated. The mother of the water eerily suspended her human-like head and upper body above the surface, as she zigzagged with remarkable speed.

Mama Dlo ran a golden comb through her long, black hair and said, "From Talparo tuh Nariva, and Oropouche tuh Shark River, de water is mine — de creatures call meh mudder. Yuh come from tong, tuh bring violence an' murder; buh yuh make ah mistake, tuh t'ink Dlo is ah pushover. Yuh come fuh Bouchon, buh he is meh lover. Yuh better swim quick-quick-quick, 'cause ah ent takin' no prisoner. Yuh hear meh? Swim quick-quick-quick, ah ent takin' no prisoner."

In the torrential rain, Kaya and Wendy swam for their lives against a tide that threatened to wrench them away from the riverbank. Telepathically, the couple actively willed each other on. They desperately grabbed hold of the smooth, drenched rocks of the riverbank, but one last desperate glance confirmed that Mama Dlo was upon them.

52

A WOMAN SCORNED

Effortlessly emerging from the wild water of the raging river, Golsha Zigg in the guise of Mama Dlo, quickly shed her half-snake vestiges to become a beautiful African woman exuding grace and poise. Ornate tattoos decorated her dark face, and she strode on long, perfectly shaped legs. Mama Dlo continued to comb her luxuriant hair, which fell well beyond her thin waist and shrouded her stunning nudity. Kaya and Wendy inched away from the grim Niburian shape-shifter. They clawed, crawled and then stumbled clumsily on the muddy riverbank. After she had muttered something unintelligible, Wendy's eyes rolled back in her head. She collapsed. Barely able to contain his terror, Kaya rose to unsteady feet and shakily stood his ground, facing the dark, grandiose woman standing before him in the pouring rain.

"What ah brave, brave boy yuh are, Hezekiah Abaniah," said Mama Dlo with derision, and her eyes glowed red.

"Ah not afraid of you," said Kaya, and his knees trembled, and his hands shook.

"Yuh should be, Hezekiah. Yuh should be," said Mama Dlo, in a honeyed tone.

Mr Rapp, if yuh could hear meh, ah really need yuh help now….

Mama Dlo raised her right arm, opening her hand to reveal her plasma weapon — a skin-coloured glove with a silvery-blue disc set in the palm. Kaya focussed. A sinister smile perverted Mama Dlo's pouty lips, and her fiery eyes narrowed as much as Kaya's fearful eyes widened. Convinced that his only effective weapon was his mind, Kaya braced himself for a battle of wills with Golsha Zigg, the deranged Niburian that now assumed the form of Mama Dlo. Wendy was dying, Kaya felt it. But he needed to banish fear. He needed to focus. That fateful time, when controlling his dread meant the difference between life and death, was upon him.

Kaya assertively asked Mama Dlo, "Why yuh doin' dis?"

Taken aback, Mama Dlo paused momentarily. "Because I can," she cackled, in a thoroughly witch-like fashion.

"Is dat why yuh kill meh gran'fadah?"

Mama Dlo's manic smile gradually faded, and she assumed a sombre, reticent demeanour.

Lowering her weapon and momentarily losing her strong, Trinidadian accent, she said sadly, "I didn't kill Ekon, it was Agnes...."

Mama Dlo began to cry. And, in amazement, as lightning flashed and thunder rolled, Kaya watched her slowly transform into another black woman — one that was even more beautiful. Mama Dlo became Agnes Talbot, the persona Kaya's grandparents once knew.

"I didn't mean to kill your grandfather," she said, between sobs. "It was a mistake, a terrible mistake. I just wanted him to love me. Oh, Ekon.... Poor Ekon...."

For a brief moment, Kaya believed he could seize control of the situation. However, without warning, the Mad Renegade flew into a bitter rage.

She screamed, "Why didn't he love me? I plundered his mind to become the vision of beauty he so desired, yet he ignored me. Despite the promise of wealth, longevity, and pleasures of the flesh beyond his wildest imaginings, he humiliated me. I was his perfect match, yet he spurned me. Why? Why do you think your grandfather did that, Hezekiah?"

"Well, ahm...." said Kaya, flabbergasted.

"I sense you find intelligence as irritating as I find stupidity," said Agnes with impatient disdain. "Come now, surely you know why."

Yeah, yuh damn mad, thought Kaya.

However, he told Agnes, "Miss Talbot, maybe he didn't t'ink he was good enough fuh yuh."

"You may have noticed I am neither a doe-eyed schoolgirl nor a wizened old maid," said Agnes condescendingly. "In time, I married a man worthy of my affection, so please refer to me as Mistress Hall."

And, with those words, she unwittingly divulged her secret to Kaya. He recalled hearing similar words uttered from the lips of a woman he thought he knew. For several years, Golsha Zigg had hidden in plain sight, in the seaside town of Coconut Grove. And now, Kaya knew her secret identity. He knew exactly where she lived. Kaya had controlled his fear, but he could no longer control his rage.

"Meh gran'fadah see right through yuh," said Kaya, clenching his fists. "He love meh gran'mudder, not you. So, yuh kill him. Yuh kill both ah dem."

Agnes shouted, "They humiliated me! I am a superior being; they should have worshipped me, but instead they humiliated me!" And then, in a soft sweet voice, Agnes spoke as if sharing a secret with her closest friend. "But don't worry, I have been rescuing your grandfather, he will live again. Years ago, I gathered his genetic material and after several failed attempts I finally made a breakthrough. I have been cloning him, and this time he will love me. But, you see, there is so very little to work with.... Not nearly enough to induce successfully accelerated growth; not nearly enough to sustain his fragile life. That's why I need you, Hezekiah. You are Ekon's only surviving male relative, and I need your lifeblood. I need to transfuse your life force. So you see, you must die, Hezekiah, so that my Ekon could live."

Lying in the mud, drenched in rain, Wendy groaned agonisingly.

Agnes looked upon Wendy with contempt. "We can't have your little Osirian trollop telling tales, now, can we?"

Agnes raised her hand to reveal her palm weapon, which she callously aimed at Wendy.

"No!" yelled Kaya.

In desperation, he mentally generated a short, sharp telekinetic burst that pushed Agnes's arm a split second before she fired. The plasma bolt missed Wendy, electrifying the ground adjacent to her.

"Insolent fool," said Agnes delivering a devastating slap with the back of her hand.

Kaya landed in the mud, four metres away.

"I could swat you like a fly," said Agnes, coldly.

"Coulda, woulda, shoulda," said Kaya, defiantly.

He immediately launched another psychic assault, and Agnes temporarily developed double vision. Undeterred, she tried to blast Wendy again, but Kaya delivered a stronger telekinetic shunt that pushed Agnes backwards. To her growing exasperation, her aim once again missed Wendy. However, she focussed her considerable psychic faculties on Kaya. Kaya briefly felt as if his head was on fire, but he counterattacked by convincing Agnes that she could not see.

Dat is how she kill Kerwin, thought Kaya, and blood trickled from his nostrils.

He scrambled to Wendy's side and found to his dismay that she was only barely breathing.

Mr Rapp, now would be ah good time....

Angry and frustrated, Agnes ran towards Kaya. She attempted to land several punches, but Kaya avoided each and every one. Agnes placed her palm on Kaya's forehead, intent on frying his skull. He quickly twisted backwards and drove the back of his head into the bridge of Agnes's nose. That really made her angry. And, with a mighty roar, she transformed into a Soucouyant, engulfed in raging flames that steamed and hissed in the pouring rain.

The Soucouyant cried, "You an' yuh harlot will never go home, yuh blood an' yuh bone ah go make meh own. Now yuh go reap what you have sown, yuh blood an' yuh bone ah go make meh own."

Mr Rapp, ah beg yuh; please save meh from dis woman bad poetry....

In the guise of the dreadful Soucouyant, Golsha Zigg, the deranged Niburian shape-shifter, stood before Kaya — engulfed in a shroud of steam and flame, poised to deliver a lethal blast of plasma energy from her palm weapon. Suddenly, high above them, two black triangular objects emerged from the thick thunder clouds and began to bombard Golsha Zigg's hovering escape pod with energy rays. Momentarily distracted, the Soucouyant shrieked with anger. Kaya seized this opportunity to retrieve his slingshot, quickly.

"Yuh wan' meh tuh play Goliath tuh yuh David, silly boy?" cackled the Soucouyant.

"Damn right," muttered Kaya, who swiftly loaded and fired.

His shot was true, and the steel ball bearing hit the flaming witch right between her eyes. She howled in astonished agony. Kaya had sensed that the effectiveness of the Mad Renegade's protective shield, which was generated by her modified escape pod, had become intermittent following the aerial attack. The Soucouyant turned her nefarious attention to the unknown vessels that hovered above, and she willed her pod to return lightning-like plasma fire to its attackers. Kaya shot her again, hitting her on her left cheek, and again on her chin. With a growl, the Soucouyant unleashed lightning bolts from the palm of her hand.

In spite of Kaya's formidable protective shielding, the direct plasma strike broke three of his ribs and sent him into cardiac arrest. Wracked by unendurable pain, and knowing he would soon die, Kaya saw the reassuring faces of the women he had loved most in his life — his mother Josephine, his cousin Raya, his grandmother Mama Flo, his grandaunt Tantie Rose, Raima Khan and Wendy Wong. Before the long darkness took him, Kaya caught a brief glimpse of two ocelots leaping upon the crazed Soucouyant as she prepared to deliver her coup de grâce. Kaya heard the Soucouyant scream, and that was the last thing he heard.

53

DEATH IN THE AFTERNOON

Panic-stricken, utterly disorientated, Kaya painfully regained consciousness, only to discover that his nightmare had not yet ended. He was not where he expected to be. He was no longer face to face with a folkloric monstrosity on a secluded riverbank in a desolate, rain-drenched ward of the Azura National Park. He was somewhere else — naked, submerged and obliged to breathe an oxygen-rich liquid instead of air. Fearing he had been captured by Golsha Zigg, Kaya tried, in vain, to escape the confines of the fluid-filled metal alloy pod that now completely imprisoned him.

"*Calm yourself, Hezekiah,*" came a familiarly sonorous voice.

"*Mr Rapp, is dat you?*" cautiously projected Kaya.

"*Yes.*"

"*Prove it....*"

"*At this moment, I am not inclined to humour you.*"

"*Yeah, dat'll do....*"

"*Despite my explicit warning, you engaged Golsha Zigg in combat, and—*"

"*Mr Rapp, wha' really happen tuh meh?*"

"*You died.*"

"*Die?*"

"*After sustaining a direct plasma strike, you suffered cardiopulmonary arrest, which resulted in your clinical death for a duration of six minutes. Nevertheless, I revived you. The regeneration process has repaired your broken bones; and, although it was somewhat challenging, I have successfully reversed both your ischemic brain injury and cardiac trauma. I am no medical practitioner, so this is something of a personal triumph.*"

"*Oh-ho, ah had a heart attack. T'anks fuh savin' meh,*" projected Kaya.

Buh maybe yuh could learn tuh use smaller words, he thought.

"*Your injuries would have been irreversible, were it not for your shielded attire. You should consider avoiding the Azura Forest altogether; I may not always be on hand to save you from your misadventures within its boundaries."*

Kaya projected his consciousness beyond the confines of the liquid-filled regeneration pod that housed him. In his mind's eye, he confirmed that he was within the now familiar interior of the Captain's Cutter.

"Where's Wendy?"

"Don't be alarmed, your hybrid friend is quickly recovering in the regeneration pod next to yours. I have successfully treated her brain injury."

He know she Osirian, and he still bring she here. He's ah good man. He wouldn't let nobody suffer, thought Kaya.

Kaya had not heard Wendy's thoughts for some time, and he worried, but he kept his innermost feelings secret.

"Meh mudder OK?"

"Yes, I was able to protect her. I am sorry I could not come to your assistance sooner."

"Two Osirian agents were supposed tuh watch over her."

"Indeed," projected Tolan Rapp. *"They were somewhat tardy; nonetheless I was thankful for their arrival. Under the circumstances, I had little choice but to leave your mother under their watchful eyes."*

"So, wha'ppen tuh de Mad Renegade?"

"Once again she has eluded capture, but not before claiming another victim. The noble Akeeta is dead."

"De male ocelot dead?"

"He sacrificed his life in your defence and the protection of your companion. He was my brave and loyal friend."

"Oh, Gorm, ah sorry...." projected Kaya, with heartfelt sympathy.

"Neela's injuries were not severe, but she pines for Akeeta. They had a most unusual pairing — ocelots normally part ways after mating."

Kaya felt the sadness in his mentor's thoughts. Although he had never openly shown it, he had grown quite fond of the eccentric man from Cyclo. Kaya appreciated all that Tolan Rapp had done for him, and he wondered how he could possibly repay his many debts.

"Mr Rapp, ah know who Golsha Zigg is."

"Indeed, your thoughts are transparent."

"Ah know where she livin'."

"And with that knowledge, what do you plan to do?"

"Ah goin' tuh avenge meh gran'fadah, meh gran'mudder, an' each an' every life dat evil monster take."

"So, you would be her judge, jury and executioner?"

"She kill meh gran'parents. Ah only want justice."

"Cries for justice are often the bitter laments of the vengeful."

"Somebody ha' tuh stop dat monster."

"And how will you prevent yourself from becoming the very monster you seek to destroy?"

"Ah doh expect yuh tuh understand...."

"You know nothing of my sacrifice and loss," projected Tolan Rapp with an uncharacteristic flash of anger.

"Mr Rapp, ah totally appreciate everyt'ing yuh do fuh meh so far; buh ah doh like bein' in dis coffin, an' ever since ah born, ah doh like breathin' water. Please leh meh out."

"Indeed. Your treatment, and that of your companion, is complete. But, know this, Hezekiah; Golsha Zigg is quite possibly the most dangerous being on this planet. She was originally an Osirian agent and they are best equipped to contain her."

Tolan Rapp telepathically activated the end cycle of Kaya's unusual regeneration process. And, as fresh air replaced the highly oxygenated liquid chemical compound, which quickly drained away through the pod's hidden apparatus, Kaya's nose, throat and lungs felt as if they contained fire. His head throbbed intensely, and his eyes itched terribly. Kaya painfully expelled the fluid from his lungs into the confines of the regeneration unit, from where it was efficiently sucked away. At the end of the procedure, warm jets of air comforted him, drying his skin and the interior of the pod. Momentarily, the heavy door of the unit swung open, reducing Kaya's anxiety. From his reclined position, he observed Tolan Rapp looming above him, holding his clothes, from which evidence of the day's excitement with Golsha Zigg and the clones had somehow been removed.

"Get dressed," said Tolan Rapp, with a distorted voice, as he handed Kaya his clothing. "You may experience impaired perceptions, but all your faculties will soon return to normal."

Kaya covered his nakedness with the Osirian camo-shielded body-suit, which, according to Tolan Rapp, had saved him from irreversible injuries.

"Somewhere, in Azura, gangsters holdin' meh friends at gunpoint, an' ah ha' tuh save dem," projected Kaya, unable to find his voice.

He donned his black tracksuit bottoms and white T-shirt.

"Hezekiah, this may come as a shock to you, but you are not Batman, and this is no time for comic book heroics. At this very moment, armed police are converging on the criminals holding your schoolmates."

"How dat suppose tuh make meh feel better?"

"Let the police perform their duties."

"All meh friends go t'ink Wendy an' I run away an' leave dem...."

"It would be most unwise to return to the forest now."

Something important was missing.

"Your thoughts are transparent," said Tolan Rapp, handing Kaya the necklace Wendy had given him.

"Dis is not ah transponder," projected Kaya, confidently, and he draped his neck with Wendy's Christmas gift.

"Of that I am certain," said Tolan Rapp, with a warm smile, and he activated the exit cycle of Wendy's pod.

Kaya felt mildly disappointed that she slept, fully clothed, in the Cyclan regeneration unit. Finally, Kaya took a good look at Tolan Rapp. His shimmering jumpsuit showed subtle signs of scorching and had a small rip on the left sleeve.

"Wha'ppen tuh yuh?" asked Kaya, with a froggy voice.

Kaya immediately caught mental glimpses of Tolan Rapp's recent past. Earlier that morning, while Josephine vacuumed her lounge and hummed a happy tune, Tolan Rapp engaged four Shu-Senyn clones in a life-and-death struggle in her secluded backyard. Employing an inventive combination of unarmed combat and gunplay, he eventually neutralised the formidable Setian agents. Tolan Rapp had been shot during the fray, and his subsequent regeneration treatment delayed his aid to Kaya. Looking around, within the Captain's Cutter, Kaya quickly realised that the four defeated clones each occupied a nearby regeneration unit.

"Dey dead?" Kaya asked Tolan Rapp.

"Of course not," said Tolan Rapp, matter-of-factly. "They are just very messed up. Obviously, I could not leave them lying under the mango tree in your mother's backyard."

"Yuh fight four clones by yuhself an' yuh win?" said Kaya, thoroughly impressed.

"I wish it were otherwise. Violence assails the spirit."

"Buh yuh win," said Kaya, gleefully.

"Hezekiah, during your dream training I have gone to great lengths to explain to you that winning is not everything. At this very moment, Setian and Osirian vessels are closing in on our location. They must not find us."

Suddenly, Kaya heard a mechanical alarm and immediately deduced it was the cutter's proximity alert.

"Screen on," barked Tolan Rapp in the Cyclan language, and the cutter's holographic viewscreen activated. "ENDAR sitrep."

Kaya understood the alien characters generated by the cutter's enhanced detection and ranging system. He effortlessly read the situation report that flashed across the advanced display. Kaya observed the lone approaching craft — a black, triangular object engulfed by a pall of dark clouds. To

Kaya, the large black silent Setian ship, with its pulsing coloured lights at each corner of its triangle, bore all the hallmarks of a classic UFO.

Dem Setians like black fuh so ... sometimes really dark grey....

Suddenly the cutter's interior lights dimmed and Kaya heard a high-pitched whine.

The Captain's Cutter processed an eerie transmission. "This is the voice of a Higher Authority," said the ominous Shu-Senyn. "We know you can hear us, Cyclan. You are an invading alien, and we demand your unconditional surrender. Your continued defiance is futile."

Kaya's head tingled, and he sensed there was another message, hidden within the transmission, something subtle and ever so elusive — sounds within sounds.

"We are under attack, Hezekiah. The Setians have unleashed a psychic storm, protect yourself," said Tolan Rapp, barely able to speak.

Kaya experienced an undeniable onslaught on his senses. Unable to breathe properly, he felt his heart racing and he gulped for air, gaining little satisfaction from his desperate efforts. Slowly suffocating, Kaya watched helplessly as Tolan Rapp fell to his knees, clutching his chest in agony. Suddenly, Wendy sat bolt upright. Her lucid stare filled Kaya with awe and the devastating realisation that she, not the Setian agents in the black triangle, hovering high above them, was the source of the terrible psychic assault.

"Those who claim 'winning is not everything', are usually losers," said Wendy, with thunderous and uncharacteristic arrogance.

"Those who believe winning to be everything can be expected to do anything to win — and predictability is a handicap," said Tolan Rapp, with some difficulty.

Wendy smirked. Unable to face the horror of her betrayal, Kaya bore the brunt of denial. He fell to the floor, gasping for breath, in a room filled with breathable air.

Ah cyah believe Wendy is ah Setian agent....

"I am the voice of a Higher Authority," said Wendy to Tolan Rapp. "I know you can hear me, Cyclan. You are an invading alien, and I demand your unconditional surrender. Your continued defiance is futile."

At that moment, Kaya knew that there had indeed been an infrasonic message hidden within the transmission from the Setian ship — a message meant for Wendy. But he had more pressing concerns — he was dying from asphyxiation. His pulse raced, and his blood pressure went through the roof. Kaya caught a brief glimpse of his bug-eyed reflection from the shiny surface of the nearest regeneration unit. And, just before his supine body began to convulse, he noticed that his face sported an unflattering hint of oxygen-deprived hypoxia-purple.

"Hezekiah, domo sharti exzomné!" projected Tolan Rapp in an archaic language, *"Domo sharti exzomné!"*

Domo shartee ex-zom-nay.... thought Kaya.

A lack of oxygen made concentration somewhat difficult. As his body shook uncontrollably, Kaya imagined himself floating in a crystal clear pool of warm water, and his wayward thoughts spiralled into ever decreasing circles.

Domo shartee ex-zom-nay.... What dat mean?

It seemed an eternity to him, but Kaya had only forgotten his fluency in Old Cyclan for the briefest moment.

De sleeper must wake....

The words bore deep into the recesses of Kaya's retreating mind, opening mental windows that spewed their priceless secrets. A sudden awareness of a treasure trove of trans-human abilities flooded Kaya's awestruck consciousness. In the nick of time, Kaya began to countermand Wendy's compelling suggestions. He began to regulate his breathing, properly. Kaya's lungs processed the rich air that filled the interior of the Captain's Cutter, and his oppressed faculties returned, more robust than they had ever been.

The Setians had corrupted Wendy, whose artificially-enhanced psychic abilities were far greater than Kaya had been led to believe. They had turned Wendy into a sleeper agent. Activated by their infrasonic trigger, she pursued the insidious Setian objective of capturing Tolan Rapp and the advanced technology he possessed. However, Tolan Rapp had made preparations of his own. Through dream training, he had covertly developed Kaya's most advanced trans-human talents and prepared him for inevitable psychic confrontations. Kaya's abilities were far more potent than Kaya or anyone else other than Tolan Rapp had realised. Tolan Rapp had transformed Kaya into his own sleeper agent, and *Domo sharti exzomné* was his passphrase.

De sleeper must wake....

54

SLEEPERS WAKE

As Wendy's singular intellect hacked its way through the formidable firewalls of the cutter's central processing unit, Kaya employed cunning countermeasures garnered from his mentor. At any rate, during his dream-time simulations, Tolan Rapp had not considered the possibility of Kaya falling in love with a potentially deadly foe. Love? Love changed everything. Kaya could stop Wendy, but only if it did not involve harming her. Even so, he would not permit Wendy to harm Tolan Rapp. Kaya found himself in an exceptionally difficult situation, and his dream training had not prepared him for the rising rage, which threatened to unhinge him. From the very beginning, Tolan Rapp, the Osirians, the Setians, Wendy Wong and even Golsha Zigg had manipulated Kaya. He had been the slumbering pawn they each sought to employ in an intricate web of power, politics, and paranoia.

De sleeper wake up now.... thought Kaya.

He sensed a deception, not from Wendy, but from Tolan Rapp, who had anticipated the daring Setian offensive. Tolan Rapp had a plan. In contrast, Wendy's transparent thoughts focussed primarily on determining the precise frequency of the cutter's defensive shields. And, for a moment, this puzzled Kaya.

Why she doh just lower de shields?

The ship's CPU provided Kaya with the answer he sought. The Captain's Cutter laid partially buried in the soft mud at the bottom of the Nariva Swamp, and its energy shield envelope protected it from the silty freshwater of Trinidad's largest wetland. Tolan Rapp had led the Setians to believe that this remote, east coast location on the southernmost tropic isle was his secret hiding place. His carefully chosen actions had served to misdirect them. He had a plan. Wendy, on the other hand, had a mission. A millisecond before Kaya intercepted her thoughts, she projected the cutter's shield modulation frequency to the Setians that hovered high above in their cloud-shrouded triangular ship.

"Hezekiah, I must leave you now. Try not to harm our visitors while I'm gone. We are Cyclan — it's not our way," projected Tolan Rapp.

He winked mischievously at Kaya but remained lying on the floor, where he had fallen, under the invisible yoke of Wendy's formidable psychic storm.

"Wha'?" quizzed Kaya.

Unexpectedly, Tolan Rapp rose to his feet and spoke to Wendy in a calm and authoritative tone.

"Domo sharti domoné."

Domo shartee domo-nay…. De sleeper must sleep? Buh wha' trouble is dis?

Before Kaya could intervene, Tolan Rapp drew his pistol and dematerialised in the wake of a matter transfer beam. At that precise moment, two Setian Elite Troopers appeared. Predictably dressed all in black, they wore futuristic military gear and heaved formidable firearms, which they ominously trained on Kaya. All the same, he simply sucked his teeth. And, with a dismissive wave of his right hand, he sent the soldiers careening to the floor. Kaya sedated the Setian intruders with irrepressible mental suggestions, just as Tolan Rapp had triggered Wendy's sleep with archaic Cyclan words.

Even so, she reached out to him from within a lucid dream.

"Kaya…. I'm sorry," projected Wendy.

"Nah-nah-nah, doh worry 'bout dat," said Kaya, telepathically, with thinly veiled insincerity.

"I've failed so completely in my mission to protect you, eh? Even now, I don't know when or how the Setians programmed me. I'm so sorry…."

"Sorry? Sorry, fuh what? Yuh only gimme ah headache — 'oman doin' dat since Adam 'n' Eve."

Silent tears streamed from Wendy's closed eyes, trickling over her ears and onto her headrest in the regeneration pod. Kaya watched impassively as the lips he still yearned to kiss, failed to articulate.

"I love you…."

De most popular lie ever told, thought Kaya, steeling himself — allowing the projected words to pass over without pity and without response.

Tolan Rapp's plan had succeeded. Kaya sensed it. But, at the last moment, something had gone terribly wrong.

Tolan Rapp returned to the Captain's Cutter in the silver-blue electrical haze of a transporter beam. He clasped a heavy prize close to his heart as if his continued existence depended upon it. Instantly drawing from his encyclopaedic memory, Kaya identified the object in his mentor's arms. With a few minor modifications, the stolen Setian hyperspatial initiator could transform the Captain's Cutter into a faster-than-light interstellar craft. Tolan Rapp could use the upgraded cutter to take his father's KARIN vaccine to the faraway Cosmic Sea Galaxy and the beleaguered people of Cyclo. He could stem the deadly epidemic callously unleashed by the warlord Brakis Tarn during the Second Psychic War. He could save millions from a fate worse than death; at least, that's what Kaya thought in the heady, euphoric moment before he sensed the unendurable pain and anguish that wracked his mentor.

Tolan Rapp slowly slumped to the floor, revealing a deep, cauterised wound in his back. He had been shot again. And, judging from his injury, his personal shield had not afforded him enough protection.

"Oh, no," muttered Kaya, racing to Tolan Rapp's side.

"The Setians have shiny new guns," said a dazed Tolan Rapp, with an incongruous chuckle.

"Come, I'll help yuh get into ah regeneration pod."

"No," said Tolan Rapp, gasping. "No time. You must take the ship … away from here." Pulling Kaya close, he added desperately, "Don't let my father's … life's work … be all in vain…."

"Ah won't let yuh die…."

Once again, the cutter's proximity alert began its mechanical wail. This time, its ENDAR systems detected five more black triangles en route to their location in the Nariva Swamp.

"Listen…. I've underestimated … the Setians. They would use my father's cure … to create … to create a plague here on Earth. The Setians plan … to kill most of the world's population. Do you understand?"

"Ah go stop dem—"

"You can't do it alone."

"Wit' yuh help—"

"We both know … that using the regeneration pod again … so soon … would drain all … remaining power. If you try to save me … the ship will be captured … by our enemies." Tolan Rapp sighed. It was long and painfully heavy as if he had expelled most of what remained of his dwindling spirit. "I see now, I've asked too much of you. You cannot do … what is required. I will transport you. I will transport you and your companion … as far away from here as I can."

With his mind's eye, Kaya clearly saw what Tolan Rapp had set in motion. To his horror, he realised that Tolan Rapp had activated the cutter's self-destruct sequence.

In exactly five minutes, the old cutter, all its secrets and most of the Nariva Swamp, will vaporise.

"No," said Kaya, in utter disbelief. "Wha' yuh doin?"

"There is no other way," said Tolan Rapp, and Kaya watched the life draining from his mentor's staring eyes.

"Kaya," came Wendy's voice.

He ignored her. In blind desperation, he plunged his unfettered mind deep into the advanced circuitry of the Captain's Cutter. Nonetheless, it soon became apparent to Kaya that Wendy had not discovered the cutter's shield modulation on her own. Tolan Rapp had simply allowed her to hack her way into the cutter's mainframe so that the Setians were duped into lowering their shields. But, once Tolan Rapp returned with the stolen hyperspatial initiator, the cutter's firewalls automatically reengaged, as he had planned, and its formidable shields re-modulated. The cutter reverted to the impregnably shielded fortress that had confounded Setian and Osirian forces since 1908. Kaya knew he could eventually get past the walls upon walls of complex programming that protected the cutter's CPU. But it would not be anytime soon; and, certainly, not before his sixteenth birthday. Tolan Rapp had a new plan.

In exactly four minutes, the old cutter, all its secrets and most of the Nariva Swamp, will vaporise.

"Kaya, please let me help you," came Wendy's plaintive voice.

"You were sent by de Setians tuh capture him. You were sent tuh capture me. Yuh expect meh tuh trust yuh now?"

"Kaya, unless you trust me, your father who truly loves you will surely die."

"Fadah? Wha' fadah? Yuh gone too far now."

"Listen carefully. Your grandfather was Sur Raal Mar-Rin, Fourth Baronet of the Royal House of Ebla. Sarai Ninkara, the renowned exobiologist, was your grandmother. Your father, who suffers here before you, is Sur Torian Raal, Fifth Baronet of Corona, of the Royal House of Ebla. And, if your stubborn pride allows your father to die unnecessarily, you, Hezekiah Torian, will become the Sixth Baronet."

"Mr Rapp, dat not true, right? Clones kill meh fadah, right?" projected Kaya, and he held back his tears.

In exactly three minutes, the old cutter, all its secrets and most of the Nariva Swamp, will vaporise.

"Domo ... sharti ... domoné," said Tolan Rapp.

"No, Sur Torian, with all due respect, your programming can no longer control me. I will not sleep," said Wendy, with calm resolve. "Your thoughts are transparent. You plan to beam your son and me to safety. And then, you plan to die on this ship, with only your father's legacy for company. But your plans are doomed to fail, for your son who truly loves you will never leave your side, and I will never again forsake him."

"Be still, young, naïve Osirian; do not stir the tides of fate," said Tolan Rapp, his anger almost exhausting what little of his voice that still remained.

"Once upon a time, I believed it was OK to lie to protect those I love. I was terribly wrong, eh?"

"Mr Rapp, wha' she say 'bout you bein' meh fadah, it true?"

Kaya's mentor slowly shook his head with regret and dismay. He opened his glazed eyes and said, "Forgive me, Hezekiah, for my many mistakes … and the many … things … I have failed to do."

In exactly two minutes, the old ship, all its secrets and most of the Nariva Swamp, will vaporise.

Suddenly, he held Kaya in a tight, trembling embrace, which weakened with each and every painful heartbeat.

"I am your father. I cannot deny it."

Dumbfounded and giddy with conflicting emotions, Kaya held Torian Raal, his perishing father; a man he knew as Tolan Rapp. Kaya peered into light-brown eyes that were older, wiser mirrors of his own and he mourned their dying embers.

"Tolan Rapp was my dearest childhood friend," projected Torian Raal, *"a selfless orphan who volunteered to fight with the Finns in the Winter War against the Soviets. He was shot dead on the 13th of March, 1940 — the last day of the conflict."*

"He was a young man I once knew. A good friend. A very brave soldier," Kaya recalled his father saying.

In exactly sixty seconds, the old cutter, all its secrets and most of the Nariva Swamp, will vaporise.

"Hezekiah, when you were four years old, as an added precaution, I stored the formula for your grandfather's KARIN cure deep within your subconscious. I'm confident that you will find a way to get it to our people. I

have faith in you. Your Cyclan abilities are fully awakening — use them with wisdom."

Torian Raal's arms gently slipped off Kaya's shoulders, and he used his remaining strength to clasp Kaya's trembling hands.

"The girl, Wendy, was a victim of our enemies. She has been assigned to protect you — this I know to be true. We are only human — none of us faultless; even so, true beauty transcends perfection. Go now, my son. Take with you, my love … and my pride…."

The cutter's auto-destruct sequence commenced its final countdown.

TEN

NINE

EIGHT Setian Elite Troopers materialised in the cutter, armed to the teeth.

SEVEN

SIX Setian Elite Troopers took deadly aim.

FIVE

FOUR Shu-Senyn sat bolt upright in their regeneration pods.

THREE

TWO transporter beams engulfed Kaya and Wendy.

ONE

Kaya Abaniah, aged fourteen, shouted, "No!" at the top of his lungs; and, he flooded the interior of the Captain's Cutter with danger.

55

ESCAPE FROM NARIVA

ZERO Setians were left standing in the interior of the Captain's Cutter.

Ten Elite Troopers and four Shu-Senyn fell to the floor like marionettes that had their wires cut.

Kaya had harnessed ambient energy from the ship. And, during the final second of the countdown, he channelled it into precisely targeted telekinetic bursts that stopped the self-destruct sequence and neutralised the transporter beam. Directed energy offshoots overloaded the central nervous systems of his enemies, rendering them unconscious.

Today not ah good day tuh die….

Wendy stooped beside Torian Raal. "Here, let me help him," she told Kaya.

"What it is yuh goin' tuh do?"

"The same thing I did for you that night at the waterfront in Coconut Grove. I'm a healer. That's my special talent. I'll do my best to keep your father alive until he can be regenerated. You just get the ship out of here. Your father's a bit melodramatic, but he's right, eh? We can't let the Setians capture us; they must not get your grandfather's work."

"Hurry den," said Kaya.

Wendy gently placed her fingertips on Torian Raal's temples. She closed her eyes, and Torian Raal's eyes opened in a wide, puzzled stare. He sighed as if some great intangible burden had been lifted, and Wendy slumped backwards — her face suddenly pale and haggard.

"I did my best," she said, listlessly. Her usually bright, green eyes became dull and dispassionate. "Your father's still not well, eh? But he won't die from his plasma wound; at least not today."

"Help meh get him into ah pod."

With Wendy's help, Kaya assisted Torian Raal into a regeneration unit. Exhausted, Wendy fell limply into Kaya's arms. He lifted her and carried her towards a vacant pod. She gently draped her arms around his shoulders and kissed him, impulsively.

"Wha' yuh really doin'?" projected Kaya, pulling away from the lips he still yearned to kiss.

"Just shut up and kiss me."

"Ah still vex wit' yuh," projected Kaya. But, even telepathically, he was a poor liar.

He gently placed Wendy into the regeneration unit before hastily clambering into the cutter's command pod. Kaya instinctively donned the ship's command helmet, which integrated into the commander's life-support and regeneration unit. The current crisis activated the unfettered recall of Torian Raal's relevant dream training. Kaya remembered that the impressive helmet would amplify his will and allow him limitless control over all of the cutter's key systems. He recalled how to fly the ship — he recalled flying it many times in his dreams. His father, Torian Raal, had honed Kaya's advanced piloting skills as part of his contingency plans. If he were incapacitated or killed, it would fall on Kaya to deliver the KARIN cure to Cyclo.

Kaya reclined and quickly cleared his mind. Within a few moments, he sensed the cutter's primary systems as if they were extensions of his physical body. Torian Raal's daring raid on the Setian interceptor that hovered high above had bought them much needed time. However, Kaya accessed the cutter's sensor array and immediately ascertained that the Setian interceptor had begun powering its formidable weapons. Kaya immediately applied his amplified thoughts and activated the cutter's powerful electromagnetic anti-gravity engines.

"Ladies 'n' gentlemen, dis is yuh captain speaking; strap up yuhself tight-tight-tight, dis flyin' saucer goin' tuh take off."

Kaya slowly raised the cloaked cutter from the bottom of the Nariva Swamp. He briefly hovered 20 metres above the surface of the water before ascending vertically to 40,000 feet at transonic speed. Outside the cutter, everything moved in slow motion, at least to Kaya. He executed an impossible right angle turn. And, in the blink of an eye, headed south, traversing Venezuela and Brazil without turbulence or a shockwave of any kind. He headed unchallenged, to the South Atlantic Ocean, where he briefly stopped. Wendy assisted Kaya by stripping the unconscious Setians of their weapons and communications devices. Kaya briefly lowered the cutter's cloak and transported the ten Setian Elite Troopers and four Shu-Senyn to Zavodovski Island, an uninhabited volcanic island approximately 1,500 kilometres east of Cape Horn. There, on the desolate home of 2 million chinstrap penguins, the troopers and clones would await rescue.

Since coming to Earth in 1908, the Captain's Cutter had eluded capture. Kaya's grandfather had applied his genius to the cutter's modifications, taking it well beyond its intended use. The ship was utterly invisible to radar. And, once cloaked, not even the advanced Setian and Osirian ENDAR could detect it. Kaya deliberately led those that would pursue him on a wild goose chase. Eager to remain in the shadows, the Setians would zero in on the cutter's temporary ENDAR visibility. They would quickly and quietly retrieve their troopers and clones. Sanity would prevail. The cunning Setians would avoid an armed confrontation with the Osirians, whose Atlantis Colony lay hidden in the depths of the Bermuda Triangle, and whose Pacifica Colony remained cloaked within the Mariana Trench, in the Dragon's Triangle, in the deepest part of the world's oceans.

"Wendy, ah taking yuh back tuh de Azura Forest," projected Kaya, solemnly.

"You don't trust me...."

"Gyul, ah cyah trust nobody now."

Kaya knew that until the captured hyperspatial initiator was installed, and further modifications made, the cutter's range remained considerably limited, especially after the cumulative effects of three extended regeneration treatments, multiple matter transports and cloaked hypersonic flights. He had to quickly return Wendy to the Azura Forest, before returning the cutter to its secret hiding place. He had to regenerate his father before it was too late.

Father. An hour ago, this title referred to a mysterious man Kaya had never known; a man believed to have been killed by the Shu-Senyn. Now, father meant Torian Raal — Sur Torian Raal, Fifth Baronet of Corona. King Tyrion XVI originally conferred the hereditary aristocratic honour of baronet to Kaya's brilliant ancestor, Ram Kara. The honour elevated the philosopher and statesman to the landed gentry, within the Royal House of Ebla, the third most powerful of the seven dominant royal families of the Cosmic Sea Galaxy. The honour elevated Ram Kara, who thereafter bore the Tamerian Lion sigil of House Ebla with pride, above the prestigious Knighthood of the Royal Kingdom of Cydonia, Cyclo's wealthiest province. The line of succession of the Ram Baronetcy of Corona began with Ram Kara, followed by Seti Ram, Mar-Rin Seti, and Raal Mar-Rin, from whom Torian Raal succeeded to become the present holder, and Hezekiah Torian, also known as Hezekiah *Kaya* Abaniah, became heir apparent.

Kaya's father slept in an adjacent regeneration unit. Fatigue and injury had overwhelmed him. A part of Kaya felt elated that the man, he had believed to be his surrogate father, was actually his biological father. He felt delighted that his father still lived, but another part of Kaya felt confusing bitterness. From a very young age, he believed his father to be dead. From a very young age, he yearned for the father he never knew. His emotional wounds were fresh and deep. What would he tell his mother who still pined for Sur Torian Raal? What would he tell Josephine?

56

CONFESSIONS IN AZURA

From the command pod of the Captain's Cutter, Kaya beamed Wendy down to precise coordinates within the lush, drenched, tropical greenery of the Azura Forest. There, she rendezvoused with the two agents of the Osirian Guard sent to assist her with Kaya's protection. Kaya promised to meet with them in twenty minutes, after returning the ship to its secret hiding place and initiating his father's essential process of regeneration and healing. The Osirians had tracked Kaya's teachers, schoolmates, and their ruthless armed captors, to a nearby network of caves. And, with the Osirians' welcomed support, Kaya planned to mount a daring rescue.

The Captain's Cutter was equipped with Cyclan technological advances beyond those available to the Osirians and the Setians. However, because of the use of inferior components acquired on Earth, it was also severely restricted by a limited and relatively unstable power source. Nevertheless, design improvisations employed by Kaya's grandfather, Sur Raal Mar-Rin, had ensured that the cutter eluded detection and capture for over a century. Sur Raal equipped the cutter with his greatest, most secret invention, a transdimensional field generator. This unique and wondrous device enabled the Captain's Cutter to assume a hyperdimensional state, temporarily, which allowed it to travel through the solid limestone walls of the bird cave, where it hid — cloaked and undetectable.

In the dimly-lit, futuristic, metallic-grey interior of the Captain's Cutter, Kaya leaned over his father who remained reclined in a regeneration pod.

"Mister...." he began to project but stopped abruptly.

How should he address his father? Mr Raal? Sur Torian? Father? Dad? Daddy? What should he call this man he now knew to be his father?

"Your thoughts are transparent, my brave son," projected Torian Raal, not opening his eyes. *"Go now, and rescue your friends. When I am fully recovered, we shall speak in our dreams."*

"Yes, sir," projected Kaya, impulsively.

Torian Raal smiled, weakly, as Kaya initiated the regeneration process.

At the appointed time, Kaya transported himself to the agreed place. From the silvery-blue electrical haze of a matter transfer beam, he materialised in the company of Wendy and her mysterious Osirian comrades. He masked his heightened alertness and remained ever mindful that Wendy had previously been compromised by the Setians. The dark garb of Wendy's compatriots did nothing to allay Kaya's concerns. The two Osirians wore helmets, with mirrored visors, and what appeared to be the black leather gear favoured by bikers in more temperate climes. Notwithstanding their outlandish attire, they seemed an odd couple, at least to Kaya. The first, clearly a man, was tall, lean and athletically built; however the second was obviously a teenage girl, slightly shorter than Wendy. Even though their conspicuous black suits and helmets effectively hid their identifiable features, their movements told many tales, and Kaya immediately felt an overriding sense of familiarity. He knew these Osirian agents.

Motioning to the male Osirian, Wendy said with an unusually professional tone, "Hezekiah Torian, I'd like to introduce you to my commanding officer, Agent Zero-five-zero." And, with a cocked eyebrow, she turned to the teenage girl and said, "And this is my comrade, Agent One-three-one."

"Alright, Agent Ninety-nine, where Double-O-seven?" projected Kaya to Wendy, with a measure of sarcasm.

"I'm Agent One-zero-six," projected Wendy, assertively. *"Be nice to my colleagues, Smarty Pants; they saved your life more than once, eh?"*

"Yuh know I'm ah only chile; ah doh play well wit' others."

"Pleased tuh meet yuh," said Kaya, and he offered Agent Zero-five-zero, his hand to shake.

Agent Zero-five-zero ignored Kaya's outstretched hand. Instead, he bowed low and kept his arms close to his sides; his upturned palms signified that he was weaponless. And, he spoke in a disturbingly lifeless robotic tone, with an arresting voice altered by the electronic filters of his futuristic Osirian helmet. Kaya sensed that Agent Zero-five-zero's accent had been deliberately changed, so that it sounded completely nondescript; even so, Kaya felt certain he had heard the man's voice before.

The man said, "Baraka, Hezekiah Torian of the Royal House of Ebla, may the light of the Great Spirit always shine upon you."

Taken aback, Kaya briefly hesitated. Never breaking eye contact, he bowed low and said, "Baraka, Agent Zero-five-zero." Then, turning to the teenage girl, he repeated the formal Osirian greeting: "Baraka, Agent One-three-one." Kaya addressed the Osirians when he said, "Ah accept Sur Torian is meh fadah, buh ah want tuh keep de surname, Abaniah. It's meh gran'fadah surname and de name meh mudder give meh. If yuh want, yuh could call meh Hezekiah Abaniah-Torian, buh tuh most people, I'm just Kaya."

"Henceforth, all Osirians shall respect your wishes and refer to you as Kaya. May it be written," said Agent Zero-five-zero, and he bowed low.

"May it be done," chorused the Osirian girls, and they also bowed.

In response, Kaya bowed low and did well to stifle an embarrassed chuckle.

With a measure of urgency, the four set off in the direction of the cave complex where the Paria College teachers and students were being held against their will. Nevertheless, the day's unprecedented revelations and extreme adventures left Kaya battling against the debilitating symptoms of shell shock. Torian Raal's dream training had not fully prepared Kaya for all that he had faced in such a very short span of time. How could it? However, in his dreams, Torian Raal had taught Kaya discipline. This, more than anything else, helped Kaya bear the brunt of the emotional challenges he faced. This, more than anything else, helped him to avoid a complete nervous breakdown.

Kaya applied his newfound powers of concentration. He focussed on the positives. Even though he had temporarily died, during that crazy, rainy day, he had not been permanently killed by gun-toting gangsters, albino clones, an insane shape-shifter, his brainwashed girlfriend, elite hybrid troopers or even a self-destructing flying saucer. His pretty girlfriend turned out to be just as weird as he was, and his father was still very much alive. Kaya had also discovered the secret identity of the Niburian shape-shifter known as Golsha Zigg — the alien he held responsible for the deaths of his grandparents. The rain had stopped, and black clouds no longer shrouded the sun. The day was still young; even so, there was much to be thankful for.

Ah wish ah didn't lose meh cap and meh sunglasses though. Dis sun killin' meh eyes....

As he followed the sodden, winding, forest path, Kaya silently observed his new black-garbed companions, committing the minutiae of their behaviour to his indelible memory.

"Yuh doh find it too hot tuh be wearing dat?" quizzed Kaya.

"They are Osirian stealth suits," said Wendy, "they automatically keep the body at a comfortable temperature."

"Well yes," said Kaya, shaking his head with dismay. "Ah sure nobody'll notice dem."

"We will be cloaked, we will not be seen," said Agent Zero-five-zero, his voice altered by his helmet.

Nevertheless, with his newfound Cyclan abilities, Kaya could no longer forget a voice. Pieces of a complex puzzle began to fall neatly into place, and several fortuitous occurrences, which Kaya had previously dismissed as random coincidences, were clearly not at all coincidental.

"Ninety-nine, ah feelin ah strong force surroundin' dis one," projected Kaya to Wendy, with a tinge of rascality.

Wendy effectively suppressed any telltale signs of amusement. Nevertheless, bent on confirming his suspicions regarding the secret identities of the two Osirian agents, Kaya continued his conversation with her helmeted commanding officer, Agent Zero-five-zero.

"Nobody go see yuh? Dat's assumin' nobody wearin' Setian glasses."

"Under the circumstances, it is a risk we are prepared to take," said Agent Zero-five-zero. "Local law enforcement personnel are closing in on the location of the abductors and their prisoners. An exchange of gunfire, resulting in multiple casualties, is highly likely and must be avoided."

"Babylon a gwaan like dem mek outta iron," said Kaya, with a mischievous chuckle, rendering his version of Jamaican patois, which totally surprised Wendy and the other Osirians.

"Wha' 'bout you?" said Kaya, to the teenage girl that Wendy referred to as Agent One-three-one. "So, wha' yuh t'ink gyul?"

Agent One-three-one turned her head towards Agent Zero-five-zero, then to Wendy, and finally back to Kaya. Her perplexed face remained hidden behind her mirrored visor, when she said, "I think time is running out, Kaya."

Kaya stared at Agent One-three-one, then at Agent Zero-five-zero, and then at Wendy.

"I think time is running out, Kaya," he said mockingly, impersonating Agent One-three-one.

Kaya began to laugh as if he had heard the funniest joke ever told.

"Kaya?" asked Wendy, clearly concerned.

And Kaya found her concern hilarious. The Osirians exchanged calmly confused glances.

He has lost the plot.

With some difficulty, Kaya caught his breath and said to Agent One-three-one, "Buh A-A gyul, like is regenerate yuh regenerate yuh big toe?"

To their chagrin, Kaya continued to laugh.

"What have you told him, Lian?" Agent One-three-one asked Wendy, sternly.

Turning to Agent Zero-five-zero, Kaya asked, "An' you, dread, wha' kinda ball head chat is dat?"

Agent Zero-five-zero folded his arms defensively and turned to Wendy. "Would you care to explain?"

"Wendy didn't tell meh ah damn t'ing," said Kaya, suddenly losing any trace of humour. "How long allyuh really t'ink yuh could fool meh? Ah sick an' tired ah all de lies. Ah thought allyuh was meh friends...."

Agent Zero-five-zero sighed deeply. "Kaya, I swear to you, I have always, always been your friend."

"Alright, Rasta; leh we done de chat one time. We ha' people tuh rescue."

"Kaya, we all care about you," said Wendy, and Kaya tried to ignore the unmistakable sincerity he saw in her green eyes.

"Why don't you tell him you love him, Lian?" taunted Agent One-three-one.

"Shut up, Miriam!" shouted Wendy, shocking Kaya with an unexpected flash of anger.

"Ooh, I'm sorry, did I touch a raw nerve?" said Agent One-three-one, with mock concern.

"Be quiet, the two of you," asserted Agent Zero-five-zero. "Kaya, we did what we were commanded to do. We did what was required, in order to effectively protect you."

"Take off yuh helmet, ah wan' tuh look in yuh eye when yuh talkin' tuh meh," said Kaya, firmly. "So, Delroy Brammer.... Dat's yuh real name?"

Agent Zero-five-zero, the man Kaya knew as the Rastafarian Roy Dread, removed his helmet. Gone were the natty dreadlocks, long sideburns, moustache and beard; short cropped hair and a sincere, handsome face remained. Nonetheless, this was the same man Kaya believed to be a dealer in African and Caribbean art; the man who habitually bought Josephine's most expensive bouquets; the very man who supposedly happened upon Kaya as he slept on a dark, secluded roadside at Coconut Grove's abandoned waterfront.

Agent Zero-five-zero said, "No, Kaya; I am Leul, son of San Samaria. I have been assigned by the High Council of the Osirian Colonies to protect you."

"Buh wha' trouble is dis? All dis time yuh wearin' ah wig.... Yuh ah real ball head—"

"Nah feel no way, Kayaman. Jamdown mi come fram; I an' I noh baan inna colony; I an' I noh serve Babylon. I an' I noh jesta."

"He said he's from Jamaica," explained Wendy, trying to be helpful. "Unlike me, he wasn't born in an Osirian colony—"

"Ah know wha' he say," interrupted Kaya.

"Major Samaria left Jamaica a long time ago; he doesn't normally speak this way, eh?"

"So, yuh really born in Atlantis?" Kaya asked Wendy.

"Yeah...."

"Under de sea?"

"Under the sea."

"Alright, Ariel; dat's just cool. Wha' 'bout you Meenal, or maybe ah should call yuh Miriam?"

Agent One-three-one, known to Kaya as Meenal Baboolal, unceremoniously removed her helmet. Kaya had already deduced that her nerdy, accident-prone persona had all been a clever act, and her braces, crutches and bandaged big toe were theatrical props. Now, he viewed her large brown eyes, elegant lips, and long, jet-black hair, in a new light. She was more confident, athletic, and attractive than Kaya and his schoolmates had been led to believe. Her brilliant acting performance had ensured that of all of Paria's students, she was least likely to be recognised as a hybrid possessing enhanced mental and physical abilities.

"Meh real name is Miriam. Miriam Badarian," she said. "Ah was born in Egypt, in a district south of Cairo, called Maadi, but ah grow up right here in Trinidad; ah couldn't do this mission if ah grow up anywhere else. Today, I'm Miriam, but tomorrow I'll be Meenal again. Yuh understand?"

Kaya nodded, "Yes. So, yuh parents are agents too?"

"Yes, of course. Listen, Kaya, don't tell Tom meh secret. We'll have to erase his memories, and dat could leave him with permanent brain damage. You keep my secret, and I'll keep yours."

Yuh really expect meh tuh tell any normal human being 'bout all dis? Dat alone is enough tuh gi' dem brain damage....

"Miriam, why don't you tell Kaya how much you love Tom, eh?" said Wendy, in a calm honeyed tone.

"Cease an' sekkle," said Major Samaria.

"Wha' really wrong wit' allyuh?" asked Kaya. "First is serious cloak 'n' dagger, an' now yuh bickerin'. So, wha' nex', eh? Ah just waitin' fuh yuh tuh tell meh dat every other man jack in Paria is ah alien too."

"We are not aliens, we're hybrids," said Wendy.

Kaya sucked his teeth derisively.

"Yuh know what? Doh tell meh a damn t'ing. Today, ah already get enough surprises tuh last meh ah lifetime. No more. Ah doh t'ink meh heart could stand de pressure."

57

MELIOR

After a short hike, in the hot, wet and humid Azura Forest, Kaya Abaniah veered off the beaten track, accompanied by his three Osirian protectors — Major Leul Samaria, Miriam Badarian, and Wendy Lian Wong. With their cloaks and shields activated, the barely-visible four stealthily made their way to the cave, where the Paria teachers and students were being held at gunpoint by ruthless gangsters.

"So, wha' dey really want? These gangsters too brazen, even fuh Trinidad," silently projected Kaya.

"Indeed, there is more to this abduction than meets the eye; we believe it was engineered by a Setian agent," said Major Samaria, telepathically.

"So, Cobo is ah Setian, after all...."

"Doh trouble yuh pretty head 'bout Cobo. He's just ah schupid sape," projected Miriam.

"Wha's ah sape?"

"It's a derogatory term used by some ill-advised hybrids," projected Major Samaria. *"It's a slur on Homo sapiens and an insulting reference to apes."*

"So, wha' yuh sayin'? We not human?"

"Of course we're human, eh?" added Wendy.

"Homo sapiens literally means wise man," projected Miriam.

"T'ank yuh, buh ah doh need ah Latin lesson."

"All de same, sapes are far from wise," continued Miriam. *"We're hybrids; we're better; we're Homo melior."*

"So, yuh sayin' yuh better dan me?"

"Yuh know very well that's not what ah mean. Not all Homo sapiens are sapes, an' besides, yuh father is pure Homo supernus."

"Oho.... Dat make it alright den; meh fadah is ah superior man," projected Kaya sarcastically, and he shared the memory of something Eldred Seymour Gobelyn, his white-haired English language master, once said: *"'The sad truth about bigotry is that most bigots either don't realise that they*

are bigots, or they convince themselves that their bigotry is perfectly justi-fied.' T'ink long an' hard about de biology lesson yuh just give meh."

Hidden behind her dark visor, Miriam rolled her big brown eyes. *"Thanks, Kaya. Ah was in class when Gobelyn said that."*

"We different," continued Kaya. *"We have rare talents — dat's fuh sure; buh doh fool yuhself into t'inking we superior. We not superior. We just different."*

"Every hybrid who try tuh educate these wise humans has been per-secuted; many have been murdered. Most Homo sapiens just wilfully igno-rant, they refuse tuh see Setian manipulation, and they freely become slaves tuh it."

"If yuh doh care 'bout all human beings, especially de schupid ones, you'll have ah hard time protectin' any ah dem."

"I believe a Setian agent is working with the kidnappers," projected Major Samaria, curtailing further telepathic bickering. *"Leave him to me."*

"Nah-nah-nah, doh come wit' dat. Ah have ah few bones tuh pick wit' Setian agents."

"This is a rescue mission, not an opportunity for petty revenge. We must be discreet, Kaya. Hütter's apparent resurrection already poses a problem."

"Hütter alive? Yuh mean tuh tell meh, dat was Golsha Zigg pre-tendin' tuh be Hütter?"

"Bravo, Kaya, yuh not just ah pretty face," projected Miriam.

Kaya knew the secret identity of the shape-shifting Golsha Zigg, but he opted not to share that information with the Osirians — at least, not yet.

"Agent Badarian."

"Yes, sir?"

"Walk with me." Major Samaria motioned to Miriam, and she fell behind with him. *"Lead the way, Agent Wong."*

Kaya sensed that his old friend had had enough of the fun and games. It was time for business, and Major Samaria made sure Miriam knew it.

58

CRAB AFTER DARK

Keeping to the murk of the shadows and shrouded by their incredible cloaks of invisibility, Kaya and the Osirians stealthily approached the mouth of the cave where their teachers and classmates were being held captive. Two grim-looking gangsters stood guard, armed with pistols, and Kaya recognised them as the ruthless pair Wendy had temporarily blinded. Major Samaria motioned to Miriam. In unison, the gangsters removed the bullets from their guns, threw them into the undergrowth, and then re-holstered their empty weapons. Sporting vacant expressions, they faced each other and violently slammed their foreheads together before falling to the ground in an unconscious heap.

Schupid sapes, thought Miriam, and Kaya heard her.

"Ah thought allyuh value all life?" asked Kaya, telepathically.

"Naaah…. Not me. Dat would be Lian. She sorf. And besides, dey not dead; dey just have serious buss head."

Despite Miriam's confident claim, Kaya's keen vision, quickly allowed him to ascertain that the men were not bleeding. However, they were unconscious and sported newly-formed lumps on badly bruised foreheads.

"Clear your minds, we are about to proceed," announced Major Samaria. *"May it be written—"*

"Wait," projected Kaya; and, a drop of blood trickled from his left nostril. *"It's ah trap."*

"Well, of course it's a trap," projected Major Samaria matter-of-factly. *"Agent One-three-one, proceed as planned."*

"May it be written; may it be done," responded Miriam.

Ah wish dey'd give us viridian pistols for dis job, she thought, and Kaya heard her.

Remaining cloaked, Miriam immediately drew her standard-issue Osirian pistol and gingerly jogged to the cave entrance. And, Kaya marvelled that unlike her alter ego, Meenal Baboolal, there was nothing at all nerdy, clumsy or tomboyish about Miriam Badarian. She cautiously peered into the cave.

"Entrance clear," reported Miriam, and she stealthily entered the dark. *"Are you receiving my visor's audio-visual feed?"*

"Negative," projected Major Samaria. *"Transmission jammed at source."*

"Understood. Within, there are four armed hostiles, playin' cards. De hostages are unconscious. I can smell a chemical, probably chloroform. Two students are missing from de group, Bruce de Freitas and Deron Biggs. I can hear agitated voices coming from another chamber; de two students are probably there. And now I sense a rising threat of violence. Boosting aural receptors. Mentally projecting conversation now...."

Kaya heard Deron whimpering sadly. He sounded gagged.

The leader of the gangsters said ominously, "Is ah eye fuh ah eye. Biggs kill meh bredda; now ah go kill he son."

And Kaya detected anger and stress in the leader's voice.

"Yuh'll get what yuh want, once I get what ah want," said Bruce, with cool malice.

"Hold your position and remain vigilant," projected Major Samaria to Miriam, before turning to Kaya. *"Wipe the blood from your nose, Kaya. Drops of blood will give away your position, even while you are cloaked. Now, let's go, follow my lead."*

Kaya's head began to throb, and he found it increasingly difficult to breathe normally. His intuition warned him that the Shu-Senyn were nearby; and, for the briefest moment, everything turned pale yellow, then pitch black. He stumbled and Major Samaria grabbed him with strong arms.

Unintentionally, Kaya's disembodied consciousness manifested, within the cave, invisibly hovering just above Miriam. Adjusting to his shock and disorientation, Kaya hastily performed a visual search of the interior, quickly confirming Miriam's report that their Paria College friends were indeed unconscious. Committing all to his photographic memory, he noted that the left side of Tom's jaw had been bruised, and Rev Baker sported a fresh cut above his right eye. With dismay, Kaya also noticed that Raima's cheeks were moist with recently shed tears. Kaya suddenly recalled Meenal Baboolal's award-winning essay about the Azura Forest adventure of a brave girl named Miriam.

He thought, sadly, *Papa Bois cyah save de day, he still in he spaceship regeneratin'.*

Despite months of extensive dream training, Kaya had not been able to project his consciousness astrally. And, in a matter of seconds, his out-of-body experience abruptly ended.

"*Kayaman, whatta gwaan?*"

"*Everyt'ing cook an' curry,*" responded Kaya, steadying himself on his feet. "*Ah even have de mango chutney,*" he added, disarming Major Samaria with a winning grin.

"*Noh tell I an' I noh lie.*"

"*Ah OK, buh just now we goin' tuh ha' some serious visitors, dread.*"

"*Awoah....*"

"*Buh doh feel no way, ah could deal wit' dem. Ah could handle mehself.*"

"*Awah wraang wid yu todeh? Yu dun kno', coward man keep soun' bone.*"

Major Samaria flashed a sincere smile before reverting to serious business mode. And, although Kaya fully appreciated the major's desire to put him at ease, he simply could not trust him; at least, not completely. There was simply too much at stake. So, Kaya erred on the side of caution. He hid his thoughts and did not make his Osirian companions aware of his out-of-body experiences.

Completely regaining his composure, Kaya focussed on Miriam's telepathic projection from within the cave, and he despaired.

"Take de gyul — de one yuh like. De one named Raima," said Bruce de Bulk, as cool as a cucumber.

"Like yuh ketch ah vaps, awa? Yuh done say dat one family ha' plenty money," said the leader of the gangsters.

"Listen hoss, ah not tellin yuh tuh kill de gyul or tuh mess up she pretty face. Just free up yuhself an' go where no man gone before. Take wha' yuh want and leave de rest. As long as she alive, de family go still pay de ransom. Trust meh."

"Youth man, you is de dreadist dread. Dat one ripe, an' ah sure she sweet like ah Julie mango. Ah go take ah taste right after ah slaughter de Assistant Superintendent son like ah goat."

"*We've heard enough, Agent One-three-one. Cease projections and prepare for conflict,*" said Major Samaria, telepathically.

Kaya immediately considered running ahead, but Major Samaria grabbed him firmly by the shoulder.

"*Kayaman, Crab sey 'im noh truss noh shadder afta dark, noh even 'im brudder-in-law, Lobster,*" said Major Samaria, telepathically.

He used the old Jamaican proverb to warn Kaya against hasty action, especially in the ever present shadow of danger and uncertainty in their current situation.

"Don't worry lover-boy; we won't let the big bad gangster have his wicked way with your pretty little girlfriend," projected Wendy.

"You are an agent of the Osirian Guard," said Major Samaria, tele-pathically. *"Act like one."*

"Yes, sir. My apologies, sir. With all due respect, I believe I should be the one to engage the Sarkan."

"Who's Sarkan?" asked Kaya.

"We think Bruce is a member of Ordu Sarkan, the Setian equivalent of Hitler Youth," projected Wendy.

"An' now yuh tellin' meh dis?"

"If he's Sarkan, he'll also be a stormbringer…."

Kaya sensed a sudden spike in the ambient danger. Instinctively, he pushed Major Samaria out of the path of lethal energy bolts and threw himself on Wendy, shielding her with his body.

Major Samaria recovered quickly, rolling into the undergrowth, drawing his pistol and returning fire as a second volley of plasma rays narrowly missed him. Briefly distracted, Kaya watched the lips he still yearned to kiss as they articulated words.

"Thank you," said Wendy, snottily. "Now, can you get off me?"

And Kaya saw the undisguised jealousy, in her scowling lime-green eyes.

"Dis ent 'bout Raima. Doh follow meh into de cave. Bruce lookin' fuh revenge. He plan tuh kill everyone an' blame it on de gangsters."

"What do you think you're going to do, eh?" projected Wendy.

"Trust meh," said Kaya.

He surrendered to temptation and planted a quick peck on Wendy's luscious lips. And, with that, he sprang to his feet.

"No, Kaya, wait…."

Already in motion, and anticipating every shot from the enemy, Kaya sensed the malevolent presence of the Setian agents Wendy had nicknamed Tweedledum and Tweedledee. They were Shu-Senyn Vets and Shu-Senyn Yerek — cloaked and hiding nearby in the undergrowth, still determined, as ever, to complete their mission. Fortunately, for these two clones, Kaya now knew they were not responsible for the death of his father. However, he was fourteen and still prone to the occasional bout of vindic-tiveness. Kaya seized the mind of Yerek who immediately dropped his pistol. Under Kaya's control, Yerek whacked Vets over the head with a broken tree branch.

"I do not feel very well," complained Vets.

"Forgive me, brother," said Yerek, before whacking Vets a second time. "Once again, I have lost control." And he rendered Vets unconscious with a third whack. Yerek retrieved his specialised stun device from his inside jacket pocket, placed it to his temple and said, sadly, "Oh, no...."

Yerek stunned himself and slumped to the ground with a weird grin on his face.

"Nah, Kayaman," protested Major Samaria, scrambling to his feet. "Cha!"

Kaya resisted a heavy barrage of Major Samaria's overbearing psychic suggestions, and impetuously stormed through the mouth of the cave, only to discover that a sheet of shimmering energy had flared behind him. A Setian force field had been activated. The increasingly anxious telepathic projections from both Wendy and Major Samaria were effectively blocked, and Kaya found himself trapped and isolated, within a field of shimmering black and purple rays of energy.

Wha' de hell?

Abandoning their card game, the four gangsters stood like mindless zombies. They aimed their guns directly at Miriam and Kaya, who failed miserably in bringing their impressive, collective psychic arsenal to bear.

"We're in containment fields," projected Miriam. *"Alien in origin. Ah t'ink lapys nerian powerin' dem; whatever dis is, it blockin' psychic ability...."*

"Ah tell allyuh dis was ah trap."

"Yes, Einstein, a trap for you, not me. Yuh real harden. Why yuh ha' tuh spoil everything by bargin' in here?"

"Because he t'ink he's Captain Trinidad," scoffed Bruce de Bulk, whose voice echoed throughout the interior of the cave.

He stood in the shadows at the mouth of the small grotto where poor Deron remained tightly gagged and bound. With snake-like speed, Miriam took aim, but before she could fire, Bruce deactivated her containment field and sent her careening into a limestone wall with a powerful telekinetic shunt. Miriam fell to the ground, barely conscious, only to be surrounded and recaptured by cloaked Elite Troopers. In unison, the troopers deactivated their cloaks and Kaya counted a total of eight, armed soldiers. Four surrounded his lapys nerian containment field, and four arrested Miriam. They callously removed her helmet and stripped her of every device.

Bruce said mockingly, "Bad news, Meenal; or maybe ah should just call yuh by yuh real name: Miriam. Yuh mudder an' fadah cyah come tuh help yuh, gyul. Fire bun dong yuh house dis morning—"

"Yuh lie!" screamed Miriam, and she shook her head in disbelief.

"Gyul, dey deader dan fry chicken."

"Yuh lie," repeated Miriam, swallowing the lump in her throat and not granting Bruce the pleasure of watching her sob.

"Wha' de hell goin' on here?" asked the astounded leader of the gangsters, who slowly approached Bruce from behind; and, cautiously levelled the double barrels of his sawn-off shotgun with the back of Bruce's head.

"Ah tell yuh not tuh come out here," said Bruce.

"Boy, doh make meh blow yuh head clean off yuh magga neck. Toro crazy if he really expect ah big man like me tuh take orders from ah likkle boy like you."

"Shut yuh trap," said Bruce, finally losing his cool.

Toro? thought Kaya.

He remembered just about everything, including a conversation he overheard between a taxi driver and his passengers. It was the day the police recovered the lifeless bodies of all four Mohammed brothers from the shallow, polluted water beneath Coconut Grove's rusted, dilapidated iron bridge.

"Ah hear Toro is de one yuh ha' tuh watch," Kaya recalled a female passenger saying.

"Biggs good-good padna, Inspector Thomas Oscar Raymond Ol-livierra?" said the taxi driver. *"He's ah damn crook."*

Bruce workin' wit' Toro?

"Ah know yuh was damn sick when yuh tell meh tuh go wit' de un-derage t'ing," said the leader of the gangsters. "Buh yuh sicker dan sick. Ah shoulda know yuh dealin' in Obeah—"

"Ah might be ah prodigy, buh ah ent no Obeah man, dat's fuh sure," said Bruce, regaining his cool. "And now dat ah have what ah want, yuh could just reverse-march like ah nice sape, and shoot Deron Biggs in he head fuh meh."

Suddenly dazed, the leader of the gangsters slowly lowered his weapon but briefly hesitated.

"Ah really doh want tuh have tuh tell yuh ah second time," said Bruce, calmly.

Kaya tried to intervene mentally, but Bruce simply chuckled, and the black-clad Elite Troopers brought the barrels of their grim weapons closer to Kaya's head.

Under Bruce's psychic control, the leader of the gangsters slowly walked backwards.

"And doh forget tuh shoot yuhself when yuh done," added Bruce.

The leader of the gangsters stopped, turned, and aimed his sawn-off shotgun at Deron, whose muffled, heart-wrenching weeping, sliced through the stifling gloom within the cave.

"Bruce, stop.... Ah here now — yuh have meh," said Kaya. "Dis ent 'bout anybody else."

"Zaw-zumn, kuat ifa Ki. If yuh try to interfere again, yuh friends will suffer," said Bruce, relishing his complete control of the situation.

Each of the four entranced gangsters slowly lowered their guns at Raima, Tom, Rev Baker and Gobelyn. Not willing to risk their safety by testing Bruce's resolve, Kaya watched in horror, as the leader of the gangsters slowly walked into the adjoining cave and lost to view. Deron's whimpers turned into the stifled screams of a teenage boy who knew he would soon be shot. Out of sight, the leader of the gangster's footfalls abruptly ceased, and for a tense, agonising moment, all Kaya heard was his own heartbeat. Suddenly, a bright flash accompanied the unmistakable boom of the gangster's sawn-off shotgun, and Deron Biggs screamed no more.

59

LIFE AFTER DEATH

Kaya Abaniah stood, frozen in a hyper-alert state of consciousness, arrested by the purple and black rays of a lapys nerian containment field. In the limestone cave that now ran the risk of becoming a mausoleum, Kaya anticipated the dreaded flash and boom of a sawn-off shotgun. He reluctantly awaited the unwelcome report, which heralded the leader of the gangsters' violent demise. Nonetheless, only silence — crippling in its nothingness, shattering in its encompassing void, swamped the gloomy interior of the cave with hopelessness.

Once again, Kaya experienced a throbbing headache, and he began to hyperventilate. He watched the containment field's purple and black rays transform into sickly shades of brown. A warm, tingling sensation at the base of his spine swiftly spread throughout his body, concentrating at the nape of his neck. Intense psychic energy saturated his consciousness with profound clarity. Fear and doubt evaporated. And, like a ghostly voyeur, his detached intellect dispassionately observed the fall of his physical body.

"Kaya?" shouted Miriam, restrained by Setian Elite Troopers — her big brown eyes agape and wild with concern.

Get up, Zaw-zumn. Ah ent fallin' fuh yuh tricks," announced Bruce, and he motioned to one of the troopers.

From his disembodied vantage point, Kaya watched the trooper retrieve a metallic disc from his utility belt. He aimed it at Kaya's unconscious body, and Kaya seized an opportunity to deceive the enemy. He manipulated the trooper into seeing only what he wanted him to see.

"His heart has stopped," said the trooper, his voice electronically altered by his black helmet.

"Doh make joke," scoffed Bruce. He deactivated the containment field and said, "Doh just stan' dere like ah plank, revive him."

"Yes, ca-vus," said the trooper, and he kneeled beside Kaya's motionless body. He placed the disc on his chest, and after a tense moment, he declared, "I'm sorry, ca-vus, he's not responding...."

"What do you mean, he not respondin'?"

"He's dead, sir...."

For a strained moment, Bruce stared in utter disbelief. "Yuh mean tuh tell meh, just like dat, dis cunumunu cross de line between heartache and heart attack?"

"No, ca-vus, he suffered sudden cardiac arrest."

"Clean the wax from yuh ears. That is what I said — he had ah heart attack."

"With all due respect, sir, heart attacks are due to arterial obstructions, sudden cardiac arrest is caused by electrical—"

"Shut up!" screamed Bruce.

The four mind-controlled gangsters lowered their guns, and bitter tears streamed down Miriam's face.

"It alright, Miriam. Kaya at de control...."

Employing perfect timing, Kaya assaulted the trooper nearest to him with a telekinetic shunt. The Setian flew head-first into the dank, mossy ceiling of the cave with a thud, before falling to earth in an unconscious heap. Simultaneously, Kaya willed two of the troopers to stun the four remaining gangsters. Under Kaya's psionic control, the final trooper opened fire on Bruce de Bulk, but Bruce's personal shield protected him from harm.

"Wha' de hell yuh t'ink yuh doin', Zaw-zumn?" scoffed Bruce.

Kaya said, "Schupidee, like yuh cyah see ah multi-taskin', awa?" And, he mentally directed the other two troopers to join the assault on Bruce.

A battle of wills ensued as Bruce coldly attempted to snatch away psychic control of the troopers from Kaya. Kaya felt his own reserves of psionic energy slipping away. He also noticed the telltale signs of mental fatigue in Bruce's fast-blinking eyes, increasingly irregular breathing and sporadically twitching upper lip. Bruce would eventually lose his nerve, and Kaya knew it.

Under the sustained pressure of their combined plasma barrage, Bruce's personal shield began to falter. "Stop!" he said, anger getting the better of him. He swiftly drew and aimed a dangerous-looking pistol at the unconscious body of Raima Khan. "Stop, Zaw-zumn, or I'll melt her pretty face like butter under de blazin' sun."

To further emphasise his murderous intent, Bruce fired an energy bolt, which blasted a smouldering hole a few millimetres away from Raima's head.

"I ent takin' no prisoner today," announced Miriam, whose deadly aim targeted the narrow space between Bruce's eyes. "Bruce boy, crapaud smoke yuh pipe...."

As Miriam's voice trailed off, and she stood transfixed with awe, Kaya willed the Setian Elite Troopers to cease firing.

"Ah glad allyuh ketch some sense," said Bruce, misreading the situation and flashing a smug grin. And he thought, *Like dey only just realise who dey really dealin' with....*

"Bruce, behind you...." projected Kaya.

Bruce swiftly switched his aim from Raima to Kaya. "Bazodee idiot, like yuh take meh fuh ah damn fool, awa? Yuh expec' meh tuh fall fuh da' ole trick? Yuh cyah ramajay or dingolay outta dis."

Suddenly, Bruce felt the moist caress of a warm breath on the exposed nape of his neck. And even so, his immature hubris and overconfidence got the better of him.

He thought, *In all ah dis excitement, ah nearly forget dat dotish sape didn't shoot heself.*

"Who cyah hear must feel," announced Bruce, and without turning around, he coolly tried to re-establish his telepathic control over the leader of the gangsters.

"Don't trouble yourself, de Freitas, he can't hear you. I shot him dead with his own gun," said a disturbingly familiar female voice.

Bruce spun, on his heel, to see the Niburian — Golsha Zigg. She wore no helmet but had assumed the darkly-clad guise of a grim agent of the Osirian Guard. The look of shock and terror on Bruce's face was one that Kaya would never forget.

Bye-bye, Bruce, thought Kaya.

Golsha Zigg raised her right arm. Much to Bruce's abject horror, she opened her palm to reveal the charged blue electric glow of her lethal plasma weapon. And, with a wide-eyed toothy grin, Golsha Zigg said, "Surprise...."

Bruce's terrified scream echoed throughout the cave, and beyond, as a point-blank blast of Golsha Zigg's lightning hurled him ten excruciating metres. His scorched, smouldering body rolled to a dishevelled rest near the mouth of the cave.

"So, he dead?" asked Miriam.

"No," said Kaya, "buh he well an' truly mash up...."

"Oh, what ah shame...."

Kaya initially thought he would very much have liked to batter Sergeant Bruce to a repentant pulp. However, he recalled his own excruciating experiences with Golsha Zigg's little plasma friend, and to his astonishment, Kaya felt pity and a sharp twinge of remorse as he gazed at his fallen rival. Bruce de Freitas — Bruce de Bulk. Finally, in this gloomy cave within the Azura Forest, Kaya had seen another Bruce — the not-so-quiet, not-so-mysterious Bruce. The flawed, insecure, paranoid and ultimately pathetic Bruce, whose superhuman abilities were squandered on bigotry and revenge, but, was this the real Bruce? The Setians had no qualms resorting to forced indoctrination. Maybe it was just childish jealousy, but Kaya concluded that Bruce de Bulk had no brain to wash.

He's ah damn fool, thought Kaya, and he wasted no more compassion on the hateful teen.

So much deception had unfurled in just one day — so many revelations. His father, Golsha Zigg, Wendy, Miriam, Major Samaria, and Bruce de Bulk had all deceived him together with many others. Even with his developing psychic abilities, could he ever really trust anyone?

Lightning bolts from Golsha Zigg's plasma weapon lit the cave with danger and brought Kaya firmly back to the here and now. The Setian Elite Troopers took cover behind heavy-duty energy shields and, for a while, they desperately kept Golsha Zigg at bay. Kaya briefly tried to formulate a plan to trap the Niburian within one of the alien containment fields. But she was far too erratic, far too intelligent, and far too powerful to be so easily snared.

"Kaya, if ah die, ah want you tuh adopt Snowy," projected Miriam. *"He's meh black Siamese fighting fish. Meh tantie an' meh uncle useless at pet care."*

Oh, Lawd, like Golsha Zigg ent de only crazy person here....

"Doh worry yuh head 'bout dat. Yuh mudder an' fadah not dead," projected Kaya, reassuringly. *"Is lie, Bruce lie."*

"Yuh sure? Why yuh didn't say somet'ing before?"

"Confronting a liar only creates a better liar," said Kaya, convincingly impersonating Gobelyn.

Meanwhile, Golsha Zigg moved swiftly and randomly, energetically hurling bolt after lethal bolt of lightning in the general direction of the Setians. Nonetheless, Kaya instinctively knew that her erratic attack was simply a ploy, a small part of her ruse. Despite her delusions, paranoia and acute emotional imbalance, there was a distinct method to Golsha Zigg's madness in battle. Psychic deception and misdirection were the Niburian's greatest allies. And, one by one, the confused Setians fell to the silvery heat haze of electricity that emanated from the palm of her right hand.

OK, so now we're doomed, thought Miriam, and Kaya heard her.

"Golsha Zigg crazy," projected Kaya. *"Just t'ink like ah crazy person an' everyt'ing cook an' curry."*

He wanted to boost Miriam's morale and mask his uncontrollable hatred towards the Niburian. Kaya still held the shape-shifter responsible for the deaths of his beloved grandmother and a grandfather he never knew. He still hated her, although his father had gone to great lengths to explain that Golsha Zigg's insanity was the product of Setian torture and brainwashing. Golsha Zigg was not responsible for her actions. She needed compassion and psychological care — but try telling her that.

"Float like ah butterfly an' sting like ah jep," Kaya told Miriam.

He somersaulted while Miriam cartwheeled, to avoid Golsha Zigg's erratic plasma attacks. Miriam shot the cloaked Setian field generator, bringing down the force field and allowing psychic projections from without.

"Switch off and close your eyes," ordered Major Samaria.

Something in the urgency of Major Samaria's voice got to Kaya. Without hesitation, he rolled flat on the ground and remained face-down. White light flooded the cavernous interior, so bright — Kaya found himself wondering if he had forgotten to shut his eyes. He felt painful pressure on his eardrums followed by the sound of high-pitched ringing. Kaya felt certain the Osirian Guard had used the flash grenades his father had warned him about. These non-lethal devices were used by both the Osirians and Setians to stun and disorientate. Kaya resisted the urge to throw up. He caught fleeting glimpses of the sporadic silvery-blue flashes of transporter beams and of dark silhouettes bearing arms. However, in this the most nightmarish of scenes, Golsha Zigg was nowhere to be seen. Kaya began to crawl slowly, towards where Raima, Tom, Rev Baker and Gobelyn remained unconscious.

He heard a robotic voice say, "He's here."

It was the most reassuring thing he had heard in a long time.

60

OPERATION: KANSEI

A familiar male voice said, "Rise an' shine, Kayaman."

And, Kaya Abaniah slowly regained consciousness. Facing brilliant sunshine, he regarded the tall silhouetted man with a confused squint-eyed stare, as recognition gradually brought a measure of uneasy comfort. Kaya recalled confronting Golsha Zigg in a cave, but now, he found himself seated in the dappled shade of a rainforest laurel, casually propped against its coarse trunk. He remembered that recently, the man, who now stood before him, admitted that his real name was Leul Samaria. But, Kaya had always known him as a Rastafarian named Delroy Brammer, who called himself Roy Dread. And, once again, that persona stood before him, wearing a knitted tam that covered long, convincing dreadlocks, a plain white cotton shirt, khaki trousers and old work boots. He was joined by Wendy, and Kaya very much wanted to hold her. He badly needed a hug, but more than that, he needed answers.

"Wha' really goin' on? Why yuh dress up like dat?" asked Kaya.

"Watcha-ya, I an' I haffi put on mi wata boot; Biggs an' 'im posse ah mash dong de people track inna Babylon style, ayah."

Roy Dread explained that Assistant Superintendent of Police, Uriah Biggs, was leading a heavily armed contingent of Trinidad and Tobago's Specialist Crime Branch. The Osirians had devised a ruse to eliminate all evidence of Osirian, Setian or Niburian activities. They called it, Operation: Kansei — a word of Japanese origin, used by Osirians and Setians to convey the idea of sensitivity in design. A word that alluded to the great stealth, care, and attention to detail, which would have to be employed to convincingly cover-up recent alien and hybrid activities in the Azura Forest and elsewhere. Roy Dread told Kaya that Wendy would bring him up to speed and hastily excused himself.

In parting, he said, "Boil some ginger wen yu go inside as it look like sa yu out fi catch cole."

On cue, Kaya sneezed, and he felt as if it came out of nowhere, and yet, the Osirian seemed to have anticipated it.

If yuh forget an' let yuh guard dong, is like dey readin' everyt'ing yuh t'inkin'. Ah wonder how much he really know.

Kaya saw Roy Dread join a group of men and women he had not seen before. They followed an old forest trail and were soon out of sight.

Wendy said, "The major is leading a group of agents disguised as hikers. They will guide the police to the cave where they'll find our friends." She reached into her pocket and retrieved what appeared to be a mobile phone. "Here," she said, handing it to Kaya.

"Yuh givin' meh ah Osirian phone like yours?"

"Yeah, it's a PCE, a Psionic Communications Enhancer. Most Osirian agents call it psio-comm," said Wendy, stifling her pride. "It's a transponder, mind-controlled communications device and a weapon of self-defence. It's basically the ultimate smartphone for hybrids."

Kaya said jokingly, "So what? Like yuh makin' meh ah agent now, awa?"

"Certainly not. I've been assigned to you as a shield, but obviously I can't be with you all the time, eh?"

"Yeah, dat's ah damn shame...." said Kaya, flirtatiously.

"The psio-comm's higher functions can only be used by psychics. Any unauthorised tampering will wipe the device, and it would seem like a vanilla mobile phone with a dead battery. In the unlikely event that someone successfully bypassed your sclerotic scan lock, they wouldn't be able to do anything except make an emergency call. They'd be connected to an Osirian operator and containment agents would be sent to the device location. At that point, they'd probably wish they were never born."

"Nice," said Kaya. "So, it can read de whites of meh eye."

"Yep, the front-facing camera does that automatically. It won't work if you're dead or your eyes were removed."

"Cool," said Kaya.

And, he stared in awe at this Wendy, who was not just a naïve fourteen-year-old Paria College girl. He marvelled at this Wendy of the Osirian Colonial Guard, who seemed to be fourteen going on twenty-one. He gazed in wonder at this intelligent, articulate secret agent sent to protect him, and he very much wanted to hold her. Kaya badly needed a hug, but more than that, he needed more answers.

"OK, let's go," said Wendy.

"Wait-wait-wait," said Kaya, "So, wha' really happen while ah was out?"

"There's far too much to explain. Psionic transfer is the quickest way."

Wendy reached towards Kaya's temple, but he flinched, fearing she would learn his secrets.

Kaya recalled his father's grim projection: *"Hezekiah, when you were four years old, as an added precaution, I stored the formula for your grandfather's KARIN cure deep within your subconscious."*

Nobody must know....

Wendy said, "How many times do I have to save your life before you start trusting me?"

Nobody must know....

Kaya stood up. Wendy briefly held his stare before he averted his eyes.

He said, "Ah suppose Golsha Zigg escape again."

"Golsha Zigg is in Osirian custody," said Wendy, bluntly. She turned and began briskly following a trail through the forest.

"What?" said Kaya, jogging to keep up.

"Bruce set a trap for you in the cave, eh? But we also set a trap — a trap for Golsha Zigg. There were two cloaked ships above us the whole time."

"Yuh makin' joke...." scoffed Kaya.

"Listen, you need to be prepared when Uriah Biggs and his men arrive."

"OK, buh yuh doh find it strange how allyuh capture Golsha Zigg?"

"She slipped up, and we got lucky."

"She up tuh somet'ing."

Kaya suddenly felt a bit light-headed.

Like ah really catchin' ah cold, he thought.

Wendy explained to Kaya that although he had not been injured, he suffered the ill effects of profound psychic fatigue.

"While you took your little nap, today's events threatened to become an intergalactic incident. We received direct orders from our Prime Councillor to immediately cease all hostilities towards the Setians. Their Higher Authority has disavowed what they described as the zealous actions of Bruce de Freitas and those who chose to follow his misguided lead. His 'foolhardy efforts to capture the former Osirian agent, Colonel Golsha Zigg, was not in any way authorised or sanctioned by this Higher Authority or any office under Setian Colonial control,' they said."

"So wait nuh, de Setian leaders issue de order tuh capture meh, an' now dey pretendin' de whole t'ing didn't have anyt'ing tuh do with meh at all?"

"Officially, neither the Osirians nor the Setians are aware of your existence; although we all know the truth."

"So, where is Bruce?"

"He is at the cave, in a stable condition. Our agents within the Specialist Crime Branch will see to it that Bruce is taken to an Osirian-controlled hospital. The official story will be that he was hit by lightning while a prisoner of the gangsters."

"But—"

"Our existence must remain secret, and most human beings will believe anything."

"Wha' bout Deron; and Miriam; and Hütter?"

"Deron isn't dead, eh? He's just suffering from shock. He passed out when Golsha Zigg shot the leader of the gangsters. We've had to plant altered memories to just about everyone involved. Our friends and teachers will remember that the leader of the gangsters panicked and took his own life, when it seemed inevitable he would be captured by the police. You and I are going to get Hütter. Everyone will remember that he was shot. In a few minutes, he's going to wake up on a riverbank, confused, with a massive headache and a bullet lodged in his binoculars. You'll get to save another person from drowning."

Dis gyul jealous fuh so....

"Where's Miriam?" asked Kaya.

"Miriam took a plasma hit that was meant for you."

"She ... alright?"

"She's Meenal now, don't forget that. It may be a week or so until her vision is fully restored. The official story will be that she suffered burns in the fire that destroyed her home."

"So Bruce wasn't tellin' lies, fire truly bun dong de gyul house...."

"Yeah. Her pet fish boiled; but don't worry, her family escaped with only minor injuries. We suspect Bruce's minions caused the fire."

"Ah know Golsha Zigg secret identity. Ah know who she is."

"Yes, your thoughts are transparent."

"She's—"

"Melda Petronella Mallory — nicknamed Obeah Widow by the fine students of Paria College."

"How long yuh know dat?"

"I sensed it just before you ran, into the cave, to save your girlfriend. Your thoughts are transparent. You haven't learnt to mask them properly."

"Is so? So if yuh could read meh mind, den how come yuh still vex with meh?"

"What? I don't have time for this, Kaya," said Wendy, with an angry sigh. "We don't have time for this. We have to get Hütter, eh?"

"So, ah see yuh didn't take back yuh bodysuit."

"Major Samaria believes you are still in danger, but please remember that as far as the world is concerned, there are no Osirians, no Setians, no Niburians and no Cyclans. There are no aliens from outer space, and no shadowy groups, manipulating every aspect of their blissfully ignorant existence. Only mad people or stupid conspiracy theorists believe such things. Remember that, eh?"

"Alright, Agent Ninety Nine...."

"Don't call me that."

"OK, Sugar Plum."

"I am not your Sugar Plum."

"Whatever yuh say, Gwendolyn...."

"Shut up!"

"How dare yuh? My father is Sur Torian Raal, Fifth Baronet of Co-rona, of the Royal House of Ebla. I wish tuh speak tuh yuh superiors, at once."

"I hate you; I really do...."

61

LOVE IN THEORY

As they jogged along an old rarely-used donkey track, in the hot and humid heart of the Azura Forest, Kaya Abaniah smiled inwardly as Wendy Wong angrily outpaced him. He enjoyed the fact that Wendy felt jealous, mostly because there was no real reason for her to feel any jealousy at all. That, and the fact that her luscious lips pouted, and her eyes glowed with green fire as she exuded her subtle brand of passive aggressiveness.

Effectively hiding his mischief, Kaya said, "So, yuh t'ink Miriam truly like Tom?"

"I don't know; you'll have to ask her that yourself."

"Ah t'ink ah already know de answer. Poor Tom — he really like dat gyul."

"From now on, it's Meenal, not Miriam, don't you forget that. And, pray tell, what is it you think you know, eh?"

"Ah know Meenal is ah good actress. Tom is ah regular human being, an' ah know Meenal doh have ah high opinion ah Homo sapiens. Ah wonder if she use she psychic powers to bamboozle him?"

"You know, for an advanced psychic, you really have no idea how to read people. You're a poor judge of character."

"So dat's why yuh look meh in de eye and lie?" said Kaya, in an Oscar-winning performance.

"What? What are you talking about?"

"Yuh tell meh endless lies...."

"Right. I thought we went over this, eh? I was assigned to protect you. When I first met you, did you expect me to say, 'Hi, my name is Wendy, I was born in Atlantis, pleased to meet you?'"

"Yuh didn't ha' tuh kiss meh.... Yuh didn't ha' tuh tell meh yuh love meh," said Kaya, provocatively.

"First of all, you are the one who kissed me, eh?"

"Doh come wit' dat. If ah kiss yuh, is because yuh hypnotise meh—"

"You arrogant, egotistical idiot—"

"An', yuh lie an' say yuh love meh—"

"I take it back!" screamed Wendy.

She angrily pounded Kaya's chest with her fists before he restrained her by grabbing her flailing wrists and pulling her close. At first, she struggled with Kaya as he kissed her; but her half-hearted resistance lasted only a moment. And Kaya felt her arms snake around his neck, as her hot tears rolled against his cheek.

Kaya managed to whisper breathlessly, "Dis is very unprofessional behaviour, Agent Wong," before her warm lips happily silenced him.

"You ... started ... it...." said Wendy, between hot kisses.

"Dat's because ... yuh ... hypnotise meh, again...."

"When it's time for kissing, kiss, don't talk...." she moaned.

And Kaya didn't say another word.

"When she finally came up for air, wiped her tears, and regained her composure, Wendy said, "It's been a crazy day, eh?"

"De craziest," said Kaya. "Ah doh wan' tuh fight wit' yuh no more, Wendy. Ah doh ever want tuh fight wit' yuh again," and he couldn't resist leaning forward to kiss some more. But Wendy stopped him with a playful, gentle shove of her open palms against his chest.

"Let's go, loverboy, we have to hurry. Hütter may be drowning, eh?"

"Hütter? Who is Hütter?" said Kaya, pretending to be mentally compromised.

Five minutes later, Kaya Abaniah and Wendy Wong discovered WHT guide, Florian Hütter, in a deep tributary of the Blue River, just where specialist Osirian agents had recently deposited him.

Poor Hütter.

Early that morning, Golsha Zigg had slipped unseen into Hütter's home and sedated him. She had assumed his physical form and stolen his car. And, while impersonating him, she led the Paria College WHT contingent on their fateful hike through the Azura Forest. The Osirians believed that the mentally ill Niburian actually had delusions of being Papa Bois. She had been known to pursue the father of the forest's agenda to protect all flora and fauna, and she was their prime suspect in the unsolved murders of the Mohammed brothers. They had been involved in the smuggling of endangered animals before they met a grisly end. In spite of this, Kaya had no trouble believing that Golsha Zigg's ultimate intentions were to capture him. The Osirians were also of the opinion that she somehow became aware of Bruce de Bulk's insidious plan of revenge, and possibly sought to defend Kaya. In the guise of Obeah Widow, Golsha Zigg had been protecting Kaya all along. She ensured that nothing untoward happened to the boy whose genetic code she believed held the key to unlocking the secret of successfully cloning Papa Choonks. Her inquisitive neighbour, Kerwin Duff, had seen too much, and Golsha Zigg protected her abominable experiments by resorting to psionic murder.

Golsha Zigg crazy, oui, concluded Kaya.

Muddied and bloodied, Hütter floundered very close to the riverbank. He bore the weight of a headful of false memories, as he struggled to reach solid ground. With considerable effort, Hütter slowly dragged himself out of the water, rolled onto his back, and sighed heavily. Many of the finer details of the day's events were mired in confusion and uncertainty, but he clearly remembered leading a group of Wildlife Heritage Trust hikers through the Azura Forest. He remembered being shot at, and he remembered falling into the river. Poor Hütter remembered exactly what the Osirians wanted him to remember. Hütter had been puzzled by his subsequent lack of injuries, but when he discovered a bullet lodged in the metal housing of his binoculars, he simply concluded that he had been very fortunate — very, very fortunate, indeed.

"Mr Hütter, yuh OK?" cried Kaya, and he was joined by Wendy in a convincing display of near-hysterical concern.

As Wendy helped Kaya pull Hütter to unsteady feet, she said, "We saw them shoot you. We thought you were dead, eh?"

"It's Wendy, ja? Wendy Wong and Abaniah. The two of you are a sight for sore eyes. Ja-ja…. They only managed to murder my binoculars," said Hütter, shakily displaying the bullet lodged in the metal casing. "I borrowed these from my father. He won't be pleased."

"Yuh father here in Trinidad?"

"Nein, he died in Austria, years ago."

"Ah sorry…."

"Don't be sorry, he was a miserable bastard," said Hütter, matter-of-factly. "I woke up clinging to some rocks about two hundred metres down-river. I must have passed out. Have you called the police? Where is the rest of the group?"

"We met another group of hikers. They heard the gunshots. They told us they called the police," said Wendy.

"We t'ink de gangsters took our group to ah cave, not far from here," added Kaya.

"Are you sure they're gangsters and not religious fanatics or even terrorists? What the hell do they want?"

"Money, probably," said Kaya.

"You know where this cave is?"

"Yes," said Wendy, "and the police have been given directions to it."

"We can't rely on the police; it may be a snowy day in Hell before they arrive...."

Just then, high above the treetops, a police helicopter speedily passed by.

Wendy said, "Oh, I think we can rely on the police. The gangsters are holding Deron Biggs. His father is the Assistant Superintendent.

Kaya, Wendy, and Hütter made their way to the cave where the Osirian subterfuge was an overwhelming success. Assistant Superintendent Uriah Biggs, and Inspector Thomas Oscar Raymond Ollivierra, also known as Toro, led two large teams of officers including members of the Trinidad and Tobago's Specialist Crime Branch. The law-enforcement contingent was very well armed with Heckler & Koch MP5 and Uzi submachine guns, Galil rifles and 9mm pistols. The leader of the gangsters had apparently taken his own life, and the panicked, outgunned gang members who had foolishly followed him, offered little resistance before quickly surrendering to the police. Bruce de Freitas and one of the gangsters had been found nearby, bearing injuries consistent with a lightning strike. Due to the serious nature of their medical emergencies, they had been airlifted to a nearby medical facility.

Kaya had never seen so many policemen gathered together in one place. Raima was first to spot him as he cautiously emerged from the undergrowth.

"Kaya," she cried, and she ran towards him with tears of joy. "Oh, Gawd, boy, ah thought dey kill yuh...."

In the impulsive heat of the moment, Raima trapped Kaya in a tight, warm embrace. Then, after noticing Wendy's disapproving stare, she felt an overwhelming urge to kiss Kaya. Embarrassed, Kaya turned his face at the last moment, and Raima's full lips missed his. Instead, her loving kiss clumsily collided with his blushing cheek.

Kaya quickly pulled himself away from Raima and stared sheepishly at Wendy.

"She thought ah was dead," he projected.

"You soon will be," projected Wendy.

Raima stepped away from Kaya with a self-conscious sigh, "Ah just glad yuh OK."

For a moment, she seemed lost, and Kaya felt sorry for her. He wondered if Bruce, the stormbringer, had used his formidable psychic powers to bamboozle Raima. He briefly wondered if, in spite of everything, Wendy did have something to be jealous of. The truth was that Kaya was just fourteen and for most of the last three years, his last thoughts before falling asleep were somehow connected to Raima Khan. Well, Raima Khan or computer games or exams and falling grades, but mostly Raima. He couldn't just forget her overnight or in the space of a few months. After all, he actually thought he loved her, not too long ago. He couldn't just forget Raima, although he felt he truly loved Wendy.

True love never dies, at least, that's what Mama Flo always said.

Oh, how he missed his Granny.

Tom, Gobelyn, Rev Baker, and most of the students and staff of Paria College joined Raima in welcoming Kaya, Wendy and Hütter. Kaya felt overjoyed that none of his friends had been hurt by the ruthless thugs, Golsha Zigg or the Setians.

And, when Cobo muttered, "Ah like how dey run and leave we...."

Hütter snapped, "Show some gratitude, boy. These two risked their very lives to get help. It's a miracle no one in our group was killed, ja? We are all lucky to be among the living, and you are lucky that Abaniah and Wendy Wong were able to contact the police. We're all very, very fortunate, and we should be thankful."

Cobo scoffed, "Yeah, you're right, Mr Hütter. Thanks, Abaniah. Thanks, Wendy. Maybe meh father will buy yuh both new mountain bikes." And with that, Cobo walked away. It took all of Kaya's willpower, not to use what little psychic reserves he had left to blind Cobo or burst a blood vessel in his puny brain. Kaya's father had warned him there would be times like this when he would be tempted to murder stupid people. Instead, Kaya held his breath, mentally counted to ten then exhaled. He watched as Cobo joined Mukesh and Deron who were being consoled by a female police officer. However, Kaya simply could not help himself, and he caused Deron to throw up all over Cobo.

"Stop that!" projected Wendy.

Kaya felt light-headed, and for a moment he feared that he would also throw up. He discovered that when he acted against his conscience, his psychic abilities became greatly diminished, and his formidable martial arts knowledge only fully surfaced at times of clear and present physical danger. These were the restrictions his father set, deep within his subconscious. These were the mental restraints imposed to fetter Kaya's pubescent potential to wreak havoc. There was also a limit to how much psychic activity he could engage in before fatigue nullified his abilities, and Kaya realised that he had reached that point.

"Yuh name Abaniah?" asked ASP Biggs. His clear, deep voice oozed authority.

"Yes, sir," said Kaya, cautiously turning to face the obvious source of Deron's muscular physique, pearly-white buckteeth and extremely dark skin.

He stood before Kaya, conspicuously dressed without body armour, in a dark-blue, tight-fitting short-sleeved T-shirt and tan cargo trousers, with shrewd eyes that peered from the shadow cast by the brim of his trademark Panama hat. "You're the boy who saved Ashok Khan's daughter from drowning?"

"Yeah, sir."

"You are ah fine upstanding young man, Abaniah. Ah only wish my son was more like you."

If yuh only know what ah almost do tuh Cobo.

"Thank you, sir," said Kaya, meekly, taken aback by the assistant superintendent's compliment.

"You must be Hütter, and Miss Wong," said ASP Biggs. "My people will need tuh ask you all some questions — just routine."

"ASP Biggs," said Kaya, lowering his voice, "Ah t'ink de leader of de gangsters was plannin' tuh kill Deron. Ah hear two gangsters talkin' in de bush. De leader wanted revenge. He say yuh kill he bredda...."

"Oh?" said ASP Biggs, not giving anything away. "I'll need you to tell me all you know, Abaniah. It's important. Ah believe dis abduction is directly connected tuh several recent murders."

"Kaya, what are you doing?" projected Wendy.

"Miriam didn't tell yuh? Toro is ah crook, and ah t'ink he workin' with the Setians."

"It's Meenal, and who is Toro?"

"Toro," said ASP Biggs, suddenly beaconing to Inspector Thomas Oscar Raymond Ollivierra.

"Dat's Toro," projected Kaya, with a subtle nod to the approaching round-faced, light-skinned man. *"Ah t'ink he was de one who plan de kidnapping."*

"Ah want yuh tuh take Sergeant Alleyne, Corporal Denny, and ten of your best men tuh check out another cave," said ASP Biggs. "We suspect they have endangered animals and illegal weapons stored there."

"Why Alleyne an' Denny, boss? Yuh know I have meh own people," said Toro, with a surprisingly weedy voice.

"Dey doin' ah little t'ing fuh meh, ah special operation," said ASP Biggs, "Ah believe dis case connected tuh de smugglers from Coconut Grove, de four brothers we fish out from under de rusty bridge."

"Yuh mean Ras Mohammed an' he brethren dem? Yuh think dis have something tuh do with dem?"

"Alleyne an' Denny have specialist intelligence; they investigating ah possible link."

"Alright boss, anything yuh say. If yuh say jump, yuh know I'll ask how high. I'll take Mandrake and Toe Jam with meh as well."

ASP Biggs pulled Toro aside and whispered discreetly, "Keep yuh eye open, padna. Ah beginning tuh feel all ah dis much bigger dan de small-time crooks we seeing so far."

However, with his newfound Cyclan abilities, Kaya effortlessly heard each and every whispered word ASP Biggs uttered.

"I hope you know what you're doing, Kaya," projected Wendy. *"Just remember, these people must never know who we are, eh?"*

"Trust meh," projected Kaya, masking his uncertainty. *"Toro want Deron dead. Dat bully ent no friend ah mine, but he doh deserve tuh die."*

"Things aren't always as they seem, Kaya. Just remember that."

Once Toro was out of earshot, ASP Biggs said, "Walk with meh, Abaniah. Tell meh everyt'ing you know." And, moving away from the group of captured criminals, dutiful police officers and dazed hikers, ASP Biggs asked, "Did any of de kidnappers mention Toro?"

"Yeah, sir, de leader."

"Exactly what it is he say?"

"He say he was takin' orders from Toro," said Kaya, not wanting to complicate matters by implicating Bruce de Bulk.

"Alright, Abaniah, dat's all ah really wanted tuh know," said ASP Biggs lowering his voice to a whisper. "Yuh did de right thing by tellin' meh. Who else know 'bout Toro?"

"Nobody," said Kaya.

ASP Biggs moved even closer and despite his use of extra strong mints, Kaya detected the scent of rum on his breath. "Alright. Don't tell anyone else," said ASP Biggs. "Can you do dat fuh meh?"

"Yes, sir," said Kaya.

"Let me deal with Toro."

62

NEWS AT TEN

That evening, when Kaya returned home, Josephine had been so relieved, angry and disappointed that she did not speak, except to say, "T'ank God, yuh alright, Kaya. T'ank God."

Kaya knew so much that she did not know. He knew, for instance, that earlier that morning, his father had risked his life valiantly protecting her from the insidious Shu-Senyn clones sent to capture or kill her. And when she subjected him to a mildly embarrassing, crushing hug, and subconsciously checked him for broken bones, Kaya almost choked on the growing lump in his throat. All this, in spite of his father's extensive dream training on the mental mastery of his autonomic nervous system.

Earlier that morning, Josephine had insisted that Kaya took a pocket Bible with him on the hike; and now, as he gazed into his mother's unconditionally loving eyes, he could not bring himself to explain to her how that Bible had been instrumental in saving his life. As much as he wanted to, he could not tell her that his heroic father was still alive. He dared not mention anything about the Niburian shape-shifter, and he could not speak of the Osirians or the Setians. Kaya couldn't tell Josephine much at all. It had been his longest day. No one, except maybe Wendy, could possibly have understood how long. The day's events had been as wild and extreme as his worse horror-film induced nightmare.

While Josephine drove him home, from Paria College, Kaya shared the bare minimum of the official story. And, with Carnival fast approaching, in February, he heard the panyard practice of steel bands preparing for panorama, the steel orchestra music competition held annually in Trinidad since 1963. Until he arrived home and stepped into the lounge, illuminated by the random twinkle of the new lights on the old, plastic, pine Christmas tree; and, until the warm, seductive scents of roasted chicken, Christmas ham, pastelles, and black cake greeted him, yesterday's ball seemed a lifetime ago. And Kaya had managed to forget about the festive season, completely. He felt older — much older. It was as if a decade of maturity had been compacted into a single day, and unceremoniously thrust upon him. Perhaps,

Josephine saw it in his eyes or heard it in the tone of his voice. He would never be the same again. Perhaps, this was why she sat wordlessly next to him on the large couch. Exhausted, for different reasons, they sat and silently watched as the opening sequence of the seven o'clock news played on the television screen.

"Three policemen and eight suspected smugglers were shot dead today in what eyewitnesses described as a series of daring police operations in the Azura Forest," announced the attractive female TVTNT newscaster.

"Ah thought yuh say only one gangster dead?" said Josephine.

Transfixed by the jaw-dropping report, Kaya mumbled, "Dis is news tuh me."

Tree police an' eight smugglers?

The newscaster said, "At around 4:00 PM today, over sixty policemen from various units led by chief investigator ASP Uriah Biggs, staged a daring rescue of hikers, including teachers and students of Coconut Grove's Paria College, who were on a Wildlife Heritage Trust expedition. Police had been alerted by a group of foreign tourists on a guided tour. They raised an alarm after encountering two students who fled the scene of the abduction and eluded the kidnappers for several hours. TVTNT understands that eighteen people, including the ASP's fifteen-year-old son, and an English Methodist minister and his fourteen-year-old son, were among those held hostage, tied up and terrorised, by eight heavily armed men in a cave for almost five hours. Eyewitnesses say the ordeal of the captives ended when the leader of the kidnappers turned his sawn-off shotgun on himself, rather than face arrest. The man was pronounced dead on arrival, at a nearby medical facility, and has been identified as Justin Jarro, the brother of Hyman *Kiliman* Jarro, who had been shot dead by ASP Uriah Biggs, three years ago, following the brutal murder of a prominent businessman."

Josephine shook her head with dismay. "Buh wha' trouble is dis? Yuh granny watch over yuh, oui."

"Reports say that around 6:00 PM, policemen investigating another cave in the area were ambushed by seven armed men, and there was an exchange of gunfire. Three policemen and the seven suspects were injured. They were taken to a nearby medical facility, but all were pronounced dead on arrival. The policemen have been named as Inspector Thomas Ollivierra, and Corporals John Manderson and Toby James. The seven suspects have not yet been identified."

Toro, Mandrake, an' Toe Jam dead? thought Kaya, and he felt sick to his stomach.

At that moment, Kaya's psio-comm rang and vibrated in his back trouser pocket. He stood up, retrieved and answered it, then headed towards his bedroom.

"So, wha'ppen now?" asked Josephine. "Yuh cyah sit nex' tuh meh an' talk tuh yuh girlfriend?" And, under her breath, she added, "Just remember, Mister Man, de two ah allyuh still underage."

"Have you been watching the news?" came Wendy's voice through the psio-comm receiver.

"Yeah," said Kaya.

"I overheard my parents speaking. The three policemen, who were killed, were Osirian informants, eh? Kaya, why did you tell Biggs about Toro?"

"Ah thought ah was helpin' Deron...."

"What if Toro wasn't a bent cop? What if Biggs had these men murdered, eh?"

"How come de Osirians couldn't regenerate dem? How come dey couldn't save dem?"

"Come on, Kaya, there are times when regeneration can only do so much—"

"Still, it could be ah coincidence dey get killed."

"Really? Just the three Osirian informants?"

"Dey were Homo sapiens, buh wha' 'bout de Osirian hybrids in de police force?"

"I don't know. My parents aren't telling me anything...."

"There's ah lot more tuh dis."

"You think?" said Wendy, with a hint of sarcasm.

"Ah thought ah was doin' de right t'ing, OK?"

From the television in the lounge, Kaya heard the newscaster as she said, "A large cache of illegal firearms was recovered from the scene, including six Uzi submachine guns, nine Smith and Wesson .38 revolvers and two Lorcin 9mm pistols. Officers also found narcotics with an estimated street value of one hundred thousand dollars; and two hundred animals, including thirty-three birds protected by the Convention on the International Trade in Endangered Species of Flora and Fauna."

Kaya and Wendy spoke at length about the criminal activities, police operations, and the role of hybrids, exchanging theories based mostly on conjecture, until they exhausted all feasible possibilities. Kaya voiced his concern for the safety of his mother and his close relatives, but Wendy assured him that Osirian agents had been assigned to their protection.

"The Setians won't risk another war," said Wendy. "The lapys nerian containment field is a Karellan invention, and my parents hinted that either

Sia agents of the Neph Alim Principality or their Prefect Ultimo in the Cosmic Sea, exerted pressure on the Luminata Prefectara to desist."

"So, basically, planet Earth crawlin' wit' aliens from outa space?"

"No, not really. There are abduction raids by the Greys, but we resist their incursions at every turn."

"Dey try tuh take meh mudder, when she was still small."

"There've been several ages of man. Human civilisation is much, much older than popular science believes it to be. Our ancestors came to Earth from the planet Talis, and like all Talisians, they were natural psychics; but after six millennia of exposure to the Sun's unique electromagnetic radiation, that psychic ability diminished until eventually, for almost nine thousand years, it didn't exist at all. You see, we are not like you or the Cyclans of the Cosmic Sea. The hybrids of Earth rely on artificial supplements, to counteract the effects of the Sun and boost latent psychic abilities. It's rare, but some Homo sapiens are born with superhuman potential. Some are natural psychics with no need of enhancement drugs at all. Your mother probably has untapped abilities, eh?"

"So Homo sapiens not inferior?"

"Have you ever heard me call anyone a sape?"

"Meh fadah say, de Osirians and de Setians have ah interest in meh cousin and she husband. And now dey missin'. Yuh know anyt'ing 'bout dat?"

Wendy remained silent a moment too long.

Yuh thoughts transparent, thought Kaya.

"I'm not a spy, Kaya, and neither are my parents. We are shield agents, assigned to protect. I've heard stuff, though — only rumours. I've heard that mercenaries from the Cosmic Sea were sent to Earth, to kill your cousin and her husband, but they escaped with the help of Osirian protectors."

"Escape? Escape where?"

"I've heard that they're under the protection of Osirians and Talisians, somewhere in the Cosmic Sea Galaxy."

"Listen, Wendy, Roman Doyle is ah schoolteacher, and meh cousin Raya is ah nurse, they ent de adventurous types."

"That's what I heard. If superhuman talents run in your mother's side of the family, it could explain the alien interest in your cousin."

"Ah whole lotta people worried 'bout dem—"

"What can I say?"

"So, Golsha Zigg escape yet?"

"Why are you trying to annoy me, eh?"

"Ah not tryin' tuh annoy yuh. Ah jus' cyah believe yuh really t'ink allyuh could ketch Golsha Zigg so easy."

"Golsha Zigg was an Osirian agent who had been captured, tortured and brainwashed by the enemy. She remains under Osirian care."

"She up tuh somet'ing, jus' wait an' see."

"I'll be sure to pass on your concerns to my superiors."

"Dey find de clone she was making, yet?"

"There's absolutely no reason to believe that Golsha Zigg was trying to grow a clone. She thought she was Papa Bois, not Victor Frankenstein."

"Allyuh better keep lookin', oui. She kill Kerwin because he see somet'ing at she house."

The fire at the Baboolal family residence also made the evening news. That, and the dramatic events in the Azura Forest, dominated the online discussions on the social networking websites Kaya and his college friends frequented. He lost track of time, messaging, posting and trying to take the edge off the traumatic events of the day. Just when Kaya finally began to relax, he heard the old-fashioned ringtone of the landline telephone perched on the kitchen counter.

"Who callin' dis hour?" Kaya heard Josephine mutter outside his bedroom, before she answered the call.

The time on his monitor's task bar was 10:06 PM.

Suddenly, Josephine screamed, "Oh, Gawd, no!" and Kaya heard the sound of a glass crashing to the tiled kitchen floor.

With butterflies in his stomach, he rushed out of his room to find Josephine. Dressed in her nightgown, she sat on the kitchen floor, collapsed against the refrigerator. Tears streamed from her eyes, and a mess of spilt ponche de crème and broken glass was scattered at her feet.

"Wha'ppen?" cried Kaya.

"Tantie Rose, boy … Tantie Rose had ah stroke…."

63

BOXING DAY

It was gloriously sunny, early on the morning of Boxing Day, in the sleepy, rural village of Tortuga. Kaya slowly followed Josephine up the short flight of red concrete steps, to the wide veranda of the old magnolia-coloured wooden house, which Tantie Rose had inherited from her parents. The simple, colonial dwelling, which had belonged to Kaya's relatives for over a century, had witnessed the tardy transition from kerosene lamps and candles to electrical light-bulbs. Far to its rear, at the edge of the dwindling forest, a long-disused outhouse that had been converted to a makeshift tool shed, stood as a stoic reminder of a bygone age.

In 1974, Tropical Storm Alma whisked away a small section of its corrugated galvanised roof; but, the Old Peters House, as locals called it, generally braved the elements and stood the test of time unflinchingly. With the growing success of Rose's Kitchen in the 1980s, Tantie Rose restored the front of the three-bedroom house and extended it to the rear. She oversaw the construction of an enviable six-bedroom family home, which mirrored the rustic charm of the original vernacular design. It was a good old house and a very special place. It was where Kaya was born.

He stood silently in the veranda and took in even the smallest details of the familiar front garden, with its bougainvillea, croton, fragrant wild roses and hibiscus. A pair of green-throated Caribs darted from flower to flower, stealing nectar before one plucked a hapless spider from its web and made a swift getaway. According to ancient Amerindian beliefs, humming-birds bore the souls of dearly departed locals; and, Kaya wondered if the green-throated Caribs knew his grandaunt was dying.

Beatrice opened the front door, with a painted smile, and exchanged sedate greetings; but, Kaya immediately sensed the pain that lurked behind her brave face.

"How she doin'?" asked Josephine, with a tremor in her voice.

"Hmmm…. Not too good today…." replied Beatrice. She called out, "Leandra? Cousin Kaya here," then she added softly, "Leandra ent takin' it too good."

As they slowly walked towards Tantie Rose's bedroom, Kaya became mindful of his own reluctance to endure the heartache of seeing his afflicted grandaunt.

He realised Josephine was trembling, when she asked, "Where Clarence?"

"Clarence and Robin gone tuh get some gas," said Beatrice, "it run out yesterday, yuh could beat dat? Gas run out on Christmas Day. Luckily everyt'ing was done cook already. Dis t'ing have everybody schupid, oui?"

In a very real sense, Tantie Rose filled the role of Josephine's second mother. She grew up with her; and, after Mama Flo had passed away, she had grown even closer to her. More than anyone else, Tantie Rose encouraged Kaya in his artistic pursuits; and, on occasion, Josephine even accused her aunt of spoiling her son. Nevertheless, Kaya always maintained special relationships with his grandaunts; and, much to the chagrin of his cousins, he often seemed to be everyone's favourite.

An antique oak dresser dominated the dining area, and on its upper shelves, among the expected Christmas greetings, Kaya noticed a selection of *get well soon* cards. He silently followed Beatrice and Josephine through the dated lounge, and as they filed past Tantie Rose's empty, well-worn leather recliner, he felt butterflies in his stomach. Kaya feared he would never see his old grandaunt occupy that chair again. For the first time, for as long as he could remember, the television, which normally spewed westerns all day long, remained mute. There would be no gunfights in the Old Peters House today. The man with no name had suddenly left town, and no one knew if or when, he would return.

It had been the worst Christmas of Kaya's life. Unsurprisingly, the many presents Tantie Rose received, remained unopened beneath the unlit, artificial Christmas tree. Instead of the sound of heated gunfire or the festive carols of Christmas, Kaya heard Tantie Rose's favourite record, *Sing out My Soul*, a compilation of Christian spiritual folk songs recorded in the 1970s, at Trinidad's Holy Name Convent. It featured the Goretti Group and Holy Name Convent School Choir, accompanied by non-traditional guitars, the Olympia Thunderbirds and Texaco Dixieland Steel Orchestras. As he listened to *Sing out My Soul to the Lord*, Kaya fought back the sorrow.

They entered the master bedroom, where the spicy scents of camphor, cinnamon and citronella, and the mustiness of illness and age, hung in the humid air. The old-time mosquito net canopy had been pulled aside, and Kaya saw Tantie Rose's supine form on her king-sized bed. Her eyes were closed.

She look dead already, thought Kaya, and his heartbeat quickened.

"She just fall asleep," whispered Leandra. Her glistening gaze met Kaya's, and her lips quivered. She sat dutifully on a dining room chair next to her grandmother, Rose.

"Alright leh we leave her tuh sleep," said Beatrice, softly.

Josephine said nothing. She simply left the room and burst into tears, and Beatrice and Leandra quickly followed to console her. Kaya stood a while, staring at the irregular rise and fall of his grandaunt's chest. The telltale droop of the left side of her stroke-stricken face was soul-destroying to behold, but Kaya resolved not to succumb to despair. Instead, he slowly approached his grandaunt's bed and tried to block out the sound of his mother bawling outside in the kitchen.

Kaya clasped Tantie Rose's leathery hand in his. Clinging to its welcomed warmth, he stared forlornly through the bedroom window's thin veil of net curtains. With a mixture of fascination and mild delight, his attention followed a swarm of Emperor butterflies, as they fluttered and dipped across the shady black asphalt road. And Kaya watched their distinctively iridescent blue wings bob and weave towards the fallen fruit beneath a tamarind tree. Outside the Old Peters House, life carried on as usual, blissfully unaware of the potent despair enclosed within its wooden walls. Kaya had sat alone with Tantie Rose, and his melancholy thoughts for a while, before the plaintive wails of Josephine and Leandra tugged distractingly at his heart strings.

He stood up, determined to see if there was something, anything, he could do to console his heartbroken mother and cousin.

"Where yuh goin' boy?" came a pained, slurred voice that was only vaguely reminiscent of Kaya's grandaunt's.

"Tantie Rose?"

Never opening her eyes, her pale, cracked lips uttered, "Jus' so, yuh leavin' without talkin' tuh meh?"

"Ah thought yuh were asleep," said Kaya, as he sat down beside her once more.

"Buh yuh never aks meh tuh make sure," said Tantie Rose, with heartrending difficulty. "Yuh tantie gone through boy…. She gone through…."

"Doh say dat, Tantie…."

"Put yuh hands on meh temple," she said impatiently. "Do it now before it too late."

Puzzled, but eager to please, Kaya simply did as he was told.

64

A PLACE IN THE SUN

Rushing heedlessly through a mysterious pall of dark mist, Kaya emerged, seated on his dining-room chair, in a large field of tall golden grass adorned with tiny purple flowers that swayed, and shifted in a cool, gentle breeze. The flowers produced a faint chorus of soothing otherworldly voices that unsettled him nonetheless. A deep-blue sky formed a cloudless canopy over the brilliantly lit scenery, but Kaya could not discern the source of the strange light. Despite its extreme radiance, it did not hurt his eyes. Tantie Rose was there too. Disappointingly, she remained on her bed, and all the visible signs of her affliction lingered.

Thankfully, even though Tantie Rose's speech still retained the light and shade of age, it was no longer impaired by debilitating illness when she spoke. "Meh face de same, because ah doh want yuh tuh forget wha'ppen tuh meh. Ah not gettin' any better."

"Wha' place is dis?" asked Kaya, cautiously.

"Well, boy, dis is a place in de sun. Dis is a place where ah doh ever feel pain." Somehow, her response triggered an overwhelming sadness in Kaya, and finally he broke down crying. "Doh cry Kaya," said Tantie Rose. "Just listen; listen good. Since yuh small, ah could tell yuh have de talent."

Wiping away the tears that streaked his face, Kaya asked, "Wha' talent?"

"Boy, now is not de time tuh play schupid wit' me. Yuh here now, in dis place, because yuh ha' de talent. De talent was handed dong from yuh great-great-gran'mudder, Ma Selena; an' yuh great-great-great-gran'mudder, Arienne, who was ah healer dat everybody call Mama Nen; and from she mudder's gran'mudder, Ma Mwamba, de chief daughter, stolen from Africa. When ah was still ah chile, Ma Selena tell meh de ole people call it de power, buh she prefer tuh call it de talent, and dat is wha' me an' Florence call it. Not everybody in de family have it. Josephine, Soraya an' you are de only ones wit' it, an' Josephine an' Soraya doh know dey have it." Tantie Rose shook her head when she said, "Douen try tuh take both ah dem.... From since dey were small, Florence an' I do everyt'ing tuh discourage dey talent; an', after ah while, dey jus' forget dey have it."

"So, Mammy an' Raya psychic?"

"Yes, chile, dey have de talent; buh dey not as strong as you, no-no-no, not at all-at-all-at-all. You have it de most, doux-doux. You have it more dan yuh know. Never abuse yuh talent, Kaya; an' doh forget de Lawd who make yuh. If yuh do, Gawd will punish yuh; mark meh words, Gawd will punish yuh." Tantie Rose held Kaya's gaze for a moment, and then the ghost of a wistful smile slowly appeared on her age-lined face. "Live yuh life, Kaya. It good dat yuh already find yuhself ah nice gyulfriend." Then she added with a mischievous chuckle, "She Chinee, buh she smart, an' she pretty fuh so."

"Ah doh know if ah could trust Wendy," said Kaya, softly. He lowered his eyes when he added, "Ah doh know who tuh trust anymore."

"Kaya, gimme yuh hand. Look in meh eye — look good. Now listen … ah ole … ah sick … ah dyin'…."

"Doh say dat, Tantie…."

"Buh ah not blind, chile. Ah could see in yuh eye, yuh love dis gyul. Yuh cyah hide dat from meh, ah wasn't born yesterday. An' dat Wendy? Hmmm, Papa, dat gyul love yuh. She love yuh, too-bad-too-bad. De way she look at yuh…. Yuh cyah fake dat. Listen tuh meh, Kaya. Listen tuh meh good. Doh t'row 'way love; yuh never know if yuh go find it again. Yuh ha' tuh learn tuh trust. Yuh ha' tuh learn tuh forgive. Ah didn't forgive Clarence fadah; even though dat men went dong on he knees an' beg meh, ah curse him and ah sen' 'im packin' on he way. Buh eventually, donkey years later, ah realise what ah t'row 'way; buh, yuh see, meh rubbish was another 'oman prize. Like ah damn fool, ah spen' ah lifetime bitter an' lonely. Ah run de only man ah ever love, to de open arms of anoder 'oman — somebody who was probably more forgivin' dan me. Yuh see, de more yuh love somebody, de more yuh expect from dem, and de more it hurt when yuh realise dey not perfect. Buh if yuh love dem, Kaya, if yuh truly love dem, yuh ha' tuh forgive dem — not for dere benefit, buh fuh yours. Yuh ha' tuh learn tuh forgive, Kaya. Yuh ha' tuh learn tuh forgive." Tantie Rose sighed heavily. "Now go tuh de top drawer in meh chest ah drawers. Yuh go find ah envelope wit' yuh name on it…."

Kaya glanced around to where the chest of drawers would be, had he still been in Tantie Rose's bedroom. It slowly materialised in the open field. However, whatever his grandaunt had tucked away for him did not interest him. He simply wanted her to recover and live.

"Tantie, ah could help yuh…. Ah know ah man who could cure yuh…."

Tantie Rose smiled, "Doux-doux, ah had meh time. T'ings bad fuh meh now, an' dey not goin' tuh get any better. How much longer yuh expect meh tuh spend meh days sittin' on meh La-Z-Boy recliner? Ah done see every Western dey ever make dat worth watchin'.."

"Ah could call Wendy, she's ah healer; an' ah know ah scientist who could cure yuh," said Kaya, in desperation. "Ah just want t'ings tuh be how they used tuh be."

A familiar male voice said, "Kaya, nothing remains the same. Things either move forward or backwards."

Startled, Kaya turned to see the recognisable silhouette of a man.

"Bonjour, Papa Bois," said Tantie Rose. She asked Kaya, with a chuckle, "Dis is de scientist yuh mean?"

"Yuh know him?" asked Kaya, surprised.

"Well yes. He already offer tuh cure meh. Ah tell 'im exactly de same t'ing ah jus' tell yuh."

"I've been watching over Rosemary," said Torian Raal.

"Why?" asked Kaya.

"Because, you love her; and your mother loves her; and also, because she loves you, dearly. I first saw Rosemary when your mother was still a child."

"Dat was you?"

"Yes, that was me," said Torian Raal, calmly.

"An', yuh couldn't stop dis from happenin'?"

"Kaya, I am not an angel, prophet or saint. I am simply a man."

"Ah man wit' advanced technology, and regeneration pods, right?"

"Yes."

"So why yuh cyah regenerate Tantie Rose?"

With warmth and humility, Torian Raal said, "I am simply respecting her wishes, Kaya."

"How yuh mean?"

"I've spoken to her, at length, in her dreams. She feels her time has come."

"Buh why? She not dat ole...."

"Do you want what's best for her, or what's best for you?"

"Ah doh t'ink ah could bear it," said Kaya. He averted his eyes, not wanting his father to see the tears.

"Kaya, search your earliest memories. You will recall that you existed before you became part of the persistent illusion we call life. Love is never lost. Love is eternal."

Suddenly, Kaya saw Torian Raal and Tantie Rose transform into numerous tiny purple flower petals. And, a strong gust of wind whipped them up and blew them into his face. He became more and more agitated as he fought to keep the seemingly endless stream of petals out of his eyes.

With a start, Kaya woke on the chair beside Tantie Rose's bed, and discovered that it was actually the mosquito net, which had blown across his face and yanked him out of a dream. He quickly pushed the sheer fabric aside to discover that Tantie Rose was fast asleep on her bed.

T'ank God, she still alive….

Kaya used the back of his hand to wipe his moist cheeks. And, for a while, with each laboured breath she took, Kaya watched the rhythmic rise and fall of his grandaunt's chest. He abruptly remembered that she told him to retrieve an envelope from the uppermost drawer of her chest of drawers. Kaya opened the drawer, and the distinctive scents of camphor and cinnamon greeted him. He quickly found the brown envelope among a variety of knick-knacks, a small jar of Tiger Balm, a Bible and rosary, used candles, old pairs of spectacles, and a biscuit tin filled with a handful of pre-decimal British coins. The envelope contained a bankbook, a small crucifix strung on a thin chain of gold, and a folded letter handwritten in blue-black ink with an old-fashioned fountain pen. Kaya opened the letter and realised that it had been written years ago, as Tantie Rose's handwriting, which he immediately recognised, had become almost illegible in recent times. In the letter, Tantie Rose said that she had opened a joint account with Kaya when he was a very young child. Over the years, she had put aside a *little something* every month, which he would be able to draw when he was eighteen. The money, she warned, should be used wisely, and under no circumstances should any portion of it be spent on computers or computer games. Tantie Rose claimed, she did not want Kaya to become a square-eyed zombie, like the many computer-addicted children of East Asia, she had heard so many disturbing things about. The crucifix and chain, she gave because his neck was bare. Tantie Rose ended the letter by saying, 'Be the great person you were always meant to be.'

Kaya opened the bankbook, and when he read that the balance was fifty-two thousand, three hundred and nineteen Trinidad and Tobago dollars, he gasped in shock. And as he gasped, so did Tantie Rose. Kaya watched as, without waking, Tantie Rose held her breath for a tense, agonising moment before laboriously exhaling. He anticipated her next breath, but it did not come. The bankbook slipped from his fingers absent-mindedly, and the peaceful expression, which appeared on Tantie Rose's inert face, broke Kaya's heart. He rushed to her side, calling for Beatrice; and still, his grandaunt's chest did not rise. Kaya placed his hands on Tantie Rose's temples and exerted all the psychic willpower he could muster, but it was all in vain. Panic-stricken he called for his mother, but even when Josephine frantically arrived with Clarence and Beatrice in tow, Tantie Rose did not breathe ever again.

65

GOODBYES

At the funeral home, as she lay in her open oak casket, Kaya clasped
Tantie Rose's ice-cold hands and fussed over her old-fashioned wig. He
utterly hated the wig. Alive, Tantie Rose never needed it; and, now in death,
she needed it even less. The body in the coffin, only vaguely resembled the
woman Kaya had loved and respected all his life. The sight of a housefly
walking across her eyelid made his blood boil and left the funeral director
deeply puzzled, when every electric light bulb in the building simultaneously
blew.

"Nothing tuh worry 'bout," dismissively muttered a spooky assistant,
"is just another power surge."

It rained, and rained, and rained, on the dark December day they laid to rest
Rosemary Adelise Peters, the daughter of John *Saga Boy* Elijah Peters and
Teresa Eugenia Holder, commonly called *Girlie* by all and sundry. Rosemary
was interred in the cemetery of Our Lady of Montserrat Roman Catholic
Church, alongside her grandparents, George Emanuel and Selena Peters, her
parents, and other close relatives, including her beloved sister, Florence
Ghislene, also known as *Mama Flo*, her brothers, Jonathan George, affectionately called *Sonny Boy*, and James *Jamie* Hezekiah, after whom Kaya had
been named.

Tantie Rose's old friend, Fr Geoffrey Buckley, presided over her
Requiem Mass, and when her distraught son, Clarence, could not find the
strength to deliver the eulogy he had previously prepared with love, Fr
Buckley paid tribute to the staunch woman he had known for almost five
decades. The organist and choir delivered a heartrendingly moving rendition
of the traditional Roman Catholic prayer, *Ave Maria*, which had been
adapted to a melody composed by Franz Schubert in 1825; and there was not
a dry eye in the house of God.

Tantie Rose's daughter, Christina Williams, four years a widow, left
the bitter cold of England's Birmingham, to attend her funeral high on a

rainswept ridge in Trinidad's hot and humid Central Range, filled with regret, and grief and uncertainty. Christina's only daughter, Soraya Doyle, had been missing in England for what seemed like an eternity, and Kaya did his best to try to console the inconsolable.

Relatives and friends came from far and wide, braving floods and landslides, to celebrate the life of Kaya's grandaunt who at seventy-six, many felt had died long before her time. They recalled that her father, Saga Boy Peters, had lived to the respectable age of ninety-three, and her grandmother, Ma Selena, was one hundred and four when she passed away.

Our Lady of Montserrat Roman Catholic Church, known simply to most people as Tortuga RC Church, could not accommodate all the mourners during the sombre funeral Mass. With torrential rain battering its old timber frame, many huddled together, under cover of dark umbrellas, beneath and beyond its iron-pillared entrance arcade.

Mercifully, there had been a lull in the downpour during Tantie Rose's burial. Wendy and her parents, Tom and Rev Baker, Raima, Devika, and Mr and Mrs Khan, were all there, cautiously navigating the scattered puddles and treacherously slippery Tortuga mud. Despite Wendy's disapproving stare, Raima found a tentative opportunity to hug Kaya and offer her heartfelt condolences. Once again, she told him she was sorry for hurting him, and asked for his forgiveness; and, to his surprise, Kaya found that forgiving her was not as difficult, as he had previously imagined.

"Yuh ha' tuh learn tuh forgive, Kaya. Yuh ha' tuh learn tuh forgive," he remembered Tantie Rose saying; and he smiled when he felt the yoke of resentment lifted from his shoulders to be replaced by the warmth of compassion, respect and renewed friendship.

"Yuh remember Cousin Rita from Caratal?" asked Josephine, and Kaya's total recall replayed every meeting as if they had occurred yesterday.

"You don't remember me?" said Sonny Boy's eldest daughter, Veronica.

She had immigrated to Canada in 1985 but had visited Trinidad several times since then. Of course, Kaya remembered her; he remembered everyone he had ever met.

Disguised as an elderly, white-bearded man, Torian Raal also attended Tantie Rose's funeral and paid his deepest respects.

When Josephine left Kaya's side to comfort her cousin, Clarence, who had nearly fallen into Tantie Rose's open grave, Torian Raal said softly, "Kaya, I have taken your advice."

"What advice?"

"I have accepted the professional help of your Osirian friends."

"Oho...."

"I have come to say, goodbye."

"So, yuh fix de Captain's Cutter?" asked Kaya, and he could barely swallow the growing lump in his throat.

"Yes, Kaya. Tomorrow, my journey will begin, and I will finally be taking my father's KARIN cure to the people of Cyclo."

"Dat's good news," said Kaya, unable to hide his heartbreak.

"My son, I have taught you all that you need to know, and I promise you I will return once my work on Cyclo is complete."

"OK den...." said Kaya, offering his hand to shake, and exerting every ounce of willpower he could muster to prevent the tears from flowing.

Torian Raal brushed aside his son's hand and engulfed him in a warm embrace. He whispered, "Know that I love you, Kaya. Know that I love you."

Kaya smothered his sobs in his father's shoulder. "Come back soon, Daddy," he cried. "Just come back soon."

The tears flowed, and flowed, and flowed.

66

CARNIVAL

Webs of protection, deception and misinformation had surrounded Kaya from birth; and, at fourteen, he bore the crushing weight of secret knowledge and the burden of superhuman abilities. The following weeks tested Kaya's character and maturity almost to breaking point. With Tantie Rose's untimely death and Torian Raal's hasty departure, Kaya descended into the clawing darkness of grief, loss and longing, and temptation plagued his every interaction. In theory, with no more than a glance of his awakened eyes, he could cause a fit or stop a heartbeat. He could effortlessly consign his rivals to the haze of forgetfulness and exact blinding revenge. He had the power. He had what some of his maternal relatives called, the talent.

Fortunately, Torian Raal had anticipated his son's pubescent turmoil and installed subconscious restraints. These would curb Kaya's abilities whenever he attempted to act against his conscience and values. After all, despite his talent, Kaya was still just a boy. The Osirian web of protection remained steadfast, and Kaya retained the love of family and friends. This was how he survived the storms of bereavement and the snares of psychic misuse.

For Kaya, the Carnival season brought with it happy distractions. Josephine and her old friends, Tangerine Jean Marcano and Gillian *Rumpa Pum-Pum* Henry, had joined Avengers Steel Orchestra, which had evolved from Coconut Grove Tamboo Bamboo. Fearing drummed communications would lead to island-wide uprisings, Trinidad and Tobago's Crown Colony Government banned African talking drums in 1883. And, in 1884, a year marred by the Hosay massacre in the southern town of San Fernando, the irrepressible and resourceful musicians of the twin isles began experimenting with instruments cleverly made from bamboo. By the early 1900s, at the height of the tamboo bamboo craze, rival gangs weaponised their bamboo instruments while brazen bamboo thieves decimated privately-owned fields. So it came as no surprise, when, in 1934, the British colonial authorities also banned tamboo bamboo. The rubbish bin band quickly took its place, with its rhythmic beating of biscuit and lard tins, any old iron, and, of course, liberated rubbish bins. And during its metallic reign, no rubbish bin was safe from the covetous clutches of Trinidad and Tobago's musical youth.

In the days when bottle caps were still crown corks, and the pallet-man sold icy bliss on a stick, when suckabags were all the rage, and Jab-jabs announced their eagerness to play swappay with the loud crack of a bullpistle, Grove Ragatang Iron Band rose out of the ashes of Coconut Grove Tamboo Bamboo, to evolve into Grove Steel Band, and finally Avengers Steel Orchestra. Like so many other steel bands, it emerged from the pioneering transition of animal skins to bamboo, to iron, and to steel. The steel pan, Trinidad and Tobago's unique invention and much-loved national instrument, was the only new and internationally recognised instrument created in the twentieth century.

As a precocious teenager, Tangerine Jean had earned her nickname after an ill-conceived hair-dyeing experiment went horribly wrong. From her grandfather, a Frenchman, she inherited a tan skin tone, an easy-going disposition and a defiant sense of individualism, all of which Kaya found somewhat attractive, even though she was old enough to be his mother. Rumpa Pum-Pum, a dark, stocky, round-faced woman, was so-called because of her Christmas Day birth and her ability to imbibe industrial amounts of rum. She suggested to Josephine that Kaya should join Kairi Krew's Kiddies Carnival Band. Months before, she had furnished her teenage son, Damian, with a ticket to play. However, Damian clumsily fell out of a mango tree and subsequently needed crutches. And so, during a rare moment of clarity, Rumpa Pum-Pum had a brilliant idea.

"Ah go give yuh Damian ticket half price," she gleefully told Josephine. "Kaya could jump up instead."

Kaya predictably protested, "Mammy, ah ent no kiddie, ah almost fifteen."

But Josephine correctly felt that the diversion would pull Kaya out of the moody gloom he had developed following Tantie Rose's passing.

"Well, Mister Man, yuh not playin' in any adult band before yuh reach eighteen; buh it will be good fuh yuh tuh dress up and jump up dis Carnival. Doh mind dey call it Kiddie Mas, is not just small chirren; de band have chirren older dan you. Wait an' see, ah sure yuh will like it," said Josephine, confidently.

Kaya's mother was correct. She usually was, although his teenage rebelliousness routinely prevented him from willingly acknowledging this fact.

Kairi Krew's band was called, Universal Folklore, and the king of the band was a tall, well-built teenager named Shaquille. He played Shango of the Yoruba pantheon, the double-headed-axe wielding master of fire, thunder and lightning. However, Kaya secretly wanted to lead the *Lore of the Land* section by playing Papa Bois, and he got his wish. It seemed fitting that he played the folkloric character his father had assumed for so many years, and now that Torian Raal had left Trinidad, Kaya wondered who would protect the country's endangered flora and fauna. Despite their terrifying encounter with Golsha Zigg, in the Azura Forest, Kaya had hoped that Wendy could play Mama Dglo; but, to his dismay, Wendy and her parents celebrated Carnival in Port of Spain. For this Carnival, text messaging and online chats had to suffice.

Allyuh too young tuh be spending so much time together, thought Josephine and Kaya heard her.

A dark, quiet stranger named Onieka, played Mama Dglo, but to Kaya's surprise, Shantel Butler had joined the band as La Diablesse. On the Saturday before Carnival, Kaya welcomed seeing her familiar face during the National Junior Parade of Bands in Port of Spain; and again, on Sunday, Shantel joined him at the San Fernando Junior Carnival Parade of Bands. In the past, Kaya had ignored Shantel, but after Carnival he resolved to rectify his behaviour. They would be good friends.

On J'ouvert morning, daybreak on Carnival Monday, Kaya watched Josephine, Tangerine Jean and Rumpa Pum-Pum beat their steel pans as Avengers dropped their bomb during the official start of Carnival. The Bomb, a classical or traditional tune arranged and performed with a calypso rhythm, dated back to the banning of Carnival during World War Two, when bands secretly developed their individual pieces, with the aim of surpassing their musical rivals and surprising Carnival audiences. In San Fernando, during the early morning Bomb competition, Avengers performed a frivolous rendition of the moving piece, *Somewhere*, composed by Leonard Bernstein for the famous Broadway musical, West Side Story. Mama Flo had been an avid fan of the American crooner, Andy Williams, who sang a heartfelt version of the song; and Kaya's keen vision caught the bittersweet tears in Josephine's eyes as the steel orchestra concluded the piece to rapturous applause.

Avengers Steel Orchestra followed a J'ouvert mas band, and far ahead DJ Madman Monstar unleashed the hottest soca hits from his forty-foot monster music truck. And, in the brief moments when Avengers took a break, Kaya heard the distinctive beat of Indian Tassa drums emanating from an unseen distance.

"Here Kaya, make some noise, beat dis," said Rumpa Pum-Pum, and she gave Kaya a cowbell and a drumstick. "Yuh in de engine room now."

On the hilly roads of San Fernando, the orange glow of sunlight slowly replaced the yellow hue of sodium-vapour streetlights, as Kaya played cowbell to the engine room rhythms of Avengers steel, and a happy mass of people of every description moved to the infectious beats of heady cultural mixes of local music. In this kaleidoscope of smoke, powder, bubbles, foam and water, Kaya wondered if the 1780s French settlers who introduced Carnival to Trinidad, had the slightest inkling that their whites-only masquerade balls would eventually evolve into one of the world's largest multicultural celebrations.

Among the crowd that followed Avengers, Kaya noticed a group of teenage boys that heckled the most attractive girls they could find. In the hot, humid, tropical climate, they wore inappropriate hoodies, swaggered conspicuously, and delivered the rapper-fuelled slang of American ghettos unconvincingly. It quickly became obvious to Kaya that they had never left the shores of Trinidad and Tobago. They were wannabe Yankees, fooled by music and movies that never seemed to highlight the poverty, illiteracy and general hopelessness of their not so fortunate American counterparts, adequately.

As Kaya considered psychic intervention, he noticed several groups of much older masqueraders portraying traditional Carnival characters. Fancy sailors wore ornate moulded paper-pulp headgear and danced the pachanga in embellished naval uniforms. A colony of man-sized vampire bats, in unflattering skin-fitting costumes, with grotesque, swansdown and papier-mâché headpieces that entirely covered their heads, gyrated to the music and flapped fifteen-foot wings, which made ambient smoke and powder swirl.

A variety of devils followed in their wake. Pretty Jab-jabs wore brightly coloured clothes much like those of the court jesters of medieval times. They entertained the crowds of revellers with cracks of their plaited hemp whips and paired to play swappay — whip-fighting toe to toe. Turning to the crowd, they chanted in time to their biscuit-tin beats:

> *Ah come from Hell, Jab-jab*
> *Ah know yuh well, Jab-jab*
> *So, pay de Devil, Jab-jab*

And red dollar bills were hurriedly dispensed by the parents of terrified children to the sharp cracks of the Jab-jabs' whips. Next was a band of black Jab Molassies, horned molasses devils armed with homemade pitchforks, covered from head to toe in tar, grease, oil and molasses.

"Abbasiyah comin' now; oh, Lawd no," cried a young girl, and the crowd began to scatter.

The wannabes disappeared, never to be seen again. Only the biggest, bravest Carnival spectators stood their ground. Large, muscular and widely rumoured to be of Grenadian descent, Abbasiyah had led the local Jab Molassies for the past decade and was notorious; and, as the sun rose above the corrugated steel housetops, flooding the streets of San Fernando with streaks of golden sunlight, Abbasiyah's besmeared entourage heralded his arrival with infectious African beats on large, empty biscuit tins, chanting:

Jab Molassie — yay
Jab Molassie — day-ee day-oh

And, Abbasiyah's imps, a group of local children led by his loyal friend, Goliath the Dwarf, put on a show of struggling to restrain him with heavy steel chains. His bloodshot eyes bulged, theatrically, as he growled, grunted and groaned, wordlessly threatening to smear black, oily grease on the pristine clothes of those who refused to pay his devil's due. With a smile, Kaya recalled the first time he saw Abbasiyah — a chained, black mountain of a man with oversized horns. J'ouvert, a long time ago — Kaya was only four-years-old, and he almost wet his pants.

The devils swept through the crowds, trailing tension and apprehension, cutting a clear path for the last of the traditional Carnival characters. Three piercing bursts from a whistle announced the appearance of a Midnight Robber. Dressed in black with an oversized fringe-brimmed hat, a bandolier bristling with fake bullets, replica pistols on each hip, and draped in a long black cape that bore symbols of death, the tall dark masked-man delivered his grim robber talk with eloquence, conviction and verve:

Hear my call
Oh, earth and sea
Listen well and despair
Sinners all
Shall bend their knee
Before the judge, so beware

I am a spirit of old

Death is my grandfather
Grim truth be told
I am the original Midnight Robber

I am the king of pain
The emperor of destruction
Hellfire spits my name
Charon Malefaction

There will be no rest for the rotten
No debt shall go unpaid
Your day of judgement is not forgotten
It is just temporarily delayed

By all means, party! Be merry
And do whatever makes you happy
Indulge each and every depravity
For I see all that you do, with the utmost clarity

Drink, and lust, and wine
Fools rebel
But listen well
You will pay for every crime

And when you hear the final bell
Scream and wail and cry
I know you well
And when you die
I will ferry you all to Hell

67

FAMILY FEUDS AND OTHER RIVALRIES

For Kaya, Ash Wednesday heralded the Lenten season's sombreness too soon, abruptly concluding his most enjoyable Carnival, and consigning his revelry to still photographs and photographic memories. Avengers Steel Orchestra achieved their best result for many years, placing 5th in the Large Bands category of the National Panorama; and, as an early birthday present, Josephine enrolled Kaya into a course of steel pan lessons. Nonetheless, Kaya focussed squarely on the upcoming annual Sports Day and his anticipated track and field showdown with his Mapepire rival, Cobo.

Kaya and Cobo were never friends. For several generations, there had been some friction between the Corbeaus and Kaya's relatives. The tempestuous Corbeau family history in Trinidad began with Frenchman Alexandre Gervais-Corbeau, an adventurous Roman Catholic settler. Alexandre came to Trinidad in 1795 while the island was still a sparsely-populated province of colonial Spain's Captaincy General of Venezuela. From Guadeloupe, an overseas region of France, he brought his young family and the African slaves they owned. He swore allegiance to the Spanish king in exchange for land. Cobo claimed that Kaya's third great-grandmother, Arienne, was a descendant of Alexandre's slaves. Nonetheless, according to the elders of Kaya's family, Arienne's mixed heritage included gens de couleur libres — free people of colour from the French-Caribbean island of Martinique, and escapees from the American Deep South, but none of Arienne's ancestors were ever Corbeau slaves.

Arienne inherited a 40-acre estate, adjacent to a massive sugar cane plantation owned by Cobo's fourth great-grandfather, Marius Corbeau. She lived there, in relative peace, until the mysterious disappearance of her husband, Arnaud. Prevalent rumours suggested that Marius, smitten by Arienne's beauty and coveting her fertile land, had callously arranged Arnaud's murder. Nevertheless, within a few years of Arnaud's disappearance, Marius's indentured labourers revolted, his wife committed suicide, and he suffered and died of a mysterious malady. Some claimed Arienne eventually lost everything except her beloved children, 32 demonetised pieces of eight, and an old donkey and cart. Be that as it may, she spirited her young, downtrodden family to Tortuga, a small village in the ward of Montserrat, where indigenous land tortoises called morrocoys roamed freely. At that time, Tortuga, a haven for runaways of every description, comprised a mixed agricultural community of native Amerindians, freed African squatters, and Catholic settlers of mainly Spanish or French origin. Within a year of her arrival, Arienne, who would later be known as Mama Nen, married Elijah Peters, a blue-eyed, land-owning widower. And, although their children and grandchildren subsequently lost most of the land to unscrupulous bankers or carelessly allowed it to be stolen by squatters, the Old Peters House, and the acre it stood on, still belonged to the descendants of Elijah and Arienne to this day. Despite their growing wealth and influence, illness and personal misfortune continued to dog the Corbeaus. And they believed they had been cursed by Arienne, long before the Dirty Thirties' diseases of black pod and witches' broom decimated the crops of their once-lucrative cocoa estates.

As often as possible, Kaya continued to wear three-kilogram ankle weights, determined to defeat Artimus Corbeau in the 100 metres race without the use of his talent; and every day after college, he jogged at least two laps of the main playing field. At times, Shantel Butler, Ocelot's hope for winning the girls' sprint races, accompanied Kaya; and often, much to the dismay of Cobo and other members of Mapepire House, Wendy Wong kept a watchful eye on Kaya's proceedings, and eagerly dispensed lashings of moral support to him.

Wendy had already proven her worth to the Mapepires in girls' hockey, and with her unplanned inclusion in their netball team. At the start of the second quarter of the netball game between the Mapepires and the Tayras, she replaced wing attacker Gillian Payne, who had suffered a knee injury. Wendy's blistering passes to goal attacker Abigail Frost, and goal shooter Nicole Richards, helped secure a decisive 34 -18 win for the Mapepires. In the final game, they faced Ocelot House, which had a 21- 16 victory over the Hummingbirds. Raima Khan played wing defence for the Ocelots, and Kaya spent most of the game, sunk uneasily in his chair, cringing, and praying there would be no bloodshed.

Ah wish Wendy was in Ocelot House. Ah cyah take dis pressure....
he thought, and unfortunately Wendy heard him.

Telepathically, she tried to assure Kaya that she would not *fry what's her name's brain*. Wendy explained that, unlike their Setian rivals, Osirians risked the summary termination of their enhancement-drug supplies if they were found to be misusing their supernatural abilities. Kaya remained sceptical, and he found the colourful metaphors that laced Wendy's thoughts throughout the game somewhat disheartening.

He still could not read Raima's mind, but he could read her lips; and, there was no mistaking her derogatory use of the word, *bitch*, whenever Wendy thwarted her interceptions. He had never seen Raima act so aggressively, and Wendy gave no quarter. Once his fear of a bloodbath subsided, Kaya could almost begin to enjoy watching the pretty, dark-haired, long legged, skimpy-skirted, sweat-drenched girls as they battled it out. Kaya felt torn. He wanted the Ocelots to win, but he did not want Wendy to lose. In the end, despite the herculean efforts of Raima, Shantel and the rest of the Ocelot netball team, the Mapepires beat the Ocelots 26 – 20.

The Mapepires consolidated their lead with 7,136 house points. Gold medal performances of Tom Baker and Raima Khan on the tennis court helped Ocelot House advance to second place with a total of 6,800 points. The Hummingbirds dropped to third with a score of 6,544, and Tayra House remained fourth with 6,520 points. Nevertheless, with another 3,000 points to be won in the events on Sports Day, everyone knew that all of the houses still had a chance of winning the coveted Paria College Cup. Cobo had qualified for the 60 metres hurdles, the 100 metres sprint and the 200 metres race, all at slightly slower times than Kaya, but Kaya knew that Cobo always did this to lull his closest competitors into a false sense of complacency.

An unknown had also entered the fray. Dark horse, Lyndell James, joined Paria College after the Christmas Holiday and qualified with faster times than both Kaya and Cobo. Rumour had it that Lyndell, the newest member of Tayra House, was a star footballer from St Bartholomew's College Pointe-à-Pierre, but he had yet to reveal his prowess on the Paria College football field. Lyndell, a quiet and modest young man, who kept mostly to himself, had caught the roving eyes of many of the Paria College girls, including Raima and Shantel. Kaya did not like the dark, handsome fifteen-year-old or his visibly well-developed abdominal muscles. Kaya's opinion of Lyndell had plummeted even further, when Lyndell offered him his hand to shake at the start of the 100 metres heats. Surprisingly, shaking Lyndell's hand felt like clasping a limp and slimy dying fish.

68

SPORTS DAY

The Annual Sports Day opened with a pan soloist's poignant rendering of the Trinidad and Tobago National Anthem. From the judges' booth, shaded beneath the playing field canopy, college principal Dr Gerald *Hairy* Harry led the opening prayer before delivering his trademark rousing remarks. He paid tribute to Kerwin Duff and welcomed his grieving parents, students, members of staff and honoured guests. The proceedings commenced with the judging of the March Past of the College Houses, which offered each house the opportunity to win a maximum of 300 points. The six judges were Bhekizitha Duna, Bernard Mendoza, Mrs Pearl Pascale, Rev Samuel Cyrus, past pupil and fashion designer Suzanne Hosein, and Councillor Simon Alleyne.

Honoured guests were Brigadier Joseph Solomon of the Cadet Force Division within the Ministry of National Security, Acting Chief Commissioner Eileen Bobb of the Girl Guides Association of Trinidad and Tobago, and prominent local businessman, college patron and past student, Septimus Corbeau — Cobo's father. They stood on the winners' podium, keenly observing the proceedings.

Wearing sharp, white dress uniforms and green berets, student members of the Cadet Force's Second Infantry Battalion Band led the procession, setting the pace with the beat of their military drums and the glassy clash of their orchestral cymbals. Hummingbird House followed in college uniform, sporting satin half masks, specially-made ties and shiny, white-plumed top hats, all of blue. House Captain Dylan Rush also wore a cape adorned with a large embroidered image of their mascot, the white-necked jacobin. Tayra House came next, bedecked with distinctive yellow flat-topped military style caps, and broad, satin baldrics. Their upper six captain, Kareem Ali, held a banner bearing their motto: *Industry, tolerance, compassion and equality*, below the image of their founder, Rev Dr Theodore Woolfe.

Captain Colin Sampson led Kaya and the members of Ocelot House. He held their flame-coloured flag aloft, proudly displaying their crest and motto: *Courage, bravery, loyalty and idealism*. To complement their college uniforms, they wore smart, red regimental berets and matching neck-scarves. With Tom at his side and Raima and a fully recovered Meenal Baboolal ahead of him, Kaya marched before the critical eyes of the judges. While Brigadier Solomon took the salute, Kaya caught the vindictive stare of Septimus Corbeau. The old Corbeau hatred of Arienne Peters and her progeny remained very much alive, and for the sake of Ocelot House, Kaya felt relieved that Septimus Corbeau was not a judge.

Finally, majorette Wendy Wong led the Mapepire House procession. She expertly twirled a baton and earned a barrage of applause. Wendy wore a green waistcoat, with a distractingly short, black mini dress and jacket. They bore military-style gold braid and trimmings on the front, cuffs and collar. A tall hat and knee-high boots of black, with green cuffs and gold trim, completed her stunning outfit.

In unison, Raima and Meenal muttered derisively, "Show off," and Kaya heard them, above the din of the military drums and shouts of encouragement from enthusiastic spectators.

Dressed in immaculately pressed college uniforms and similarly embellished black hats and green waistcoats, the Mapepires and their house captain, Adrian Leotaud, paraded like proud peacocks before the three judges, eyes right, smugly chanting:

Left, right, left; Mapepire's de best.

The Mapepires were good, very good. They had won the March Past the previous year, and the year before that; and, Kaya feared they would win it, yet again. Although he was proud of Wendy, he did not want Mapepire House to have another victory under their arrogant belt.

To his credit, Cobo was a great all-round athlete. On the morning of the Paria College Sports Day, he picked up two gold medals and one silver medal in the 50 metres and 100 metres butterfly, and the 100 metres backstroke respectively. For his part, Kaya earned a gold medal in the long jump. Sean Charles of 4I played the role of trainer, goading Kaya to try harder, and offering him dubious, unsolicited advice.

"Whatever yuh do, doh shake Lyndell hand, Dragon Assassin," he told Kaya. "He go steal yuh power."

Kaya's father had already warned him about psychic vampires, individuals who inadvertently or deliberately stole psychic energy from others. However, Kaya remained unconvinced that Lyndell practiced psychic vampirism of any kind.

Nevertheless, when Lyndell offered his slimy hand just before the long jump competition commenced, Kaya impulsively slapped him on the back and said with a grin, "Good luck, man."

Lyndell James dominated the long jump competition; until on his final try, Kaya narrowly beat Lyndell's best jump by just two inches.

At 12:50 PM, on the college playing field in the blistering heat, Kaya, Cobo, and Lyndell prepared for their first race, the boys' 60 metres hurdles. Kaya wore his red Ocelot vest, black shorts and red spiked running shoes with black trim. Cobo sported the Mapepire track uniform, which comprised a green vest, brown shorts and black spikes with green trim, and Lyndell stood in silent prayer, wearing a yellow Tayra vest, black shorts and black-trimmed yellow running spikes. Despite Lyndell's faster qualifying time, Kaya remained quietly confident. Like Cobo, Kaya had not run his fastest race to qualify, and although he did not doubt Lyndell's raw talent, his performance in the long jump suggested that the boy from St Bartholomew could be beaten.

From Cobo, came the customary arrogance and contempt.

"Ah beat yuh before, Abaniah. Ah'll beat yuh again," he smirked.

"We'll see," responded Kaya, calmly.

In contrast, Kaya sensed uncertainty from Lyndell. His victory in the long jump had shaken the confidence Lyndell gained from his faster qualifying time in the 60 metres hurdles. Lyndell had grown particularly concerned by Kaya's sinister sounding nickname of Dragon Assassin and the whispered claims of the Mapepires that Kaya's grandmother was a notorious Obeah woman.

At 1:00 PM, Kaya took fifteen tense seconds to settle into his blocks.

Wendy projected, *"You can do it, Kaya,"* and it took another five seconds for Kaya to regain his focus.

Eight boys held the set position, anxiously awaiting the report of Bernard *Bulldozer* Mendoza's starting pistol. In lanes, one, four, and six were Cobo, Deron Biggs, and Colin Cole of Mapepire House. In lanes, two and eight, dressed in blue sleeveless shirts, white shorts and white-trimmed blue spikes, Peter Rogers and Justin Samuel represented the Hummingbirds. Kaya remained focussed in lane three; and, Lyndell James and Kurt Minors of Tayra House occupied lanes five and seven respectively. For two agonising seconds of deafening silence, the eight boys remained poised to race, mindful of the fact that a false start would result in immediate disqualification.

Lyndell was first to react to the gunshot, leaping to his feet in cat-like fashion, with the single thought, *Ah go win.*

Kaya would later learn that the St Bartholomew boys called Lyndell, Rocket Man. And, as he dug his metal spikes into the ground and gave desperate chase, Kaya forgot all about not using his talent and winning quickly became everything. Nonetheless, at the first hurdle, he leapt too high and Cobo passed him. The second hurdle came sooner than Kaya anticipated, and the heel of his leading right foot clipped the top bar. He did not fall, but he suffered the loss of a valuable fraction of a second and veered dangerously close to Deron. Lyndell kept the lead with Cobo close behind. Kaya bridged the third hurdle perfectly, racing neck and neck with Cobo, who clipped the fourth then struggled to maintain his balance. And, all the while, Kaya heard the thunder of feet, the otherworldly din of heavy breathing, and the frantic cheers of the spectators; and the passionate thoughts of his racing rivals were abstracts of base human emotions. At the fifth and last hurdle, Kaya overtook Cobo just as Kurt Minors and Justin Samuel collided and fell; but, nothing could distract him as he gained on Lyndell in the final stretch. All too soon, the race was over; and, to his disappointment, he crossed the finish line in second place.

Kaya felt that his overconfidence had cost him a gold medal, and he dejectedly settled for appreciative pats on his back from Sean, Shantel, and Tom, thoughtful words of encouragement from Raima and House Master Gobelyn, and projected thoughts of love and pride from Wendy. Kaya stood on the second tier of the winners' podium with a silver medal on a blue ribbon draped around his neck. He entertained the consoling thought that at least he had beaten Cobo. Josephine had taken the afternoon off, leaving her flower shop in the hands of trusted employees, and her animated cheers contrasted the tight-lipped scowl of Septimus Corbeau. At that moment, there was no prouder mother than Josephine Abaniah and no father more disappointed than Cobo's.

69

THE FASTEST

The eight fastest boys of Form 4 assembled at the start of the 100 metres sprint. They were Deron Biggs, Peter Rogers, Lyndell James, Colin Cole, Kaya Abaniah, Kurt Minors, Artimus Corbeau, and David Holder. Of all the Sports Day events, the 100 metres sprint was the one Kaya desperately wanted to win. Two years ago, Kaya had beaten Cobo and won his only 100 metres gold medal. However, the Mapepires maintained that Cobo only lost because of a pulled hamstring injury, which he endured two weeks prior to that race. Last year, Kaya's best simply was not good enough, and Cobo stole the gold. Nevertheless, he was determined to win this year. Lyndell had won the 60 metres hurdles, but in the 100 metres sprint, there would be no hurdles to slow Kaya down. Having dropped to third place for the first time, Cobo was worried, and Kaya sensed it.

During the last two months, Kaya had trained harder than he had ever trained before. And now, as he stood, arms akimbo, staring down the full length of the track to the finish line, Kaya fully understood why he had not won the 60 metres hurdles. He had confronted his mistakes, and in the 100 metres sprint, he would not allow his emotions to get the better of him. He focussed on his father's dream training, and the systematic mastery of mind and body that made him fitter, stronger, and faster. The good wishes of housemates, and even the projected messages of encouragement from Wendy Wong, were dispassionately filtered out by Kaya's slit-eyed focus on victory.

Bulldozer called the boys to the starting line. He reminded them that anyone guilty of a false start would suffer immediate disqualification. It took thirty seconds for the boys to settle in their blocks while Hairy Harry urged the excited spectators to be quiet. For two intense seconds, the boys held the set position before Colin James jumped the gun. Disqualified and humiliated, he left the field, head bowed, shrouding a red face and tear-filled eyes with his right arm. Lyndell began to pray, Deron bounced up and down on the balls of his feet, and Cobo inhaled deeply before he shot Kaya a derisive glance.

Cobo's contempt slid over Kaya and fell away harmlessly, and Kaya shook out his arms and legs before returning to the starting line.

Once again, silence quickly fell upon the sports field of Paria College, and for three long seconds, seven boys remained utterly transfixed in their set position. Bulldozer fired the starting pistol, and Kaya sprang off his blocks, a hair's breadth ahead of Cobo. Miraculously, Lyndell passed them at the ten metre mark; and, between twenty and thirty metres, the gap widened. Kaya briefly entertained Cobo's panicked challenge before he found his stride. He gained on Lyndell, catching him at fifty metres; and, at sixty metres, Kaya had reached his maximum speed. He inched ahead of Lyndell, who stole a frantic glance and coaxed a final burst of acceleration from his taxed legs. Seventy metres into the race, Kaya and Lyndell were neck and neck, with Cobo hunting them down like a hungry wolf. The three were a full metre ahead of the pack. Kaya ignored the excruciating pain in his legs, the ammonia-like carbamide scent of sweaty fear in the air, and the menacing sounds of exertion that emanated from the other runners. Somewhere behind Kaya, Peter Rogers pulled a muscle and howled in pain and bitter defeat, but Kaya dismissed him, effortlessly. The fast approaching finish line completely dominated his pin-sharp mind, and Kaya battled to maintain his top speed while Lyndell's exertion gradually took its toll. Desperate to win his father's approval, Cobo growled in anguish. Kaya sank deep within himself, blocking out his mounting muscular pain and ducking into the tape. The almost imperceptible cut he received on his neck filled his heart with joy. In a desperate bid to overtake Kaya, Cobo frantically dived across the finish line but simply ended up with bruised knees while remaining in third place.

Kaya was the fastest boy in Form 4. Everything had assumed the surreal clarity of slow motion as he absorbed every minor detail of his triumph. Among the whistles, cheers, and applause, he recognised the gleeful squeals of Wendy and Raima. He spied Sean Charles, on the sidelines, jumping as if he wanted to fly. And Tom, who could not dance, was happily dancing. And, in the sea of spectators' faces, Kaya found Josephine's smile, and his superhuman eyesight stole a glimpse of the tears of joy that streamed down her proud face.

Kaya mentally prepared for a swift, controlled stop on the broad, concrete steps of the 6th Form Block, when something utterly unexpected occurred. His right foot sank into a shallow hole that had been covered with freshly mown grass. His ankle twisted, and Kaya crashed and rolled on the ground, before coming to an abrupt stop against the first concrete step.

A crescendo of laughter greeted Kaya as he slowly sat upright. He tried to stand but found that his right foot could no longer take his weight, and white-hot knives of agony forced him to remain seated.

Yuh shoulda break yuh neck, thought Cobo, and Kaya heard him.

In contrast, he distinctly sensed his mother's mounting concern. She struggled, with an urge to storm the field and smother Kaya with motherly love. Nevertheless, when Josephine failed to emerge dragging unendurable embarrassment in her wake, Kaya silently thanked God for restraining her.

"Oh, Gawd, Kaya," cried Raima, before Wendy shoved her out of the way.

"I'm here, doux-doux," Wendy projected to Kaya, as she stooped at his side. *"Let me take a look."*

A curious crowd quickly gathered around them, as Wendy gingerly removed Kaya's right shoe. He gritted his teeth in discomfort while she gently rubbed his ankle.

Wendy said telepathically, *"Thank God, it isn't broken, eh? It's badly sprained, but I can heal it."*

"Yuh sure?"

"Yeah, I'm sure."

"Wendy, wha' yuh doin'? Yuh have tuh get ready for de girls' 100 metres," barked Adrian Leotaud, captain of Mapepire House.

"Gimme a sec," shouted Wendy, angrily.

"Yuh cyah do dis, yuh cyah heal meh," projected Kaya.

"Did you hit your head? Of course, I can, that's what I do. I'm a healer. That's why I was chosen to be your protector."

"Yuh know very well yuh wouldn't be able to run after yuh heal meh."

"So what? I'm psychic remember? You tried to hide it from me, but I know all about that jerk, Cobo, and his twisted family. I know why beating him, is so important to you."

"Well, ah just beat him, didn't I?"

"Yeah.... Yeah, you did."

"Ah doh want yuh tuh heal meh, Wendy. Ah want yuh tuh race."

"Listen, we all know Shantel is going to win."

"Dat's not de point an' yuh know it. Ah want yuh tuh race."

"I love you, you know that?"

"Yup. An' ah love watchin' yuh run."

"I think you hit your head, you better get it checked out, eh?"

"Wendy!" shouted Adrian.

"OK-OK...."

"Go run yuh best race," said Kaya, and he gently squeezed Wendy's hand.

"OK, Dragon Assassin," replied Wendy, with a dimpled grin.

And, as she trotted away, Kaya imagined that her gracefully swaying hips whispered, *"See you later, alligator."*

Kaya noticed Raima watching the way he admired Wendy. He could not read her thoughts, but he did not have to; he recognised the haunted look of jealousy when he saw it.

Tom said, "I think now would be a good time to retire, Abbers," and he helped Kaya to his feet.

"How yuh mean?" said Sean Charles, "Come boy, come, we go freeze yuh foot an' ban' it up."

Colin Sampson said, "Fellas, we have forty-five minutes before de 200 metres. Grab yuh shoe, Abaniah, after yuh collect yuh gold medal we'll take ah good look at yuh ankle. We need de points, hoss; de Mapepires still killin' us."

"Where Dragon Assassin shoe gone?" asked Sean Charles. "Allyuh see ah red shoe?"

Kaya's heart sank. He knew exactly where his shoe was.

"De Mapepires take meh shoe...."

"Buh wha' trouble is dis?" said Colin Sampson. "Somebody gettin' serious cut tail here today."

As the Ocelots began to work themselves up, Mukesh emerged, bearing Kaya's right shoe.

Colin Sampson grabbed Mukesh by the neck of his vest. "Wha' yuh doin' wit' de man spikes, Mapepire boy?"

Kaya immediately noticed that Mukesh sported a freshly administered black eye. In fact, everyone noticed it.

"Let him go, Colin," said Kaya. "He didn't take meh shoe."

Colin released Mukesh but continued to glare at him.

"Here, Abaniah," said Mukesh; and as he handed Kaya the shoe, Kaya quickly grabbed his hand.

In an instant, Kaya probed Mukesh's mind. As he suspected, Cobo had taken his shoe, but Mukesh challenged Cobo and was punched in the face for his audacity. And, if not for Adrian's intervention, Mukesh would have received more than just a punch in the face.

"Wha' de hell yuh doin, cuz? We doh move so," Adrian told Cobo. "Doh bring shame tuh yuh house an' yuh family."

"T'anks, Mukesh," said Kaya, and Mukesh avoided his piercing stare.

"So, Abaniah, we even now?"

"Yeah, man. We even," said Kaya, amused that saving a life had been compared with returning a shoe.

Once again, Kaya stood on the winners' podium, but this time he occupied its highest tier; and it was none other than Septimus Corbeau who placed the gold medal around his neck.

"Well done, Abaniah," he said as he shook Kaya's hand.

Then, to Kaya's shock and amazement, Septimus Corbeau projected, *"Congratulations. Right now you are a hero; but, given enough time, every hero falls out of favour. Yes, little man, I know who you really are."*

Kaya feigned oblivion. Perfectly hiding any hint of alarm, he continued to shake Septimus's hand, graciously.

Septimus turned his attention to Lyndell James and presented him with a silver medal. Cobo received his second bronze medal of the day, but his father said nothing when he shook his hand, and he did not even look him in the eye.

Kaya wondered how much Septimus Corbeau knew about him; and, he wondered if, after all, Cobo also had what Kaya's elders called, the talent.

Before the start of the 200 metres sprint, Gobelyn and Colin Sampson ensured that a first aider attended to Kaya's ankle.

"Abaniah, you've been injured, so I won't ask you to compete," said Gobelyn. "The Mapepires are a competitive lot, with a fierce sporting tradition; but, this year, we have a real chance of taking the Paria Cup from them."

"Breds, we really need de points," said Colin Sampson.

"Wit' dis ankle, ah doh know if ah could win, buh I'll do meh best," said Kaya.

"That's the spirit lad; our best is the most anyone could ask of us."

"Look, Abaniah, forget de pain, forget de ankle, and just win de damn race. Ah know yuh could do it," said Colin. "Beat Cobo wit' ah sprain ankle, an' de Mapepires cyah come back an' say dat he faster dan you."

Undeterred by his bandaged sprained ankle, and the Corbeaus' bitter contempt, Kaya assembled with the other competitors at the starting line of the 200 metres. Peter Roger's pulled muscle prevented him from participating, so Kaya took his mark with the six remaining qualifiers. In lane one was Colin James who had been disqualified from the 100 metres, in lane two Deron Biggs, Lyndell James in lane three, Kaya in four, Cobo in five, David Holder in six, and Kurt Minors took his mark in the seventh lane. Kaya had never won the 200-meter sprint, which had always been his hardest race. It called for greater speed endurance, and Kaya found the curved track challenging.

For three arduously silent seconds, Bulldozer kept the boys in the set position, before the deafening report of his starting pistol, signalled them to fly. First, off the blocks, was Cobo, desperate to make up for previous losses and eager to please his pompous father. Kaya gave chase, the curvature of the track putting additional strain on his injured ankle. He worked hard to dismiss the bolts of white-hot pain that shot up his right leg. At twenty metres, Cobo still held the lead and Kaya had almost forgotten about Lyndell, who inched closer on the inside. Kaya ignored the agony of each stride and began to run as if his life depended on it. At fifty metres, he was neck and neck with Cobo, with Lyndell still hot on his tail.

Between fifty and seventy metres, Kaya continued to accelerate with the three leaders, a metre ahead of the other runners. One hundred metres into the race, Kaya maintained his top speed while Cobo's face betrayed the first telltale signs of panic. Little by little, Kaya drifted ahead, and Cobo's panic became anguish. Halfway down the home straight, Kaya had not slowed down, and his rivals began to buckle under the pressure.

The scenery took on a yellowish hue, as Kaya's pain reached its unbearable peak. Kaya could barely feel his right foot, and he feared he would blackout. With just twenty metres between him and the finish line, Kaya finally began to falter. With each stride, his lead decreased. Tears of agony streamed from his squint-eyed grimace. With each step, his right ankle dipped into molten lava. He carried on.

Ah have tuh win.

On either side of him, Lyndell and Cobo began to duck.

Ah have tuh win.

Kaya ducked into the finish line, and instinctively his right arm shot up — his finger pointed to heaven.

Ah win!

Elation, relief, and agony descended on Kaya as he decelerated into a pained trot and awkward hobble. From the sidelines, Colin Sampson grabbed him with powerful arms and lifted him off the ground.

"Yuh win, Abaniah, yuh win!"

Moments later, when Colin released Kaya and he took a much-needed breath, Wendy smothered him with a tight embrace, kissing him roughly on the cheek.

Kaya held onto her warm body until Tom said, "Get a room."

Gobelyn shook Kaya's hand. "Well done, young man."

Suddenly, all about Kaya were Ocelots eager to either shake his hand or pat his back. Dejected, Cobo left the scene, red-faced, head bowed.

Lyndell shook Kaya's hand. "Good race, man."

Lyndell completed the 200 metres race in second place, ahead of Cobo, who was third; and, Cobo's humiliation in the track events could not be more complete. Wendy placed fifth in the girls' 100 metres sprint, but she had excelled in swimming, earning three golds and one silver. Shantel completely dominated the girls' track and field sports, receiving gold medals in the broad jump, 60 metres hurdles, 100 metres sprint, 200 metres race, and 400 metres relay. With 297 points, the Mapepires won the Paria College March Past. Hummingbird House were second with 295 points, third were the Ocelots with 294, and the Tayras were in fourth place with 292 points.

Finally, the time came for Hairy Harry to announce the final house results and the winner of the Paria College Cup.

"In fourth place, with a total of 7,139 points, Hummingbird House," announced Hairy Harry, and all were jubilant, except the disappointed Hummingbirds. "In third place, with a total of 7,234 points, Tayra House."

The Tayras, who had been last at the start of Sports Day, welcomed the news; and it took a while before everyone settled down.

"In second place," continued Hairy Harry, "with a total of 7,799 points, Mapepire House; which means that, with a total of 7,828 points, Ocelot House wins the Paria College Cup."

In the euphoria that ensued, Rev Baker produced a silver flask and said, "Gobbers, I think this happy occasion calls for a little tipple."

Impersonating Rev Baker, Gobelyn said, "Happiness is not to be found at the bottom of a bottle or from the tip of a needle; it is not to be found amidst a cloud of smoke or within a sugar-coated pill. If you look for it in these places, you will find naught but despair."

"Oh dear, I suppose it's just you and me, Mr Johnnie Walker," said Rev Baker, and he took a sip from his flask.

"You didn't say you were packing Scotch," scoffed Gobelyn, "I thought the ruddy thing was filled with wine."

"Kaya, I need you to help me with something," projected Wendy.

"What, now?"

"Yes, Kaya, now."

"Where?"

"Follow me."

Kaya followed Wendy off the playing field.

"Hey, Abbers, where are you going?" shouted Tom, and Kaya saw Meenal distract him with animated conversation.

"Where we goin' Wendy? Meh foot killin' meh."

Wendy did not respond, she silently walked ahead of Kaya, towards the bike shed.

70

FEVER

In the bicycle shed, away from prying eyes, Wendy kissed Kaya; and, very soon, he forgot about the pain in his ankle.

When she finally came up for air, she said, "I have some good news."

"Yuh parents gone away fuh de weekend?"

"Don't be silly, eh?" said Wendy, and she punched Kaya in the shoulder.

"Oww.... Dat hurt."

"I have news from Cyclo," said Wendy.

Kaya's eyes widened with anticipation, "Meh fadah alright?"

"Your father is fine—"

"De cure work?"

"It worked. They're calling him the Hero of Cyclo."

Kaya swept Wendy off her feet and twirled. They laughed happily; until suddenly, he kissed her. Not breaking the kiss he gently lowered her until finally her feet touched the ground.

And, moments later, when he tried to break the kiss, Wendy projected, *"Don't stop."*

Eventually, Kaya broke the kiss. He tucked his chin on her shoulder and held her close, cheek to cheek, enjoying the warmth of her loving embrace.

"Ah miss him," projected Kaya.

"I know, doux-doux.... I know.

"You'll see him again, Kaya," said Wendy, staring into his dewy brown eyes. " I know you will."

Wendy stooped at Kaya's feet, placing her hands on his swollen ankle.

"Yuh doh have tuh do dat," said Kaya.

"I want to," said Wendy, and she used her ability to heal Kaya's injury.

"Ah love yuh," projected Kaya.

"I know," said Wendy, with a chuckle. "I'm psychic."

On the 14th of May, Kaya celebrated his 15th birthday. He spent the day in the company of his best friends, Wendy, Tom, and Meenal; and that evening; they treated him to a newly-released American science fiction blockbuster. The two couples did not see much of the movie; and, after it had ended, they left the cinema, all smiles, with turned up collars that covered the love bites on their necks. Kaya was truly happy, happier than he had ever been. And, more and more, his psychic abilities grew.

The college year ended; and, a rainy night, in the first week of August, saw Josephine ill with a high fever. She lay awake on her bed, covered in a thick woollen blanket, drenched in sweat and shivering uncontrollably. Experiencing fresh waves of feverish chills, she slowly reached for the glass of water on her bedside table, but Kaya picked it up and gently held it to her chapped lips. Josephine gulped the tepid water past sore swollen tonsils, and when she had satisfied her thirst, Kaya placed the glass back on its bedside perch.

She sighed while Kaya adjusted her pillow. With a low, croaky voice, she said, "Buh look how yuh lookin' after me now, boy."

"Yuh should sleep," said Kaya, with a loving smile.

"Hmmm…. Ah had ah dream," said Josephine, softly. "Ah saw yuh father."

"Where yuh see him?"

"Somewhere. Somewhere strange. De sky was ah funny colour, an' he was surrounded by one set ah people — endless, sick people. He was givin' dem medicine or something. What a strange dream…."

Kaya remained silent. He wondered if he should tell his mother the truth.

"Yuh want tuh know something funny?"

"What?" asked Kaya, and his heartbeat quickened.

"Ah could always tell when yuh father was going tuh call. Ah could sense him."

"Really?"

"Yes, really."

"Ah sense him at Tantie Rose funeral," said Josephine, with a faraway look on her face. And then, turning to Kaya with a puzzled expression, she said, "Ah could sense him now. Who was dat old man yuh were talkin' to?"

"Old man?"

Josephine gently placed her hand on Kaya's face and stared lovingly into his eyes. "Yuh soundin' like a parrot, boy. What it is yuh t'ink yuh protectin' meh from?"

Kaya did not want to break the solemn promise he made to his father, and he did not want to lie to his mother. He simply did not know what to say; and, in the end, he reluctantly mumbled, "Ah sorry, Mammy—"

Suddenly, a deep earthy voice interrupted Kaya. "No, it is I who should be sorry."

Silvery-blue flashes preceded a loud crack of thunder, and the bulb in Josephine's bedside lamp simultaneously blew. Kaya immediately felt a presence in the darkness. Poised to defend his mother, he turned to see an ominous silhouette of a man. Unmoving, the intruder stood in the room, surrounded by a faint electric glow.

"Torian?" whispered Josephine, in abject terror.

The man said, "Yes, Josephine; do not be afraid, it is Torian."

"Daddy?" said Kaya, with cautious anticipation.

The man stepped forward and paused revealingly in the light that shone through a gap in the drapes. Kaya instantly recognised his father, but he also realised that his father was not actually there.

"Oh, Lawd, ah must be dyin'," cried Josephine.

"No, Mammy, yuh have a fever and yuh delirious, but yuh not dyin'," said Kaya, and he waved his hand through the projected image of his father. "Dis is not ah ghost; dis is ah hologram."

"Josephine, what Kaya says is true," announced Torian Raal. "You see before you a psychic projection, facilitated by our Osirian allies. Only my consciousness is with you now; but, I assure you, I am very much alive."

Kaya watched as Josephine's terror gave way to elation, and then to the anguish of a broken heart. "Why?" she sobbed. "I loved you.... How could you abandon me?"

"Please. Forgive me," said Torian Raal, his voice coarse with emotion. "I sought only to protect you."

"All dese years, ah thought you were dead...." said Josephine, as if talking to herself. "I loved you. Yuh know ah loved you, an' yuh left meh alone wit' yuh son."

Josephine sobbed bitterly, and her raw confusion and self-pity prompted a coughing fit.

"Son, please show your mother all that she must know," said Torian Raal.

"But—"

"Your mother has suffered for far too long because of me, and I cannot bear to see her suffer a moment longer. I am guilty of a great crime,

Kaya. I broke the heart of the only woman I have ever loved. There are not enough words, in any vocabulary, which could adequately explain what has been. So, show her, Kaya.... Show her everything. It is what must be done."

Kaya held Josephine's hand, focussed and projected. *"Mammy, yuh could hear meh?"*

Josephine continued coughing for a while, before tightening her grip on Kaya's hand.

"How yuh doin' dis?"

"Tantie Rose call dis de talent. We get it from Mamma Nen."

"Nen?"

"Lemme show yuh."

Kaya placed his fingertips on Josephine's temples and whispered, "See what ah see. Know what ah know."

It took just fifteen minutes of dream time for Kaya's merged consciousness to show Josephine the truth.

"Yuh father is ah alien."

"Yes, Mammy."

"Why yuh didn't trust meh, Torian?"

"The danger was far too great, and I could not bear to lose you."

"But yuh still lose meh, Torian...."

"Only if you cannot forgive me."

"All dese years, ah know yuh were watching over meh. Ah thought it was yuh spirit. Ah forgive yuh ah long time ago. Ah love yuh den, and ah still love yuh now."

With a lump in his throat, Torian Raal said, "As soon as I can, I will return."

"Yes, ah know," said Josephine, "an' ah will be waiting for yuh."

"Kaya. Son. All of my relatives, entire generations have fallen to KARIN. You and your mother are all that I have. You are the light in my darkness; but alas, I am needed here on Cyclo. There is much still to be done, but I will return to Earth, to you, to your mother."

"I know," said Kaya, softly, and a single tear rolled down his cheek.

"Know that I love you," said Torian Raal, and the holographic transmission began to falter. Farewell, Kaya. Farewell, Josephine. Until we meet again.... Know that I love you.

The transmission ended. Josephine pulled Kaya into an embrace and sobbed loudly. "He's alive.... He's alive."

Eventually, in the early hours of the morning, the thunderstorm passed, Josephine had stopped crying, and she began to give in to the calming cobwebs of sleep.

Suddenly, she sat; bolt upright, with a start.

"Kaya?"

"Yes, Mammy."

"Exactly what it is you an' Wendy were doin' in de bicycle shed?"

APPENDIX I

PARIA COLLEGE FACULTY
from the notes of Thomas Andrew Baker

Dr Gerald Harry – (Hairy Harry) Principal / Religious Knowledge

Bhekizitha Duna – (Shaka Duna) Vice-Principal / Dean

Eldred Seymour Gobelyn – (Goblin) English Language

Cyril Williams – (Silly Willy) Caribbean History / Debating Society

Melda Petronella Mallory – (Obeah Widow) European History

Paco Jimenez Calabazo – (Poco Calabash) Spanish

Amita Abilash – (Miss Cutlash) Visual Arts / Photographic Society

Lucien Talman – (Lucky Shortman) Physics / Chess Club

Pandaros Hooghly – (Oogly Panda) Chemistry

Noreen Adams – (Spexy) Geography / Tennis Club

Allister Shen – (Master Shen) Mathematics / Music

Pranit Prakash – (Car Crash) Office Management / Principles of Business

Hugo Balgobin – (Haemoglobin) Biology / Cricket Club

Mrs Pearl Pascale – (Miss Mow Dem) Information & Communications Technology

Maurice George – (Georgie Porgie) English Literature / Christian Fellowship

Bernard Mendoza – (Bulldozer) Physical Education

Ranjit Gulzar – (Ranjit) Groundsman

APPENDIX II

PARIA COLLEGE HOUSES
from the notes of Thomas Andrew Baker

Ocelot

Founder: Rev Dr Conroy McKenney
Master: Eldred Seymour Gobelyn
Captain: Colin Sampson
Mascot: Ocelot. **Colour:** Red. **Element:** Fire. **Ideal:** Passion.
Motto: *Courage, bravery, loyalty and idealism.*

Mapepire

Founder: Erebus Apophis Corbeau
Master: Lucien Talman
Captain: Adrian Leotaud
Mascot: Bushmaster. **Colour:** Green. **Element:** Water. **Ideal:** Emotion.
Motto: *Wisdom, ambition, achievement and resourcefulness.*

Hummingbird
Founder: Errol Hume
Master: Allister Shen
Captain: Dylan Rush
Mascot: White-necked jacobin. **Colour:** Blue. **Element:** Air. **Ideal:** Ideas.
Motto: *Reason, creativity, intelligence and communication.*

Tayra
Founder: Rev Dr Theodore Woolfe
Master: Amita Abilash
Captain: Kareem Ali
Mascot: Tayra. **Colour:** Yellow. **Element:** Earth. **Ideal:** Stability.
Motto: *Industry, tolerance, compassion and equality.*

APPENDIX III

A: HEZEKIAH ABANIAH - PARIA COLLEGE TIMETABLE
from the notes of Miriam Badarian

FORM 4P Kaya Abaniah	1 8:10-8:45	2 8:45 - 9:20	3 9:20 - 10:00		4 10:25 - 11:00	5 11:00 - 11:35	6 11:35 - 12:10		7 1:10 - 1:50	8 1:50 - 2:30
MONDAY	ICT	ENG	RK	**B**	BIO	BIO	ART	**L**	SPA	SPA
TUESDAY	MATHS	MATHS	ENG	**R**	ICT	ICT	LIT	**U**	ART	ART
WEDNESDAY	GEO	GEO	PE	**E**	SPA	CARIB. HIST	MATHS	**N**	BIO	BIO
THURSDAY	ENG	ENG	RK	**A**	GEO	GEO	LIT	**C**	EURO. HIST	EURO. HIST
FRIDAY	SPA	CARIB. HIST	ART	**K**	ICT	ENG	MATHS	**H**	LIT	LIT

B: PARIA COLLEGE - FORM 4 STUDENTS BY HOUSE
from the notes of Miriam Badarian

OCELOT:
Kaya Abaniah, Richard Achong, Meenal Baboolal, Bobby Babooram, Tom Baker, Alison Bond, Shantel Butler, Julie Changiah, Sean Charles, Penelope Farmer, Peter Farmer, Barry Gangasingh, Anthony Griffiths, Charmaine Hennessy, David Holder, Petal Jackson, Michael James, Raima Khan, Christine Murray, Derek Parish, Kevin Porter, Teddy Rodriguez, Lisa Samuel, Corinne Scott, Basdeo Singh, Amanda Soong, Sandra Tate, Paula Walters.

MAPEPIRE:
Mukesh Ahriman, Denzil Bari, Mervin Beharry, Deron Biggs, Keron Brown, Colin Cole, Artimus Corbeau, Kerwin Duff, Selwyn Duncan, Colin Francis, Abigail Frost, Raul Gomez, Melissa Grantham, Paula Lyons, Kylie Maynard, Gillian Payne, Kiara Persad, Motilal Persad, Indira Ramroop, Martin Reece, Nicole Richards, Geoffrey Rose, Prakash Singh, David Skinner, Patricia Smith, Penelope Tate, Derek Taylor, Brent Wong, Wendy Wong.

HUMMINGBIRD:
Rita Baldeo, Kevin Beharry, John Byno, Linton Crawford, Felix Chung, Ian Davis, Amy de Gourville, Nina Fuentes, Dwayne Gopaul, Farisha Grant, Pedro Hernandez, Michelle Hunt, Kenneth Lee, Pamela Martin, Denise O'Connor, Rudolf Ramesar, Susan Ramjohn, Ricky Ramlogan, Kevin Rampersad, Peter Rogers, Justin Samuel, Nancy Samuel, Peter Sharpe, Gerald Shelton, Mark Simon, Beatrice Taylor, Marlon Weekes, Roxanne Williams.

TAYRA:
Jenny Ali, Gail Angelou, Eve Appleby, Melody Ashby, Faye Asher, Mark Bailey, Daryl Boothe, Elizabeth Crosbie, Kimberly de Gannes, Cheryl Edwards, Yasmine Gosine, Lyndell James, Dexter Jones, Whitney Jones, Curtis Joseph, Keith Lynch, Kurt Minors, Samantha Mohan, Dale Montano, James Moore, Anthony Palmer, Helen Ramjohn, Errol Ramkissoon, Jonathan Singh, Patricia St John, Curtis Tang, Paul Tikasingh, Whitney Walker.

APPENDIX IV

SELECTED EXCERPTS FROM
THE PERSONAL JOURNAL OF THOMAS ANDREW BAKER
Compiled by Major Leul Samaria

31st September,

It's Independence Day — a public holiday, here in Trinidad and Tobago. So far, so good. Life in Trinidad is great. The people are really friendly, and the sky is always blue — except when it rains. It's rainy season now,
but so far it's been OK. No storms or hurricanes.

I had just one uncomfortable experience. One day, on the way to college, two local boys approached me. They were around ten-years-old.
      The shorter one said, "Yuh real far away from home, Yankee."
      I politely told him, "I'm not American. I'm English."
      "Oh, is so?" said the taller one. "Well, yuh far away from Piccalilli."
      I told him I didn't like Indian pickles or any pickles, for that matter.
      But he said, "Pickle? How yuh mean?"
      I realised he had no idea I was being sarcastic, so I simply told him,
"Piccadilly is in London, I'm from Oxford."
      The shorter boy said, "Yuh leave de cold tuh come here, an' look
how de sun ha' yuh face red-red-red."
      I said, "Listen, I'd love to stop and chat, but I'll be late for college."
      "Alright Paria man, doh leh we keep yuh," said the taller boy. "Wha'
time it is now?"
      I was beginning to feel just a bit uneasy, so I said, "It's around quar-
ter to eight."
      "Yuh sure?" said the shorter boy. "Check it nuh, check it."
      "I don't have a watch," I told him.
      "Ah sure yuh ha' a smart phone," said the taller boy, with a dodgy
look on his face.
      I hadn't realised that Maureen, our housekeeper, was running an er-
rand and saw what was going on.
      "What allyuh t'ink yuh doin?" she growled and grabbed each boy by
the ear. "Doh leh meh ketch yuh harassing de Reverend son, ever again. Yuh

hear me? Ah not afraid tuh cut yuh tail. Yuh mudder is meh good friend, an' when I tell she wha' allyuh gettin' up tuh, ah sure she go make sure yuh cyah sit dong fuh a week."

Maureen released the boys, and they ran off, never looking back.

"Yuh really ha' tuh be careful talkin' tuh strangers, Tom," she said sternly, "Yuh jus' come an' yuh doh know de place yet."

I didn't argue, I simply thanked her, and off she went, her shiny red shoes clacking down the street.

12th October,

I've noticed that Trinidadian Creole and Jamaican Patois often include mispronounced English or French words and phrases, with African or other grammatical rules applied. When speaking Creole, many Trinidadians substitute *th* with *d*. So *the* becomes *de* and *this* becomes *dis*. Also, *th* can be just *t* as in *three*, which is often mispronounced *tree* or *thank*, which is mispronounced *tank*. There is also a noticeable tendency to drop the *d* at the end of some words; *and* is usually pronounced *an'*, and *friend* is *fren*. Tenses are often ignored — "I watched him as he walked down the dark road," is likely to become — "Ah watch him walk dong de dark road." Although English-based, I have found it difficult getting to grips with Trinidadian Creole, but daily prayers seem to be working.

Jamaican Patois is even more difficult, and I doubt I will make much progress as even the Trinidadians have some difficulty understanding it. Anyway, I noticed that the few Jamaicans, I've met, don't pronounce *h*. So *heart* becomes *art* and Hugh Roy becomes *U-Roy*. Kaya introduced me to a real Jamaican Rastafarian named Roy Dread. When he spoke to Kaya, I did not understand anything he said. Trinidadian Rastafarians are much easier to understand.

17th November,

Trinidad and Tobago's Hindu community recently celebrated Divali, which is a public holiday here. The celebration is very much family-orientated and the festivities involve stunning, nocturnal displays of small, lighted clay lamps, which are filled with oil to signify the victory of light over darkness and good over evil. Firecrackers are also used to ward off evil spirits.

APPENDIX V

B FOR BODYGUARD

ORIGINAL MONOLOGUE
by Hezekiah Abaniah

Behold! Before you, a bawdy bard, cast begrudgingly, betwixt and between, as both benefactor and bandit by the biliousness of fate. This brazen beauty, no banal by-product of blustering bravado, is the badge of a bitter battalion, now beaten, banished. However, this benign, buccaneering bondsman of a bygone barony, stands with bated breath; bewitched, beguiled and burning to beat these belligerent, barbarian brutes, boundlessly bent on butchering blameless babes. Your bona fide bodyguard, forever your bastion; neither bedlam nor bureaucracy shall blunt my bayonet, broadsword or battle-axe. My blood, my brawn and bone, I bequeath you. But, bravura banter briskly becomes brainless balderdash. So, permit me to add with respect that it is my very good fortune to make your acquaintance. I am your humble servant, B.

PLAIN ENGLISH MONOLOGUE
by Miriam Badarian

Look! Here I am, a raunchy poet, cast reluctantly in the unresolved position of both patron and thief by an unpleasant destiny. The shameless beauty of this is not the result of an exaggeration of courage on my part, but a clue that I was once a member of a disaffected group that no longer dares to fight. However, as a kind-hearted adventurous bounty hunter, from a once prestigious place that no longer exists, I stand under your spell, anxiously eager to beat these aggressive, uncultured thugs, who are enthusiastically committed to harming innocent children. In good faith, I am your bodyguard, and I will always defend you. No confusion or complication will ever prevent me from using all my faculties to do so. Without hesitation, I will lay down my life for you. But, my brilliant speech is quickly becoming mindless rubbish. So, permit me to add with respect that it is my very good fortune to make your acquaintance. I am your humble servant, B.

A SELECTIVE GLOSSARY OF
OBSCURE WORDS, NAMES & UNUSUAL TERMS

A

A-A: *(ay-ay)* [Trinidadian] Expression of indignation or surprise. Usually said very quickly as an exclamation, or very slowly in a questioning manner.

AGOUTI: *(ah-gootie)* Large South American rodent, hunted and served as a delicacy in Trinidad.

AGUE: *(aig-you) Acute fever.*

AH: [Trinidadian] *I.* Also used as pronunciation of *a.* Example: "Ah want tuh buy ah bread."

AH TRUE: [Jamaican] *It is true.*

ALLYUH: *(all-yuh)* [Trinidadian] *All of you people.*

ARAWAK: Indigenous people of the West Indies. Earliest known inhabitants of Trinidad.

ASP: Assistant Superintendent of Police.

AWA: [Trinidadian] *Or what?* Example: "Like yuh schupid, awa?" — "Are you stupid?"

AX: [Trinidadian] *Ask.* Example: "Ah want tuh ax ah question."

B

BABOOMAN: [Trinidadian] *Bogeyman.* A mysterious old man of Indian descent, with long hair and a beard, dressed in a dhoti and often feared by very young children. Usually seen in rural areas, carrying a sack over his shoulder, and using a staff, walking from village to village to attend Hindu prayer ceremonies.

BABYLON: [Rastafarian] *Police.* The establishment. Western society. Corrupt elite. An ancient world power, which, according to the Christian Bible, oppressed God's people. God's enemy, which he will destroy.

BACCHANAL: *(back-ah-nal) Scandal.* Confusion. Heated argument. Wild party or FETE.

BACHAC: *(bah-chak)* [Trinidadian] *Leaf-cutter ant.* Large, black or red soldier ant.

BA' JOHN: [Trinidadian] *Bad John.* Bully. Tough guy.

BAZODEE: *(bah-zo-dee)* [Trinidadian] *Giddy.* Being dizzy or confused by an attractive member of the opposite sex.
BELAIRI: *(bela-eerie)* [Talisian] *Beautiful bird.* Land of the Beautiful Bird. Tobago. The Blue-crowned Motmot, which only exists in Tobago.
BREDDA: [Trinidadian] *Brother.*
BREDS: [Trinidadian] *Brethren.* Brother.
BUH: [Trinidadian] *But.*
BULLPISTLE: [Trinidadian] A long, elastic whip made from the stretched and cured penis of a bull.
BUSS: [Trinidadian] *Burst.*
BUSS STYLE: [Trinidadian] *Show off.* See CUT STYLE.
BUNKS MI RES': [Jamaican] *Take a nap.*

C

CALYPSO: [Trinidadian] *Song.* Topical, often humorous, and on any subject. Usually composed for, but not limited to, the Carnival season. Frequently employs double entendres.
CALYPSONIAN: [Trinidadian] *Singer.* Someone who sings calypsos.
CARIBANA: [Canadian] Previous and more common name of the Scotia-bank Toronto Caribbean Carnival, held each summer in the Canadian city of Toronto, Ontario.
CA-VUS: [Setian] *Sergeant.*
CEASE AN' SEKKLE: [Jamaican] *Stop and settle down.* Calm down and relax.
CHA: [Jamaican] Expression of disappointment, impatience or vexation.
CHEN PI: *(chen pee)* *Dried orange peel.*
CHIRREN: [Trinidadian] *Children.*
CHOONKS: [Trinidadian] *Sweetheart.* Term of endearment or affection, originally used to describe a chubby individual. Abbreviation of CHOONKALUNKS.
CHOONKALUNKS: [Trinidadian] Term of endearment or affection, originally used to describe a chubby individual. Also CHOONKANTS, CHOONKS, CHUNKS.
CHOW-CHOW: [Trinidadian] Traditional pickled relish made with cauliflower, carrots, onions, runner beans, sweet peppers and pimento peppers, usually served with Christmas ham.
COCKROACH HAVE NO RIGHT IN FOWL PARTY: [Trinidadian] Avoid situations where you are unwelcome or could risk being snubbed.
COMESS: *(com-ess)* [Trinidadian] *Confusion.* Commotion. Confused situation. BACCHANAL.

CORBEAUX: *(cobo)* [Trinidadian] *Black Vulture.*

CÔTÉ-CI CÔTÉ-LÀ: *(cotay-see cotay-lah)* [Trinidadian] *This side, that side.* Rumours. Long-winded, irrelevant or unimportant conversation.

CRAPAUD: *(krapo)* [Trinidadian] *Large frog or toad.*

CRAPAUD SMOKE YUH PIPE: [Trinidadian] *You are most certainly doomed.*

CROTON: Tropical garden plant and houseplant, with variegated leaves of green, yellow, orange, red or crimson, in a wide variety of shapes and sizes.

CUNUMUNU: *(koo-noo-moo-noo)* [Trinidadian] *Simpleton.*

CURRANTS ROLL: [Trinidadian] Currant-filled, diagonally cut, rolled pastry—usually flaky with a hint of cinnamon.

CUT STYLE: [Trinidadian] *Show off.* Behave or display in a showy or conspicuous way.

CUT TAIL: [Trinidadian] *A beating.* See LICKS.

CYAH: *(keeyah)* [Trinidadian] *Can't.* Cannot.

D

DADDY BOUCHON: *(Daddy boo-shaw)* [Trinidad and Tobago Folklore] *Father of the Forest.* See PAPA BOIS.

DAT: [Trinidadian] *That.*

DINGOLAY: *(dingo-lay)* [Trinidadian] *Dance.* Gyrate in an elaborate or provocative way. Make of oneself a pompous display.

DERE: [Trinidadian] *There.*

DEES: [Trinidadian] *These.*

DEY: [Trinidadian] *There.* Their.

DNA: *Deoxyribonucleic acid.* Nucleic acid consisting of double-stranded nucleotides that carries the genetic information determining the makeup of all known living organisms and many viruses.

DOH: [Trinidadian] *Don't.*

DOMO SHARTI DOMONÉ: *(doh-mo shartee doh-mo-nay)* [Old Cyclan] *The sleeper must sleep.*

DOMO SHARTI EXZOMNÉ: *(doh-mo shartee ex-zom-nay)* [Old Cyclan] *The sleeper must wake.*

DONG: [Trinidadian] *Down.*

DONKEY YEARS: [Trinidadian] *Ages.* A very long time.

DOTISH: *(doh-tish)* [Trinidadian] *Doltish.* Stupid.

DOUEN: *(dwen)* [Trinidad and Tobago Folklore] Lost soul of child who died before being baptised. Characterised by feet that are backwards-facing with the heel at the front. Lures children into forest.

DOUX-DOUX: *(doo-doo)* [Trinidadian] *Sweetie.* Term of endearment of French origin.

DREAD: 1. [Jamaican] Rastafarian. 2. An adjective meaning ruthless, evil or cold-hearted. 3. [Trinidadian] Various, often contradictory, meanings including: cool, outstanding, bitchy, talented, and friend. See HOSS. Can also imply a phrase, for example, "Nah, dread," which means, "No, I cannot believe this."

DREADIST DREAD: [Trinidadian] *Badass.* Most outstanding and talented individual. Coolest of the cool. Baddest of the bad.

DUNCEY-HEAD: [Trinidadian] *Stupid.*

DUPPY: *(dup-pee)* [Jamaican] *Ghost.*

DUS' IT: *(duss it)* [Trinidadian] *Leave.*

DUS'IN' IT: *(duss-in it)* [Trinidadian] *Leaving.*

E

ENDAR: [Cyclan] *Enhanced Detection And Ranging system.*

ENT: [Trinidadian] *Ain't.*

EVERYT'ING COOK AN' CURRY: [Jamaican] *All is well.*

F

FADAH: *(fah-dah)* [Trinidadian] *Father.*

FAMILY: 1. Relative connected by blood or marriage. 2. [Trinidadian] Polite way of addressing an unknown person, especially female.

FETE: *(fett) Party.* Social gathering.

FLIM: [Trinidadian] *Film.* Movie.

FLYING LOW: [Trinidadian] Speeding excessively in a car.

FREE UP: [Trinidadian] *Relax.*

FROUPSY: *(froopsie)* [Trinidadian] *Nerdy.*

G

GIMME: [Trinidadian] *Give me.*

GORM: [Trinidadian] *Gosh.*

GREYS: Small, grey-skinned extraterrestrials with large heads and very large, black eyes. See SIA.

GYUL: *(gheeyul)* [Trinidadian] *Girl.*

H

HAJIME: *(haji may)* [Japanese] *Begin.*

HIGHER AUTHORITY: Ruling class of descendants of alien-human hybrids striving to dominate and enslave mankind. See SETIANS.

HOSAY: An Islamic festival observed by Shia Muslims in Trinidad, commemorating the martyrdom of Imam Hussein ibn Ali, the grandson of the Prophet Muhammad. Multi-coloured model mausoleums are paraded in the streets, accompanied by the beating of Tassa drums, before being ritually offered up to the sea.

HOSAY MASSACRE: In 1884, in anticipation of civil unrest during Carnival in Trinidad and Tobago, and following riots and frequent strikes on local sugar plantations, the British colonial government enacted the Peace Preservation Ordinance, which prohibited large street parades and torchlight processions. It also authorised the banning of drum beating, horn blowing, and the use of any noisy instrument. That year, the government also issued regulations preventing Hosay processions from travelling on any public highway. Nevertheless, thousands took to the streets of San Fernando for Hosay on Thursday, 30th October. They were met by the police, supported by British troops. After the Riot Act had been officially read, shots were fired to disperse the crowds, resulting in twenty-two deaths and over one hundred wounded.

HOSS: [Trinidadian] *Horse.* Mate. Buddy. Good friend. Partner. See PADNA.

HYSKOTH: [Osirian]. *Karellan.* A fierce hybrid race of humans engineered by rogue Talisian scientists. See KARELLAN.

I

IRIE: *(I ree)* [Rastafarian] Powerful, excellent, feeling great.

I AN' I: [Rastafarian] Me, myself and I.

I-MAN: [Rastafarian] *I.* Reference to self.

INNA: [Jamaican] In a. In the.

IS SO: [Trinidadian] *That is the way it is.* (Statement). *Is that right?* (Question).

I-WAH: [Rastafarian] *Hour.*

J

JA: *(ya)* [German] *Yes.*

JAB-JAB: [Trinidadian] *Devil-devil.* Patois derived from French diable-diable. Traditional pretty devil mas player of Trinidad and Tobago Carnival, usually dressed in bright costumes often featuring horizontal panels of alternating colours, armed with a BULLPISTLE or plaited hemp whip. Distinguished by a mesh mask, horned skull-cap and breastplate. Jab-jabs demand money from their audience by chanting ominously, "Ah come from Hell, Jab-jab; ah know yuh well, Jab-jab; so pay de devil, Jab-jab." In the past, rival groups of Jab-jabs would PLAY SWAPPAY or violently clash on the streets, cracking their whips and exchanging blows.

JAB MOLASSIE: [Trinidadian] *Molasses devil.* Patois derived from French diable mélasse. Traditional devil mas player of Trinidad and Tobago Carnival, usually dressed in shorts or trousers cut off at the knees, a horned cap, a wire tail, and armed with a homemade pitchfork. The entire body is daubed in tar, lard, grease, molasses or red, green or blue pigment with which the Jab Molassies threaten to besmear spectators unless they are paid in cash. Metal chains and shackles are often used to restrain one of the Jab Molassies in a band.

JACK SPANIARD: [Trinidadian] *Paper wasp.* Can be very aggressive, especially if nest is threatened. Very painful sting, usually resulting in swelling. Also JEP.

JAGABAT: [Trinidadian] *Slut.* Promiscuous individual.

JAMETTE: *(jah-met)* [Trinidadian] Loud, crude, vulgar woman of low moral standards.

JEEZ AN' AGES: [Trinidadian] Exclamation of surprise, shock, dismay or disbelief.

JEP: *(jepp)* [Trinidadian] *Paper wasp.* Also JACK SPANIARD.

J'OUVERT: *(joo-vay)* Large street party, which starts early on the Monday morning that marks the beginning of Carnival in Trinidad and Tobago.

JULIE MANGO: [Trinidadian] Sweet, juicy mango with deep orange flesh and green skin blushed with crimson. Not fibrous or starchy. Trees can grow to over 30 feet in height. See STARCH MANGO.

JUMBIE: *(jum-bee)* [Trinidad and Tobago Folklore] S*pirit.* Demon.

K

KAIRI: *(ka-yiri)* [Talisian] *Hummingbird.* Land of the Hummingbird. Trinidad. [Arawakan] Island.

KARAILI: *(ka-riley)* [Trinidadian] *Momordica charantia.* Extremely bitter vegetable grown in Trinidad and Tobago.

KARELLA: A planet on the outer rim of the Cosmic Sea Galaxy. Originally a penal colony of the Talisian Commonwealth, Karella is the home world of genetically engineered human hybrids from Earth. The Royal Dynasties of Enki, Seti, Wotan and Arat originated in Karella.

KARELLAN: A thing or human being of or from the planet KARELLA. Descendant of Talisian/Kian hybrids originally banished to the planet Karella by the High Council of the Talisian Commonwealth. Also HYSKOTH.

KARIN: [Cyclan] *Karellan Immunodeficiency Nanovirus.* Virulent, highly infectious nanoviral weapon based on Cyclan technology and developed by the Karellan military. Its illegal use by invading Karellan forces loyal to Brakis Tarn is considered the main cause of Cyclan fatalities during the Cyclan Genocide of the Second Psychic War.

KETCH: [Trinidadian] *Catch.*

KI: (key) [Talisian] *Earth.*

KOLMÅRDEN: *(cole-mordaan)* [Swedish] A large forest that separates two of Sweden's main agricultural areas—the provinces of Södermanland (so-dimunlund) and Östergötland (oster-yoetlund).

L

LA DIABLESSE: *(la dja-bless)* [Trinidad and Tobago Folklore] Demonic, well-poised woman with a hideous face, which she hides with a large-brimmed hat, and one human foot and one cloven hoof, which she hides with a very long dress. Lures men to their doom in secluded forests.

LADKI: [Urdu] *Girl.*

LAPPE: [Trinidadian] *Agouti paca.* Largest rodent in Trinidad, highly prized as wild game.

LAPYS NERIAN: *Black Stone.* Hardest substance found in the Cosmic Sea Galaxy. Exists as an extremely rare, black, single crystal alloy, and as an equally rare naturally occurring crystal.

LAPYS VIRIDIAN: *Green Stone.* Priceless substance that exists in the Cosmic Sea Galaxy as an extremely rare, green, single crystal alloy, and as an equally rare naturally occurring crystal from the distant moon of Spiro Majur.

LEGGO: [Trinidadian] *Let go.*

LICKS: [Trinidadian] *A beating.* See CUT TAIL.

LIKKLE: *(lickle)* [Trinidadian] *Little.*

LILY OF THE NIGHT: *Stephanotis floribunda.* Madagascar jasmine. Tropical, woody-stemmed climber, which produces clusters of white, highly scented, waxy, star-shaped flowers, popular for bridal bouquets and wreaths.

LIMBO: [Trinidadian] Dance, usually to the beat of African drums, featuring performers bending backwards from the knees and shuffling forward below a long stick held progressively lower by two others.

LIME: [Trinidadian] Informal get-together of a small group of people.

LUMINATA PREFECTARA: *Prefects of Enlightenment.* An extremely powerful, clandestine organisation believed to be indirectly controlled by the Neph Alim Principality.

M

MAGGA: [Trinidadian] *Skinny.* Very thin.

MAMA DLO: [Trinidad and Tobago Folklore] *Mother of the Water.* Half African woman — half anaconda snake, also known as Mama Glow or Mama Dglo whose name is derived from the French, maman de l' eau. Protects flora and fauna in or near local rivers. The female counterpart of PAPA BOIS.

MAMAGUY: *(mama guy)* [Trinidadian] *Deceive.* Attempt to get something using flattery.

MAMA YO: [Trinidadian] Exclamation of surprise. See PAPA YO.

MANICOU: *(manee-coo)* [Trinidadian] Small to medium-sized opossum hunted in Trinidad.

MAPEPIRE: *(mah-pay-pee)* [Trinidadian] *Venomous pit viper.* [Carib] Matapi. Snake. Either of two species of poisonous vipers found in Trinidad. Mapepire balsain or fer-de-lance. Mapepire zanana or bushmaster — the largest pit viper in the world.

MASH: [Trinidadian] 1. *Crush.* Step on. 2. *Go away.* Usually shouted at dogs.

MASH UP: [Trinidadian] *Break up.* Destroy. Damage.

MAUBY: *(more-bee)* Popular beverage made with sugar, tree bark extract and still or sparkling water. Sweet with a bitter aftertaste. Consuming large amounts can cause diarrhoea.

MIDNIGHT ROBBER: Traditional mas character of Trinidad and Tobago Carnival, inspired by West African griots—historians and storytellers, American cowboys, Mexican bandits, and Brazilian cangaceiros. Character-ised by an oversized hat with a wide, fringed brim, a long cape usually adorned with various symbols of death and calamity, and armed with swords or pistols. Midnight Robber is easily identified by his *robber talk*, a boastful, mocking speech, often laced with threats and rendered in a manner imitative of the historical slave master's vocabulary and mannerisms.

MIGHTY SPARROW: One of the most successful and famous calypsoni-ans of Trinidad and Tobago. Also known as the *Calypso King of the World.*

MILO: *(my-low)* Chocolate and malt powder, usually mixed with hot or cold milk to produce a beverage popular in Trinidad and Tobago.

MORROCOY: [Spanish] *Turtle.* Local name for Trinidad's vulnerable land-dwelling tortoises. Usually the yellow-footed tortoise, but sometimes the similar red-footed tortoise.

MUDDER: [Trinidadian] *Mother.*

N

NEPH ALIM: *Cloud Scholars.* The Neph Alim Principality. Enlightened beings of the clouds. Mysterious race believed to control the SIA and LUMINATA PREFECTARA.

NIBURIAN: An ancient race of highly advanced alien beings. According to Karellan folklore, the Niburians were shape-shifters who had the power to give humans of their choice the gifts of wisdom, prescience and astral projection.

NOW FUH NOW: [Trinidadian] *Immediately.*

NOWHERIAN: [Trinidadian] *Vagrant.* Someone of no fixed abode.

O

OBEAH: *(obee-ah)* [Trinidadian] Witchcraft and folk magic originating from West Africa.

OH-HO: [Trinidadian] An expression of comprehension, surprise, derision or mock astonishment.

OOGLY: [Trinidadian] *Extremely ugly.*

ORDU SARKAN: [Ancient Setian] *Youth Army.* Elitist Setian paramilitary youth organisation comprising male alien-human hybrids aged 14 to 19, indoctrinated into racial domination. Motto: Kuat ifa Ki—the strong shall inherit the earth. Also SARKAN.

OUI: *(wee)* [French] *Yes.*

OSIRIAN: A thing or human being originating from descendants of alien-human hybrids striving to protect mankind on Earth.

P

PADNA: [Trinidadian] *Partner.* Mate. Buddy. Good friend. See HOSS.

PALLET: [Trinidadian] *Ice lolly.* Milk, ice-cream or fruit flavoured frozen lolly.

PALLET-MAN: [Trinidadian] *Ice lolly vendor.* Traditionally sold pallets from a bicycle cart.

PAPA BOIS: *(papa bwah)* [Trinidad and Tobago Folklore] *Father of the Forest.* African man with cloven hooves. Protects flora and fauna in local forests. Similar to Pan, the Ancient Greek god of the wild.

PAPA YO: [Trinidadian] Exclamation of surprise. See MAMA YO.

PARANG: [Trinidadian] Popular music of Trinidad and Tobago origin, of Spanish, Venezuelan, Amerindian and African heritage; largely sung in Spanish and performed by visiting serenaders during the Christmas season, often in exchange for food and drink.

PASTELLE: [Trinidadian] A traditional Trinidadian Christmas dish, made from cornmeal dough, filled with a spicy mixture of minced beef, pork, peppers, onions, olives and raisins, wrapped in banana leaves, tied and steamed to a light crust.

PAWI: *(pa-we)* [Trinidadian] *Trinidad Piping Guan.* Species of large, black, turkey-like bird, close to extinction, which is found only on Trinidad.

PCE: [Osirian] *Psionic Communications Enhancer.* Psychic-controlled mobile communications device, incorporating transponder, flashlight and non-lethal defence ray emitter, disguised as a basic mobile telephone. See PSIO-COMM.

PELAU: *(pay-lau)* [Trinidadian] Popular local dish made with rice, pigeon peas, meat or chicken. Cooked with herbs and coconut milk; coloured and flavoured with burnt sugar.

PLAY SWAPPAY: [Trinidadian] *Fight with whips.* Usually between rival JAB-JAB groups.

POMMERAC: (pom-marak) [Trinidadian] *pomme Malac (Malaysian apple).* Red or pink-skinned, pear-shaped fruit, with white flesh surrounding a large seed. Originally from Malaysia, Vietnam, Sumatra and Java.

PONCHE DE CRÈME: [Trinidadian] Christmas eggnog made with eggs, sweetened condensed milk, evaporated milk, rum, Angostura bitters, lime zest and grated nutmeg, served ice cold.

PONE: [Trinidadian] Sweet, rich, moist, pudding. Usually made of cassava, sweet potato, sugar and coconut.

POT HONG: [Trinidadian] *Pot hound.* Mongrel. Mixed-breed street dog.

POUTINE: *(poo-tinn)* [French-Canadian] Common Canadian dish made with French fries covered with fresh cheese curds, and topped with brown gravy.

PREFECT ULTIMO: Absolute leader of the LUMINATA PREFECTARA. See NEPH ALIM.

PSIO-COMM: [Osirian] See PCE.

R

RAMAJAY: *(rama-jay)* [Trinidadian] *Birdsong.* Sing, act or play in a flamboyant, frivolous or attention-seeking way. Instrumental solo or improvisation. Swearing or being boisterous for a lengthy period.

RNA: *Ribonucleic acid.* Nucleic acid consisting of a single strand of nucleotides involved in protein synthesis in all living cells and the transmission of genetic information in certain viruses.

ROAD MARCH: The most-played song during the Trinidad and Tobago Carnival parades.

ROARING LION: One of the pioneering calypsonians of Trinidad and Tobago. Well known for his very long, successful career and lion-headed cane.

ROYAL HOUSES: *Royal Dynasties.* The seven dominant royal families of the Cosmic Sea Galaxy:

ENKI *(en-key)*
Sigil: Arosian Ten-Shi.
Colours: Black & Gold.
Motto: *Angels Defend Us,*

SETI *(setee)*
Sigil: Beast of Typhon.
Colours: Red, White & Black.
Motto: *Death Before Dishonour.*

EBLA *(eb-lah)*
Sigil: Tamerian Lion.
Colours: Red, Gold & Brown.
Motto: *Brave Not Fierce.*

WOTAN *(woe-tan)*
Sigil: Snow Wolf of Utak.
Colours: Black, Grey & Silver.
Motto: *Cold Is Our Ally.*

XAAN *(sahn)*
Sigil: Eno Fire Wasp.
Colours: Purple, Yellow & Bronze.
Motto: *Fear My Sting.*

KAITO *(kai-toe)*
Sigil: Orinx Dragon.
Colours: Green & Bronze.
Motto: *The Flames And The Fury.*

ARAT *(ah-rat)*
Sigil: Varian Silver Hawk.
Colours: Dark Blue & Silver.
Motto: *We Come From Above.*

S

SARKAN: [Ancient Setian] *Youth.* See ORDU SARKAN.
SCHUPID: [Trinidadian] *Stupid.*
SCHUPIDEE: [Trinidadian] *Stupid individual.*
SCIENCE: [Jamaican] *Witchcraft.* OBEAH.
SCIENTIST: [Jamaican] *Witchdoctor.* Sorcerer. Occult practitioner.
SCOOCH: [Trinidadian] *Dodgeball.*

SETIAN: A thing or human being originating from descendants of alien-human hybrids striving to dominate and enslave mankind on Earth.

SHU-SENYN: (shoe-seneen) [Setian] *Agent.* Cloned agent of Seti. Man in Black.

SIA: *(see-ah)* [Cyclan] Visitor. Small, grey-skinned extraterrestrials with large heads and very large, black eyes. Commonly called GREYS.

SKYLARK: [Trinidadian] *Mess about.* Act in a playful manner. Indulge in tricks, pranks, and horse-play or be inattentive, careless or deceitful. Neglect duty.

SOLO: [Trinidadian] Local brand of non-alcoholic beverages, available in several flavours including orange, grape, banana, kola champagne, and cream soda.

SORREL: *Hibiscus tea.* Popular herbal tea made from Hibiscus sepals, usually served cold.

SOUCOUYANT: *(soo-ku-yah)* [Trinidad and Tobago Folklore] Old, demonic, vampiric woman. Often travels in the form of a fireball. Obsessed with rice.

STAR: [Jamaican] *Man.*

STARCH MANGO: [Trinidadian] Small variety of mango with sweet, creamy, fibrous or starchy flesh and yellow skin when ripe. One of the three most popular mangoes in Trinidad and Tobago, together with the JULIE MANGO and doux-doux mango.

SUCKABAG: [Trinidadian] *Sucker bag.* A sweet fruit-flavoured drink, frozen in a small clear plastic tube.

SU-SU: *(sue-sue)* [Jamaican] *Gossip.*

SWELL UP YUH FACE: [Trinidadian] *Pout.* Look angry.

T

TABANCA: [Trinidadian] *Lovesickness.* Physical and mental symptoms typically associated with the absence of a former lover or with unrequited or rejected love.

TALIS: Capital planet of the Talisian Empire.

TALISIAN: A thing or human being of or from, the planet TALIS.

TANTIE: [Trinidadian] *Auntie.*

TAMBOO BAMBOO: [Trinidadian] *Drums of bamboo.* Tamboo is derived from French, tambour, meaning drum. Instruments made from bamboo stems of different lengths and weights, rhythmically beaten with sticks, and pounded on the ground, by musicians of African origin in Trinidad and Tobago for Carnival parades, folk dances, stick-fights, wakes, and other celebrations.

TAMPEE: [Trinidadian] *Weed.* Wacky backy.

TAY MO: [Cyclan] *Open Hand.* The Way of the Open Hand is an ancient martial art developed in the Ryac Islands on the former 16th Cosmic Sea Planetary Colony of Baris, renamed Cyclo, planet prime of the independent Cyclan Confederacy of Neutral Planets. It was developed partially from the indigenous martial arts of the Ryac Islands called Tay, which literally means *hand*, and from Arashi Paksa the traditional martial art of the Talisian armed forces. Tay Mo utilises both striking and grappling, while specialising in speed of movement and minimal dependency on physical strength in close-range combat.

TAYRA: *(tay-ruh)* [Trinidadian] Indigenous omnivore from the weasel family, also known locally as the high-woods dog or chien bois because of its dog-like bark. Lives in the tropical forests of Trinidad.

TEN-TOE TURBO: [Jamaican] *Feet.*

TIMBITS: [Canadian] Doughnut holes sold at Tim Hortons, a Canadian restaurant franchise specialising in coffee and doughnuts, founded in the 1960s by Canadian ice hockey player, Tim Horton.

TOBAGO: *(toe-bay-go)* The smaller of the two principal islands of the Republic of Trinidad and Tobago.

TONIC: 1. A medicinal substance taken to produce vitality or a feeling of wellbeing and vigour. 2. [Trinidadian] Paraquat. A quick-acting herbicide and weed killer, extremely poisonous to humans if ingested, and notoriously used to commit suicide.

TREATY OF VERSAILLES: Peace treaty, at the end of World War I, which ended the state of war between the Allied Powers and Germany. It was signed at the Royal Château de Versailles, in France, exactly five years after the assassination of Archduke Franz Ferdinand, on 28 June 1919.

TSUZUKETE: *(tsoo-zoo-keh-tay)* [Japanese] *Continue.*

V

VAMPIN': [Trinidadian] *Flatulence.* Producing an offensive odour.

VAPS: [Trinidadian] *Fit of madness.* Sudden inexplicable behaviour or movement. To suddenly act in an excited or uncharacteristic manner. Example: "He ketch ah vaps."

VETS: [Setian] *Six.*

VEX: [Trinidadian] *Vexed.* Angry.

W

WATA BOOTS: [Jamaican] *Waterproof boots.* Waterproof work boots or rain boots, usually used in farming.

WHA' SCENE YUH ON? [Trinidadian] *Why are you acting that way?*

WINE: [Trinidadian] Suggestive dance typified by rhythmic, exaggerated, circular and side to side movements of the lower torso, hips and pelvic region.

Y

YAME: *(ya-may)* [Japanese] *Stop.*

YARD: 1. Courtyard. Garden. 2. [Jamaican] Home. House. Residence.

YEREK: [Setian] *Three.*

YUH: [Trinidadian] *You.* Your.

YUH FADAH HEAD: [Trinidadian] Expression of irritation or annoyance.

YUH HARDEN: [Trinidadian] *You are stubbornly disobedient.*

YUH MAKIN' JOKE: [Trinidadian] *You cannot be serious.*

Z

ZAW-ZUMN: [Ancient Setian] *Abominable one.*

ZUG UP: [Trinidadian] Cut badly. Uneven, careless, cutting of anything.

About the Author

Wayne Gerard Lionel Trotman is a British writer, filmmaker, artist, photographer, blogger, composer and producer of electronic music.

Born in the Republic of Trinidad and Tobago, Trotman studied at Presentation College, San Fernando, under the late former principal, Brother Michael Samuel, whom he described as one of the greatest human beings he had ever known. He won the *Presentation College Art Prize* twice—1979 and 1982. During the early 1980s, Trotman won several national art prizes in Trinidad and Tobago. His artwork during this period consisted largely of comic book illustrations and acrylic or oil paintings.

In August 1984, Trotman moved to England to study art and design at the *Heatherley School of Fine Art* in Chelsea, London. In 1985, his work was chosen for the *London Youth Festival Exhibition*. Between the late 1980s and mid 1990s, Trotman produced compositions for *British Sky Broadcasting (BSkyB)*; as well as low budget independent film productions. He completed his second feature film script entitled *Ashes to Ashes* in 1994; and, in 1995, his short film — *London: Metropolis of the Future* premiered at the *British Short Film Festival*. Trotman, who is trained in several martial arts disciplines, directed, co-produced, scored and edited the British independent film, *Ashes to Ashes*, in 1998—arguably the world's first digital feature film and Britain's first martial arts movie. He also played the film's lead role of Gabriel Darbeaux and used real martial arts weapons, including the nunchaku or two-piece rod.

In 2006, Trotman co-produced a training DVD, which tackles the cause of anxiety and panic attacks: the *fight or flight* response. Between 2006 and 2009, he wrote his epic Psychic Wars sci-fi novel: *Veterans of the Psychic Wars*; and in 2012 he released the eBook, *Ashes to Ashes: Screenplay*. Also in 2012, Trotman became *Kingston upon Thames Adult Intellectual Chess Champion*, in what was his first and only British chess tournament. January 2014 saw Trotman at number 1, on the *Reverbnation* electronica chart for the UK and 6th globally. He has maintained a Top 40 presence throughout 2014. In January 2015, he released *Kaya Abaniah and the Father of the Forest*, another thrilling instalment from the Psychic Wars universe.

Chapter One of:

VETERANS OF THE
PSYCHIC WARS

WAYNE GERARD TROTMAN

www.redmoon.co.uk

Chapter 1

Roman Doyle activated his Bluetooth earpiece as he walked towards the cashpoint machine. The tall, twenty-five-year-old black man had a lean, athletic build and cast a long shadow from the amber street lamp a few metres away. Roman knew the wisdom of observing his shadow, especially when he walked the streets of North London late at night.

Seven years ago, observance of his shadow saved him from grievous bodily harm. Roman noticed his shadow swiftly approached by another, broader and shorter. Raised high, its thick arm bore a long thin object.

The stocky criminal, equipped with a metal pipe, did not know his potential victim was an accomplished martial artist. Had he known, he would have attacked the much larger businessman who barrelled past fifteen minutes before. At merely seventy kilograms, Roman seemed an easier target.

The astounded thug found himself the recipient of a shattered nose from a gyaku zuki reverse punch, and two broken ribs from a dwet chagi spinning sidekick. The mugger sailed through the air, and seconds later, slammed onto the kerb—unconscious.

A cool, relaxing summer breeze, starkly contrasted the urgently vibrating mobile phone in Roman's right jacket pocket.

It's very late.

This call was no surprise. He knew the caller; her striking Nubian features had suddenly flooded his thoughts seconds before the phone's mechanical response.

She's probably wondering where I am, he mused.

To an onlooker, Roman would seem schizophrenic as he spoke into the discreet receiver.

"Hello?"

The husky, playful tones of a familiar female voice reassured him that his intuition was yet again correct.

"Roman. Where are you Roman?"

It's Soraya.

Her mild Trinidadian accent immediately conjured up pleasant memories of his early childhood on the tropical island; vivid memories of swarms of brightly coloured butterflies surrounding him.

"I'm at a cash-point," said Roman, quickly scanning the secluded street.

He removed a leather wallet from his trouser pocket, slipped a debit card from it and guided the plastic into the slot of the silent cashpoint machine. The screen refreshed instantly:

ENTER PIN:

- - - -

"I've been thinking about you," Soraya said, and Roman recalled how similar her brown eyes were to those of his mother.

"Uh-huh?"

"I've been thinking about your name—Roman, such a strong, sexy name."

"Hmmm," he responded with a hint of sexual provocation.

"But I also like Moses," Soraya added unexpectedly.

A furrow suddenly appeared in his dark brow. He typed the last digit and the screen refreshed again, prompting him to enter the required cash amount.

"Soraya, we've had this conversation.... I'd like to pass on my name," Roman divulged with more than just a tinge of irritation.

"But Moses so much better dan Junior," she claimed, not bothering to speak the Queen's English.

Roman typed **2 0 0**, then pressed **ENTER**.

"So we'll call him Romeo. This is the fourth time we've had this discussion in as many days Soraya; it's late, and I'm not in the mood."

The debit card emerged from the slit in the machine with a low mechanical whirr and Roman returned it to his wallet.

"Romeo sound so—tragic," Soraya's playfulness now giving way to disappointment.

From his rooftop vantage point, with long black hair wildly billowing in the wind, a darkly clad man with Oriental features spied Roman through the viewfinder of an extremely sophisticated pair of binoculars. The ever-changing illuminated characters on the screen were thousands of years older than the Great Pyramid of Giza.

Even though Roman stood three hundred metres away, the display captured his every move with startling clarity. Betraying exceptional stealth, the man retracted the binoculars, tucked them within his black tunic, and silently leapt off the roof into the murkiness below.

"Honey," Roman said, grabbing the cash dispensed by the machine, "I thought we decided that we'd call him Roman? Moses will be his second name."

Soraya responded, "We'll talk about it when yuh get home. Doh forget meh peanut butter yuh know."

"Okay," a smile traced across Roman's face.

I almost forgot.

He quickly counted ten twenty-pound notes, placed them in the wallet, and returned the now bulging billfold to his trouser pocket. Roman proceeded across the seemingly deserted street, briskly heading towards his dark grey BMW E87 hatchback parked sixty metres away.

"An' de ice cream," Soraya added.

"Okay, Sugar, I'll be home before you can say rum 'n' raisin."

"Bye," she purred.

"Bye."

He pressed a small button on his Bluetooth earpiece ending the call.

In an eerie snake-like fashion, five large men with Oriental features and shaven heads emerged from the darkness. They followed Roman, who remained oblivious to the menacing shadows, which gradually converged on his own.

With a wry grin, Roman anticipated the reward that awaited him if he found rum 'n' raisin ice cream and peanut butter after 1:00 AM.

Yes, Soraya would be most pleased.

Soraya, his wife of just eleven months, was two months pregnant. This was their secret. They had not told family or friends. During the past week, Roman developed the belief that profound changes in Soraya's hormone levels were the cause of these strange cravings.

Still smiling to himself, he suddenly experienced a sharp pain in his head.

What the hell?

Surprised, he winced and pulled the earpiece off his ear.

Maybe the earpiece is faulty.

Then, to his shock, Roman noticed a drop of blood at his feet and re-alised that he also had a nosebleed. Quickly tugging a neatly folded handker-chief from his back trouser pocket, he mopped the blood from his nose.

Ominous, whispered voices seemed to come out of nowhere, adding terror to Roman's unfolding nightmare—voices that grew louder within his mind, until they became a roar. Suddenly, he heard an inhuman cry, like a thunderbolt cleaving through the branch of a majestic oak tree.

Turning swiftly, he saw two of the five men charge. A gust of wind whisked the bloodstained handkerchief from his grasp as the pair approached with bewildering speed.

Before Roman could react, the men somersaulted over his head in unison. They landed three metres behind him. The other three stood their ground, glaring at him with undisguised malice.

Stunned and dizzy, Roman tasted blood as his nose continued to haemorrhage. His handkerchief sailed through the air unnoticed until someone shrouded in darkness snatched it from the wind.

For a painfully tense moment, Roman stood perfectly still. Two men blocked his retreat; three stemmed his advance. Characters, which seemed better placed in a graphic novel than on the streets of London, effectively surrounded him. Their outlandish weather-beaten clothing bore symbols that Roman could not decipher.

Suddenly feeling a surge of adrenaline, his experience with the mug-ger seven years ago flashed through his mind.

Roman reassured himself that at twenty-five years of age, he now weighed a healthier eighty kilograms, and through continued training, he attained third dan black belts in Shotokan Karate and Taekwondo. Roman felt certain he would achieve fourth dan grades in both forms before his twenty-sixth birthday. In the ancient arts of Karate and Taekwondo, the black belt not only signified maturity and proficiency, it also symbolised the wearer's imperviousness to darkness and fear.

Three years ago, not satisfied with the well-known Japanese and Ko-rean arts, Roman commenced training in Muay Thai Boxing and Chinese Wing Chun — a fact, which many of his competition rivals were unaware of. This he felt gave him an additional edge. Confident in his abilities and proud of the many tournaments he had won, Roman held the opinion that few men could withstand a motivated assault incorporating all four styles.

Muggers beware.

However, *these are no ordinary muggers.*

Each man weighed over one hundred and fifteen kilograms, yet Ro-man had the impression they could sprint one hundred metres in under nine seconds. They moved with precision and perfect equilibrium. Their toned bodies, dark green tunics, leather utility belts and tall boots screamed military training.

Who are these guys?

The man at the centre appeared to be their leader. He stepped forward. In response, Roman took one stride back, quickly glancing over each shoulder at the men to his rear. The leader motioned with authority and his four henchmen stood frozen. In unison, threatening smiles appeared on the faces of all five antagonists.

Roman shot to full alert status and the leader's sinister grin transformed into a cold stare. Suddenly, metal rods slipped from under the leader's sleeves into his enthusiastic hands.

This could be serious, thought Roman.

The leader rolled one of the rods to Roman's feet and held the other firmly in his right hand. Then, with a flamboyant flourish, he stretched out his arm. His foot-long baton instantly extended three feet each side. The other men stood back in silent anticipation as their leader moved another step towards Roman.

One on one—how sporting.

Roman did not pick up the staff at his feet.

Instead, he shouted defiantly, "Listen, I've worked really hard for my money!"

Without further ado, the leader attacked, and Roman narrowly evaded his furious blows. In a fast-flowing movement, he picked up the shaft from the floor, activated it and counter attacked. But very soon, a relentless whirlwind of impossible force drove Roman into desperate defence. To his surprise, every parry threatened to crumble his wrists and elbows.

The sharp clamour of metal violently striking metal resonated across the surrounding streets of North London. Dizzy and distressed, Roman tried unsuccessfully to break the circle, but the four mountainous henchmen prevented any escape. They forced him to resume his battle for survival with a much stronger opponent.

This is no ordinary mugger.

Roman could not recognise the man's fighting style. It seemed a confusing mix of practically everything and nothing at all; at least nothing that Roman had encountered in his martial arts training.

Somehow the man anticipated Roman's every move. The blows Roman received, as a result, made his intolerable headache even worse. The throbbing flow of blood from his nose adversely affected his vision; and, for the first time in his life, it dawned on Roman that he would be clubbed to death.

During the fight, Roman failed to notice that his driving licence had fallen out of his coat pocket. Even if he had noticed, he could have done little about it. A devastating blow to the back of his head temporarily robbed him of his sight. Three blows followed in quick succession, forcing him to his knees, barely conscious and utterly defenceless.

The ease of his defeat seemed beyond comprehension. He tried to speak but his mouth failed to cooperate.

Take the car, take the phone, take my watch, and take the cash. Take it all; I just don't want my wife to be a widow....

The leader retracted his staff and smirked confidently. In unison, strange blades slid from the sleeves of the other four men into their eager hands. The four advanced collectively with a cry—arms raised, about to strike Roman.

The leader raised both arms, and his men stopped dead in their tracks. They froze momentarily then retreated with a sinister reluctance.

Roman's sight slowly returned. He used the long metal weapon in an attempt to stand, but an unseen force oppressed him. An invisible yoke prevented him from becoming upright.

Then, in an almost theatrical manner, the leader stretched out his right arm towards Roman and he instantly fell prostrate to the ground. Roman clutched his throat with his right hand; and to his astonishment, strangled himself.

Other Titles by Wayne Gerard Trotman

VETERANS OF THE PSYCHIC WARS

ASHES TO ASHES: SCREENPLAY

www.waynegerardtrotman.com

www.redmoon.co.uk